WILLOW MARSH

JO CASSIDY

ISBN (Paperback): 978-1-948095-17-4

ISBN (eBook): 978-1-948095-18-1

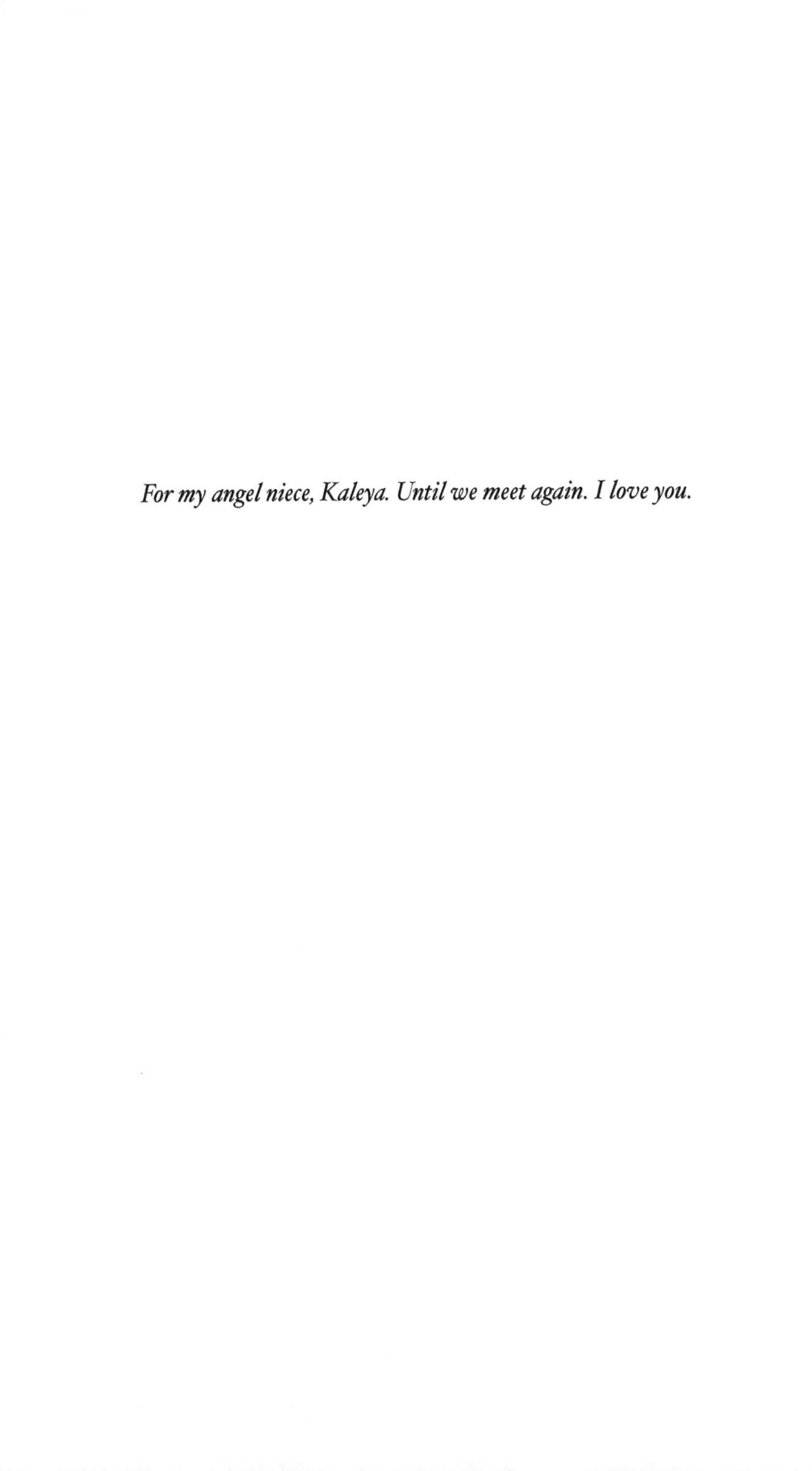

For my angel niece, Kaleya. Until we meet again. I love you.

I'd been trying to contact my mom ever since the night of the crash, but it's difficult to speak to the dead. None of my séances worked. Amá always told me to never give up, so I kept trying, knowing the sound of her voice could solve my worries.

Like most back yards in Willow Marsh, the woods lay behind the property line, filled with thick birch and willow trees. The frosty air pricked at my skin as I stared up at the dark clouds. If it was this cool during the day, I didn't want to imagine what it was like at night. I ducked between a couple trees, wishing I had a jacket. I didn't want to risk sneaking back to get it, though. Dad could come back any minute.

A small clearing opened among the trees, revealing an area of damp soil with scattered grass. When I kneeled, the cold, wet earth saturated my black jeans, sending a shiver through me. I took three red candles out of my backpack and placed them in a triangle on the ground. With shaking hands, I struck a match and held the flickering flame over each wick, waiting for it to ignite. Closing my eyes, I breathed in the aroma of cinnamon, letting it soothe me.

"Amá, it's Tessa." I waited. She had taught me how to contact the dead when my abuela passed away. It would've helped if I had someone with me, but people tended to freak out when I used the word séance.

Especially my dad.

Staying connected to the dead, honoring them, and always remembering them was part of me and my culture. Everything I loved and held dear to my heart was my family – and two of them were gone because of me.

I needed to focus. I pictured her in my mind – dark curls, friendly brown eyes, and her smile: always knowing, always laughing. "Amá, are you there?"

A gush of freezing wind brushed by me at the same time a light force, almost like a weight, pushed into me from all angles. My fingers scraped along the damp earth as I hurried to stand, sensing something nearby.

Tessa. My name rushed by with the breeze in a soft, sweet tone.

I whipped around, searching between the weeping branches for Amá. My low ponytail – heavy from the weight of my thick hair and the green scarf holding it back – swished with every sweep of the head.

Tessa.

"Amá?" Had she finally come? I rushed back to the candles, kneeling before them, bouncing and shaking at the same time. "I'm here. Please talk to me."

The flames danced, and a chill crawled up my back, snaking onto my neck. Frost engulfed the leaves on the ground, and I watched as each one froze over in a slow motion tidal wave. I dug my dirty fingers into my jeans just to have something to latch onto. My ragged, deep breaths created a cloud of mist in front of me.

I stood, my wobbly legs almost making me collapse. My eyes darted around in search for the source of the cold. A bird whistled above me, piercing and loud, the sound echoing through the woods and vibrating my skull.

Swirls of dark colors took over my vision, followed by a series of images. An old, rusted key. A willow tree etched into stone. White flash. A brown and black bird with black, beady eyes and a sharply pointed orange beak. Black flash.

The intensity of the images forced me to my knees. A presence drifted to my side at the same time a bone-chilling energy pressed into me. The bitter power ripped out any trace of happiness inside, leaving something hollow in its place like I'd never experience joy again. My skin tingled all over, fear icing its way through my veins to the point I could barely move. The small bird landed next to me and craned its neck, looking at me with its beady eyes, just like from the image. At the same time it cawed – a lilting song that was captivating – heat radiated under my skin, replacing the cold and thawing my bones.

Lungs burning, I pushed my palms against my forehead until everything stopped. My eyes throbbed, lids twitching with each heartbeat. Whatever evil had been there was gone. I took a few breaths to calm down before I peeled my eyes open one at a time, afraid of what possibly awaited me. The forest stood in contemplative silence, the frost on the leaves gone and the candles blown out. The bird was nowhere in sight.

I wiped away the dirt on my hands, thinking I'd see a change in myself. Something inside felt different. But my light brown skin looked the same as always. I traced the long, thick scar on my right hand, running between my thumb and index finger, remembering the crash.

For a while, I stayed rooted on the cool ground in confusion, trying to figure out what I had done wrong. Nothing like that had happened before. My previous séances had been calm and peaceful.

When I noticed the time on my phone, I collected my candles and bag and forced myself to weave back through the trees and to the moving trailer outside the house. If Dad found out that I tried to contact Amá, I'd be grounded for the rest of my life. Luckily, he hadn't come back from running his errand, giving me time to collect myself.

He'd tried to get me to go with him, but I wanted some time to have my séance, so I told him I needed to call my best friend back home and wanted some privacy. Dad had taken the car but left my duffel bag, so I had something to sit on. I fished out my favorite maroon hoodie with a Día de los Muertos skull on it. My abuelo had bought it for me for my last birthday, and I wore it every chance I got.

I tightened the scarf holding my hair in a ponytail. It was one from Amá's huge collection. I'd started wearing them after the crash to feel connected to her. The scar on my hand glared at me, reminding me of what I'd done. I quickly found another silk scarf in my duffel bag and wrapped it around my wrist, hooking it over the web of my right hand.

I sunk onto my bag, placing my hands over my face. I had to act like my normal self so Dad wouldn't get suspicious. He couldn't know the terror I'd just faced. Even though the evil had vanished, my heart was still trying to find a normal rate. I took deep breaths, thinking of my mom and brother – they always brought me back to my serene place.

Since Amá and Felix's deaths, acting had almost become second nature so I could get the worriers off my back. It was easy to appear fine on the outside, when, inside, I was slowly falling apart.

CHAPTER 2

Tugging my hood over my head, I watched Dad open the front door with a rusty crowbar he'd found in the garage. I stood on the porch, keeping a safe distance from the house. The hinges groaned in protest as Dad yanked the door open. A dense, freezing current that smelled almost sour drifted out from the cracks.

"See?" Dad threw down the crowbar and dusted off his hands. "Easy."

"No, Apá." I pulled on the strings of my hoodie until the material cinched around my face. "Keys would have been easy. A house built in this century with a functional door would have been easy."

Dad's cracked lips turned up into a fraction of a smile. "The realtor didn't have keys. The previous family left in a hurry." He ran his hand down his face. "Tessa, this is our home now. Besides, donde quiera que moramos, siempre seremos familia." He cut off sharply on the last word. The saying reminded him of Amá. He looked up, blinking back tears from his watery eyes before he walked into the house.

Wherever we dwell, we will always be family. My parents' motto they developed after we left Mexico to move to Skokie, Illinois. Now we'd come to Willow Marsh, leaving Skokie, Leya, Amá, and Felix behind.

But I couldn't pack a city, my best friend, and two people buried six feet under. So, I went empty-handed and empty-hearted with Dad.

My cell phone vibrated in my hoodie pocket. A grin broke out on my face when I saw it was a text from Leya. I loved that even though two states were now between us, we could still communicate daily. Well, more likely hourly knowing us. She was the one thing that kept me sane.

Leya:
I hate Mr. Garby.

Tessa:
:) what happened this time?

He wouldn't extend the
due date on my paper.

Why do you need more time?

I'm in mourning. My best friend
LEFT ME. I need time to adjust.

*Moved.

LEFT ME.

MOVED. Speaking of,
I'm outside the new digs.

And?

And I may not survive the night.

"Tessa?" Dad poked his head out the door, his thick, ungelled hair sweeping with the movement. "You coming in?"
"Yeah."

Gotta go. Parental needing me.

Call me later.

I hurried down the front steps, snapped a picture of the house and sent it to Leya. It had been less than twenty-four hours since Dad and I had closed the door on our U-Haul and I'd said goodbye to Leya. I already missed her like crazy.

The glint of Amá's family ring on my left pointer finger caught my eye. The sides were bronze, and on top rested an intricately carved pink dahlia that housed a secret container. Inside rested a lock of my great-great grandmother's hair. Amá gave me the ring on my fifteenth birthday. She said the ring would always keep us bonded together. I stroked the smooth bronze on the side before I climbed back up the porch steps.

The cold, stale air hit me when I crossed the threshold. Cobwebs and dust decorated the house. I brushed my finger over a table in the entryway, rubbing the dirt between my thumb and index finger.

"How long has this place been vacant?" My voice echoed through the corridor. "I'm surprised it's still standing."

Dad used his shoulder to shut the door as best he could. The use of the crowbar had caused some damage. "Not sure." He paused, taking in the place. "It's going to need some work."

"More than some." Rounding the corner, I walked into the living room. White sheets haphazardly covered all the furniture like it had been done in a hurry. The walls were bare, dust outlines of previous clocks and frames visible. The yellow and orange flowered wallpaper made me quirk an eyebrow at Dad. "Nice decor. So glad I get to live through the sixties since I didn't get the chance the first time they were around."

"Try the seventies." He pinched the bridge of his nose. "It's pretty bad, isn't it?"

"It's terrible." I drew back the thick, orange velvet drapes. When I pulled up the shades, light filtered through the dirt-covered window.

A screech from my left made me jump. Two bats came out from behind a book shelf, flapping and shrieking as they searched for darkness.

Dad took off down the hallway, disappearing from my sight.

"Seriously?" I called out as I ducked behind the couch. "You're running away?"

A minute later he came back, holding a broom. "I needed reinforcement." He swatted at the bats, making them huddle in a dark corner on the ceiling. "Open the front door."

With a prayer of courage, I left the coverage of the couch and sprinted to the door, swung it wide open, pushed myself into the wall, and lifted my arm to shield my eyes. "It's open!"

Dad grunted, mumbling under his breath. Moments later, the bats squealed by, and I slammed the door, holding it closed with my back. "How many more unwanted residents do you think we're going to find?" I shook out my hands and gagged before I rejoined Dad in the front room.

Lowering the broom, he smiled. "A lot, I'm afraid." He pointed his thumb toward the hall. "If you thought this was bad, wait until you see the kitchen."

Somehow, the kitchen managed to be worse. The cupboard doors that were still there hung from their hinges but threatened to fall off at a sneeze. More cobwebs and dust clung to every surface. The appliances, yellow, green, and orange in color, looked even older than the seventies. Broken glass littered the yellow daisy linoleum.

Dad yanked a sheet off the table, sending the dust in a panic. He grimaced at the surface. "Rat droppings."

"We need to bomb this place." I plugged my nose to try to avoid the stench of mold and dead rats.

"I'm sure it's fine. I'll call a bug guy in the morning." Dad had his sturdy hands on his hips, surveying the room like he could fix it with his eyes.

I pointed to a dead mouse curled up in the corner. "I'm talking atomic. Blow this house to smithereens. We've probably caught ten different diseases since we walked inside."

"Drama queen." Dad narrowed his light brown eyes, but a tiny smile pulled at his lips.

The creek of the front door being opened echoed down the hall. "Knock, knock!" High heels clanked on the wood floor. A curly-haired blonde woman stepped into the kitchen, her spray tan verging on orange. She pointed her thumb behind her. "Your front door seems to be broken."

Tucked in the crook of her arm was a tan and white Pomeranian with a pink glitter collar. The dog's tongue stuck out, her wide, brown eyes taking in the kitchen. She was an adorable ball of fluff.

The lady's black dress clung to her small figure, showing off her curves and perfectly sculpted cleavage. Even though she was dressed like a twenty-year-old, the lines on her face and arms told me she was probably in her late forties or early fifties.

She held out her manicured hand toward Dad, her smile

revealing flawless, white teeth that were probably as fake as her boobs. "I'm Barbie. You must be Mr. Isaacson."

Barbie? I held in a sigh. She had to be kidding.

Dad stepped forward, his eyes darting to her boobs before they settled on her eyes. I threw up a little in my mouth. He gave her hand a little shake. "Yes, but call me Alec. It's nice to finally meet you in person, Barbie." He gestured to me. "This is my daughter, Tessa."

I yanked down my hood and pulled my hair, so the ponytail rested over my shoulder. I didn't want to creep her out by being hidden under the protection of my hoodie.

Her smile faltered as she glanced at me, but she covered it up just as quick. "Ah, yes, I remember you mentioning her when we talked on the phone. Hello, there." After giving Dad a lingering look over, she scratched her dog's neck under the collar. "This is Fluffsies."

Fluffsies answered with a squeak of a bark.

Barbie motioned over her shoulder, but then snapped her head in surprise at the empty entryway. She rolled her eyes. "Graham!"

Dad looked at me, his eyebrows furrowed. I answered with a shrug because I knew as much as he did.

A guy around my age came in, shuffling his feet, his head down, shaggy brown hair falling over his eyes. He had on a dark hoodie that was a little too big for him. His jeans fit him perfectly, though. He popped out a skull earbud from one ear, letting it fall against his chest. Rock music blared from it, but I didn't recognize the band.

Barbie put her hands on her curvy hips. "Well, don't just mope there. Say hi to our new neighbors." She looked at Dad, undressing him with her eyes.

Dad was good looking, well-built, and usually wore nice button-down shirts and fitted jeans. I knew ladies would be attracted to him. But I didn't want to witness stuff like that so soon after we lost Amá – especially not from Barbie.

She absentmindedly pointed her finger behind her. "This is my son, Graham. Same age as Tessa." Tearing her seductive blue eyes away from Dad, she looked at me. "Your father told me you're a junior. So is Graham. He'll be able to show you around school."

Graham slowly lifted his head, his green eyes blinking rapidly as he stared at me, open-mouthed. I suppressed a smile. A warm, tingly sensation erupted inside, causing me to fist my hands like I could stop it from exploding out my fingertips. Something about him charmed me.

Dad held out his hand to Graham. "Nice to meet you."

Graham still stared at me, his blinking eyes showing no signs of slowing down. Barbie finally slapped his arm to get his attention. "Manners. Shake this nice man's hand."

Graham took Dad's hand and shook it. "Hi, ss...sir."

Barbie motioned to me. "Now shake the young lady's hand."

I leaned forward, causing Graham to back into the doorframe. Shooting a sidelong look at Dad, I reached out my hand. "Nice to meet you, Graham."

After a few awkward moments, Graham finally extended his hand, wiping it on his jeans before he did. When our hands clasped, I could feel his shaking. Despite the scarf wrapped around part of my hand, the heat from his hand soaked into me.

Graham licked his lips, his blinking eyes darting from my eyes to my mouth, to my eyes, and back to my mouth. "Hi."

Barbie cleared her throat. "You can let go now." She rested her hand on Dad's bicep. "Sorry about him. We don't get a lot of new residents here." She blocked her mouth with her hand so Graham couldn't see and mouthed, *He's slow.*

Graham had cowered back at her words. I wanted to

punch her, but I refrained. Decking the realtor within an hour of stepping into Willow Marsh was probably not the best first impression. But I tucked the option away in case a situation presented itself again.

Dad pulled his arm away from Barbie and gave Graham's shoulder a small squeeze. "I'm sure Graham's a wonderful young man. I'm excited to get to know him better."

Graham stood straight at Dad's words, the smallest of smiles landing on his wet lips. Fluffsies watched the entire exchange panting and wagging her tail that was curled onto her back.

"Me, too," I said, smiling at Graham. "It'll be nice having someone to show me around town and school." I still didn't like the fact I had to move in the middle of my junior year and make new friends, but I suddenly had an overwhelming need to protect Graham. He'd probably been verbally abused his whole life.

Barbie glanced around the kitchen, her smile strained. "How do you like your new home? Best place money can buy here in Willow Marsh."

"This is the best available house here?" I frowned at the rat droppings on the table and rubbed my forehead. "That's comforting."

A strangled laugh came from Graham, but he lowered his head the moment his mom looked at him, anger in her eyes.

When she turned her eyes to me, pride swelled up in them, and both she and the dog lifted their chins a little. "You'll find that Willow Marsh is a wonderful place to live. A prominent family used to reside in this home. It's an honor to live here." If they had been such an important family, why had they left in such a hurry?

Dad shot me a warning look, knowing I rarely dropped things, but I ignored him. "What happened to the family? From the looks of it, they've been gone for a while."

"They moved." Barbie turned her attention to Dad, changing the subject. "What can we do to help you settle in?"

"Well, I'm thinking this home needs to be fumigated," Dad said. "Is there someone in town who can do that?"

Barbie brushed her hand along her cleavage. "Willy Heathrow can do that for you. I'll call him first thing in the morning. For now, you and . . ." She narrowed her eyes at me.

"Tessa," I offered.

Barbie forced a smile. "You and Tessa can stay at our place until this home is deemed safe to live in." She said it like she hoped it would be a long time before that happened.

"Don't you have a hotel in Willow Marsh?" I asked. No way I wanted to stay under the same roof as that woman.

"The owners are on vacation." Barbie's eyes went wide when she saw the dead mouse in the corner. She quickly changed her focus, glancing at her watch, a gold piece with diamonds encased around it. "It's getting late, and you two must be tired. Let's head to my place and get you settled in for the night." After another head to toe undressing of Dad, Barbie left the kitchen, snapping at Graham to follow. He gave me a blinking glimpse before he put his earbud back in and left.

When they were out of the kitchen, I crept to Dad, keeping my voice low. "You can't be serious, Apá. Where did you find her?"

"She's the only realtor in Willow Marsh." Dad ran his fingers through his thick hair. My looks came from my mom, but the thickness of my hair came from Dad. It was a beast to keep tamed.

"I'm not staying at her place." I glanced back at the kitchen entryway to make sure they weren't nearby. "I can already see her 'accidentally' walking into your room at night, completely naked." I shuddered, rubbing my arms.

Dad frowned. "She wouldn't do that."

"I wouldn't be so sure of that," I said under my breath. "Especially since you didn't tell her about Amá."

His unfocused eyes landed on the dirty linoleum. "I told her your mom was out of the picture, which is true." He peeled his gaze from the floor. "I thought we decided to not let people know."

"Right." I folded my arms. "So, let's pretend Felix never existed and Amá has been out of our lives for years." He had a point, but I was still coming to terms with their deaths. Not talking about them at all tore my heart into a million pieces.

Dad gently squeezed my arm. "Tessa, this will give you a chance to start over and not think about the accident. We can tell people when you're ready. As for right now, we can't stay in this house, and the motel is not an option, so we're staying with Barbie and Graham for a night." Dad sulked out of the kitchen, closing the conversation.

I fingered the scarf on my hand, right above where my scar was. Pretend like Amá and Felix never existed. At least then the town would never know the truth of what happened that night. All I had to do was don a mask and live a never-ending masquerade.

A cool draft swept through the kitchen, causing my scarf and hair to swing around. I checked for an open window, but they were all sealed shut. So was the door leading to the back yard. The breeze swirled faster, circling around me, making me sway where I stood. Reaching out my hand, I took hold of the counter and gripped it tight. Seconds later, the wind stopped.

Paper rustled near my feet. I bent down to find a thin envelope addressed to the Barnett Family. The return address just said *G*. I started to crumple the envelope in my hand, but something stopped me. After smoothing it out on the counter, I folded it, and then placed it in my hoodie pocket.

"Tessa?" Dad hollered from the front door. "Are you coming?"

The thought of staying with Barbie added to the anxiety building inside. "Yeah." I forced myself down the hall.

The sudden breeze, plus the séance gone wrong, left a cold sensation in the pit of my stomach like a bad omen. Willow Marsh could be the death of me.

CHAPTER 3

The Dixon family had a tiny off-white house with chipped paint and a few missing shingles. Strings of weeds covered the yard, and only a portion of the chain-link fence still stood. They didn't have a guest room, so I didn't understand why Barbie thought we should stay with her.

Dad and I each brought in a bag with our necessities. We set them in the carpeted entryway while Barbie gave us a tour. There wasn't much to see. Front room, kitchen, bathroom, Barbie's room, Graham's room. All small and with furniture as old as the house we'd just got, if not older. Nothing matched, like they had gathered random items over the years from a thrift store. Most of the drawers in every room had missing handles or hung crooked.

We ordered some pizza for dinner. Graham said nothing the whole time, just kept his head down, his fingers drumming on the table. He had his earbuds wrapped around his neck. He'd been listening to music until his mom barked at him to turn it off.

When she wasn't feeding Fluffsies, who sat in her lap,

Barbie kept reaching over to touch Dad, or she'd bat her fake eyelashes at him. His smile was strained through it all, trying to be a polite guest. I had to force my pizza to stay in my stomach from the disgusting display.

After dinner, Barbie snapped her fingers at Graham. "Show Tessa to your room."

Graham shuffled toward the hall, so I picked up my bag to join him.

"Do you ww...want tt...to be on tt...top or bottom?"

My shocked eyes landed on Graham, not sure if I'd heard him right. I'd have to get used to his stuttering.

His face flushed when he realized what he'd asked. "Of the . . ." He stepped inside his room and pointed to the bunk bed against the wall.

A pine scent filled the room. There were jeans, T-shirts, hoodies, and boxers covering the floor. He had nothing hanging on his walls and no knickknacks, which surprised me. All he had on his dresser was a digital alarm clock with fading lights, and an old boombox straight from the eighties.

"I'll sleep on top. I'm sure my dad won't want to climb up there."

Graham took the bottom pillow and switched it with the pillow on the top bunk. "Better pillow."

"Thanks." I searched for a place to put my bag, but couldn't see any carpet.

Noticing my problem, he moved some of his clothes out of the way, creating a spot for me to set my bag. "Ss...sorry. Didn't know anyone ww...would be ss...staying here tonight."

"No worries," I said, setting it on the floor. When I looked at him, he licked his lips and lowered his eyes, blinking wildly.

Dad strolled into the room and smiled wide when he saw the mess. "Oh, yeah, this brings back memories."

Graham stuffed in his earbuds and hurried out of the

room, knocking into his dresser on the way out. Dad watched him retreat and then turned to me. "I didn't mean to scare him off."

"I'm pretty sure it was me, not you."

Dad placed his bag next to mine. "Well, you're a lot prettier than I am." He nodded his head toward the door. "Why don't you go see if you can get him warmed up to you? He didn't say a word during dinner." His eyes flickered toward the door, and he kept his tone low. "Probably because his mom wouldn't stop talking."

I snapped a picture of the bed and sent it to Leya with the caption: *Daddy and I get to share a bunk bed!* "This sounds like a secret mission."

"If you choose to accept, of course," Dad said.

"Only if I get to work with Jeremy Renner." I wiggled my eyebrows, making him laugh.

Graham was on the old, brown couch in the family room, watching the local news, though he didn't seem to be interested. With how fuzzy the screen was, they probably didn't get many channels.

He listened to his music as he stared blankly at the TV. They'd added fluffy bright blue accent pillows as if to mask the fraying couch. Even though I sat on the complete opposite side, he scooted closer to the edge of the couch, as if those extra two inches could save him from catching my cooties.

I waved my hand to get his attention. After a few seconds, he took out one earbud and held it in his hand. I asked the first thing that came to my head. "Do you have any siblings?"

Beating his long fingers against his leg, Graham kept his blinking eyes on the TV. "No. Yes. I . . ."

He didn't know? I turned toward him, hoping to show I was harmless and friendly, but he pushed himself into the side of the couch and used a pillow to create a barrier between us.

Tucking my legs underneath me, I opened my mouth to mention Felix but stopped myself. Bringing him up would unleash a lot of questions I wasn't ready to answer. Not yet. "So, you do have siblings?"

He stopped drumming his fingers and finally looked me in the eye, still blinking fiercely. "Brother."

"Older? Younger? Does he live here, too?"

He lowered the volume on the TV with a huge remote that was being held together by duct tape. "Older. He died three months ago. Accident."

Instinct made me want to reach out to him, tell him I understood his pain, but I held it in. "I'm so sorry, Graham. That must be hard."

He nodded in response.

"What about your dad?" I didn't see any photos of an older man in the family room. In fact, I hadn't seen any pictures of Graham's brother either. They kept their decorations and possessions to a minimum, as if they could leave at a second's notice.

His leg bounced as he tapped his fingers against it. "He died ww...when I ww...was young."

Leaning my elbow on the arm rest, I stared at Graham, taking him in. He seemed nervous, but I wasn't sure if it was because he didn't know me or because I was a girl.

Even though we just met, I felt a connection to him. We both shared the loss of family, and the remaining parent didn't understand us all that well. The guilt inside clawed at me, wanting to scratch its way to the surface. I should have been the one in the grave, not them. I wished I could talk about it with Graham, but that meant taking off my mask and revealing the truth – I wasn't ready for that.

He glanced over at me, blinking and drumming.

My phone rang, so I pulled it out of my hoodie pocket,

grateful for the interruption of an awkward moment. Leya wanted to video chat, so I hit accept. "Hey."

Leya wiggled her sculpted eyebrows at me. "Hey, your beautiful self." Her sultry tone washed a comfort over me. It was like we were in the same room, though we were hundreds of miles away. She had her braided hair down, falling around her round face. Her pink lips were really glossed, like usual. "I saw the picture you sent me of your new home. Congrats. So, do you have to share a room with a rodent, or do you get your own space?"

Fiddling with a pillow on the couch, I smirked. "I requested my own room, but we'll see what happens." I turned to look at Graham. "It's my best friend, Leya."

He'd been staring at my phone cover, which had a blue and green Día de los Muertos skull on it. I'd found it one day when I was shopping with Leya. It matched the one on my hoodie, so I had to get it.

Graham blinked in acknowledgment of my statement. He turned back to the TV, lowering the volume even more.

"Hello?" Leya's self-assured voice rang out from the phone, and I looked at the screen to see her big, brown eyes glaring at me. "Who are you talking to that's not me? I asked you a question."

I suddenly wished we weren't doing a video call. I pulled the phone closer to me so she could see less of the background. "Oh, just someone we're staying with. What did you ask?"

Her eyes darted behind me, trying to take everything in. "Where are you? And why are you sharing a bunk bed with your dad?"

"With the realtor who found our home. The bunk bed is the only option," I said. Out of the corner of my eye, I caught Graham staring at me, intrigue in his blinking eyes. His fingers continued to beat on his leg.

Her mouth turned into an O. "What's he like?" She leaned in close. "Can I see?"

"She," I said. "It's a she."

Leya twisted her head to the side. "Ooh, la la." She smacked her lips. "Hot? Single? Children? Please tell me she has an extremely gorgeous son so when I come to visit you, I can flirt with him."

Red climbed up Graham's neck to his cheeks as he covered his hair with the hood of his sweatshirt. I thought about ending the video call and just chatting, but there was no going back now.

"She does, but I have dibs," I said, winking at Graham. Taking the pillow from beside me, I threw it at his head. He caught it and held it against his face, making me smile.

Leya pouted. "He's right there, isn't he?"

"Yep." I tried to pull the pillow from Graham's face, but he held on tight.

"You so suck," Leya said. "Let me see him!"

Graham groaned, laying his head against the back of the couch, keeping the pillow on his face. I turned the phone, so she could see that he was hiding.

She sighed. "Text me and tell me the truth. Every juicy detail." She started speaking loudly. "How hot he is, how old he is, and how kissable his lips are."

Graham somehow sunk farther into the couch.

I choked on a laugh. "Will do."

"Later." Leya blew me a kiss.

I did the same. "See ya." I so missed my other half. We were like twins separated at birth, which was probably good for our families. Both of our bold personalities would be difficult to handle under the same roof.

I tucked the phone into my hoodie pocket and then reached forward, shoving Graham playfully on the arm.

"You're going to have to get used to having me around. You won't get rid of me that easily."

Graham lowered the pillow, his face bright red. "G...guess I'll have tt...to tt..try hard."

When his smile got bigger, I laughed, and he soon joined me. For the second time in weeks, warmth filled me – both times from being around Graham. I forgot how nice it felt to laugh.

"You two should get to bed." At the sound of Barbie's condescendingly pleasant voice, my laugh and the warmth evaporated, leaving a tight coil in my stomach in its wake. She stood near me with her arms folded, wearing a tight tank top and shorts that barely went to the top of her skinny thighs. "It's late."

"Right." I stood, brushing past her.

Dad was in the hallway, his eyes lingering a little too long on Barbie. He flinched when he saw me, probably embarrassed to be caught. "Tessa. You going to be okay if I don't go with you to school tomorrow? I have a lot to do with the house."

"Don't worry about it." I held my arms against me, trying to stay calm. Thinking about Felix and then seeing Dad check out another woman a couple months after Amá had died was sickening. "I'm not ready to go to school yet."

Dad came close to me, keeping his voice low so only I could hear. "I think it will be good for you to get back to school. I've let you take the past few weeks off. You have a chance at a fresh start here."

My fists clenched at my sides. "Don't expect me to get over them as easily as you did. It's not like they moved away, Apá. They died." I shouldn't have taken my anger out on Dad, but he was in the line of fire at the moment.

He cleared his throat right as Barbie appeared in my vision, cramming us in the hallway. She picked up Fluffsies from the ground and held her against her chest. "Graham can take you to school tomorrow. Despite his problems, he can still drive rather well. You won't be in any danger."

Grief consumed Dad. His shoulders slumped as he ran his hand down his face. I gave his other hand a squeeze and mouthed *I'm sorry*. He nodded before he shuffled past us and went outside, probably to calm himself down.

Barbie took the opportunity to lean in close to me, which was easy since there wasn't much room to begin with. With her amber and musk scent, her perfume was probably named *Smoldering Passion* or *Erotic Seduction*. "Listen, Jessica . . ."

"Tessa . . ."

"I know my son is a little slow, but please don't try to take advantage of him." Barbie tucked some loose hairs of mine behind my ear, her fake fingernails scratching my skin, making me shudder. Her tone – while trying to appear motherly – had a strained edge to it. "I saw you flirting with him in there. He has a sensitive heart and is nowhere near being ready for a relationship of any kind, so it's best if you stay away."

I opened my mouth, but she sauntered away – Fluffsies in tow – before I could say anything. Even if she had stayed, how would I respond to that?

After I dry-heaved out of disgust, I hurried into the bedroom and got ready for bed.

CHAPTER 4

I tried to calm myself and focus on positive things, like the fact we only had to be there for one night. I smiled at the bunk bed. Felix would have been thrilled to sleep on top. Staying in a strange place with weird people would have been an adventure for him. He found the positive in everything.

My eyes traveled to the scarf covering the scar on my hand. I deserved so much more than a scar, but it was a constant reminder of what I'd done.

When Dad came back inside, I hugged him. "I really am sorry. I shouldn't have taken my anger out on you."

Dad kissed my forehead, bringing me back to my safe place. "It's okay. We've both been through a lot. But we need to stay a team. You're all that's left of my family."

"I'll go to school tomorrow. You're right. I think it will be good for me."

After Dad fell asleep, I got Felix's stuffed green and black T-Rex out from my bag and tucked it under my arm. I always hoped having the dinosaur with me would help with my nightmares, but they still came.

Every night I dreaded bedtime. Up until the second I had to climb into bed, I focused on anything and everything else, trying to put my mind in a happy place. But the night of the crash haunted me. It didn't matter if I meditated before, repeated my mantra, said a prayer, or controlled my breathing, I couldn't get rid of the terrifying dreams.

I was transplanted back to the night my world ended. Rain pelted the windshield so hard, I thought it would shatter. It thundered in my ears. Then came the horrifying screams, the stench of death suffocating me as I fought for control of the car. Sometimes I couldn't see what was going on; I just heard the noises and smelled the terror, which was somehow worse.

My normal nightmare switched in the middle of the night.

I stood in a dark forest with rotting black trees, a small bird flying overhead, rain crashing down, soaking me through. I trembled from the freezing cold, my teeth clattering together. Swallowing my fear, I tried to move, but fuzzy black vines climbed out from the ground and grabbed my legs, rooting me in place. When I tried to open my mouth to scream for help, the vines flew up and laced through my skin, sewing my mouth shut.

Suddenly a high wind started up, circling around me and yanking at my hands like it wanted to take me away, but the vines wouldn't let it. A raspy, sinister voice whispered my name as the air tugged at my hair, my clothes – every piece of me. The air and earth fought for my body, and I worried it would rip me in two.

The force of the wind blew the rain away, sucking it from my clothes, leaving me brittle and dry. I watched in horror as the skin on my arms and hands disintegrated into ash and floated away.

I woke, curled up in a ball, gripping the blankets and dinosaur. Sweat soaked my baggy clothes and sheets. My lips and mouth went dry as I panted through a panic attack. Closing my eyes, I focused on controlling my breathing and relaxing my muscles. *Control. Steady. Calm.* My therapist in Skokie told me to repeat that every time I had a bad dream or anxiety attack.

I unwrapped the silk scarf from around my wrist and used it to tie back my damp hair. Finally calm, I climbed down the bed and sneaked out of the room, not wanting to wake Dad.

Graham was sprawled out on the couch in the family room, fast asleep. He had one arm hanging down and the other covering his eyes. He wore his hoodie with the hood up. Just the sight of him sleeping so peacefully shaved off a layer of my anxiety.

I tiptoed into the kitchen, hoping to get a drink of water. I didn't want to wake Graham, so I kept the lights off, but I had no idea where the cups were. The first two cupboards I tried were wrong.

Suddenly the kitchen light flipped on, and my hand went to my chest as I spun around.

Graham held up his shaking hands. "It's just me." He'd put his hood down, and his earbuds rested around his neck. His flannel pajama bottoms had a hole in the knee.

It took a moment to quiet my heart. My mouth and throat were still dry from my panic attack.

"Are you okay?" he asked in a low voice.

I stared at him for a moment, watching his eyes blink fiercely and his fingers tap against the counter. Forcing myself to nod, I lowered my hand. "Bad dream." My voice was rough.

"Do you ww...want ss...some ww...water?"

Closing my eyes briefly, I rubbed my eyelids. "That would be nice."

While I waited for Graham to fill the glass, I repeated my mantra in my head. *Control. Steady. Calm.*

"Tt...tessa?" Graham held out a glass, his hand shaking as the water sloshed around.

I took it from him, offering a soft smile. "Thanks." The cool water raced down my dry throat like it couldn't get to its destination fast enough. Within seconds, I had downed the whole glass.

With a huge smile of awe, he took the glass from me. "More?"

"No, thanks," I said, but the thought of falling back asleep didn't sit well with me. More nightmares would come if I did. I eyed the small, round kitchen table. The light wood had been nicked in many places. "Do you mind sitting with me for a moment? I'm not ready to go back to sleep, and I don't want to be alone."

He took a seat at the kitchen table, resting casually in his chair. "Tt...tell me about home. Leya."

I sat down in the chair across from him, placing my hand on the table for support. It wobbled under my weight – one of the legs was shorter than the others. "Leya is extremely shy and quiet."

"I noticed," he said, smirking.

"We've been best friends since the first grade." I caressed the side of the family ring on my finger, thinking of Amá. My midnight chats used to be with her. "Leya was born in Haiti, me in Mexico, and somehow we both ended up in Skokie, Illinois of all places."

Graham blinked wildly. "Naturally." A smile pulled at his lips. It looked good on him.

Amá would say it was fate Leya and I both ended up in Skokie. "Leya keeps me sane. Whenever I'm in a bad mood, she can talk me down."

"Ww...why did you move here?"

To get away from the memories of Amá and Felix. To start over. "Dad got a job here."

"Contractor." His fingers tapped the table. His eyes held more information behind them, but I didn't press it further. "Ww...why did he look here?"

I lifted my leg onto the chair and rested my chin on my bare knee. "Not sure on that. He just said he wanted somewhere different." He'd been searching online for new jobs, and he stumbled across an opening in Willow Marsh.

Graham went to the cupboards with a slight spring in his step, grabbed two mugs, and made us some hot chocolate. Marshmallows included.

When he sat back down, some hot chocolate swished from his cup and down the side, landing in a small puddle on the table. With a clenched jaw, he used a towel to clean up the mess. His hands hadn't stopped shaking. I couldn't help but stare at them. Graham sat back in his seat and sighed.

"Ww...we don't know."

"Don't know what?"

He grimaced. "Ww...why I ss...shake and tt...twitch. Doctors did lots of tt...tests. They think it could've been a defect from birth."

My shoulders drooped in fake disappointment. "And here I thought you were nervous because I'm so beautiful." I sighed, way over the top. "There goes my ego."

His tight lips spread apart in a smile before he chuckled, light and smooth. I could definitely get used to that sound.

I glanced at the clock on the microwave on the counter. Only a few more hours until sunrise. I should have probably let Graham get back to bed, but I wasn't ready to face the darkness.

Graham tapped the table to get my attention. "Tt...tell me about Ss...Skokie."

He let me rattle on for another hour. He would never know how much that meant to me. He also wouldn't know how much I held from him. How much I wanted to tell him but didn't because I wasn't ready.

When I was a kid living in Mexico, I used to play with my grandparents' mask collection. My abuelo loved to collect them from all over the world. I'd put them on and pretend to be someone else for the day. They always told me I could be anyone I wanted to be, but to always be the best version of myself when facing the real world.

Graham and the rest of Willow Marsh didn't need to know all my sins so my secrets would keep piling up as my masquerade continued.

CHAPTER 5

Graham's old Ford two-door truck rumbled into the parking lot of Willow Marsh High. From the look and the smell wafting from the crack above the passenger side window, they'd freshly done the pavement. All the lines were blinding white.

Having Graham with me made going to a new school a whole lot easier, especially since Dad couldn't make it. Though Graham twitched from nerves, he had a calming effect I desperately needed.

My anxiety crept in the moment we stepped out of his truck. Most of the time, I could put on a smile and manage being out in public, being polite and talkative to everyone around me. Sometimes, though, I wanted to be alone. A part of me wished I could wear one of my abuelo's masks and pretend to be someone else forever. Then I wouldn't have to worry about slipping up.

I reached back, grabbed the free part of the scarf hanging from my ponytail, and set it over my shoulder, twirling the silk in my hands to give them something to do.

Graham and I looked like we'd coordinated outfits with

our hoodies, dark jeans, and Converse shoes. If everything had been the same color, I probably would have changed. But Graham didn't strike me as the type who'd own a pink hoodie. At least I hadn't seen one on the floor of his room.

The tall, white columns in front of the school added to the charm of the brown brick building. It looked old, like from a completely different century, but had held up well. All the rectangular windows were exactly the same size, all neatly arranged and stacked on top of each other perfectly, like the whole thing had been carved from a magazine.

A bronze statue of a bull terrier on the front lawn caught my eye. A small brown and black bird – similar to the one in the forest – landed on the statue's head. When I blinked, the bird was gone.

Graham paused at my side. He had one earbud in, the other resting against his chest, heavy rock music drifting from it. "That's Ss...Sallie. Our mascot."

I arched an eyebrow. "The Willow Marsh Bull Terriers? That's quite the mouthful."

He scratched the back of his head. "No bull. Just tt...terrier. It's from the Civil Ww...war."

"Ah." I smirked. "The only Civil War I like to research has to do with Captain America."

"Better brush up on the real one if you're gg...going tt...to live here."

I scrunched my nose. "You sound like my dad. He loves all that history stuff." I stared at the statue. "It's one of the things that drew him here."

Graham nodded in understanding, and then looked at me. "Ready?"

Taking a few deep breaths, I stared at the front doors of the school. They were only metal and glass, but to me, they were intimidating. On the other side sat a whole new world. New teachers and students. Different schedule.

I hated change.

"Control. Steady. Calm."

Graham ran his shaking fingers through his brown hair, his voice low. "What's that?"

"Huh?" I hadn't realized I'd said it out loud. "Oh. Uh. My mantra, I guess. Helps me with change and my anxiety." I'd told Graham a lot during our middle of the night talk, so he knew about my anxiety.

He'd told me all about his nerves and twitching, something he couldn't control. Turned out we had a lot in common. He hated change as well.

"I like it." He stuffed his fingers into his pockets. "Control. Ss...steady. Calm." He glanced at some students who passed us before he whispered. "I might need to change the middle word."

"Hey, Graham, I never thanked you for last night. For staying up and talking to me."

He shifted where he stood, like he was itching to move. "I understand. Happy tt...to help."

"Would I freak you out if I hugged you?" I'd wanted to hug him after our talk, but Graham didn't seem to respond well to touch.

He tensed as he fiddled with his earbuds, his blinking eyes finding the ground.

"Just thought I'd ask. If you ever change your mind, let me know." Pushing the silk hanging on my shoulder to the back, I moved toward the school and Graham followed. "So, I'm going to assume holding my hand for comfort is out of the question as well?"

Graham threw back his head and rubbed his eyes with his thumb and pointer finger. "You're kk...killing me," he said with a groan.

I almost worried he wouldn't get my sarcasm, but he laughed. We pushed open the doors and walked into Willow

Marsh High with ease. My shoes squeaked across the linoleum as we entered the wide hallway. Cases lined the walls, a ton of trophies filling the space. Either Willow Marsh was good at a lot of things, or they just handed out trophies for everything.

"Look, Scram has a girlfriend." A deep voice came from behind us, and Graham went rigid. "How much you paying her?"

I turned around, determined to tell the guy off, but stopped short in surprise. Standing there in a tight Henley shirt was the most gorgeous guy I had ever set my eyes on. About a head taller than me, he had a light tan, was well-toned, and had a square, firm jaw. My eyes were torn between the guy's brown eyes and very kissable lips.

His demeanor changed when he saw me. His body relaxed, and he stared straight into my eyes, causing my cheeks to flare.

Graham cleared his throat next to me, so I turned to him. Sadness tugged at the corner of his light green eyes, and a faint frown rested on his lips. From the nickname, I assumed this guy was never nice to Graham, and I had stood there, checking him out.

The guy stepped forward, his eyes intent on mine. "Have we met before? You seem familiar." A tropical scent filled my nose, making me wonder if it was his shampoo or a cologne. Either way, it smelled good.

Hello, hotness, a sudden voice inside my head said. I tensed, not recognizing the sultry tone. Where had it come from?

"Me llamo Tessa." My voice came out more breathless than I wanted. I had no idea where the Spanish had come from, but it brought me back to starting school in Mexico as a kid.

He stuck out his hand, which I took in mine way too fast.

"I'm Blake." His thumb stroked my hand, right above my scar. "Make my day and tell me you just moved here."

I'd been so nervous for the day, I'd forgotten to wrap a scarf around my hand. I worried about his thumb finding my scar since I didn't want to talk about it. His one-sided smile made my unease melt. "Yep."

"Lucky me." His eyes searched mine. "Are you sure we haven't met?"

I'd remember meeting him. "Positive." At least I managed more breath in my voice.

Blake still held my hand, and when I tried to pull away, he took a step closer, his body inches from mine. "Let me show you around."

Staring into his deep brown eyes made it hard for me to think. "Alright." Wait. Graham. I turned to where he'd been, but he'd left. Letting go of Blake's hand, I looked around, but couldn't see Graham anywhere. "Where'd he go?"

Blake put his arm around my shoulder. "Don't worry about him. He's the last guy you want to make friends with, trust me. I'll take you to the front office, and we'll get you a schedule."

I kept searching the crowd for Graham, hoping to spot his hood or shaggy hair. I stuffed my hands in my hoodie so I wouldn't think about my scar. I tended to notice it more than other people did. To me, it was a spotlight shining in the eerie night.

"So, where did you move from?" Blake asked.

"Illinois." I finally became aware of other students in the hall, talking and laughing before they had to go to first period. The weight of Blake's arm around my shoulder felt heavy with all the curious eyes following us.

He smiled, revealing a dimple on his right cheek. "From those gorgeous eyes and your Spanish, I was expecting something more exotic."

I returned the smile. "I was born in Mexico and get most of my looks from my mom. But my Spanish is rusty." Inside, I cringed. I'd mentioned Amá and let my guard down within minutes of meeting Blake. I hoped he wouldn't ask any questions. It would be a while until I was ready to talk about Amá or Felix.

As we passed others in the hall, they all looked at me, sizing me up. I bet they didn't get a lot of new students. A few girls frowned when they saw Blake's arm around me. With my left hand, I adjusted my bag on my shoulder, taking the opportunity to shrug away from him. I didn't need enemies on my first day.

"Are both your parents from Mexico?" he asked.

My eyes kept searching for Graham, but I didn't see him. "Just my mom. Dad's from Illinois."

Blake held the door open for me as we headed into the front office. He managed to talk the counselor into putting me in most of his classes. I guess he had a way of charming anyone he talked to. Normally, that would turn me off. But something about the way he talked and carried himself captivated me. I found myself laughing at everything he said and forgetting my anxiety completely.

Maybe the new school wouldn't be so bad after all.

CHAPTER 6

Blake stayed by my side all morning, introducing me to all the teachers and his friends. There were too many names and faces to keep track of, so I just smiled through it all.

When we arrived in fourth period, I saw Graham sitting in the back of the class. His head was down, his fingers drumming on the desk. I hadn't seen him since he disappeared before school started. After checking in with the teacher – an older gentleman who looked seconds away from retiring – I went straight to the empty seat next to Graham, ignoring Blake. I heard him say something about having some students switch seats so I could sit by him, but I wanted to talk to Graham. I'd felt so bad for abandoning him, especially after he'd stayed up all night talking to me.

Setting my bag down on the floor, I took the seat next to Graham and hoped no one else sat there. "Hey, you. You disappeared on me."

He kept his eyes on the table and ignored me. I wanted to put my hand on his arm, but the gesture would freak him out. When I turned toward him, he moved away, putting his arm on the table to block me out. The teacher started class, and I tried my hardest to pay attention, but I kept looking at Graham. I needed to find a way to communicate with him, and I wasn't sure about the school policy on cell phones in class.

A few years ago, Felix lost his voice from a cold, so we wrote notes to each other. Then we kept on doing it for fun when we were bored.

I pulled out a piece of paper from my backpack and wrote *I'm sorry.* I slipped it on the table, maneuvering between Graham's arm and torso so he could see it. He tensed at first when he saw my hand, but he drew back his arm and stared at the paper.

Tapping one hand on the table, he reached into his bag and grabbed a pen. He wrote something and pushed the paper back to me.

It's okay. He shrugged like it was a common occurrence. Had he been teased and shut out his whole life?

With a glance at the teacher to make sure he wasn't paying attention, I wrote another note. *Let me make it up to you. Let's go do something tonight.*

Like what? Graham wrote.

What's there to do in this town?

Nothing.

I smiled. *There has to be a movie theater or mini golf or something.*

There's a bowling alley.

Perfect.

I don't bowl.

I flicked his arm and saw a tiny smile form on his lips. *Then it should be easy to beat you,* I wrote.

I said I didn't bowl, I didn't say I didn't know how. I'll cream you. Graham had very neat handwriting. Perfect, actually.

You're on.

"What's going on back there?"

I looked up to see the teacher staring at us, his hands on his hips and his eyes narrowed. The heat from Blake's intense gaze bore into me, but I kept my focus on the teacher.

Graham hurriedly tucked the note into his hoodie pocket.

I sat tall. "I was just asking about the bathroom rules. Do I need a pass or something?"

He pointed a wrinkly finger at the door. "Just raise your hand and let me know. Bathroom is right down the hall on the left."

"Thank you, sir." I flicked Graham on the arm just for fun before I stood. I paused in the doorway so I could look back at him. He had a smile on his face as he stared at the note under the table.

With a smile of my own, I stepped out into the empty hall, heading for the bathroom, when a breeze picked up. It swirled around me, just like it had done in my dream, then continued down the hall. The whirling white wind – in the shape of a small tornado – floated through the air. It beckoned to me, like it needed to show me something. Intrigued, I followed it, passing my classroom and around the corner. The wind stopped in front of a tall brown locker, bouncing a little in the air before it slithered through the cracks of the locker door.

The locker shook, the metal rattling, the contents pounding against the sides like they were being thrown around. Above me, the hallway lights flickered. I glanced around, but no one was in sight. My shaking hand went to the locker handle. I had no idea what was inside or if I was ready for it, but I had to know. Right as my skin touched the metal, the latch lifted without any effort on my part. The breeze flew out, smacking into me before it evaporated like it had never been there.

As I regained my bearings, I looked inside, expecting to

see lots of stuff from all the commotion the wind had caused, but only an old, rusty key sat in the middle of the locker. A part of me wanted to pick it up, but I shook with nerves. It was the same key that flashed through my mind yesterday in the woods when I'd tried to contact Amá. She'd shown it to me – or someone had.

My hand rested on the locker shelf, slowly inching toward the key. It was just a key, but for some reason, I was afraid to touch it. What if something happened when I did? I knew that was probably silly, but how had it even gotten there? Before I could make up my mind, a rush of wind swept into the locker and blew the key into my hand.

Chills covered my arms and legs, causing me to shake and almost drop the key. It was icy to the touch. I looked it over, noticing how old it had to be. It was thick, bronze, and the top was incredibly detailed. My finger traced along the pattern, the design familiar. It almost looked like a dahlia. My eyes went to the family ring on my finger.

Wind flew past my ear. *Tessa.* A woman's voice, soft and airy.

"Amá?" I whirled around, my eyes frantically sweeping the hallways, but I saw no one. The lights flickered again until they went out, leaving me in sudden darkness. Lightning outside lit up the hall as my eyes adjusted to the dark. Thunder boomed, followed by thick raindrops clanking on the roof.

A cool sensation traveling through the blood in my arm caught my attention. My skin rippled and protruded, light blue pulsing underneath. Before I could touch it, my arm returned to its normal state. Had I imagined it?

Doors to the classrooms opened, and students filled the hall, using their phones to light the way. I stuffed the key into my pocket and was about to shut the locker door when I saw a name scratched on the inside of the door. I switched on the flashlight on my phone and held it up to the name. *Ellington*.

"Tt...tessa?" Graham's sudden voice behind me made me jump and whirl around, holding my lighted phone out in front of me. "Did you gg...get Tt...trenton's old locker?" He threw up his hands when he saw my panicked eyes. A smile formed on his lips. "I ss...startle you a lot." When I didn't lower my phone, he motioned to it and whispered. "Mind not shining that in my eyes? Especially with the skull staring at me."

Shutting the locker door, I lowered my phone and smiled weakly at Graham. "It was open. I actually don't think they ever assigned me a locker."

"Do you have your paper from the front office?" He blinked fast and hard.

I reached into my pocket and pulled it out, glancing it over. "Does it say on here?"

He stepped close to me, our arms almost touching. He was getting more comfortable with me. He pointed to the bottom corner. "Right here."

The number matched Trenton's, or Ellington's, locker. "Huh. This *is* my locker."

"Here's the combination." Graham pointed to it on the paper.

It had opened on its own before, but when I tried to pull up on the handle, the door didn't budge.

"They keep them locked," Graham said in a whisper.

"It opened before," I said. "Who's Trenton?"

"A friend of mine," he said, still whispering. "His family moved a few months back. Your dad bought their house."

"Oh." I used the combination to open the locker. When I searched for Ellington's name on the door, only the smooth brown metal stared back at me. "That's odd."

"What's odd?"

If I mentioned I'd seen a name and now it had disappeared, he'd think I was crazy. Maybe I'd imagined that as well. My eyes went to the clock on the wall. "Everyone left their classrooms. School isn't over yet." The lights were still out.

Graham pointed to a window down the hall. I walked to it, looking outside at a nasty storm. The rain pelted down in huge, quarter-sized drops. Lightning ripped through the sky, illuminating the trees that rocked with the howling wind.

"Willow Marsh gets these storms every now and then," he whispered. When he kept his voice low, his stutter went away. "They're sending everyone home. We should probably get out of here before it gets worse."

I looked into his blinking eyes. "So, no bowling tonight?"

He shook his head in response.

Thunder roared, and I jumped. Graham laughed, so I hit his arm. "I'm not used to these kinds of storms, okay?" Taking him by the arm, I steered him toward the main doors, stopping when we got there. Rain and wind assaulted the glass, making it hard to see out. I pulled up the hood of my sweater, tucking my ponytail and scarf inside. "Listen, this is kind of freaking me out, and it looks like you can barely see in front of you out there, so I'm taking your hand until we get to the truck."

I slipped my hand into his, keeping a light grip. I watched his eyes, ready for him to panic, but he surprised me by interlocking our fingers and stepping close to me. He leaned down, probably so I could hear his whisper over the storm. "Hold on tight and stay close. It'll be worse once we're out there."

He didn't wait for a response before he pulled me out into the storm.

CHAPTER 7

Sleeping became my most dreaded part of the day. The nightmares were always lurking under the covers, their spiteful eyes anxious for me to close mine so they could take charge.

My therapist in Skokie gave me a prescription to help me sleep, but I hated to take it. The pills somehow magnified the dreams, each scene more piercing in sound and sickly in color than the last. The drugs weighed me down and made it harder for me to break free.

Every dream was the same. Wet pavement, the tires sending water flying everywhere, high winds shaking the car, and rain pelting against the windshield to the point it started cracking, just like my heart had done that night. The car hydroplaning, swerving us all over the road, and jolting me. Amá wailing and Felix crying. Complete and sudden loss of control.

My world coming to an end.

I woke in a mess of damp sheets, sweat dripping down my face and back. My wet hair clung to my neck, and I shivered, fighting back tears. It was only a matter of time before I completely broke down and would never want to face the world again. Dad and my therapist told me over and over again that it wasn't my fault. So did Leya. But neither their words nor my head could convince my heart.

Being careful not to wake Dad, I grabbed my exercise clothes and went to change in the bathroom. Though it would be freezing, I put on a tank top and shorts. It would motivate me to move. Instead of using my scarf, I left it wrapped around my wrist and used a band to pull back my hair.

Outside, the storm had completely passed. The trees were calm, and only a few clouds floated in the dark sky. The sun was asleep with the rest of the town.

Unfortunately, we were still stuck at the Dixons'. Our house needed a lot more work than Dad had thought, so I wasn't sure how long we'd have to endure Barbie. At least that meant more time around Graham – shy mannerisms aside, he was pretty hot.

As I started my run, I opened the playlists on my phone and found Bob Marley. Felix's favorite.

I didn't check the time before I left, but it was early morning. Normal people slept during that time, but I couldn't. Running cleared my mind. My muscles being on fire kept me alert and strong.

I ran wherever my feet took me. Down Main Street, past the old, cottage-style houses, and then to our new house. The whole place was tented off, the circus colors matching with the joke of a house, so I kept going. My pink and black Nikes pounded on the pavement as my muscles burned.

Soon the wooden, chipped *Thanks for visiting Willow Marsh* sign came into view. Below it were the words: *Freedom is ours.* There were some rifles carved into the sign, presumably from the Civil War. Seemed like most things in town had something to tie in with it.

A little bird perched itself on the sign, its glossy eyes staring straight at me. As I drew closer, it opened its sharp beak and whistled, making me cringe. Was it following me around? Or did Willow Marsh have an infestation of creepy little birds?

I pushed myself harder, my legs digging into the wet pavement, and my arms pumping, until I passed the sign, not wanting to ever stop. Thick willow trees lined both sides of the road, and I couldn't see past them. I kept on going, hoping for some freedom that wouldn't be found. There were no street lamps, so the only light came from the moon and stars. I ran down the center of the road, something I'd never do back home or before the crash.

My lungs and muscles ached and screamed for me to stop. I ran a little farther until my legs were about to collapse. Standing in the middle of the road, I panted, holding a cramp in my side, and staring up at the stars. Bob Marley sang in my ears.

Felix.

I missed him.

Amá.

I missed her, too.

So much it hurt worse than the fire burning in my muscles.

Tears escaped, falling unashamed down my cheeks as sobs racked my chest. Bending over, I put my hands on my knees, fighting for air. How would I live with them gone? Why them?

Why did I have to survive?

I held my arm up to my mouth, using the scarf wrapped around my wrist to stifle my cry. Bright lights made me look up. A car came toward me, slowing down as it got closer. I stepped off to the side of the road, expecting them to pass, but they stopped next to me.

The window rolled down, and a middle-aged man in a uniform leaned out, his hairy arm resting on the door of his cruiser. 'Willow Marsh Sheriff' was painted on the side of the car, along with a gold badge. He was about to say something, so I took out my earbuds, letting them fall on my shoulders, but then he looked me over. Opening the door, he got out of his car and rushed over to me. "What's wrong?" His voice was deep and scratchy, adding a layer of authority to him. His hand rested on the grip of the gun as he scanned the area, probably looking for the cause of my breakdown.

I still hadn't composed myself. Anxiety consumed me to the point that tingles flared inside, and I couldn't breathe right. Turning my back to him, I covered my mouth with the scarf and tried to force myself to stop crying and control my breathing.

Don't be so dramatic. The voice again. A darker, silky, inner voice. Maybe I'd already gone crazy and didn't know it.

The sheriff's firm hand suddenly landed on my shoulder, and he kept it there while I cried. He must have realized I wasn't in any danger; I was just freaking out. Closing my eyes, I took a deep breath, willing myself to calm. *Be strong*, I thought. *Control. Steady. Calm.*

My breathing finally evened, and the tears stopped. I wiped them away with the scarf and turned to face the sheriff. I had no idea what to say. There was no sane reason for a teenage girl to be in the middle of the road, early in the morning, sobbing uncontrollably. "Sorry. I..." My mind went blank.

Lowering his hand, the sheriff glanced up and down the street, his hands resting on his waist, just above his belt. "Why are you out here all by yourself?" When his intense, brown eyes found their way back to mine, I noticed how familiar they were. Same square jaw. Same jet black hair. Natural light tan from spending lots of time outdoors. Blake.

"Just out for a run." Bob Marley sang out from my shoulder. I took my phone out of my pocket and pressed stop.

The sheriff raised a thick eyebrow. "This early in the morning?"

I wiped my cheeks with my hands, getting rid of the last of my tears. "Couldn't sleep." The cold ran over me, and I wished I'd brought a jacket.

"I don't think we've met." He held out his hand. "Sheriff Hayes."

My scarf was saturated with sweat and tears, so I unwrapped it and took his hand in mine. His gaze lingered on my scar, and I quickly yanked my hand away, putting it behind my back and clenching my fist. "Tessa Isaacson."

Recognition passed over his face. "Oh, yes, the new family in town. You and your father, correct?"

"Yes." Small town. No secrets, which could be very bad for me.

"Are you hurt?"

"What?" Now that I had finally calmed, my senses came back, taking in the overwhelming smell of cigarette smoke from the sheriff. I took a step back, my sneakers splashing a little bit of water from a puddle.

"You were crying," he said.

Lies. I needed to get better at telling them. "Just missing home and my friends. I have anxiety." Or be overly honest to a stranger.

"Well, this is your home now." Sheriff Hayes got a pen and business card from a pocket inside his jacket and scribbled something down before he handed it to me. "That's the number for Rita Hastings. She's the local therapist. I think you'll really like her. Give her a call."

His writing was hard to decipher. I flipped the card over and saw his name and number. He'd found me crying, and his immediate response was sending me to a therapist?

Men, dark-inner-me said. I pushed her away.

Taking the card, I slipped it into my pocket along with my phone. "Thanks."

"Also," he said, looking down the road, "try not to run in the middle of the street. We wouldn't want you getting hurt." His intense gaze landed back on me.

"Noted."

Amusement flashed in his eyes. "Let me give you a ride back. You ran a pretty long distance."

When we got in his car, I buckled up and watched the sun paint the sky orange and pink as it continued to rise. After a few miles, I realized he wasn't kidding. I really had run a long way. The car stank of cigarette smoke, so I rolled down my window to get some fresh air. I turned to him, noticing so much of Blake in him. "What are you doing up this early?"

Sheriff Hayes arched an eyebrow, but a faint smile appeared on his lips. "Unfortunately, that's the duty of the sheriff. The law never sleeps."

I played with the scarf in my hands. I'd have to clean it as soon as I could. Thank goodness Amá had a huge scarf collection. "You have duties outside Willow Marsh?"

His face remained passive as he answered. "Sometimes."

I couldn't stop staring at his jaw and eyes. "Do you have a family?"

"Yes." Sheriff Hayes turned off the radio. It hadn't been loud, so I didn't know why he felt the need. "Wife and two kids."

I picked a piece of lint off my tank top, trying to be casual. "Son?"

He stole a glance at me before he grinned. "You met Blake."

"Yes. He looks just like you." I went to touch my ring, but my finger was bare. I didn't like to wear the family ring on runs.

He rubbed his hand over the stubble on his cheek. "What about you? Do you look more like your father or mother?"

"My mom." I needed to change the subject before I let something slip. The sheriff finding out my secret could be disastrous. "So, are there decent running trails in Willow Marsh? That might be better than the road."

Sheriff Hayes' mouth turned into a small smile, his eyes humored. "There are, actually. Blake and I trail run every weekend. I'll give Blake a map to give to you at school."

We crossed back into the city limits.

"Uh, I'm staying with the Dixon family, so you can drop me off there. Our new house is pretty old and needs to be fumigated. Along with other things." I added that last part under my breath.

At the mention of the Dixons, Sheriff Hayes' face darkened. "How do you know the Dixons?" His tone was almost accusatory, like I'd done something wrong.

I didn't want to get caught up in their drama. I scooted closer to the door to widen the distance between us. "Barbie helped us find the house. She offered her home until things can get cleaned up."

He stayed in a fierce silence until we reached the Dixon house. He put the car in park and handed me another business card. "This is the number for the Willow Marsh Inn. Tell them I sent you, and they'll let you stay there free of charge until your house is ready."

"I thought they were on vacation." That was what Barbie had told us.

"They're back."

The thought of getting away from Barbie was enticing, but the sheriff's grim attitude intrigued me more. "They on your wanted list or something? It'll only be a few more days, I'm sure. Barbie doesn't seem to mind." Because she wanted to get in Dad's pants.

"Tessa, right?" Sheriff Hayes asked, turning toward me, and resting his hand on my headrest.

I nodded.

"I'm going to cut to the chase." He glanced out the window at the Dixon's small house. "I love this town. But we have a few ... unsavory characters. Unstable is a better word." He pointed to the paint-chipped front door. "Two of them live there. Be careful of them. Graham may seem like a nice, shy boy, but I assure you, he's not." He plastered a smile on his face, the corners of his eyes wrinkling. "Blake, he'll be a good friend for you. I'll have him drive you to the Willow Marsh Inn after school. I'll give your dad a call and let him know of the new arrangements. We'll get your stuff moved out of the Dixon house today so you won't have to worry about it."

Dark-inner-me scoffed. *First a therapist, now this?*

While I agreed with her, the fact that she kept popping up in my mind at random times was freaking me out. I wanted to ask her where she came from, but that would be admitting she was in there, messing with me.

"Sheriff, that's very kind of you, but I'm sure it's not necessary."

He held up his hand. "I assure you, it is. Best not to argue with the sheriff, right?" Another forced smile.

This town and people gave me the creeps. Opening the door, I jumped out, the biting cold welcoming over the iciness radiating from the sheriff.

I put on my own forced smile. "Thanks, Sheriff, for the ride. I'll look for Blake at school for the map. Have a *lovely* day." I shut the door with more force than necessary.

Why did the sheriff hate the Dixon family so much? Maybe Barbie was an ex of his.

I texted Leya.

Are you awake?

I watched the sheriff drive away. I hated not having Leya close so we could talk face to face. My phone vibrated in my hand.

Leya:
Are you kidding me?
It's freaking early!

That's the bright eyed
girl I needed to hear from.

You're so lucky you're
in another state, otherwise
I'd kick your sorry trash.

I met the sheriff, who just
happens to be Blake's dad.

What?! Is he as hot? Wait,
why did you meet the
sheriff? Did you get arrested?
Should I call you? Do you
have to share a cell?

Couldn't sleep. Out for a run.
Sheriff gave me a ride back
to Graham's. And, ew, so not
comparing Blake to his dad.

We seriously need to set
some ground rules as to
what warrants an early

text. I'm going back to sleep.

I sneaked inside the Dixon home, shutting the door as softly as I could.

"Tt...tessa?" Graham adjusted himself on the couch, propping himself up on his elbow. "Ww...where ww...were you?" He drummed his fingers along the side of his flannel pants. He had his hood up, and his shaggy hair fell over part of his eyes, but I could see enough to detect the uncertainty and the lack of confidence they held. He didn't give me a dangerous vibe.

His eyes quickly ran down me, over my tank top and shorts. With the way Graham looked at me, I felt more exposed. But for some reason, I liked it.

I shook the thought from my head. "Went on a run."

You should run away from him, dark-inner-me said.

Even though the sheriff had warned me to stay away, the fact that dark-inner-me didn't want to be around Graham made me want to get closer. I put on my mask of confidence and sauntered to the couch, stopping at Graham's side. I flipped his hood back so I could see his eyes better. "Bowling? Tonight? If there's no storm, of course."

Graham's blinking almost went out of control as he stared at my hand that had touched his hood. For the first time, I noticed how long his eyelashes were. They'd make any girl jealous. He tried to speak, but nothing came out. He eventually nodded.

"Great." I smiled at him before I went to get ready for the day.

Masquerades could be quite enjoyable if done right.

CHAPTER 8

Graham's fingers beat along the peeling steering wheel on the way to school, his eyes darting over to me every now and then. I hoped I hadn't come on too strong earlier. The last thing I wanted to do was scare him away.

I turned up the rock music blaring from the speakers. It usually tended to calm Graham down. I had no idea how to tell him I'd be staying at the inn. It didn't seem fair to him to bail and not give him a heads up.

I was twirling my phone in my hand when it buzzed.

Dad:
Sorry I missed you this
morning. Headed out early
to work on the house.

Tessa:
Get it done ASAP. I miss
having my own bed.

I know how you feel.
I'm doing my best.

I met the sheriff.
He said we can stay at
Willow Marsh Inn for free
until the house is ready.

That's the best news I've heard
since we moved here. I need
to get away from Barbie...

I laughed, choking it down when I saw Graham looking at me. "My dad. He can be funny sometimes."

Have a good day at school.
Love you.

Love you.

Graham turned into the school parking lot, finding a space near the back. He tended to stay away from the crowd, and I didn't mind. When he reached for the metal door handle, I stopped him.

"Graham, wait."

He lowered his arm, adjusting his body to face me, his eyebrows raised in curiosity. He licked his lips, his eyes flitting to mine a couple times. Warmth rose in my cheeks. I'd never kissed a guy, and I'd never wanted to. Graham was making me rethink that.

I played with a loose piece of fabric on the truck bench, trying not to get too flustered. "I wanted to let you know that my dad and I will be staying at Willow Marsh Inn until our house is ready."

He blinked at a fast rate as he drummed his fingers along his leg. "Ww...why?" His lips were pursed in disappointment.

Slowly, I scooted toward him. I kept my movements small and steady to not scare him. He watched as I placed my hand on top of his and kept his eyes there while I talked. "It's nothing against you." *Definitely against your mom.* "We didn't want to intrude, and the inn offered us a place for free."

His hand shook under mine. I took a firmer grip, causing him to reduce his shaking until he stopped. His eyes grazed my lips before they settled on my eyes, and his blinking slowed. He whispered to stop his stutter. "I've liked having you around."

"I've liked it, too." I gave his hand a small squeeze. "Thank you for listening to me and being a friend."

"Thank you for being nice to me." Graham returned my hand squeeze. He leaned toward me, his curious eyes on my lips. My heart rate quickened. I liked Graham, but I wasn't sure how much, or in what way. I was in such a bad place. And with him, was he just wanting to kiss me because I was the first girl who paid attention to him? We hardly knew each other, yet I'd never felt as comfortable with another guy as I did with him.

A horn honked outside. In a swift motion, Graham opened the door and stumbled out, running his shaking fingers through his hair.

The horn had been for someone else. I had to hold in a laugh as I got out of his truck and shut the door. He had started sulking toward the school, and I hated to see him like that, so I jogged to catch up to him. I needed to ease the tension. "I'm so going to kick your butt at bowling tonight." I linked my fingers together and stretched them out in front of me. "I went a few times as a kid, so I totally have it down."

Graham's shoulders loosened as he laughed. "Tt...trust me, I'll ww...win."

"There you are." Blake jogged up to me, giving me a hug, his tropical scent reminding me of sunscreen and trips to the lake with my family. "I didn't know you were a runner. I know tons of places we can go." He pointed at the tree-covered hills behind the school. They were large, but not mountains. Something I could handle. "Some of the best trails are back there."

Somehow, the sight of him made my head go cloudy. I didn't know how to control it. "Hey, Blake." Why did I always sound so breathless when I said his name?

Blake glanced at Graham. "Hey, Scram, you can do just that. Scram."

How could a guy go from amazing to a total prick in a matter of seconds? "Blake, don't talk to him like that."

I thought Graham might disappear again, but he stood tall, facing Blake. "It's up tt...to Tt...tessa."

A smile found its way to my lips. Seeing Blake and Graham side by side with Graham not cowering back let me get a decent look at the two of them. Blake had a natural hotness to him with his smoldering eyes and that dimple. He was confident and charming. But he could be a jerk.

Graham was unsure of himself. He didn't wear designer clothes or have a lot. But a girl could melt into a puddle from his natural smile. And there was something in his humble manner that made me feel comfortable with him − like I could trust him. In that moment, with the way he was looking at Blake with rare confidence, it was kind of sexy.

I needed to talk to Leya.

I'm here, dark-inner-me said. *And I can tell you exactly which one I want.*

I tensed at her voice. Why was she in my head? Maybe it

was something in the water in Willow Marsh causing me to go crazy. Or it was another power altogether.

Blake shoved Graham in the chest, bringing me back to the reality in front of me. He towered over him. "Stay away from her. My dad already took care of getting her out of your house. Now I'm going to make sure you don't hurt her. We don't need another *accident* happening."

Accident? What accident?

Fear flashed on Graham's face, but then he calmed, and he looked at me, probably waiting to see my response. When I stood there in confused silence, disappointment – and maybe some regret – crossed his eyes. Shaking his head, he took off, trudging into the school and out of sight.

Blake's arm was around me in no time as he steered me toward the front doors. "Sorry about that." He must have sensed my anxiety, because he dropped his arm and held up his hands to show his innocence. "I'm not trying to scare you, Tessa. But my dad was right with everything he told you about Graham. You can't trust him. He's unstable."

So was I. My frantic eyes searched for Graham in the hall. I wanted to ask about the accident. I knew all about those. But he'd disappeared.

Focus on Blake, dark-inner-me drawled. My hands balled into fists, trying to control my anxiety. It was scary that she'd become so present.

"Don't worry about him." Putting on a smile, Blake set a map in my hands. I tried not to stare at the adorable dimple on his cheek. "I've highlighted the best trails." He pointed to one on the left-hand side, his arm brushing against mine. "I thought we could go to this one on Saturday morning. At the top, there's a gorgeous view of Willow Marsh. I think you'll love it."

I stood in the hallway, trying to gather my thoughts. He'd already planned an outing for us? It had been less than an hour since I talked to his dad. I opened my mouth to tell him I wasn't sure if that would work, but his flirting eyes on mine made me pause. Heat flushed my cheeks.

"What time should I pick you up?" Blake brushed away a few strands of hair that had stuck to my lip gloss. "I'm an early person, but not as early as you." His smile. How could a girl think straight with his lips pulled like that?

"Uh..." The bell rang overhead, interrupting us.

Blake put his arm around my shoulder again. "We can talk about it later."

Just as long as we see him again, dark-inner-me said with a hopeful sigh.

I wasn't sure where she'd come from, or who she was, but the voice stalking my mind needed to go.

Dark-inner-me giggled. *I'm going nowhere, sweetheart.*

CHAPTER 9

During fourth period, Graham wouldn't talk to me. I tried passing him notes, but he'd crumple them up and throw them back. I hated that I was letting Blake ruin whatever relationship I had with Graham.

The teacher had his back to the class, writing something on the board, so I texted Leya. She'd know what to do.

> Need to talk. 2 guys.
> Don't know what to do.
> HELP!

My phone buzzed seconds later.

> WHAT? OMG! Call me!

> Can't. In class.

> Don't drop that information
> on me and then tell me you
> can't talk!

Sorry. Call you as
soon as school ends.
Miss your crazy face.

During lunch, I told Blake I had to go talk to a teacher but instead went to find Graham. When my search inside the school came up empty, I checked outside.

"You're disgusting!"

I turned toward the voice and saw a spunky girl shove a squirrelly guy in the chest. She must have sensed me staring, because she looked at me, the anger in her eyes turning into hope.

"Are you the new girl?" she asked. She had dyed bright red hair that looked like she cut it herself, choppy all around, but she pulled it off. I could definitely see the Latina in her beautiful brown eyes. She rushed over to me and played with her black tongue ring like it was second nature. The sun glinted off the gold cross hanging from her neck.

"Yes." I smiled at her seconds before she threw her arms around me.

"Thank the Lord!" She hugged me tight, swaying back and forth.

Her friend walked over. "Don't mind Corrine. She has issues." She yanked on the back of Corrine's loose T-Shirt.

Corrine let me go but kept her soft hands on my arms. She shot her friend an affectionate glare like they sassed each other all the time. "Excuse me for getting excited about having someone new in town." Corrine nodded her head at her friend. "Jade has no manners, so she shouldn't be talking."

Jade had her hair dyed blue, with piercings on her nose, lip, eyebrow, and multiple on each ear. A tattoo of some black birds resided on the inside of her wrist. They looked like they were flying away to freedom. She folded her arms. "Tess or something, right?"

"Tessa," I said.

"I'll stick with Tess."

I motioned to the squirrelly guy. "What did he do to make you so mad?"

Corrine put her hand on her hip. "Something completely inappropriate, which I'm so not repeating. The only reason he's getting away with it is because he's Jade's boyfriend." When I started to back away, she stepped with me. "Where you headed?" She moved the cross pendant back and forth on the chain.

I continued to walk backward, tightening the scarf holding my hair back. It had come loose during the bear hug. "Looking for a friend."

"Name." Jade's hazel eyes were bored.

"What?" I asked, stopping.

Jade raised her voice, talking slowly. "What's the name of your *friend*?"

"Graham."

"Dixon?" She pointed behind me. "Try the shed in back of the school. That's where the loners go."

Corrine slapped Jade upside the head. "That's no way to talk about her *friend*."

I turned and hurried away as they argued. Behind the school, I found an old shed, the wood shaving away from years of neglect. The hinges moaned as I forced the door open.

Smoke immediately welcomed me. I sniffed and then grimaced. It was a combination of cigarettes and marijuana. I pressed the scarf wrapped around my wrist against my nose and breathed in the smell of lilacs. When my eyes finally adjusted to the dim lighting, I saw a mix of guys and girls staring at me, all with looks wondering why I had the audacity to step into their space. I tried to ignore them as I looked around for Graham.

His curly mess of hair caught my attention in the back corner of the shed. He was sitting on a makeshift bench, his head down, tapping his fingers on his leg. Earbuds were perched in his ears. His lips moved, but they weren't singing a song – he was talking to himself. I popped out an earbud, and he looked up in surprise, his calm eyes going wide when he saw me. I'd taken him from his happy place.

Graham wrapped his hand around the earbud dangling against his chest. "Ww...what are you doing here?"

He was sitting in the middle of the bench, so I motioned him to move over. He debated for a moment, but he finally slid down, making room for me.

I sat down, coughing. "How can you stand it in here?"

A small smile landed on his lips. "I like the calm of it all."

"Are you going to ignore me forever?" I asked. Amá always told me to get straight to the point.

He hummed along with the rock music coming from his headphones. The motion looked like he was trying to go back to his safe place, so I gave him a minute. He finally spoke, but wouldn't look me in the eye. "I don't like him."

Blake.

Delicious, dark-inner-me said. *Let's go find him.*

Shut up! I shouted back. *Who are you?* I rubbed my forehead, wishing I could rub her away.

I'm you, dark-inner-me said. *The rational version.*

That didn't seem likely. I noticed Graham was staring at me, waiting for my response. I pulled at the strings on my hoodie. "That's understandable. Has he always teased you?"

He slowly nodded, his fingers creating a melody on his leg. "For as long as I can remember. But the ladies love him. Along ww...with everyone else."

I almost commented on him using the word 'ladies,' but then realized it was easier for him to say than girls or women.

"Listen, I'm just trying to get to know people in this town

before I pass judgment. You of all people should understand that."

He looked at me. "That's fine. I'm just letting you know how I feel about him. He's a manipulative jerk. One day you'll realize it." He played with the cheap, black watch on his wrist. "Or not. Ladies are always fooled by him."

I leaned my head against the wall behind me. "I'm not like most girls." Well, not usually. Blake brought out someone else in me. "Graham, I still want to be your friend."

He leaned his head back as well. "*He'll* let you?"

"He doesn't own me, and there's no way he can tell me who I can and can't be friends with." No way would I let a guy control me like that.

"I wouldn't be so sure of that." He lifted off the bench, so I yanked him back down by the arm of his hoodie.

Sheriff Hayes said I couldn't trust Graham, but Graham said I couldn't trust Blake. I didn't know who to believe. Honestly, everyone seemed a little shady to me. But I didn't want to give up on Graham just yet.

I eyed the scarf covering my scar. "What accident was Blake talking about?"

Graham's hand balled into a fist. "Nothing." His tone was sharp, closing off the topic.

I changed to another one. "Is there something about Blake I should know about?"

He blinked several times before he answered in a whisper. "I thought you wanted to figure it out on your own." He put his earbuds back in, stood, and left me alone on the bench in the smoke-filled shed.

A guy stumbled toward me, a lazy smile on his thin lips, so I bolted out of there, catching up to Graham. I ran in front of him, making him stop and let out a huff. He took out his earbud, looking at me expectantly.

"Are we still on for tonight?" I'd been itching to get out. I hoped it would take my mind off things and maybe for once I could feel normal.

He ran his fingers through his hair, and his focus went to the lightly cloudy sky.

I tugged a string on his hoodie. "Graham, my life is beyond complicated right now. I want to get out and have some fun. The only person I want to do that with is you."

Red covered his cheeks as his hand went to the string I'd touched, his voice trembling with surprise. "Really?"

"Really." I pushed him lightly on the arm. "Pick me up from the inn tonight at seven."

"Where are you going?" Jade's bored voice broke up our moment.

I whipped around to see her standing there, her blue eyebrows up in anticipation of my answer. Corrine bounded up next to her, a twinkle in her eyes like she was excited to see me.

"We're going bowling," I said, my words drawn out in confusion.

Jade sucked on the ring around her lip. "Not much of a bowler, but what else is there to do in this stupid town? We'll see you there."

Jade walked away before I could respond.

Corrine grinned. "I seriously haven't been bowling in forever, so this should be interesting. See you tonight!" She jogged back to her friends.

I turned to Graham with my eyebrows furrowed. "Did they just invite themselves to go out with us tonight?"

He chuckled. "It's Jade."

The bell rang, signaling the end of lunch. I backed away from Graham, my hands in my hoodie pocket, and a sultry mask on my face. "You should smile more often. It looks good on you."

Leaving Graham standing there with a red neck and

cheeks, I went to my class wondering if I'd completely lost my mind. I had a voice in my head and was toying with two guys who were possibly dangerous. Or were at least hiding secrets.

The whole masquerade and not knowing who to trust thing was giving me a thrill it shouldn't have.

CHAPTER 10

After school, Blake dropped me off at the Willow Marsh Inn. The owners had a room ready for Dad and me, and the sweet, old wife took me straight to it. True to his word, the sheriff had our bags sitting on the beds in the room. I was a little sad I didn't get to see Barbie's reaction when he showed up to take our stuff.

I tried calling Leya, but it went to voice mail, so I texted her, my ring clinking against my phone case with the movement.

> Where are you? We
> need to talk guys.

Choir practice. Sorry.

> This is more important!

Trust me, I agree. But Miss
Jennings doesn't think so.
In fact, she's yelling at me

right now. *shakes fist*

Gah. Lame.
Call me later.

Dad brought dinner to the inn on the way home from work. The smell of penne and garlic bread made my stomach rumble. He tossed me a bottle of Dr Pepper.

I pressed the frosty plastic against my cheek. "Where did you get this?"

"The market in town." He pulled out another bottle from his bag. "Got one for myself, too."

"I think the market is my new favorite place in Willow Marsh." There was no table, so I plopped down on the blue velvet couch, swung my legs up, and placed the paper plate on my stomach.

With a chuckle, Dad went into the bathroom and changed into basketball shorts and a T-shirt. When he came back out, he turned on a basketball game, the volume low. It was an old box TV I didn't know they made anymore. "How was school?"

I finished the bite of bread in my mouth. "Fine. I'm going bowling tonight with some new friends."

"That's good to hear." He wiped his chin with a napkin. "I think it'll be good for you to get out." He hadn't shaved in a few days, so a small beard was forming. He'd always kept it shaved smooth because Amá liked it that way. I was kind of curious to see what he looked like with a full beard.

I dipped my bread into the creamy garlic sauce on the plate, careful not to let the scarf on my wrist touch it. "How are the renovations coming?"

He took a few bites of his penne before he answered. His eyes drooped – it had probably been a long day for him.

"Great. I think we'll only have a few days left here, then we can sleep in our new home."

The thought of having my own space, my own bathroom, made me smile. I loved my dad, but being cooped up with him in a tiny space was too much. "Was Barbie mad when you left today?"

"At first. She wanted an explanation, but then she saw the sheriff and went quiet."

I pointed my fork at him, a piece of penne dangling from it. "Maybe we should have him be a mediator every time we're around her."

Dad choked on a piece of food for a second before he grinned. "That's not a bad idea."

I finished off my plate, scraping up every morsel, and then dished myself some more. It was surprisingly good for takeout.

"How's the new job?" I asked, sitting back on the couch. I rubbed my arm back and forth on the velvet for a second, loving the feel.

He'd been offered a position as the city's private contractor, doing mostly construction jobs and fixing up old buildings. He'd been an architect in Illinois, doing all the planning and mapping, but he missed the days of the hands-on work. He started out working for a construction company before he'd received his degree and began his career. In Willow Marsh, he'd be able to do both.

"So far, so good." He flipped the remote control around in his hand. "Sheriff Hayes showed me all around town and took me to my office on Main Street."

"You have your own office? Fancy."

He shrugged it off. "It's nothing much. Tomorrow I'll be working at our home, updating the kitchen. The tent should be off by then."

I adjusted myself on the couch so I could face him. I'd

been wanting to talk to him about Amá and Felix, but I was never sure how to bring it up. Dad wasn't one to talk about his emotions a lot. But I needed to get it off my chest. "Do you think about them? Amá and Felix?"

Dad turned to me, surprise flashing on his face. The dark circles under his eyes matched mine. He'd probably been sleeping as well as I had, which wasn't very much. "Of course. All the time." His face softened, most likely sensing my sadness. "How are you holding up?"

I poked some penne with my fork. "Not too well. It just hurts so much. I want to hear their voices again." Biting back a sob, I set my plate on the end table next to me.

Dad swung his legs so he could sit up on the edge of the bed. He leaned forward, placing his hand on mine. "Tessa, I know how you feel. Give it some time. The pain will slowly subside."

"But not go away?" I whispered.

"I don't think anyone can ever fully get over the loss of a loved one." He squeezed my hands. "But you focus on the good times and use that love to guide you forward." He wrapped me up in his arms. "I love you, Tessa. I miss your mom and brother every day, but I'm glad I still have you."

I buried my face in his chest and breathed in his soapy scent. "I love you, too, Apá."

He held me for a while before my emotions became too much. I pulled away, grabbed my bag, and went into the bathroom. I stared at myself in the mirror for a while. Wisps of hair poked out from my ponytail. I pulled out the blue scarf and ran my fingers through my hair. Not much could be done to save it. I hadn't bothered with makeup since that fateful night, so my dark, tired eyes were painfully obvious. Maybe wearing makeup again could be part of my masquerade so no one could ask about my state.

Sighing, I stared at the bag next to the sink. I needed to

try to talk to Amá again before I went completely insane. After I placed the three red candles on the counter, lighting them one by one, I turned off the bathroom light. I silenced my cell phone before I began.

Closing my eyes, I took slow, deeps breaths and pictured Amá in my mind. I whispered so Dad wouldn't hear, but also to set the mood. "Amá, it's Tessa. Can you hear me?"

The noise from the TV broke my concentration. I did my best to block it out. "Amá, are you okay?"

Heat grew inside, warming my blood. A tingling sensation coursed through me as an overwhelming blanket of love surrounded me.

Tessa, mi amor, Amá whispered.

My eyes flew open, hoping to see her, but I was alone. The flames from the candles dimmed, and I found myself leaning forward. "Amá, don't go. I need to apologize."

I focused on the warmth in my soul. "I'm sorry. I never meant to hurt you or Felix." A presence drifted to the side of me, the weight of it tethered to me tight. Amá was in the bathroom. I wanted to hold her and feel her arms wrap around me like they used to. "I miss you, Amá."

Suddenly, a white wind swirled around the room, ending my contact with Amá. There were no windows in the bathroom. Panicking, I watched as the air jumped to each flame, stretching across the distance, and blowing them out one by one, leaving me in darkness.

The heat left me, replaced by a frosty current running through my veins that made me shudder. I wrapped my arms around myself, though it did nothing to warm me.

One candle lit on its own. A cool breeze wafted from the mirror like I'd stepped into a freezer. The mirror crackled, ice covering every inch as another wick lit. The flames stretched out, lighting the other candle, and towering way higher than they should have been able to go. The fire melted the ice on the mirror, creating a dozen streams of tears running down the glass.

Thick fog rose from the ground, climbing until it reached the ceiling and occupied the entire bathroom. Unable to see, I stretched my arms in front of me and tried to feel around for the door. My skin rippled like something was crawling underneath my skin, and the cold continued to run through my veins. Even though I was terrified, I touched my skin and forced myself to keep my fingers there as my skin moved up and down in a slow, steady movement. When I pushed, it was soft and squishy like slime. I was beyond grateful for the darkness and fog so I couldn't see what was happening to me. At least I could pretend it was all in my mind.

The cold fog kissed my skin. Each breath was an intake of tiny icicles diving down inside, wanting to freeze me from the middle.

Dark-inner-me growled in the distance like she wanted to come forward, but couldn't. Some force was stopping her. My skin pulsated faster, the ripples painfully pushing at my skin. My body was having a war inside, two forces fighting against one another – the icy presence and dark-inner-me.

With the clashing forces inside, the buzzing on my skin, the ice inside my body and out – I worried I might shatter into a million pieces.

Suddenly, the fog evaporated. No trace of it remained in the bathroom. The ice within me dissolved as the presence left. I quickly flipped on the light before I held out my arms and looked them over, but I couldn't see a difference in my skin. I let out the smallest breath of relief. When I looked up, I choked back a scream.

On the mirror, letters were formed with ice: HELP.

I stumbled backward, hitting into the side of the tub. My legs flipped out from underneath me, and I fell into the tub, my head smacking into the wall and my body thudding on impact. I laid still for a moment, groaning and rubbing the back of my head.

Dad ran in moments later. He glanced around the bathroom, his concerned eyes settling on me sprawled in the bathtub, my legs dangling over the edge. Reaching down, he wrapped his arms around me and helped me out of the tub.

"Tessa, what happened?"

I was shaking too much to answer. No way he would understand, or even believe me. I was having a hard time believing it myself.

My eyes went to the mirror. The word had disappeared.

Dad looked at the counter, his concern turning into anger. "Tessa, not this séance stuff again." He blew out each candle with more force than necessary. "I told you to stop. It's not healthy. You can't contact your mom, okay?" He waved his hand in front of my face. "You still with me?"

"Yes." I licked my dry lips, my tongue sticking to my skin for a second. "Sorry."

"Tessa, this is dangerous. Promise me you'll stop this nonsense." His intense eyes bore into mine. He wanted me safe, and I completely understood. Too much had happened to us. "Promise me."

With everything going wrong, it was probably a good idea to lay off anything séance-related for a while. He waited until I nodded before he took the candles and left the bathroom. I looked at the empty mirror once more before I ran out after him.

CHAPTER 11

Graham held up three steady fingers, rubbing in the fact that he'd bowled three strikes in a row. A turkey in a navy blue Civil War uniform danced across the screen, mocking me and my pathetic skills. Since we'd started, I had knocked over one pin. One.

It was only my third time bowling in my life. The previous two times were for friends' birthday parties when I was younger.

I picked up a purple ball from the return and shuffled to the lane, trying to ignore the smell of musty carpet. I'd opted for a lighter ball, hoping it would be easier to handle. The scarf on my hand made it hard to grip the ball, but I didn't want to take it off because then I would have to stare at the scar all night. I'd chosen one of Amá's cloth scarves instead of a silk one. The purple flowers on it matched the bowling ball.

Glancing over my shoulder, I smiled at Graham, trying to sound surer than I was. "Prepare to be blown away." I narrowed my eyes at the lane and released the ball. It thunked hard on the ground and bounced into the gutter.

A very slow, deliberate clap came from behind me. Putting

my hands on my hips, I turned to Graham. "We can't all be professionals like you." I tried again, the bowling ball staying on the very edge of the lane, falling into the gutter right before it reached the pins.

Jade went next, knocking over a grand total of five pins. As Corrine lined up for her turn, Jade sat next to her boyfriend, Marcel. He was a short guy, skinny, and wore black square-rimmed glasses. He kept his black hair in a fro on top, with the sides shaved off. A tattoo peeked out from his shirt sleeve, but I couldn't tell what it was.

Marcel leaned forward, his forearms resting on his legs. He had a small piece of wood in one hand, the other using a carving knife. According to Jade, he whittled things everywhere he went. He was currently working on a bowling pin.

"How you liking Willow Marsh?" Corrine asked as she sat down. She kicked her feet up and rested them on the small table.

Marcel tucked the wood and knife in his jeans pocket and then went up for his turn.

I shrugged. "It's small, and the people can be kind of forceful." I glared at Jade, but it turned into a smile when she threw popcorn at my head. I retrieved the fallen pieces from my shirt and ate them.

"We know what we want." Jade tossed some popcorn into her mouth. "And we take it. Nothing wrong with that." She'd worn a hooded utility jacket in an army green but hadn't bothered taking it off, even though the heater was on in the bowling alley.

My phone buzzed in my back pocket.

Leya:
Can we talk now?

With one of the guys.

Call you later tonight.

YOU'RE KILLING ME!

You'll live.

Leya sent a photo of herself, her braided hair pulled back, glaring and shaking her fist, making me laugh out loud. Even when she tried to be stern, she couldn't pull it off. She had the brightest smile that always reached up to her fun, brown eyes. Everyone loved her the minute they met her. She was the life of the party and made everyone feel included. I missed her so much.

Corrine leaned over my shoulder. "Who's that?" Her breath smelled of buttery popcorn.

"That's my best friend, Leya."

Corrine played with her tongue ring and pointed to Leya's picture. "She's beautiful."

I tucked the phone back in my pocket. "Oh, I know. Guys wouldn't give me a second glance when she was around."

"You're prettier." Graham's quiet voice filled my ear. He blushed when I looked at him. He pushed up the sleeves of his forest green shirt. "Ww...watch and learn." He grabbed his ball from the return and lined up, giving me a nice view of his butt. I found myself biting my lip, so I cleared my throat and turned away from the others, hoping they couldn't see the red on my cheeks.

He's no Blake, dark-inner-me said.

I was hoping to go the night without her showing up. If my séances hadn't been going so wrong, I'd probably look up a way to rid your body of spirits, if that's what she was. There had to be another way to release her without giving the other side a chance to torment me.

Since my back was to the others, I took a moment to talk to her.

Seriously, who, or what, are you? I asked.

DIM clucked her tongue. *Apparently, someone who has better taste in men.*

I ignored her insult since Graham was getting ready to throw the ball. I had limited time.

What do you want? I asked.

She snickered. *You know* who *I want.*

The way she said it, possessive and sultry, made me shudder. Graham's ball soared down the lane, which meant I'd have to talk to DIM later.

Go away, I responded.

The ball crashed into the pins, toppling them all over. Graham pumped his fists into the air and then held up four fingers.

When he saw me frowning, Graham picked up my ball and motioned for me to join him, his bottom lip sticking out in a pout to match mine. I narrowed my eyes at him, and he chuckled, lighting up his eyes. DIM had no idea what she was talking about. Graham was hot.

I fake sulked to his side, knowing no matter what he told me, I'd still suck. He set the ball in one of my hands, then took my other hand and placed it over the holes, positioning my fingers where they needed to be. His strong hand shook on mine, and up close I could smell his soap. It had a woodsy scent. Pine. It reminded me of his room.

He ran a finger across my scarf and whispered. "It might be easier if you took that off."

If I took it off with him watching, it would draw attention to the scar. "It's fine."

"Okay." He stepped back and pointed to the ground. "Line up ww...with the middle dot. Make ss...sure to kk...keep your arm ss...straight."

With a deep breath, I pulled my arm back like he'd showed me, then let it fly forward, the ball leaving my hand. It landed softer that time and kept on the lane. When the ball collided with the pins, four fell down.

I did a little dance, and then threw my arms around Graham. "I hit them!" When I noticed he wasn't hugging me back, I released him, blushing. "Sorry. I got a little excited."

"You two need to get a room," Jade said, munching on some popcorn. "Might help Dixon loosen up a bit."

Graham slouched in his seat, his cheeks and neck completely red. I'd embarrassed him, which made me feel terrible.

My second attempt hit two more pins, but Graham didn't notice. I took a seat next to him, trying to keep a safe distance. His leg bounced as he drummed his fingers along it.

"So," I said, looking at Jade, who had just finished her turn. "Have you all lived in Willow Marsh your whole lives?"

"Unfortunately," Jade said, tugging on the cuffs of her jacket.

Corrine came back, pointing at Marcel to go. That time he left the wood and knife on the table before he jogged over to the ball return, a lightness in his steps.

Corrine looked at me. "It's nice to finally have someone new here. Most of the time, people just disappear from Willow Marsh."

"You may be next." Jade snapped a picture of Marcel bowling, smirking at her screen.

Closing her eyes, Corrine made the sign of the cross. "Don't say stuff like that. Now I'm going to end up like the Barnett family."

I stiffened. The envelope I'd found in the kitchen was addressed to the Barnett family. "How did they *end up?*"

Marcel sat down, and all four of them exchanged a look that said *how much do we tell the new girl?*

Graham took his turn, cutting the conversation short. His ball plopped on the ground and immediately found the gutter. I heard him swear under his breath as he went again, only hitting two pins that time around. I figured the best thing to do would be to not make a big deal out of it.

I took my ball and lined up again, positioning my fingers like Graham had shown me. I ended up knocking down seven pins between my two tries.

Graham had his head down, beating his fingers on his leg.

I sat down next to him, resting my hands on my knees. "I just knocked over seven pins, and you completely missed it. That was a record for me." He still wouldn't look at me. "If I keep this up, I might win, and then I could buy a shirt that says, 'I beat Graham at bowling,' and wear it everywhere I go."

His drumming slowed, and so did his blinking. He fingered his earbuds that he'd taken out of his hoodie pocket. He normally kept them around his neck, but they interfered with his bowling.

I gently bumped my arm against his. "Remember, you can't get rid of me that easily."

When Graham's turn came, and he didn't move to get up, I picked up his ball.

"This is way heavier than I expected," I said. "I'm going to bowl for you and make certain I win."

He stopped drumming but didn't look up.

"Fine." I went to the lane, bent my knees, getting ready for a granny toss. The ball slipped from my grip, falling with a thump below me. I bent to pick it up again, but Graham beat me to it, his hands brushing across mine.

"That's the ww...worst form ever."

I threw out my arms. "Well, let's see what you got, Mr. Professional."

Graham shooed me out of the way and bowled another

strike. He smiled triumphantly, his face glowing with a calm surety that clashed with the sullen mask he normally wore. I needed to find a way to bring it out more often.

The bottle of Dr Pepper suddenly caught up to me. "Where's the restroom?" I asked Corrine.

She pointed to the back corner of the bowling alley. "Over there."

Graham put his hand on my arm before I walked away. He kept his voice in a whisper. "We don't really know what happened to the Barnett family."

"They disappeared?" I whispered back, even though I didn't need to. It felt weird talking at a normal volume when he whispered.

Graham shrugged, but sadness touched his eyes. "Maybe. Trenton would have mentioned to me that they were moving." He rubbed the back of his neck. "They just up and left. His phone was disconnected the next day."

"Weird. I'm sure there's a reasonable explanation for it." Unless they were caught up in all the craziness Willow Marsh had to offer. But I didn't want to worry him. I leaned in close and tugged on one of his hoodie's strings. "I would apologize for hugging you, but you need to get used to it."

I don't know why I loved toying with him so much, but I did. I couldn't help myself around him. He brought out a version of me that hadn't made an appearance since well before the accident – and I liked that version.

It didn't require a mask.

CHAPTER 12

I'd just turned on the faucet, running my hands under the warm water, when a soft masculine voice I didn't recognize swept past my ear.

Tessa.

"Please, not again," I said in a hushed tone, turning off the water. I couldn't handle it. There was no way the presence could have followed me. I'd ended my séance back at the hotel.

Tessa. A little louder, a rough edge forming in the tone.

Air swirled around me in a white tornado. My long hair flew in all different directions, blocking my view. The wind moved faster, the sound thunderous in my ears. Maybe someone would hear it and come running. Then I wouldn't be the only one seeing it, and I'd have proof I wasn't completely crazy.

Tessa. So loud and full of static. I lifted my arms toward my ears, but the wind pushed against them, holding them down.

Lights flashed above me as the sound of electrical currents cracked in the room. Wind tugged me in every direction. I had to grip the counter to keep from falling over. My sweaty fingers slipped along the surface, making it difficult to grasp. Closing my eyes, I tried to focus on my breathing. *Control. Steady. Calm,* I thought.

Help me! The voice boomed, shaking me right to my core, my chest tightening to the point it was hard to breathe. I tried to move toward the door, wanting to flee, but the wind held me in place. I just wanted it all to end, and whoever was haunting me to leave. How could I possibly help them?

The tornado pushed against me like an invisible compactor. My lungs burned, and I gasped, fighting for air. Tiny spots danced in my vision as I became lightheaded. The lights went out, and again, with no windows, I was left in complete darkness. Panic throttled me – I needed to get out.

I summoned every ounce of strength I had left in me, ready to scream my head off, when, abruptly, the wind stopped. The sudden lack of force sent me stumbling back, smacking into the wall between the stalls. The weight of a presence entered the room like they'd finally been able to break through. It was as if the wind was their force trying to cross over to the human side.

The lights flickered back on with a buzz, but they were dim, barely lighting up the room. Little misshaped pieces of frozen water floated in the air. Just like at the motel, fog filled the bathroom, starting from the ground and snaking around my body, its icicle teeth biting my skin. Life pulsed from the fog like an evil entity. Goosebumps broke out all over me, and not just from the sudden cold.

How had it followed me? The voice didn't sound like Amá. In front of me, words formed on the mirror with a low screech, like someone was writing through the condensation.

Ellington.

My eyes focused above the name. Behind me, a vague figure of a man stood there, sunken and tired. He wore a navy-blue uniform with gold buttons, reminding me of a soldier. The bottom half of his body was fog. It pulsated like a heartbeat.

His mouth opened, but his lips never moved. *Help me,* a faint voice said. His withered hand reached out, landing on my shoulder.

The lights flickered, casting an eerie yellow glow to the icicles floating in the air. The fog below the man rushed in to consume me, fighting its way into my mouth and ears, seconds before everything went black. I stumbled around, searching for the door, for a way out.

Tessa. The voice was back to a whisper as the fog retreated from me.

My hand collided with the door knob, jarring a few of my fingers. I yanked open the door and stumbled out, stifling a scream.

I frantically searched for Graham. He had his hand on a bowling ball, moving toward the lane, but he looked back, like he'd been watching for me. Our eyes locked, and mine cried out to his. He immediately put down the ball and ran to me.

I went straight into his arms, holding on tight, and never wanting to let go. Burying my face into his neck, I shook uncontrollably. The air around me vibrated like Ellington was still there. The skin on my arms and hands undulated, tingling me. Queasiness rolled in my stomach, and I wanted to sit down, but I didn't want to leave Graham's arms.

Voices sounded around me. Jade. Corrine. Marcel.

I ignored them and held on to Graham. His shaking hand stroked my hair.

"Shhhh." His warm lips pressed against my ear. "It's okay, Tessa. You're safe."

For a few minutes, I fought to calm down, gripping the

back of his shirt. Sweat slid down the small of my back, even though my insides were still icicles.

I was losing it – going out of my mind. I needed help.

Or Blake, DIM said.

No. I snapped.

Pretty please? DIM whined.

No!

The voice made me angry, but it also helped me fight my fear. I pulled back a bit, forcing myself to look up at Graham. He placed his slightly sweaty hands on my cheeks. The heat felt nice against my cool skin. He made sure to whisper to control his stuttering, but it also added a calmness I desperately needed.

"What happened, Tessa?"

"I need to get out of here." Tears trickled out, going down Graham's hands, but he didn't flinch.

"Want me to take you back to the inn?"

"No." I needed fresh air and a place where wind was a naturally occurring thing. I licked my lips, trying to wet them. My deep breathing had left them dry. "Somewhere outside. Public."

Confusion crossed over his eyes, but he nodded. "Whatever you want."

Corrine put her hand on my arm. "What happened in there? You're pale as a ghost."

I trembled. "I'm just tired. Haven't slept well."

"Someone who's *just tired* doesn't freak out like that." Jade came close, tilting her chin down and raising her eyebrows. "You on something?"

"No." It would explain my behavior and maybe rationalize what had just happened.

Corrine and Jade exchanged a look – they didn't believe me.

"What's up with your eyes?" Jade asked.

Inside, a current ran under my skin, like small waves covering every inch of me. My hands went to the skin under my eyes instinctively. "What's wrong with them?"

Corrine leaned in, examining my eyes. "There's blue swirling with the brown."

"That's so freaking awesome," Marcel said. All four of them huddled around me, peering into my eyes.

I looked down, making them all step back. I wished I had a mirror so I could see what they were talking about. How could a color be swirling in my eyes? My arms still rippled and for a small second, I lost feeling in them.

"Can I have some of whatever you had?" Marcel asked. Both Jade and Corrine hit him on the arm. "Ouch!"

My hand flew up and slapped him across the cheek. My eyes went wide in horror. I had not done that on my own. My arm wouldn't go back down. It was like something held it in place. I had to use my left hand to force my right arm back down. One last wave travelled through me before I was myself again.

That felt good, DIM said.

I was too stunned to respond.

Marcel held his hand against his cheek, looking at me with as much surprise as Jade and Corrine.

"Ww...we're leaving," Graham said, putting his arms around me and snapping me back to reality. "You can finish ww...without us." He didn't wait for a response. He kept a steady arm around me, helped me into my hoodie and Chuck Taylors, and then escorted me toward the doors.

Before we left, I looked over my shoulder and mouthed "I'm sorry" to the others – their gazes glued to us in shock – though it wouldn't fix what I had done. What DIM had done.

Graham helped me into his truck. I sat in the middle, leaning my head on his shoulder as he drove.

CHAPTER 13

Graham parked along the curb on Main Street near an ice cream parlor with a giant, plastic chocolate shake in front of it. It took a while before I could scoot out of the truck. Graham wrapped his arm around my waist and guided me to the sidewalk. I was still trying to figure out what had happened at the bowling alley. I wasn't sure what freaked me out more: that Ellington was now following me, or that I randomly slapped Marcel. What if he'd been holding his carving knife? Things could have ended with someone accidentally getting stabbed by that jagged little thing.

The one person I really needed to talk to was dead, leaving me all alone to sort out the mess. I could talk to Leya, but she wouldn't know what to do – not like Amá would.

I sat outside at a freezing metal table while Graham went inside and bought us some ice cream. The inside had an old-fashioned feel with the pink chairs and tables, and high pink stools in front of the large counter. But I wanted to be outside.

Willow Marsh was as chilly as Skokie. All the shops

looked like they had been there since the early nineteen-hundreds with their hand-painted signs and white columns, but just like the school, they were all in good condition.

Taking Amá's dahlia ring from my pocket, I slid it back on my pointer finger, and my tense muscles relaxed a little.

The streets were quiet, with just a few people walking by every now and then. They would all smile at me and say hello as they passed. No one said anything to Graham after he came out with the ice cream, but a few nodded at him in acknowledgment.

"Are you ss...sure you don't ww...want to ss...sit inside?" He had his earbuds back around his neck.

The thought made my stomach churn. I needed the fresh air and the public. Maybe nothing would haunt me where others could see. "I'm sure." I didn't want to talk about what happened in the bathroom. I couldn't explain it without sounding crazy. "What's your brother's name?" I asked before taking a bite of my rocky road ice cream. Felix's favorite flavor.

Graham flinched, then stuffed a large bite of mint chip ice cream in his mouth. I waited for him to swallow. He wiped at his mouth. "Greg." He said it clearly. Normally he had a problem with G's.

I lifted my legs and rested my feet on the empty chair next to me. If I had been ready to talk about it, I would have told him Felix was the biggest Iron Man fan on the planet. He even had Iron Man's mask painted on his ukulele. Felix also had an uncanny ability to devour a dozen of Amá's tamales in a matter of minutes.

"How old was he?" Taking a purple scarf from my hoodie pocket, I pulled my hair back into a ponytail.

"Twenty." His voice was low.

The moon shined bright in the clear sky. One nice thing about Willow Marsh was that you could see the stars no matter where you went. Well, when there weren't clouds hogging up the sky. "What did he do? Was he working or in school?"

He pushed his ice cream around, his face sullen. A part of me wanted to change the subject, but I wanted to know how much I could trust Graham. "He ww...worked."

"Cool." I took another bite of ice cream and stared up at the sky, trying to sound casual. "What did he do?"

When Graham didn't respond, I turned to him, noticing he was staring at me with intent eyes. He was angled toward me, his spoon hovering over his cup.

"You okay?"

"I don't like tt...talking about it." He chucked his unfinished ice cream in the trash bin behind him before he put in an earbud in the ear opposite me and pressed play on his phone.

I set down my ice cream on the table. "I'm sorry. I thought it might help to talk about it, but we don't have to." He drummed his fingers, his blinking fierce. My brain tried to find something to talk about. Considering how he responded to the mention of his brother, I figured I shouldn't bring up his dad.

The wind picked up, causing my ponytail to sway. I tensed for a second, but then remembered we were outside where wind was normal. There was nothing ominous about it. I played with the scarf on my wrist. Graham's silence increased my anxiety. Did I dare bring up what happened in the bathroom? Or with the locker? He would think I'd gone insane.

I didn't want to push him away. I felt broken inside, leaving me so confused. Normally I talked with Amá or Leya when things got hard. But I hadn't been able to find the time to really talk to Leya.

"Do a lot of people disappear from Willow Marsh?" I asked.

He sat back in the chair and clasped his hands, resting them on his stomach. "You ww...want tt...to know the tt...truth?"

I swirled my ice cream around in the cup with my spoon. "Yes." I wanted to know more about the town my dad dragged me to, far away from my best friend.

"There's been a lot more disappearances than usual." He whispered, shutting out his stutter.

"Do you know why?" My eyes stayed on the slowly melting ice cream. The marshmallow swirled with the chocolate.

He scooted closer to me, his voice getting quieter. "I have a theory. But it won't make sense to you."

I forced myself to look at him and closed the distance between us. My heart raced from being so close. "Try me."

He didn't pull away. "Legend has it there are Civil War relics buried deep under the city." His eyes darted around the empty street before they settled on me. "One of the founding families, the Harrisons, have been searching for the treasure for years. Along with lots of other citizens. It seems like the ones that were getting close to finding answers are the ones that have disappeared."

"Like, they just up and leave, or no one can find them?"

He stared at his clasped hands. "No one can find them."

"Do you think the Harrisons are behind it?" A breeze swept by me, wrapping around me like it had a purpose. I had this overwhelming feeling someone was watching me – or maybe a spirit roamed nearby.

"Maybe," he said. "They used to be filthy rich, but have blown through their inheritance. They could be desperate enough."

A middle-aged woman wearing a pink apron shuffled out and wiped off the table next to us. Her eyes focused on Graham and me like she knew what we had been talking about. Graham used his boot to push his chair away from me, the metal grating the sidewalk. Scratching the back of his hair, he cleared his throat, looking anywhere but at me. My shoulders drooped at the distance between us.

I stood and threw my ice cream away, my stomach unable to handle any more. The lady finished her fake table wipe down and left us alone.

If it were true about the relics under the city, it would definitely give people a motive to do something drastic, like make a family disappear.

I thought of Ellington in the soldier uniform. Maybe he'd been involved with the war, or died during it. If that were the case, he could still be tethered to Willow Marsh in some way and needed my help severing that connection.

A brown and gray bird with an orange beak landed on top of the giant plastic shake, staring down at me, and I shuddered. The same bird. I hugged my arms around me, wishing I had something more than just my hoodie.

"Tessa?" Graham whispered.

"Yes?"

His blinking eyes looked up at me. "Why did you freak out at the bowling alley?"

I stared at him, watching his eyes search mine. "It's complicated."

The bird bounced a little as it whistled, and then it flew away into the night.

"I understand complicated." He kept his voice low.

A small smile formed on my lips. "I know. But you'll think I'm crazy."

Graham's eyes went to his drumming fingers. "Aren't we all a little crazy?" He looked like he was about to say something else, but he suddenly glanced behind me and went as pale as a ghost.

CHAPTER 14

A handsome man – though hardened from probably a life of bad choices – stopped next to our table, reeking of alcohol. He held an open bottle of Jack Daniel's in his hand, not bothering to hide it in a brown bag or anything, like he didn't care who saw him with it.

"Nice night, isn't it?" His tone was creamy and rich. He tilted his scruffy neck back, glancing at the sky. He looked to be in his early forties, his greasy brown hair slicked back, and had a thick, brown beard that rounded his chin. He leaned close to Graham, his lopsided stance and the disturbing glint in his light blue eyes causing my stomach to clench. He had a flannel jacket over his old, tattered shirt.

Two younger men stood by him, both slightly dazed, yet somehow totally present. The older of the two, probably in his late thirties, quirked his head at me, his eyes the same color as the others. They had to be brothers. His eyes held a clouded emptiness behind them, though, like he was void of emotions. He looked me over like he was trying to calculate how he could take me apart and then reassemble me.

I trembled and stepped away, closer to Graham. I debated

whether or not to sit back down, but I didn't want to give these men any advantage over me.

"You're Greg's little brother, right?" the bearded man asked in a smooth, even voice. "Also starts with a G." He bent down, getting so close, his nose almost touching Graham's cheek, that it made Graham shrink back. "Ggg...gggg...graham."

The other two men chuckled in a deranged melody. The one hadn't taken his eyes off me – in fact, he barely blinked. All three of them were pale as the moonlight, like if they were to stand in the sun all day long, they'd still remain that way.

"Hey, Reed," Graham said, his voice tight.

Reed slapped Graham's shoulder with a brotherly squeeze. "You and I need to have a little talk." He sat down in a chair next to Graham and leaned back, resting his arm on the back of the chair. His lips ticked. "You and your brother have some unfinished business with me. Since he's gone, you're going to have to help me out."

Graham kept his head down, his leg bouncing like crazy. His fingers pounded on his jeans at an even faster rate.

Reed kicked Graham in the leg. "I do hope you're paying attention to me."

When Graham didn't respond, Reed leaned forward, casually grabbed Graham's neck, and pushed the side of his face into the table with a lot of force. His tone remained like honey. "Graham, you answer when I talk to you."

"Let him go!" I pounced toward Graham, but the youngest one stepped between us and shoved me back. He clucked his tongue, waggling his lanky finger at me. He was the tallest of the guys, his sharply pointed jaw covering up some of his long, slender neck.

Out of the corner of my eye, I saw a couple coming toward us. When they saw what was happening, they crossed the street and pretended like they didn't see anything.

"Cowards!" I yelled. That made them skitter away faster.

I hoped Reed would see them and stop, but he continued, unfazed that people could see what he was doing. It made me wary of how far he would go in public. I tried to push forward again, but the tall guy wrapped his gangly arm around my waist and threw me back with a stunning amount of strength. I banged into the window of the ice cream parlor, snarling at the man the whole time. He just chuckled and winked in response.

Graham grunted from being pushed into the table. Reed kept a tight grip on him. "I want my stuff." He wiped a crumb from his jacket with his free hand. "Where is it?"

"I...I... don't know." Panic filled Graham's voice.

Reed lifted Graham's head and slammed it into the table, causing Graham to cry out. Spit dripped down Reed's beard. "Wrong answer." He lifted Graham's head again, about to slam it back onto the table, but Graham twisted his body to get out of Reed's grip.

Graham took my hand and whispered in my ear. "Run." There was a fierce edge to his voice that surprised me.

"Lars. Ace," Reed said, snapping his fingers at the others.

Graham yanked me away, but we only got a couple feet before the other two men stepped in front of us, blocking our escape. Graham and I had our backs to the store with nowhere to go.

Reed stood, glancing me up and down like he was noticing me for the first time. He ran his hand along the side of his beard, his lips twitching to the side. With the malicious twinkle in his eyes, I knew why Graham had cowered back. There was something downright terrifying about him.

"I don't think I've seen you around before." Reed sauntered up to me, his body leaning to the side as he did, causing me to back into the window of the ice cream shop. The store owner bristled out, closed the door, and locked it from the inside.

What was wrong with these people?

"Don't touch her." Graham squished his body between Reed and me.

I tried to wrap my fist around the back of Graham's hoodie to keep him close, but Lars and Ace grabbed Graham by the arms and yanked him away from me, holding him back.

Reed put his hand on my hip and pushed his body into mine. His whiskey breath was borderline murderous. He pressed his mouth to my ear, his soft beard scraping my jaw line and tickling my neck. I turned my head, but he took his other hand and clamped it around my throat, holding me in place. His finger trailed along the scarf holding my hair back. "What's your name, sweetheart?"

Get away from him, DIM whispered. *He's bad news.*

I pounded my fists on his arms, but it just caused his hand to tighten around my throat. Grabbing his hands, I tried to pry his fingers away from my neck. When that didn't work, I clenched the flannel sleeves of his shirt and yanked on them. My legs thrashed around as I tugged on his arms. He just watched me the whole time with a lackadaisical expression.

"Leave her alone!" Graham shouted clear and firm. He jostled away from the others and threw himself at Reed, fighting to get him off me. The tallest guy, Ace, took Graham by his hood and yanked him away like a puppet. Graham roared and pushed toward me again, but Lars joined in, that time the two of them struggling to keep Graham at bay.

"Don't let him go again," Reed said, his head tilted to the side so the others could hear.

Lars removed one hand from Graham and brushed away some hair that had fallen into Graham's eyes. Graham scrunched his face at the guy, obviously weirded out by the gesture.

"You need to learn something, little girl," Reed breathed into my ear, his voice airy. "I run this town, so if I want to play, you can't say no."

I continued to kick, but it was useless. My fingernails dug into his hands as I clawed at him. The harder he squeezed my throat, the more lightheaded I became, my vision going blurry.

Out of the corner of my eye, I saw the scarf on my wrist. Maybe if I could loosen it, I could use it on Reed's throat to wrench him away from me. My hand fumbled on the material as I tried to set my wrist free.

All of a sudden, the pressure on my throat released as Reed was ripped away from me, his body flying back, but a warped smile on his face. I dropped to the ground, my knees banging against the cement. My hand went to my throbbing throat, rubbing it.

I had expected to see that Graham had somehow managed to rescue me, but instead I looked over to see blue custom Nike Air Force's and designer jeans. Blake had Reed in a headlock.

"What the hell do you think you're doing, Reed?" Blake seethed, the veins popping out of his neck and forehead.

Reed struggled out of Blake's grip and stumbled back, banging into the table. He stood up, straightening out his jacket. "Just saying hi to the new girl."

"You don't get to touch her." Blake stepped up to Reed, standing tall, using his height to his advantage. "Are we clear?"

Graham bent down next to me, put his arm around my waist, and helped me stand. I trembled as I tried to control my breathing. My neck ached. His kindness contrasted with the violence so much that I wanted to melt into him. I wrapped my fists around his hoodie and pulled him close, his presence calming my racing heart. Air finally eased its way into my lungs so I could breathe normally. Graham kept his steady hand on the small of my back, the other hand tangled in my mess of hair as he held me against his chest.

Reed smoothed back his hair, letting out a laugh. "Just messing around, kid." He pointed at Graham. "I'll be in touch." He grabbed his Jack Daniel's from the table, motioned for Lars and Ace to follow, and the three of them slunk down the sidewalk.

Blake hurried to my side, completely ignoring Graham. He put his hand on my arm and looked at me like we'd known each other forever, and he was genuinely concerned about my well-being. "Are you okay?"

Releasing Graham's hoodie from my death grip, I rubbed my neck and shook my head. "Who was that?"

"Someone you don't want to mess with." Blake stroked my arm. He too made my heart race, but so differently. He lifted my chin awkwardly so he could inspect my neck.

Moving my chin away from him, I put my arms around me. Graham had stepped back from us, watching, but not saying anything. I hated that he'd gone from standing sure to cowering the second Blake came near me. I needed Graham to stay strong, but I wasn't sure how to tell him that without embarrassing him even more.

Blake shrugged out of his jean jacket and draped it around me. He rubbed his hands up and down my arms. "I'm so sorry that happened to you, Tessa." He turned to Graham, his eyes heating with anger. "What were you thinking, letting her be around them?"

Graham slapped his fingers against his leg. "Ww...what ww...was I thinking? It's a ss...small tt...town, Blake. They can ww...walk anywhere they ww...want."

"It wasn't his fault," I said to Blake. "They showed up, and Graham tried to stop them."

Blake glared at Graham. "I told you to stay away from her. This is what happens when people are around you."

"Blake, don't take it out on him. I'm fine," I said, even though my neck still ached, and I had no idea what had just happened – or why. "Just drop it."

Blake looked at my neck, his eyes softening. "He left a mark." His thumb brushed against my neck, sending shivers through me. Something about the guy made me go crazy. I couldn't think straight. "Let me take you home."

Yes, please, DIM purred.

Shut it, I said.

"Graham can take me." My voice was quiet and shaky. I trusted myself more around him, especially if DIM could take control of me and do things with Blake I so didn't want to do.

"I don't mind, really," Blake said.

Headlights lit up the area, making me lift my arm to shield my eyes. Sheriff Hayes slowly stepped out of his cruiser, eyes darting up and down the street, his hand resting on the top of his gun. "What happened here?"

"Reed attacked her," Blake said, motioning to my neck.

I motioned to the red mark on Graham's cheek. "He attacked *us*. Along with Lars and Ace."

The sheriff checked the markings left on my throat, his squinting eyes taking them in. "How are you feeling?"

I rubbed my throat. "Sore. But I'll be fine. Graham's probably in worse shape."

Sheriff Hayes turned to Blake. "Take her back to the inn. Make sure she gets inside safe." He looked at Graham and rubbed his jaw. "You and I need to talk."

Blake put his arm around my shoulder. Graham's eyes

went to the ground, but not before I saw the anger flare. His hands balled into fists, and his jaw tightened.

"Seriously, Graham couldn't have stopped it all on his own," I said. "We were outnumbered." I glanced at the ice cream shop where the lady was now doing a fake wipe down of the window so she could see what was happening. "No one tried to help us in any way. They all just watched it happen."

"What about the Harrisons?" Blake asked his dad, pretending like I hadn't said anything.

"I'll take care of them," Sheriff Hayes said. "You take care of Tessa."

I startled at the mention of the name. The family that was probably behind the disappearances. "Harrison?"

Sheriff Hayes nodded. "You'll get to know their family soon enough. Just try to stay clear of them if you can." He stepped close to me so no one else could hear. "And stay away from Graham. I warned you, Tessa. I don't want this to happen again. You could get seriously hurt."

The sheriff waited for me to nod before he sat down next to Graham, and they talked in low voices.

Blake instantly guided me away to the passenger side of his electric blue Ford Mustang GT, complete with white racing stripes. Pretty nice car for the sheriff's son. He opened the door and helped me in. I had to hold onto his jacket, which was draped around me, so it didn't fall off. I would have slipped my arms inside the sleeves, but jean jackets weren't really my thing, nor did I like the idea of fully accepting help from Blake.

We didn't talk the entire ride. I didn't have the energy for it. A ghost had attacked me, then a man assaulted me, and people had looked the other way. On top of everything else, the sheriff didn't even ask me if I wanted to file a complaint. Maybe moving to Willow Marsh had been an even worse idea than I thought.

What would I do about Graham? I liked him. He made me feel comfortable and normal. I was getting the feeling that if I spilled everything to him, he'd listen and understand. But there was no way the sheriff and Blake would let me be around him now. Not after this.

Blake opened the car door for me when we got to the inn. I had been so deep in thought, I hadn't noticed we'd stopped.

Taking a gentle hold of my arm, Blake helped me out of the car and to the door of my room. He rubbed my arms. "I'll pick you up tomorrow morning for school. Try to get some rest."

"Thanks, Blake. For the ride and stopping Reed." I shuddered at his name.

He put his arms around me and pulled me into his chest. "I'll protect you, I promise. Reed and his brothers won't be able to hurt you as long as I'm around."

His tropical smell filled my senses. Being in Blake's arms was so much different than Graham's. With Graham, it felt right. Easy. With Blake, though, it felt protective, almost like ownership. I had a feeling my freedom would be limited with him around.

Blake reminded me of one of Leya's exes, Jayden. He was gorgeous, and you could get lost in his eyes. Every word he said made you melt and forget life was happening around you. But he was controlling. Sometimes I felt like Jayden viewed Leya as a possession. I could see Blake doing the same.

Pulling back, I went to take off his jacket, but he stopped me. "You can give it back to me in the morning." He leaned in, trailing his finger along my cheek. "Sleep well." He faltered for a moment when he looked into my eyes. "Your eyes."

Were they still changing color? "Yeah?"

"They're blue." No more swirling. The blue must have overtaken the brown. Blake sucked in a sharp breath. "You sure we haven't met before?"

Why did he keep asking me that? "We haven't met before."

He relaxed and drew in close. I couldn't tear my eyes away from him. His smile captivated and intrigued me. Blake was trouble – more trouble than Graham.

His warm lips pressed against mine. For a moment, I was too surprised to do anything. I'd never been kissed before. But then my lips were moving against his, hungry for more. His lips were soft, tasting like oranges, and before I could stop it, my tongue ran across his bottom lip.

Yes, yes, yes. DIM laughed.

I shoved Blake away from me, gasping for air. I swear, for a moment, that heated moment, DIM had taken over me again.

Blake looked confused. "I'm sorry. Apparently, I misread the situation."

"I just..." I pressed a shaky hand to my clammy forehead. "It's been a crazy night. I'm exhausted." I opened the door to the room. "We just met, Blake. We shouldn't..." My eyes clouded for a moment, and a cool current ran through my veins. Something was terribly wrong inside me. "Goodnight."

I slammed the door, pressed my back against it, and tried to catch my breath. What had just happened?

CHAPTER 15

The slam of the hotel door caught Dad's attention. He scrambled from his bed, almost falling over, and rushed to my side. "What's wrong?" His concerned eyes went to my neck, widening when he saw the mark Reed had left. "What happened to you?"

I scooted around him so I could sit down on the couch. "I was attacked."

"What?" Dad sat down next to me and examined my neck. I flinched at his touch, the pain making me squeamish. "Are you hurt anywhere else?"

"No." Every part of me buzzed, still high on adrenaline from everything that had happened.

A whistle blared from the TV. Dad snatched the remote control from the bed and muted the basketball game he was watching. Then he grabbed a water bottle from the mini fridge. "Who attacked you?" He kneeled before me, a tenderness in his eyes that put me at ease.

"Some creep named Reed Harrison." I took a drink of water, grateful for the coolness against my dry throat. "He wanted something from Graham, but I don't know what."

He reached into his shorts' pocket and retrieved his phone. "I'll call Sheriff Hayes."

I gently placed my hand on his. "He already knows. He showed up and said he'd take care of it." My neck throbbed as if the pressure of Reed's strong hand was still wrapped around my neck.

He hesitated, his scrunched eyebrows and pursed lips telling me he still felt the need to do something, but he eventually nodded and tucked his phone back in his pocket. "I'm glad you're okay." He smoothed out my hair. "As for Graham, I want you to stay away from him."

I almost dropped the water bottle. "He's my friend, Dad. Remember? My only friend here." The corner of his eyes creased in anger, so I continued. "This is what you wanted. Me making friends."

His nostrils flared. "Not with Graham. Sheriff Hayes told me about him today. You need to stay away from him."

My fist tightened around the bottle. "Sheriff Hayes talked to you about Graham? What did he say?" Why did the Hayes men keep interfering with my life?

"That he's dangerous." Dad ran his hand down his face, pulling a little at his skin. "Promise me you'll stay away from him."

I couldn't keep that promise, but I was holding a masquerade. I kept my tone cool and even. "Sure. The sheriff's son, Blake, drove me home. He's giving me a ride to school tomorrow. Not Graham."

Goody, DIM said.

You and I need to have a little chat, I said. *Later.*

Looking forward to it.

That made one of us.

Dad sighed in relief. "Good. Tessa, if this Reed guy comes near you again, call me. I'll be there as soon as I can."

My phone vibrated in my pocket, so I pulled it out. Leya's

bright smile lit up the screen, and all my anxiety turned to joy. She was exactly who I needed to talk to. "Dad, it's Leya. I'm going to go outside and catch up with her."

He lifted an eyebrow. "You can't talk in front of me?"

I kissed his forehead and stood. "Of course not."

"Don't go far," he said. "Not after what just happened." He slowly stood, his body tense, his troubled gaze reluctant to let me go. I didn't blame him – not after everything we'd been through.

"I'll be right outside the door. Promise." Smiling at him, I opened the door and stepped out into the cold. If it hadn't been so dark, I would have video chatted with Leya so I could see her face. Problem was, she wouldn't really be able to see mine. And she'd probably lecture me about being outside in the dark.

My phone was warm against my ear from being in my pocket. "You have no idea how much I miss you."

"Same here, sugar," Leya drawled. "Tell me everything. Now!"

As I caught Leya up on Graham and Blake, I found myself wandering around to the back of the inn toward the willow trees. Their branches were full and thick, and I couldn't see past them. Clouds covered the sky, creating darkness all around. A little bit of light buzzed from a lantern attached to the back of the inn.

"So, which one is cuter?" Leya asked with a scandalous tone.

"By typical standards, Blake." I ran my fingers across my lips, remembering his kiss. "Leya, he kissed me."

"What?" A sharp rustle pierced the speaker, and then her voice came on again. "Sorry, I dropped the phone because I was in so much shock. You just met him! He kissed you? How was it?"

Closing my eyes, I thought back to the moment. "I don't

know. There's something about him that drives me wild and makes me not think straight. But it doesn't feel right." And I wasn't entirely sure *I* had been the one to kiss him, which was wrong in so many ways.

DIM snickered, but I ignored her. I wouldn't let her distract me from my call with my best friend.

Leya groaned. "Reminds me of Jayden. Maybe you should stay clear of him. Tell me about Graham."

Graham's triumphant face at the bowling alley entered my mind, making me smile. "He's different and thoughtful. He's got this cute charm about him that I really like."

Her incredulous tone dripped through the phone. "Do they put something in the water in Willow Marsh? Because this so doesn't sound like you. You're like anti-guy or something."

"I'm not anti-guy." I kicked at a pebble on the ground as I paced near the trees. "I just hadn't met anyone worth my time."

"And now you have." I could hear the smile in her voice. "I want to meet him and shake his hand. I never thought you'd meet your match."

I stepped into the trees, feeling comfort in the shelter they provided. "Unfortunately, Dad, Blake, and the sheriff don't want me near him. They say he's dangerous."

"Dangerous? How?" She munched on something. Probably Cool Ranch chips, knowing her. When I didn't respond right away, Leya spoke up. "Tessa, tell me whatever it is you're hiding from me. Now."

A rustle in the trees made me turn my head. I searched through the thick branches but couldn't see anything. My maroon Chuck Taylors squished against the soft earth as I moved around. "I honestly don't know. But Blake once mentioned an accident."

She munched some more. "What kind of accident?"

"I'm not sure. But they keep saying I could be hurt from being around Graham." I stuffed my free hand in my hoodie pocket, hoping to warm it up. The night had only grown colder. At least my hand holding the phone had some coverage from the scarf.

She stopped chewing. "Like physically hurt?"

My eyes scanned the area, trying to find what had caused the noise, but all I could see were the branches of the willow and birch trees. "I don't know. Maybe? When Blake mentioned the accident in front of Graham, Graham got a terrified look in his eyes, like just thinking about it scared him."

The light flapping of wings sounded above me. A small brown and black bird landed on a willow branch not far from me. It had to be the same bird. The coloring and size were identical, down to the sharp, orange beak and skinny, black legs. "Even if they're right and he did hurt someone, who am I to judge? My accident cost two people their lives." The mention of Amá and Felix tugged at my heart. "I miss them so much, Leya."

"I know, hun," she said with a gentle tone. "I wish I could be there to hug you."

"Me, too."

The bird blinked at me, and then took flight like it wanted me to follow. I wasn't sure if it was curiosity or the hope that it was somehow connected to the other side, but I tagged along, keeping my eyes trained on it.

"I know you're a great judge of character," she said. "Make sure you sort it all out before you go making any rash decisions."

The bird flew farther into the trees. I had no light to guide me – just the sound of flapping wings. "Hey, Leya?"

"Yeah?"

"You still believe in ghosts, right?" My foot connected with a rock, and I stumbled, making me cry out in shock.

Leya screamed. "Seriously, Tessa? Don't ask me about ghosts, and then yell like that!" When I didn't say anything, she whistled. "You still there, sugar?"

"I'm here." The bird's flapping sounded farther away, so I picked up my pace, hoping I wouldn't trip on anything else. "So, I take it you do believe?" I was sure I'd seen a man in the mirror, trying to communicate with me, but it was hard to explain that to others.

"I believe anything is possible." Her voice had a lot of air, like she was trying to calm herself down from me scaring her. "I like the thought of loved ones staying with us after they depart."

"This isn't Felix or Amá." The bird finally stopped, perching itself on a tree.

"Then who?" Her voice sounded skeptical.

I waited for the bird to do something else, but it just sat there, not moving, looking straight ahead. "Someone named Ellington."

"Ellington?" Her voice perked up. "That sounds mysterious."

"I guess." My eyes searched the trees, but darkness consumed the area. The moon and stars were still covered up by the clouds. Thunder roared overhead, but I hadn't seen a flash of lightning, probably thanks to the trees.

"Have you actually seen a ghost?" she asked. "Wait, are you still taking your medication? It made you loopy before the..."

"NO!" *Control. Steady. Calm.* "You know I stopped taking the pills." I'd tried to stay clear of my anxiety meds after the night of the crash, turning to running to help find a release.

"Just asking." She sniffed. "No need to get all defensive."

Thunder boomed, shaking the ground beneath my feet.

The bird cried out in a melody that was eerily sweet. "I'm sorry. But strange things have been happening to me, Leya. I've been hearing someone whisper my name. I saw a man in the mirror tonight. He was standing behind me."

"Did he say anything?" She sounded scared.

I swallowed. "Help me."

She let out a loud breath into the receiver. "That's just downright freaky. Promise me you'll go see someone. Do they have a therapist or like a priest or someone you could go talk to?"

The willow branches around me swung back and forth as the wind picked up. "Yeah. The sheriff gave me a therapist's number."

"Call her first thing tomorrow." She paused. "Okay, where are you? It's so freaking loud."

"Outside, in the trees behind the inn." I glanced back toward where I thought the inn was, but I'd become disoriented. I couldn't see anything through the trees. Dread settled in my stomach when I realized I didn't know how to get back. "Would this be a bad time to bring up that a scary-looking man attacked me tonight?"

"And you're alone in the woods?" Leya swore in Creole. "Are you out of your mind? Tessa, get back to the inn. With your dad. To safety."

Wind swirled, spinning me around and around where I stood. My world became dizzy. The bird whistled loudly and flew to my side, spiraling in the wind with me. My ponytail whipped around, my hair and the scarf smacking into my face and obscuring my view. I tried lifting my arm so I could wipe the hair away, but the wind kept it glued to my side. My other hand gripped tightly onto my phone. Was a spirit trying to enter our realm?

"Tessa?" Leya yelled through the phone.

Thunder boomed from every direction. I tried to hang on

to my phone, but the force of wind and my spiraling motion caused it to slip from my grasp. The bird nipped at my hair, and I screeched. The wind suddenly stopped spinning and started pushing and pulling at my hair and clothes. I stumbled around, trying to stay on my feet.

"What do you want?" I screamed as loud as I could, but my voice got lost in all the noise.

Wind smacked into the center of my chest, sending me flying backward. I collided with the ground, fallen tree branches stabbing my back. I clawed at my neck as I fought for air that had been sucked from me. Something below me scraped along my back like it was moving.

There was a small clearing among the trees, letting me see. High in the sky were thick, dark clouds.

Rain fell in big droplets, smacking against my face. The wind stopped. The bird sat on a branch, staring down at me. It tilted his head to the side and whistled, trying to get my attention.

Fog rose from the damp earth, only creating a thin layer this time, instead of filling up the area. Maybe being outside gave it more room to spread. I looked around, waiting for Ellington, but I didn't see him anywhere.

Something sharp poked my back, and I twisted to my side. I skimmed around the twigs for solid ground so I could push myself up, trying not to think about how dirty my Día de los Muertos hoodie was getting. My right hand brushed against something hard. Lightning filled the sky, casting a spotlight on what had poked me.

Next to me, four crooked fingers stuck up from the earth, the decaying skin falling away from the bones right before my eyes. Screaming, I crawled away, no longer caring about the mud caking my clothes and scarves. I scrambled to my feet and ran. The darkness and rain made it hard to see. My Chuck Taylors kept slipping on the slick leaves and mud.

I had no idea where I was running or if I was going the right direction – all I could think about was getting back to safety and away from the bird and the possibility of ending up in the ground myself. I'd lost my phone, and the trees obscured the sky, so I had no light. But I pushed on, trying not to think about what I saw and how it had got there.

Fire ignited in my legs and lungs, warning me to slow down, but I couldn't. Tears joined the raindrops on my cheeks. A fallen tree came into my view at the last second, but I had too much momentum to stop. My shins collided with it, tearing my legs and hurling me into the muddy ground. I could only roll onto my side and curl into a ball.

Hail pelted every inch of me in a vicious attack. My right shin stung. Even though the thought of moving made my body cry in protest, I shifted so I could see my leg. Blood trickled down it, soaking my socks. Removing the scarf from my wrist, I shook off the mud and tied it around my leg, more for the pressure than anything.

I needed to force myself up. I couldn't stay there in the forest. Not in the storm, or with the bird, or a human hand most likely connected to a dead body. With shaky arms, I pushed my palms into the mud and lifted myself off the ground, standing on wobbly legs.

Tessa. The soft, female voice came from the right. I turned my head to see a white glowing orb the size of a tennis ball floating in the air.

The wind had picked back up, trying to push me away from the floating orb, but I took unsteady steps onward. Every time I wanted to give up, every time I paused, the orb pulsed – it's bright light growing – and said my name.

Tessa.

I kept going, pushing myself farther through the trees and the pain, even though every step brought me closer to my legs finally giving out.

Tessa.

A small gap in the trees showed me the light on the back of the inn. Adrenaline surged through me, lifting the weight of my tired muscles, and I ran straight toward the inn.

Straight into the arms of Dad.

CHAPTER 16

Dad swept me into his arms, held me close against his chest, and carried me back to the inn. After he set me on the couch, he tried to stand, but I threw my arms around his neck, crying. The image of the decaying hand flashed through my mind. I wanted to say I'd imagined it, but it was so real. I swear the bird had led me there.

My stomach rolled as I pictured the flesh falling away from the bone. I quickly pushed away from Dad and scrambled to the nearest trashcan, unloading my dinner.

"You're okay, sweetie." He kneeled down beside me and stroked my wet hair. When I'd finished, he gently rocked me in his arms, waiting patiently for me to calm. I heard his phone buzz a few times, but he ignored it, focusing all his attention on me.

After a few minutes, my breathing steadied, and the tears stopped. Dad kissed me on the forehead. "I'm going to grab some towels from the bathroom. I'll be right back." He got to his feet and took his phone, dialing someone as he hurried to the bathroom. "Leya, I found her. She's fine. A little distraught and banged up, but okay. I'll have her call you when she's feeling up to it. Thanks for reaching out to me."

Dad came back, helped me back onto the couch, and wrapped a towel around my shoulders. It did little to warm me. I needed a blanket and a hot shower.

"Leya called me and told me something was wrong." He wiped some tears off my mud-streaked cheeks. "What happened, Tessa?"

Dad had never believed in the supernatural. He wouldn't understand what had happened to me, so I had to leave most of it out. "I was out in the trees talking to Leya when I tripped. On the ground, I saw..." I trembled at the thought of the fingers sticking out of the dirt.

"You saw what?"

I placed my hand on my mouth, fighting back a dry heave. I took a few breaths before I spoke. "A hand. I think there's a body out in the woods."

He snatched his phone from the bed and dialed, stroking my hand while he did. "Sheriff Hayes? This is Alec Isaacson. Sorry to call so late, but my daughter may have found a body in the woods behind the inn." After a few exchanged words, Dad hung up the phone, turning his attention back to me. "The sheriff is on his way. He wants to talk to you if you're up to it."

Thunder rattled the windows. The heavy rain sounded like rocks against the glass. Dad rubbed his hand down his face. "He probably won't be able to search tonight. Way too stormy." He put his arm around my waist and helped me stand. "Maybe you should go quickly rinse off in the shower. The hot water might be soothing."

"A shower does sound nice right about now." I pecked him on the cheek and hobbled to the bathroom.

I put my ruined jeans and shoes in a wet heap, letting Amá's scarf that had been wrapped around my leg fall on top.

Even if I somehow managed to get the blood out, it would still be a reminder of what had happened and what I saw. I didn't see any tears in the hoodie my abuelo gave me, so it was salvageable.

Fighting through tears, I washed off my ring under the warm water running from the sink. Mud was stuck in every crevice, the pink dahlia hardly recognizable. I scrubbed until every speck was gone.

I turned the water in the shower as hot as it would go, heating my skin in the best way possible. The feeling of dread and being powerless needed to be washed away. Something bad was happening to me. I was seeing and hearing things – going out of my mind. Leya was right; I needed to talk to someone.

The door to the bathroom opened. "Tessa, I'm setting some clean clothes on the sink for you. Take all the time you need." The door closed, trapping in the steam.

Grabbing a wash towel hanging around the showerhead, I scrubbed at my hands and legs, wiping away the mud. Sucking in a sharp breath from the sting, I wiped at the cut on my shin, trying to remove any excess dirt. A thin layer of skin had been removed. Maybe the inn would have a first-aid kit. Ours was still packed away in the moving trailer.

After a good fifteen minutes, I forced myself to leave the shower since my skin had wrinkled. I slipped into my T-shirt and sweats slowly, hoping to drag out the time until I'd have to talk about what happened. I rolled up the right leg of my sweats to leave my scrape exposed. I'd ruined enough clothes for one night.

I washed my face and brushed my thick hair, working through the snarls. The mirrors were still steamed up from my hot shower.

Like a finger was dragging across the mirror, letters formed in the condensation. My eyes darted behind me in the mirror, thinking I'd see someone, but no one was there. When the movement on the mirror finished forming the message, my eyebrows scrunched in confusion.

Trenton.

Graham's friend. The guy who had my locker before me. The body in the woods, did it belong to Trenton? Was someone trying to tell me that? The bird had led me to the location, and a ball of light got me safely back to the inn. I didn't know who was helping me, and who wanted to hurt me.

A knock on the bathroom door made me jump. "Tessa?" Dad. "You almost done in there? Sheriff Hayes and Blake are here."

Blake? Why had he come? "Yeah. Just a second." When I looked back at the mirror, the name was gone, and the mirror had cleared.

Hurry and finish, DIM said in an excited tone. *So we can see Blake.*

Did you take control of me earlier? I asked, trying to hold back my annoyance.

You mean, did your rational side do what your weak side couldn't? That answer is yes.

My fist tightened around the handle of my brush. *You need to stop doing that.*

If you'd stop letting me, I would. DIM giggled. *But we both know you enjoy it. Don't deny yourself life's pleasures.*

I took a deep, shaking breath. *You're not the one in control here. I am.*

She tsked. *You so sure about that, darling?*

I didn't have time to argue with her anymore. I ran the brush through my hair before I joined the others in the room.

Blake and Sheriff Hayes were sitting patiently on Dad's bed. The couch was now covered in mud and blood, thanks to me. Dad sat across from them on my bed.

The sheriff had his uniform on, as usual. Blake was just in a muscle shirt and shorts like he'd been working out before the call.

The second Blake saw me, he pushed up from the bed and enclosed me in his arms. "You've had quite the rough night." He smelled strongly of sweat, confirming my suspicion.

"Yeah." That's all I could force out. It was weird having him hold me like that with our dads watching. I kept my arms at my sides, which probably made it more awkward.

Sheriff Hayes had to clear his throat before Blake would release me.

The sheriff pointed at my leg. "That doesn't look too good." He tossed Blake his keys. "Get the first-aid kit out of the trunk."

While Blake was outside, I recounted as much as I could without talking about the bird, the wind, or the ball of light. Which didn't leave much to tell.

"Are you certain it was a hand?" Sheriff Hayes asked, writing down what I had said in a small notepad.

The hand would give me nightmares for a long time. "Yes."

Blake bounded into the room like a man on a mission. He rushed to my side and knelt down. Before I could react, he had his cold hands on my leg, the first-aid kit open, and he was cleaning the scrape. I sat on my hand to hide my scar.

"What were you doing out in the woods?" Sheriff Hayes eyed me, his eyebrows coming together.

"Out for a walk." For some reason, I didn't want to bring Leya into it. Blake was already too invested in my life. She was one treasure I could keep to myself, at least for the moment.

Sheriff Hayes' eyes crinkled in amusement. "You like to go places you shouldn't, don't you?"

I tried to keep my tone even. "I was just going for a little walk. I didn't know the woods were off limits."

"They're not." The sheriff stole a glance at Blake. "My son has a similar sense of rebellion in him."

Blake shrugged a shoulder. "I like a little adventure. So what?" He placed a large Band-Aid over the scrape, his hands being gentle.

Sheriff Hayes stood, tucking the notepad inside his jacket. "We'll come back tomorrow morning before school, and maybe Tessa could walk me out to where she thinks she saw the hand?"

Dad put his arm around my shoulder. "Do you think you could handle that?"

"I think so." It wouldn't be as terrifying during the day, especially if I weren't alone.

Blake gave me another hug before they left, going back out into the storm. I felt bad for making them brave the weather. Hopefully, they'd get home okay.

See, you do care, DIM said.

About the welfare of human beings? Of course I do. I'm not evil.

DIM cackled, making me tremble.

It took me forever to fall asleep. I tossed and turned for hours. The second I drifted off, the nightmares played. First, Ellington in his war uniform. His sullen eyes were begging and pleading for help. I asked what he needed help with, and all he talked about was finding a box.

Flutter.

I was back in the car at the steering wheel. Mom next to me in a beautiful red dress. Felix with a white dress shirt and red tie, singing in the backseat. The bird perched on my shoulder. Rain pelted against the windshield, obscuring my view. Wind shook the car, sending it swerving all over the wet road. I'd finally regained control of the car, my fists tight on the wheel, when I thought I saw something in the street.

I slammed on the brakes, turning the wheel to the left until I lost complete control. The car flipped over and over and over again. Mom yelled, Felix screamed, and the bird whistled.

My world went black.

CHAPTER 17

Sheriff Hayes and Blake showed up early in the morning. The sun had barely woken up. I hadn't been able to fall back asleep after my nightmare, so I was dressed and ready to go. I'd wanted to go on a run, but I didn't need another lecture about being out on my own. After a few shakes on the shoulder, Dad finally woke and joined us outside.

Blake stayed right by my side as we trudged out into the woods. The ground was still damp from the rainstorm. Trying to remember which way I had gone was difficult. It had been so dark that I'd had no bearings on my location. We were able to track some of my muddy footsteps I'd left on the ground.

Out of the corner of my eye, I saw the bird following us. Sheriff Hayes walked to the left, but the bird whistled and flew to the right.

"I think it was that way," I said, pointing my finger.

Blake looked up at the willow tree where the bird was perched. "I hate those birds." His gorgeous eyes found mine. "They're called vampire finches. Suck the blood from other birds. So disgusting. They aren't even native to this land, but of course, they'd end up in Willow Marsh."

Of course. Willow Marsh apparently attracted the crazy.

He squinted at the bird. "Probably a female with the brown coloring."

I tilted my head to the side, studying him. For once there wasn't arrogance or confidence on his face – just a genuine sureness that caught me by surprise. "You seem to know a lot about birds."

Blake chuckled. "Just the vampire finch. When they're all over your town, you get curious."

We continued through the woods. I watched the bird, going where it went. She'd stopped on a branch when light reflected off something on the ground. "My phone!" I ran to it, picking it up, and scraped off the mud, revealing the skull on the case. When I tried to turn the phone on, nothing happened. The rain had ruined it.

"Looks like you're going to need a new one," Dad said over my shoulder.

"I have an old one you can have." Blake took the phone from me and slipped out the sim card, turning it over in his hand. "Hopefully it will work." He handed the phone and card back to me.

"I need everyone to take a few steps back." Sheriff Hayes' tone was authoritative.

We all turned to him. He was staring at the ground. My eyes followed his gaze, landing on the bony hand that stuck out of the ground. It was real. The skin had been bitten off by something. I'd seen it peel away from the bone, but I thought I had imagined that part.

Dad put his hand on my arm and guided me away from the area. "That was disgusting."

I rubbed my arms, trying to get some warmth. "Imagine

falling on it in the middle of the night, during a storm. Terrifying."

Sheriff Hayes was on the phone, giving directions to his deputies. "Get the coroner out here as well."

It didn't take long for everyone to show up. Dad, Blake, and I stood off a ways, watching them work. As they removed the dirt from the area, by the condition of the body, it was obvious that it hadn't been there long.

Blake sucked in a sharp breath. "No." He stepped toward the body, getting close when his dad pushed him back. "Dad, that's…"

Sheriff Hayes nodded, his eyes grim. "I know."

"You know who it is?" Dad asked.

Both Blake and the sheriff looked over at Dad. Blake's eyes went to me before he rushed over, wanting a hug. I held him but didn't know why.

Because it feels nice, DIM purred. She popped up at the most inopportune times.

Sheriff Hayes rubbed his hand along his jaw and stepped close to Dad. "He went to school with Blake. We thought his family moved a few months ago, but maybe not."

"Sheriff!" A deputy called out. "There's another body over here!"

The sheriff ran out of sight.

"Trenton." It came out quiet, but Blake heard me.

"Yes." Blake backed out of our embrace enough to look at me, a frown on his lips. "It's Trenton."

CHAPTER 18

News as crazy as finding a dead body in the woods, especially that of a local teenager everyone had known, spread within the hour.

When Dad, Blake, and I hiked back to the inn, there were tons of citizens gathered around, trying to get past the police tape and into the woods. A few locals the sheriff trusted were standing guard, holding up their arms and making sure no one crossed the line.

Dark clouds filled the sky, the chance of rain on the horizon. It added an extra layer of gloom to the already depressing day. I tightened the scarf holding my hair back, wishing I could transport myself back in time where the past few months were never real.

Blake's friends swarmed to him, wanting to hear every detail, giving me a chance to sneak away. A strong dose of him left me woozy.

"Has your episode passed?" Jade's dry voice was surprisingly comforting to hear.

I whirled around to see Jade standing there with the hood

of her jacket up, covering her colorful hair. She had her hands shoved into her jacket pockets.

"What?" I asked.

Corrine and Marcel stood on either side of her, both bundled up in the early morning chill. Corrine offered up a sympathetic smile, probably not envious of what I had discovered. Marcel took a step back, creating a larger distance between us, and I didn't blame him.

Jade shifted her weight to her hip. "You totally freaked out on us last night. My crazy aunt used to do the same thing. Mom called them 'episodes.'"

Corrine glared at Jade. "Nice. Didn't she end up in a mental institution?"

"Yeah." Jade put her arm around Marcel's waist, trying to move him forward, but he stayed in place. "She actually committed suicide last year."

Corrine slapped Jade's arm. "What's your problem? She just found a dead body in the woods!"

I rubbed the goosebumps on my arms, remembering the hand reaching up from its shallow grave, and my nightmares that followed.

"I'm sorry about last night," I said to Marcel. It was weird that it had only been twelve hours since that had happened. It felt like a lifetime ago. "I don't know what came over me." But I did, and I wished there was a way to rid myself of her.

Marcel rubbed his cheek where I'd slapped him. "I've had worse from Jade." She responded by punching him in the gut, and he grunted. "See?"

"Are you okay?" Graham's soft, calm voice sounded behind me.

Without thinking, I threw my arms around his neck. For a moment, he stood stiff, but he finally loosened up and held me close. I breathed in his pine scent, and for the briefest moment, I relaxed. "I'm so sorry about Trenton. I know he was your friend."

Graham sighed into the side of my hair. He twirled the end of the scarf holding my hair. "I can't believe you found him . . . like that. How are you feeling?"

"Awful. Graham, I don't know what to do."

"About what?" Jade asked, suddenly in my view, her amused eyes dancing between Graham and me. "Don't you two go all lovey-dovey on us."

Graham dropped his arms, so I stepped away, but I wished he was still holding me. I smoothed out the scarf on my wrist. "Nothing. It's not important."

"Did they really find the whole family?" Graham asked, his blinking eyes on the cracked asphalt. One skull earbud was in his ear, the other falling on his chest. He had his hood up like most everyone there. They were always prepared for the rain.

"Yes." I slid my hand into his, and he linked our fingers, igniting a longing and desire I'd never felt before. It was exhilarating, if only for a fleeting moment before I was brought back to reality.

Sheriff Hayes and his deputies had continued to search the area, uncovering Trenton's mom, dad, little brother, and little sister. I overheard the coroner say something about 'blunt force trauma to the head.' I'd broke at the very thought, unable to hear anymore, and excused myself. Dad and Blake had decided to follow me out as well.

Graham's hand shook in mine, but it was from the grief of losing a friend, not nerves. I gave it a gentle squeeze and rubbed his arm. "I'm so sorry, Graham."

"Who would do something like this?" Marcel asked, his nose scrunched in disgust. He adjusted his glasses and stared into the woods.

Tears and mascara slid down Corrine's cheeks as she clasped her cross pendant in her hand. "Three kids. That's just wrong."

I wanted to know why the bird had shown me the burial site. Had Amá sent it? I needed to talk to Leya.

"Hey, Graham," I said. "Could I borrow your phone? Mine died last night." I flinched at my word choice.

Jade let out a laugh, giving her an excuse to wipe away some tears. She wasn't as stoic as she let on.

Graham handed me his phone, and our fingers and eyes lingered on one another. His cheeks ignited, and so did my heart. He fiddled with his earbuds. "Leya?"

"Yes." Letting go of Graham's hand, I stepped off to the side, close to a birch tree, and dialed her number.

She picked up after a few rings, her voice eager. "Tessa, please tell me this is you. If this is some stupid telemar..."

"It's me." I missed her so much.

Leya let out a long breath. "Thank goodness. What happened last night? And whose phone are you calling from?"

"Graham's." I filled Leya in on what happened. I made sure to get out of ear range of everyone so I could tell her everything. They didn't need to know about my crazy.

"It's your mom," Leya said as soon as I was done. "I know it. She's helping you."

Out of the corner of my eye, I caught Blake watching me. He stood with his arms folded, making his muscles bulge, and his eyes darted between Graham and me. I stepped farther away from it all and into some willow trees for coverage. "How does finding five dead people in the woods help me? It's only given me nightmares."

"Tessa." Leya took a deep breath. "Think. There has to be a reason. If anything, that family needed to be found. No one knew they were dead. Now it's known. Their extended family can have closure."

"Yeah." A light rain started up, landing softly on my head, so I tugged my hood over my hair. The smell of rain in the forest was something I could get used to. "I'm wondering if it has something to do with the Harrison family. Maybe Reed killed them."

"Reed? As in the guy who attacked you last night?"

My eyes drooped, so I rubbed them with my palm – the lack of sleep was catching up to me. "Yep. Graham said he didn't trust their family."

"Why would Reed murder an entire family? That seems extreme, don't you think?"

"I don't know." A flutter of wings made me look up. The vampire finch sat on a rain-covered branch, staring down at me. "This whole town is crazy."

Jade wandered over to my side, bumping my arm with hers. "Stalker alert." She nodded her head at Blake. "The guy is so messed up."

"Who was that?" Leya asked, a slight trace of jealously in her tone.

"Her new best friend," Jade said into the receiver.

I pushed her away. "It's Jade. I go to school with her."

Leya sniffed. "I don't like her."

"You haven't even met her." I sighed. There was no point in arguing with Leya. Or Jade. Put together in a room, they'd either love or hate each other. Probably both.

Jade yanked the phone from my grasp and put it on speaker phone. "We need to talk about why Blake's looking at Tessa like he owns her."

"How is his head positioned?" Leya asked, all business.

"What?" I ran my thumb over the smooth bronze of my family ring.

"Chin down," Jade said, squinting at him. He stood a few paces from his friends, right next to the Willow Marsh Inn sign. "Eyes somewhat of a glare. Possessive."

I took the phone back from Jade, but kept it on speaker phone, holding it out in front of me. "How can you even tell that from here?" Blake had lined himself up so he could see me between the trees, but he was still a good distance away.

"It's true." Corrine joined us, smiling wide at the phone. "Hi, Leya! This is Corrine."

"Hi!" Leya said. "I so wish I was there right now. What's Blake wearing?"

Jade scratched the back of her head, the birds on her wrist moving with the motion. "Ripped jeans. Red Henley T-shirt. Jean jacket like he's forgotten what decade it is."

I threw out my free hand. "What does that have to do with anything?"

"Wow," Leya said, hurt in her tone. "I feel like all our years of friendship has failed you."

"Don't be too hard on yourself." Jade glanced me up and down. "I'm sure Tess isn't an easy subject."

Leya chuckled. "Ain't that the truth."

Graham and Marcel joined us. Graham stood close enough to me that I could feel the heat radiating from him. "Ww...why is Blake looking at you like that?"

"See!" Corrine smirked, her hands on her hips. "Even the guys notice."

Marcel held up his hand. "I didn't notice. I don't look at Blake Hayes." He puckered his lips and kissed Jade on the cheek. "He's not my type."

I took a moment to glance at Blake, but his focus was on his friends around him.

"Tessa," Leya said. "Take me off speaker phone."

I did as told, holding the phone against my ear. "You're off."

"Do you trust everyone standing next to you?" Leya asked.

I glanced at them one by one. Marcel, I still didn't know well, but Jade would be picky with who she dated. Jade, I definitely trusted her. Even though she was brutally blunt, she was honest. Corrine, I did as well. I felt a connection with her. She was raw, in a good way.

Graham? There were still things I needed answers to, but deep inside, I knew I could trust him. The feeling I had when I first met him was of warmth and charm.

"Yes," I finally said.

"Good. Put me back on speaker phone."

I pressed the button and held out the phone. "You're on."

"Listen up, Willowites," Leya said in an authoritative voice. "Tessa is my best friend. I love her like a sister. It kills me that I can't be there, so I need all of you to promise me you'll take care of her."

Corrine pulled her head back in a way that said, *You didn't need to ask.* "No problem, Leya. We got it."

Jade rubbed her face on the sleeve of her jacket. "Yeah, whatever." But she meant it.

"Done." Marcel put his hand around his arm and flexed, showing off his non-existent muscles. The guy was incredibly skinny, which I hadn't noticed until then. He was wearing skinny jeans that highlighted his bird legs. "I've got this taken care of."

Jade pushed his arm down but held a smile on her lips.

Graham's calmly blinking eyes settled on mine, his jaw tight in determination. "Of course."

"Good," Leya said, relief in her tone. "As for Blake, how do you feel about him?"

He's sexy as hell, DIM drawled.

Of course, she'd chime in.

"Major douche bag," Jade said, glaring over at him. "Total prick. Can't stand him."

"Same here." Corrine rolled her eyes and scoffed. "He can't keep a girlfriend for longer than a minute. Total player."

Don't listen to them, DIM said. *Jealousy is such an ugly trait.*

Marcel adjusted his glasses. "He's a typical spoiled kid. Gets what he wants." He wiggled his eyebrows and winked at me. "Right now, he wants Tessa." He elbowed Graham and lifted his chin. "But Graham and I won't let that happen."

Jade swore under her breath, kicking at a stick on the ground. "He only wants her because she's a shiny new toy. He'll play with her and then chuck her in the trash when he's done."

What's wrong with playing with shiny toys? DIM chuckled. *They're fun.*

Seriously. Shut. Up, I said. She was way too much of a distraction, and I didn't want to slip in front of all of them.

"Good to know," Leya said. "Graham? You never responded."

"Does it matter ww...what I think?" Graham stared at the damp soil beneath our feet. He wore thick military-type boots that looked like they'd weathered a lot of storms. I'd probably have to invest in some myself. My Chuck Taylors were practically ruined from all the mud and rain.

"Of course it matters!" Leya yelled. "You're the most important vote."

Corrine tilted her head to the side and pursed her lips. "Hey, now. Just because they're all doe-eyed for each other doesn't mean his opinion is worth more than ours."

"It kind of does," Marcel said with a one shoulder shrug.

Jade clucked her tongue. "Yep. Girls get stupid over guys." She narrowed her eyes at Marcel. "Except for me."

Marcel nodded and pointed at her. "True that. This girl owns me."

Graham's face looked as hot as mine felt. I could feel the blush rising. "Alright, that's enough."

Graham stepped closer to me and the phone. His blinking eyes calmed. He kept his voice in a whisper. "I hate him.

Tessa knows that. He would never treat Tessa with the respect she deserves."

"Why are we whispering?" Leya asked. "Is Blake close? Can he hear us?"

Graham turned around to hide his face from us.

I took the phone off speaker and moved away from everyone. "He whispers to stop the stuttering. Didn't I tell you that?"

"No!" Leya sounded mortified. "Tell him I'm sorry. Wait, put him on the phone so I can apologize directly to him. Wait, no, he'd hate that."

"Just don't bring it up again," I said. "It'll be fine."

Closing my eyes, I took a deep breath, smelling the fresh rain on the willow trees. It was a small solace to be found in the whole ordeal.

"Tessa?" Leya asked.

The longer I was away from her, the more I missed her. I needed her there with me. I needed Amá and Felix. "Yes?"

"Please be careful." She sniffled. "I don't want anything to happen to you. Keep a safe distance from Blake."

A few tears of my own escaped, but from the pain of missing her. Of missing my family. "That might not be easy. You know Dad wants me to be friends with him."

"You need to talk to your mom. She'll know what to do."

"I can't." I put my hand over my eyes. "She's dead, remember?"

Leya sniffed a few times. "You know what I mean. You can communicate with her. So do it."

I wasn't sure if I wanted to try another séance with all the crazy things going on – it could just make it worse.

"Tessa?" a deep voice said.

I turned around to see Blake standing incredibly close. His tropical smell mixed nicely with the rain.

Yummy, DIM said.

"Shut up," I said through clenched teeth. I wanted to strangle her.

Blake flinched. "What?"

Marcel, Jade, Corrine, and Graham were all shooting daggers at him with their eyes. Blake didn't seem to notice. Or he didn't care.

I shook my head, giving him a light smile.

"Was that Blake?" Leya whispered.

"Yes," I said. "I'll call you later."

"With what?" Leya asked. "Your phone's dead."

"I'll get another one, I promise." I turned away from everyone, kicking at a fallen willow branch on the ground. "I miss you." I wrapped my arm around myself, wishing I could hug her.

"Miss you more." Leya blew a kiss, then hung up.

I mumbled a few swear words to get them out of my system before I forced myself to turn around. "Hey, Blake."

He stayed close to me, even though Jade and Corrine tried to position themselves in the way. It was an awkward, tight square.

"Who were you on the phone with?" Blake asked, his eyes only on me.

"Just a friend." That was all he was getting out of me.

"My friends and I were going to grab some breakfast," Blake said. "Want to join us?"

The thought of food made me sick. Not after everything I'd seen out in the woods. Not after the nightmares. "I'm not hungry."

Dad walked up at the most inopportune time. "Tessa, you should go with Blake and his friends. It will be good to get your mind off things." He and Blake exchanged a look like they had talked about me behind my back. Oh, that made me like Blake even less. How had I let myself get so wrapped up in his charm?

I think we both know why, DIM said.

I know, I said. Having DIM in my head made the attraction stronger. Maybe it was her and not me. I needed her out. *Who are you? What do you want? And don't give me some crap about being another version of me.* No way I'd gone *that* crazy. At least I didn't want to believe I had.

You'll have to find out those answers on your own, sweetheart, DIM said. *You're a smart girl. You'll figure it out soon enough.*

"I'm not hungry," I said.

Corrine put her arm around me, her cold cheek pressing against mine, but it was still warmer than being with Blake. "We'll hang with her for a bit."

Dad kept his eyes on me, his tone firm. "Tessa, go with Blake."

Everyone stared at me, waiting for my response. Most of their eyes were wide in surprise at Dad's forcefulness. I didn't have the energy to argue with Dad. I didn't want to fight with him. We were both in bad places.

"Fine." I handed Graham back his phone, my thumb stroking his hand, and walked away from the group. Blake and Dad followed behind me.

Before I got into Blake's Mustang, Dad kissed me on the forehead. "Thank you."

"Don't go planning stuff behind my back," I said, leaning on the open door. "I can take care of myself."

"And I told you to stay away from Graham." Dad placed his hands on my cheeks in a loving way, softening me ever so slightly. "I haven't changed my mind. Blake's your friend now. His friends are your friends."

I quivered. "You're supposed to be my father, not my owner."

Dad took a step back, hurt in his eyes. "I am being your

father. I'm trying to protect you from someone who could seriously harm you. You need to trust me on this one."

"Whatever." I got in Blake's car and slammed the door. Dad watched us drive off, wearing a frown and his eyebrows drawn together in concern.

CHAPTER 19

When Blake dropped me off after breakfast, workers were still behind the inn, sifting through the crime scene. I stood there for a moment, my unfocused eyes on the yellow tape, and recounted everything that had happened. The hand, bodies, and the ball of light – it didn't seem real.

I wanted to contact Amá. I was wary about doing another séance, but I needed to find a way to get rid of DIM, and figure out what Ellington wanted. Amá was the only one who'd know what to do.

I waited until late that night when Dad started snoring before I sneaked out of the room and into the chilly night. The sky was clear, the stars and moon giving off the only light. Lifting my hood, I walked out into the trees, retracing my steps from the night before.

A few yards in, a rustle sounded behind me. I turned and scanned the area, my racing heart sending a gush of warm blood through my veins. A white light bounced up and down in the distance, growing larger as it came closer to where I stood.

Was Amá already here? Maybe I wouldn't have to have a séance and risk something else going terribly wrong.

The frustrated tone that carried through the trees told me otherwise.

"Are you sure she's out here?" Jade asked.

"Leya said she would," Corrine snapped. "Go back to the car if you're going to act like this. Or better yet, walk home."

Corrine and Jade appeared through the willow trees, both holdings lit candles in their hands.

"Why are you here?" I asked.

Jade glanced at her candle. "I just want to let you know I don't believe in this crap." She had the hood of her jacket up, as usual.

Corrine shrugged. "Leya told me you wanted to contact your mom. We wanted to help." When I gave her a confused look, she grinned. "She called Graham and asked for my number. She only wants to help and doesn't want you to do this alone."

Jade snorted. "For the record, nothing is going to happen. You can't talk to the dead."

"Yes, you can," Corrine said. The flame from her candle illuminated her beautiful face. "You should hear the stories my mom and grandma tell. They'll make you shiver like you'll never be warm again."

"But that's what they are." Jade drew out the next words. "Stories. Fictional."

"Seriously, Jade, let me have this for once." Corrine held the candle in front of Jade's annoyed face. "Why don't you go hang out with Marcel? He has way more patience with you than I do."

Hearing them argue made me wish Jade would leave. Amá always said you couldn't contact the dead when your emotions were high. You needed to be steady. *Control. Steady. Calm.*

It would be nice to have Corrine so I wouldn't be alone, but how would I be able to ask Amá about Ellington or DIM in a way that Corrine wouldn't understand what I was talking about? I wasn't ready for her or Jade to find out about that part of me.

I snatched the candle from Jade's hand, sending a drop of wax to the ground. "I agree. Go be with Marcel. You're ruining the vibe." Turning my back on them, I moved farther into the woods, away from the inn and safety. Leaves crunched behind me as the two of them followed. Of course Jade would stay.

The good thing about them coming was now I had candles. Dad had thrown my others away. I didn't know what I'd expected to do without them. Just hope and pray for the best, I guess.

After a couple minutes, I stopped in the middle of some leaning birch trees. The storms probably made it hard for the skinny trunks to stand straight. I cleared some dead leaves from a small patch of wet earth and set my candle on the ground. Corrine put hers next to mine, pulled another candle out from her zippered hoodie pocket, lit it with a lighter, and set it down, creating a triangle.

"So, what are we supposed to do now?" Jade asked, staring up at the trees. She used the back of her hand to cover up a yawn.

"Everyone stand behind a candle." I chose the one I put on the ground. Jade and Corrine selected from the other two. Crossing my ankles, I sat down, leaves crinkling under my weight. My skin tugged around my scraped shin, but I did my best to ignore the sting. Corrine sat in front of hers, back straight and taking a deep breath.

Jade swore. "You can't expect me to sit on the wet ground." When Corrine and I ignored her, she swore again and plopped down, landing with more force than necessary.

Corrine and I held hands and reached our other hands out to Jade. She glared at them for a good ten seconds before she finally gave in, swearing multiple times as she grabbed our hands. Hers slipped right out of mine.

She motioned to the blue silk scarf on my hand. "Can you take that stupid thing off? I can't get a good grip."

"No." I held my palm out toward her. "Just take it, Jade."

With a sniff, she grasped onto my hand, squeezing hard. "Why do you wear it, anyway? Is that some weird fashion in Illinois?"

"It was my mom's." I closed my eyes, trying to calm myself. I focused on my senses. The rustle of trees in the wind. The cool air pressing into my hoodie. The smell of wet earth not long after rain. Jade's unnaturally deep breathing. A vampire finch whistling in the distance. Cinnamon wafting up from the candles.

"Amá," I whispered. "Amá, I'm here."

Jade snickered. I opened my eyes in time to see Corrine whack her on the arm.

"Ouch!" Jade rubbed her arm. "I'm sorry. It's funny. She's talking to a dead person." She played with her blue lip ring, running her tongue along it. "Maybe you could contact Trenton's family while you're at it. Ask them who killed them."

I dropped her hand and pointed back toward the inn. "Leave. Now."

"Don't get so ornery," Jade said in a sharp tone.

I leaned forward, resting my hand on my knee and looking her in the eye. "I'm not kidding, Jade. I don't want you here. You'll ruin it."

Her lips were in a tight line, but her eyes softened. "I'm sorry. I'll stop."

It took me a minute to calm myself. Once my heart had steadied, I took Jade's stiff hand and tried again. "Amá. Are you here? Can you hear me?"

Nothing.

"Amá, it's Tessa. I need to talk to you." The candle's flames grew wide in front of me. The wind picked up, sending a cold rush of air sweeping by. "I need help."

A funnel of warm wind circled around me, and then weaved its way between the three of us, moving in a snakelike manner. The tip of the air funnel caressed my ear, heating it.

Tessa.

"Did you hear that?" I asked. I'd heard it before – multiple times. Same calm, loving tone. It had to be the same person. A woman.

"Hear what?" Corrine asked, her tone skeptical.

Tessa. Whoosh.

I could sense her nearby, a weight floating next to me. So many emotions hit me at once. Relief. Sorrow. Anticipation. Joy. Pain. Regret. They swarmed inside, battling with one another, each one wanting control. I reached out and latched onto the anticipation.

"Amá, I'm here," I said, my hands shaking. "Something crazy is happening to me, and I don't know what to do. People are communicating with me." And possessing me.

Tessa. I'm here.

Amá. It had to be her. She'd finally come.

Corrine's and Jade's hands had stiffened in mine as they stared at me, confusion in their eyes. Jade's mouth moved, but I'd tuned her out. Nothing she said could possibly help.

The flames from the candles flickered. They jumped high, then swayed from side to side. I watched them move, hypnotized by their dance, and found myself swaying with the motion. The wind joined in, creating a pocket of air above the candles and adding to the heat.

Tessa. The sweet and intoxicating sound came from the wind pocket. I couldn't drink it in fast enough.

"Amá, how do I stop it?" Letting go of Jade and Corrine, I

leaned in close, my hands on my knees, feeling the heat from the flames on my neck. They'd become taller and thicker, demanding attention. "How do I send them back to the other side?"

Jade and Corrine both muttered something, but their voices sounded like they were far down a tunnel.

Suddenly, the flames became so small I could barely see them. She couldn't leave me – not again. There was so much more to say.

"Amá! Don't go!" Tears started to fall as I clasped my hands together. My thumb pressed the family ring deep into my skin, the dahlia leaving an impression on my skin. "I don't know who to trust. Tell me who to trust!" I'd been so torn since coming to Willow Marsh. Everyone seemed to be holding secrets, but so did I.

The flames flew up, licking my skin, sending me stumbling back and rushing to get on my feet. Those candles shouldn't have been able to produce that much light.

Something evil drifted next to Amá – I could sense it deep inside. Its distorted aura fought for control, wanting to shove Amá away and take over.

The pocket of wind caught fire, the sight horrifying, yet captivating. Wisps of flames slithered out from the wind pocket in an enchanting dance. My feet moved toward it, though my head and heart told me to run. I needed to get closer. I reached my hand out, my fingertips inches from the ball of fire. Heat seared my skin, and I welcomed it. I deserved the pain.

There was something else I needed to know. "Amá. Can I trust Graham?"

Small drops of rain fell from the sky. The fire sizzled at each drop. The ball of flames expanded, growing larger and larger. Someone's freezing hands grabbed my arm, tugging me away, but my body and soul kept trying to push forward.

The ball grew and grew, the light overbearing. I shielded my eyes with my arm. Amá lost her power as the evil spirit grew stronger. Rain fell harder and thicker, pelting me all over. Steam surrounded the ball of fire.

Another malevolent entity lurking nearby circled Amá's presence – dousing her warm love with a bitter cold hate until she extinguished – and pushed against my chest like a spear. With a loud pop, the ball exploded, sending embers everywhere.

"No!" I screamed. "Amá!"

Darkness filled the area, rain clouds concealing the moon and stars. All three candles had gone out. The warmth inside me evaporated, replaced by a cool sludge that slowed me down. It wriggled through me, pushing at my skin and trying to take control. It took its time, working its way into every crevice of my body.

Drops of rain splattered all over us. The wind turned cold and picked up, circling around me, Jade, and Corrine. We backed into each other and linked our arms together to keep us steady. The wind moved so fast, around and around like a hurricane, sending my hair and the ends of the scarf smacking into my face. I couldn't open my eyes or mouth because of the force. Hot air worked its way through my veins, dissolving the sludge that pulsated until it had disappeared.

Suddenly, the wind stopped.

"Let's go!" Jade screamed. She and Corrine scrambled to pick up the candles on the ground, mud and leaves flying around.

Corrine yanked on my arm. "Tessa, we need to get out of here!" The rain had turned to hail, almost the size of pennies.

Jade took off, heading back toward the inn. Corrine ran after her, but tripped on a fallen log, sending her candles flying. She hurried to grab one while I went for the others. Corrine ran after Jade, not looking back.

I stood in the area, knowing I needed to leave, but not wanting to go just yet. Amá had been there. If the evil spirits hadn't shown up, would she have answered me?

My clothes and hair were completely soaked. Each strike of hail felt like a stab on my cold skin and another hole added to my heart.

"Amá," I whispered. "I love you."

It took every ounce of energy in me, but I forced myself to turn around and move toward the inn, pushing against the wind and rain. I'd only gone a few feet when my candle flickered on, despite the water falling from the sky. Something rustled on the ground. I shakily held out the candle, trying to get a better look. Leaves crawled across the mud, forming letters, creating words.

I gasped, the candle slipping from my scarf-covered hand. Instinct kicked in, and I quickly caught the falling candle with my other hand.

In damp leaves on the ground, it read, *Be wary of who you trust.*

A gush of icy wind sent the leaves into a frenzy, scattering them through the air. I ran out of the woods before anything else could happen.

Jade and Corrine were huddled together, waiting for me outside of the inn. They shivered in the cold, soaking wet. My shaking hands fumbled to get the key into the door and open it.

Dad snored from his bed, giving no sign that he'd heard us come in. I softly padded into the bathroom and grabbed towels for all three of us. I was about to go back out when Corrine and Jade came in the bathroom and shut the door.

"What happened out there?" Corrine asked. She ran the towel over her choppy hair. Red soaked into the white towel from her fresh dye job.

"You saw," I said, peeling off my wet hoodie. "My mom

contacted me." Other spirits had shown up, and something had crawled through me like I was a cave to dwell in.

Jade and Corrine shared a skeptical look. Corrine's eyes were soft. "Tessa, nothing happened, aside from the storm."

"What?" I used my towel to squeeze water from the end of my ponytail. "No, the candles went crazy. Wind gushed all around us. My mom said my name multiple times."

Jade rifled through my bathroom bag, throwing the contents onto the counter. "Where are the drugs?"

I snatched the bag from her. "What?"

Jade yanked on the bag, trying to take it back. "The drugs, Tess. Are you taking medication? Something to calm yourself?"

"I'm not taking anything." I'd stopped taking medications after the accident. I wanted nothing to do with them or their side effects.

"Tessa." Corrine gently placed her hands on my arms. "Yes, it got a little windy, but it was from the storm, not someone contacting you. This is a typical, nasty Willow Marsh storm."

Pushing her hands off me, I placed my shaking hand on my forehead and sat down on the toilet lid. "No. I saw it. I saw the flames move and the leaves." They'd spelled something. I saw it. "I saw it." I'd felt the spirits. I'd felt the change inside. I wasn't crazy.

DIM whistled in my head. *Someone's losing it.*

"Not now," I said to DIM.

"Fine," Jade said with a huff. "We'll talk about this later."

"Maybe after you get some rest?" Corrine knelt in front of me. "You're probably just tired. Your imagination is playing tricks on you." She ran her white tongue ring across her lips. "I really hoped it would work."

Jade tapped her fingers on the counter. "I told you it wouldn't. You can't talk to the dead because *they're dead.*"

"I just need to be alone," I whispered.

Jade took Corrine by the arm and left me alone in the bathroom. I curled up in the corner, hugging my legs close even though it caused the scrape on my shin to sting. "I know what I saw. I know what I heard."

You heard what you wanted to hear, DIM said.

"No. It was real. Amá was there."

Was she? DIM asked, a lilt in her tone. *Your friends didn't notice anything.*

"I'm not crazy." I sniffed and wiped my nose with the scarf on my wrist. "They just aren't connected to the other side like I am."

Keep on telling yourself that, sweetie pie. Won't make it true.

"Just go away." I rocked myself, the motion soothing.

I'll always be here for you, DIM said. *Always.* She started humming "Masquerade" from *Phantom of the Opera*. A chill flew through me, and my stomach rolled. I wasn't crazy.

CHAPTER 20

My nightmare came back in full force that night. The séance brought it to life. The dream of the accident went on longer; the screams were even louder, the wind faster, and the rain harder. A hand reached up from the middle of the road, its bony finger beckoning to me, causing me to swerve and lose control.

I shot up, panting, and holding the damp sheet against my chest. I could have sworn I'd been screaming when I woke, but when I looked over at Dad, he was sound asleep on his stomach, his face smashed against his pillow, not aware of my state.

Instead of attempting to fall back asleep, I went on a run. No matter what Sheriff Hayes had told me, I ran down the middle of the street, out of town, toward the sunrise. Tears mixed with my sweat as I pushed myself along.

Someone or something had been haunting me, I'd been attacked, yet I still went out on my own. A part of me wanted the punishment. I deserved to die as well. Plus, living recklessly was a thrill. A high.

When my lungs and muscles were on fire, close to burning

me down, I stopped and caught my breath. I felt around in the zippered pocket of my running shorts and found the business card with Rita's number, along with the new phone Dad had gotten me. I didn't even glance at the time when I dialed her number, but I knew it was early – way too early.

She answered on the second ring. "Hello?"

"Ms. Hastings?" I asked, still panting.

"Yes, who's this?" she asked, a calm tone showing no signs that it was odd for me to be calling her at the early hour.

"Tessa Isaacson." Even though the cold air bit at my skin, sweat slid down my face and back.

"I was expecting your call. Please, call me Rita."

I lifted the bottom of my tank top and used it to wipe sweat from my upper lip. "I was wondering if we could talk." Dryness scratched my throat. I needed water.

"Why are you out of breath?" Rita asked, still calm and smooth.

Turning back toward Willow Marsh, I started for town with my hand on my hip. "Out on a run." Adrenaline coursed through my veins, invigorating me. Nothing beat a runner's high.

"This early in the morning?"

"I couldn't sleep."

"Come by my office after school." She sounded alert, like she had been awake already. "I'm in the city building on Main Street. You'll find me listed on the directory."

Ignoring the burn in my legs, I pushed on, walking at a brisk pace. "Thanks."

"I look forward to meeting you. See you later." Rita ended the call.

I put my phone and the card in my pocket and ran back to the inn with a lightness in my step.

B lake dropped me off at the city offices after school. He didn't ask why I was going there, which I appreciated.

Rita's office was easy to find. After looking at the directory, I took the elevator to the second floor and found the wood door with her name on a gold plaque. I opened the door, expecting to enter a waiting room, but I stepped right into her office.

"Lo siento! I didn't know this led directly into your office."

Rita stood from her chair, smiling at me, revealing her straight teeth. She looked to be in her early fifties, with brown, curly hair that went just below her ears. Reading glasses were on top of her head, snuggled into the curls. Around her neck, she wore a gold chain with a teardrop pearl. She had a subtle beauty that made her seem friendly and approachable. My whole body eased in her presence.

"Don't worry," Rita said. "Please, come in and sit down." She motioned to the gray couch next to her desk. Her tone was as soothing as her demeanor.

As I sat down, I looked around her office. All the white and gray furniture looked new and in perfect condition. White bookshelves lined the wall opposite the couch. Tons of books filled the space, with some photos and plaques scattered throughout.

In the center of the bookshelf was a framed photo of Rita, a man, and a golden retriever.

"That's my husband, Hal, and our dog, Brewster," Rita said, following my gaze to the photo. "He's extremely friendly and loves everyone he meets. He does have a bad habit of jumping up on people. He gets overly excited."

"Your husband, or the dog?" I took off my black Chuck Taylors and tucked my legs under me, getting comfortable on the couch.

Rita lightly laughed as she rolled her chair out from around the desk and scooted near me, but keeping a comfortable distance. She set a pad of paper and a pen on her blue slacks. "How are you liking Willow Marsh?"

Shrugging, I played with the strings on my hoodie. "Still getting used to it. It's different from home."

"How so?" Her gaze dropped to my hands, causing me to stop messing with the strings.

"Smaller. Quieter. No privacy."

She crossed her legs. "Do you want privacy?"

I eyed her, not sure of how much to say. But I wanted to talk to someone. It was why I'd gone to her. "The world doesn't need to know everything about me."

She gave a small nod in understanding. "How's your dad adjusting to the move?"

I hadn't actually talked to him about his thoughts on moving to Willow Marsh. I focused too much on myself. I rubbed the cotton scarf on my hand. "I'm not sure. I'll have to ask him."

She jotted something on her pad, highlighting her wedding ring. It was a simple gold band with a white pearl on top. "How's your relationship with him?"

"It's complicated." So I'd stop fiddling with them, I stuffed my hands under the sides of my legs.

She sat there, waiting for more. She made me more comfortable than my therapist back in Skokie. Her eyes were trusting.

But Amá, or someone, had told me to be wary of whom I trust.

"Dad struggles with my anxiety." Amá knew how to handle me. I debated whether I should tell Rita about Amá and Felix, but I wasn't ready.

"How long have you had anxiety?" There was no judgment in her eyes, and I liked her for it.

"Years. Since middle school." I leaned back on the couch.

She thought for a moment before she asked her next question. "How are *you* adjusting to the move?"

I wasn't. I didn't have a home anymore. While I loved Skokie, and Leya was still there, Amá and Felix weren't. Willow Marsh definitely didn't have a cozy vibe. I felt lost and alone. "Just trying to do the best I can."

"Why did you move?"

Just running from the reminders of Amá and Felix and the accident. I took my hands out from under me, fingered the scarf on my hand, and shrugged. "Dad wanted a change?"

Her eyes danced in amusement. "A question is not an answer. You can tell me the truth when you're ready." She scribbled on her paper before she went on.

"Your call this morning," she said, taking the glasses that rested on her head and putting them on, "it was early." She glanced at her phone. "Quite early. Is this normal for you? Being up before dawn?"

Nodding, I stared out the window behind her, spinning the ring on my finger. The blinds were open, letting me see Main Street and the few cars passing by. "I have a hard time sleeping, so I go on runs. It helps my anxiety."

Out of the corner of my eye, I saw Rita lean forward in her chair. "What do you do on your runs?"

"Listen to music." My unfocused gaze followed an elderly couple walking hand-in-hand down the sidewalk.

"What kind?"

"Reggae, usually." It was Felix's favorite. I could feel Rita looking at me, but I continued to stare out the window.

"What else do you do to help with anxiety?"

Play Felix's ukulele. It made me feel connected to him. "Take deep breaths. I have a mantra I like to repeat."

An old, beat-up Chevy truck pulled up along the curb outside. A camo pattern ran down the center of the otherwise black truck. Its gigantic wheels raised it obnoxiously high in the air. The door opened, and the driver slinked out. Reed. I tensed at the sight of him, ready to bolt. He looked in the side view mirror and smoothed out his long beard and greasy hair.

"What's wrong?" Rita asked.

I turned to her, noticing concern in her eyes.

"Your demeanor just changed." She looked out the window, but Reed had already disappeared from sight.

I ran my thumb over the dahlia on my index finger, thinking of my family. "Have you ever felt like someone is watching you?"

Her right eyebrow shot up. "You think someone is watching you?"

"No. Just wondering." I balled the cuffs of my hoodie in my hands, covering every inch of my skin. Bringing up dead people talking to me probably wasn't the best idea on the first visit. Or ever. People had a hard time with it.

Rita didn't seem satisfied with my response, but she didn't push it further. "What's your mantra?"

"Control. Steady. Calm." I looked back outside but still didn't see Reed. He must have gone inside one of the stores. My heart rate had quickened just thinking about him. Concern for Graham built up inside. I wish I could talk to him.

"I like that. Keep using it." Rita glanced over my face as if trying to read me. "Why did you come to me?"

Shock rippled through me. Why would she ask that? "I needed to talk to someone."

She sat back in her chair, took off her glasses, and perched them on her head. "Tessa, I feel like you're keeping things from me. If you want this to work, you need to open up."

I looked down at my fisted sleeves. "Don't you have

secrets? Ones you know you can't tell anyone?" I forced myself to look up.

Her eyes held intrigue. "Of course. But sometimes secrets weigh us down and make us forget who we are."

Or they keep us safe.

Rita smiled at me, the gesture comforting and genuine. "Tessa, I want you to know you can call me anytime. Day or night. I'd also like to see you a few times a week. After school work for you?"

I tucked my phone in my jeans pocket. "Yeah. That will be fine." I slipped my feet back in my shoes.

Suddenly, the door opened, and Reed stepped inside the room, a twisted smile on his lips. He wore the same flannel jacket from the night I met him.

"I told you to knock before you come in," Rita said in a sharp tone. Her gaze darted between Reed and me, probably sensing my unease.

He completely ignored her. "Well, hello, sweetheart," Reed said, looking at me, his sweet tone causing me to squirm. He held out his arms and slowly rolled up his sleeves, one at a time. "I don't think I got your name. I just know you're Graham's girlfriend." A thick scar ran down his arm going from his elbow all the way to his wrist.

"You're dating Graham?" Rita asked me, intrigue in her tone.

I twirled the strings on my hoodie. "We're just friends."

The twitch of Reed's lips told me he thought otherwise. "Tell him I'm stopping by tonight to get my things. I'll be by around eight." His gaze travelled over me, his milky blue eyes drowning in fascination. "Aren't you going to tell me your name? Or did they not teach you manners where you came from?"

He's seriously disgusting, DIM said, her tone strained. *Why is he standing so close?*

I narrowed my eyes as I stood up and took a step toward the door. "They taught me to stay away from creepy men."

DIM chuckled. *That's my girl.*

He smiled, rubbing the back of his neck before he turned a slightly possessive gaze to Rita. His tone was as calm and airy as a spring breeze. "Was this a one-time thing, or will my appointments be pushed back from now on?" He loosely folded his arms. "Actually, can we just cancel them altogether? I think I've been . . ." He pursed his lips, thinking. Then a smile tugged at the corner of his thin lips. "Fixed."

"You know I can't do that, Reed," Rita said. "Unless you want to be the one to tell Judge Billings." She motioned for Reed to sit down, her unsure eyes finding their way to mine. I moved to get out of his way, and he stepped past me, his smooth finger trailing across my waist as he did.

"Hope this means we'll be seeing each other every day, sweetheart," he whispered in a velvety tone, his thick beard brushing my neck, before he plopped onto the couch, kicking his boots up on the cushion.

I hurried out without looking back.

CHAPTER 21

Dad and I enjoyed a very thick, Chicago-style pizza for dinner, almost as good as the places in Chicago. I'd already called and talked to Leya, recounting my whole day. I didn't spare the smallest detail, because when I tried, she knew I was leaving something out.

Dad had turned on the TV and found a basketball game to watch. He'd switched into his pajamas – a plain white tee and blue cotton pants. He stacked some pillows against the headboard and leaned up against them.

"Apá," I said, putting my legs up on the couch. I gently pressed my jeans, right over the bandage on my shin. The sting wasn't as bad as it had been.

"Yeah?" His eyes were glued to the TV.

"How are you doing?"

Dad glanced over at me. "Okay. I have a lot on my mind." His eyes fluttered back to the TV. "I'm excited about our house. I did a lot of work on it today, including your bathroom and bedroom. You're going to be happy with the updates."

"I sure hope so." I looked at the screen on my phone,

checking for a response from Graham. I'd texted him and told him we needed to talk. An hour had passed, and he still hadn't responded.

Blake would have responded right away, DIM sang.

What's it going to take for you to go away? I asked. *Permanently.*

Oh, you'd just have to become sane again. Good luck!

I snarled at her before I shoved her into the back of my mind.

"What about you?" Dad asked. "How's school going?" With a water-dampened napkin, he wiped at some pizza sauce that had spilled on his white tee. He finally gave up, crumpled the napkin, and chucked it in the trash can on the other side of the room.

I twirled the phone around in my fingers. "So far, so good. Blake and his friends have been really nice to me." The guys I met had been. The girls shot me daggers.

"Staying away from Graham?" He swore at the TV, mad at a basketball player he couldn't control.

"Yes."

Graham hadn't been happy with me. I'd hung out with Blake and his friends at school, ignoring him, Jade, Corrine, and Marcel. They threw glares and swear words at me all day. Well, only Jade swore. But if people saw me with them, word would somehow get back to Dad. "Are you liking Willow Marsh?"

Dad pressed mute on the remote control. "For the most part. I'm slightly worried that I picked the wrong place. I hope finding dead bodies was a one-time thing. Why all the questions?"

I wasn't sure how he'd react, but I wanted him to know. "I met with a lady today. Rita Hastings. She's a therapist."

"Ah." He turned the sound back on and watched the game. He hated therapists. Any doctor, really.

My phone buzzed, saving Dad from a tirade. One day, he'd have to open up to the idea that I needed to talk to someone. Graham had finally responded.

Graham:
What's so important?

Tessa:
I saw Reed today.

Did he hurt you?

The fact that he asked that let me know he didn't hate me completely. It also confirmed why I liked him so much.

No. He wanted me to give you a message.

What is it?

He's coming tonight around 8 to pick up his "stuff."

...

Hello?

Did he say anything else?

No.

Thanks for letting me know.

So, what are you going to do?

...

Graham?

...

Sighing, I grabbed my Nikes from under the couch and slipped them on. I thought about asking Dad for his car keys, but I wasn't ready to get behind the wheel. Graham wouldn't come to get me, and there was no way I'd ask Blake.

Oh, yes, DIM said, sneaking back in. *Ask Blake.*

Willow Marsh wasn't that big, but it was probably still a fifteen minute walk to Graham's house from the inn. There was no way Dad would let me leave again after what had happened the night before. I waited until he went to the restroom so I could sneak out.

Are you ignoring me? DIM asked.

Once outside, I texted Leya so someone would know where I was going. My phone lit up, her bubbly face on the screen.

You can't ignore me forever, darling Tessa.

Shaking my head, I pressed the decline button, put the phone in my pocket, tightened the scarf holding back my hair, and broke out into a run.

CHAPTER 22

I arrived in front of Graham's house five minutes before eight. Reed's jacked-up truck wasn't on the street, so I jogged to the front door and knocked. Dad had called me, but I didn't pick up. I hoped he wouldn't come searching.

Barbie answered the door in a low-cut V-neck shirt, anger passing over her face when she saw me. Fluffsies – who was cradled in her arms like a baby – barked at me in excitement, but then saw Barbie's face and switched to a low growl.

"You have a lot of nerve showing up here." Barbie tried to shut the door, but I put my arm on the door to stop it from closing. Her eyes widened in shock.

"I'm here to see Graham." Using my shoulder, I pushed my way inside and jogged straight to Graham's room, ignoring Fluffsies' cries.

Graham stood near the window, peering out. He was leaning on a wooden bat, his stance casual like the bat was a part of him, and I tried not to think about the fact that it was kinda sexy. "Ww...what are you doing here?" He kept his focus outside the window.

"I wanted to make sure you weren't going to do anything stupid."

Barbie waltzed up to the door with Fluffsies in the crook of her arm. "Get out of my house."

"Graham," I said, eyeing the bat, "what do you think you're going to do? Beat them?"

He turned his gaze to me, some hair falling over his intent eyes. "If I have to."

Barbie scoffed. "Don't be silly, Graham. You don't know how to use that thing."

"Shut up!" Graham yelled.

Fluffsies kinked her head to the side, her tongue sticking out as she made a noise that almost sounded like a *huh?*

Barbie opened her overly-glossed lips to say something, but I shoved her out of the room and slammed the door, locking it. She pounded on the door, her shrill tone and Fluffies howl grating on my nerves.

"You should seriously install soundproof walls and doors." I kicked at the door, but they didn't stop.

Graham went back to looking out the window, and his hand tightened around the bat. "They're here."

I put my hand on the one that held the bat. He flinched at the touch, but I kept my hand firm. "Graham, don't answer the door."

"They'll find another way in if I don't." Graham yanked his hand away from me and walked over to the door.

I got there before he did, my back against the door, blocking it with my body. "I'm not letting you do this. Those men are dangerous. We should call Sheriff Hayes."

The doorbell rang, a low buzz like it was running out of juice.

He pulled his jaw tight. "I'm not calling your boyfriend's father to help me. I can tt...take care of myself." He put his hand on the side of my shoulder and tried to push me out of the way, but I held steady. "Tt...tessa, move. I don't ww...want to hurt you." His hair fell over his eyes, sticking to his long eyelashes as he blinked. I had to stop myself from reaching up and sweeping his hair off to the side.

Pushing myself away from the door, I took a step toward him, causing him to step back. I closed the distance, placing both my hands on his cheeks. "Graham, please. I'm begging you." My voice quivered.

The doorbell rang again, followed by pounding on the front door that seemed to have a melody.

His green eyes looked past me, blinking wildly. "I'm ss...sorry. I have to do this." Taking a firm hold of my hands, he moved me away from him and opened the bedroom door. His eyes were on the carpet. "You should leave." He popped in both his earbuds and stretched out his neck before he disappeared into the hall.

I followed him out, hearing low, angry voices at the door, along with Fluffsies barking.

Reed forced his way into the house, his body leaning, shoving Barbie in the process. He stopped when he saw Graham and me, and he righted himself. His light blue eyes went to the bat in Graham's hand, and Reed grinned, rubbing his hands together. "Put that away. You won't need it."

Lars and Ace flanked his sides, but not before Ace locked the front door. Lars' white shirt was so thin, I could see through it.

"Lars, take care of her," Reed said, waving a hand at Barbie. "Ace, lock the back door."

Lars slinked to Barbie's side and wrapped his hand around her skinny arm, lifted her from the ground, and tossed her on the couch like a doll. His head cocked to the side as his emotionless eyes found mine.

Whistling, Ace strolled over to the sliding glass door in the kitchen, making sure it was locked. He cupped his hands over the glass to look outside, and then gave Reed a lopsided smile. His button-down flannel shirt was perfectly pressed, contrasting with his brothers' sloppy appearances.

"Don't tt...touch my mom." After popping out an earbud, Graham took a step forward, his hand tightening on the bat.

"We aren't going to hurt you if we don't have to," Reed said. His placid gaze meandered over to me, and he offered me a closed-lip smile that made my toes curl.

Graham positioned himself between us, blocking Reed from my view. His steady hand reached behind him and landed on my waist. His voice was low and threatening. "Greg didn't leave anything here, so you can leave."

Reed waggled a finger at Graham as he sauntered over to the kitchen, opened the fridge, found a beer, and popped the cap off with the counter top. After he took a drink, he rejoined us in the living room, pushing up on his tiptoes for a second, almost in giddiness.

Barbie stayed still on the couch with her eyes down and Fluffsies in her lap. Lars loomed over them, his greasy hair hanging low on his forehead. He flexed his hands like he was itching to touch her – not in a rough way, but how he'd looked at me when we first met, and he wanted to see how I was put together.

"Listen, I just want my stuff." Reed took another drink and wiped his mouth with the sleeve of his unbuttoned flannel jacket when a little bit dripped down his beard. "Greg had it, he lived here, so his stuff is here. So where is it?"

"There's nothing here!" Graham yelled.

"We got rid of everything," Barbie said from the couch, her voice low and shaking. Her normal arrogant personality was nowhere to be found. A small amount of terror danced in her eyes. "Took it to the dump."

Reed finished off the beer, tossed the bottle in his hands a few times, and then threw it against the wall, shattering it into pieces. His chest heaved in and out as he drew deep breaths, but his rich, buttery tone stayed steady. "Don't lie to me. No mother would get rid of all her son's possessions." He tucked in his white undershirt, and then smoothed it out. "Where's his stuff?"

When Graham and Barbie didn't say anything, Reed tsked and disappeared down the hall, searching the rooms. Graham tried to follow him, but Ace hurried over and shoved his hand into Graham's chest to stop him. Ace puffed out his chest and rested his hand on top of his large, silver belt buckle with a snake on it, the fangs bared. His pointy chin jutted out like he was daring Graham to make another move – like he *wanted* him to.

Crashing and thudding echoed down the hall as Reed searched the rooms – the whole time casually singing "The Way You Make Me Feel" by Michael Jackson.

I looked to Graham, wondering if he thought the singing was as weird as I did. He was lifting the bat, but Ace stopped him, snatching the bat away from him with ease. Ace swung the bat in a couple circles like he was warming up, whistling the same tune as his brother. His large hands rubbed the grip of the bat before he rammed it into the back of Graham's legs, sending him to the floor.

Barbie screamed out, getting up from the couch, but Lars put his palm on her forehead and pushed her back down. It was the first time I'd seen her show concern for her son. The fear in her eyes grew as she clung to a whimpering Fluffsies.

While the guys were distracted, I backed toward the door, unlocked it, pulled my phone out of my back pocket, and dialed 911.

Reed's heavy boots skipped back down the hall. He threw his arms wide. "Come on, guys. Where's his stuff?"

I slipped my phone back in my pocket. "It's not here," I

said, making sure to be loud. "None of Greg's stuff is at the Dixon's house, okay, Reed? So just leave."

Reed calmly walked over to me, running his hand along his beard with a small cackle rising. He pinned me against the front door, his palm under my chin, and his thin fingers tapping my cheek. His other hand landed on my stomach. Pushing my head into the door, he slid me up, slowly lifting me off the ground until my feet were dangling just above the carpet.

Graham yelled, followed by a crunch of the bat hitting him. He screamed out in pain. My hands went up to Reed's, trying to pry his fingers away. I flailed my legs around as I scratched at his skin.

Do something, Tessa, DIM growled. *If you don't, I will.*

I waited until Reed was looking at his brothers before I reached behind my head and untied the scarf holding my hair. I wrapped the ends around both hands and pushed the scarf into Reed's neck until he loosened his grip on me. Using all my strength, I jammed my knee into his groin, and then elbowed him in the face when he bent down. My scarf slipped from my grasp and fell onto the carpeted entryway.

DIM squealed in joy. *Yes!*

Turning around, I opened the front door and ran.

"Stop her, please," Reed sang out.

I knew I could outrun them – I was fast. But the Dixons didn't take care of their yard, and I stumbled on some pavers that were covered by weeds. Someone jumped on top of me, knocking me to the ground. Two large hands turned me onto my back, and Lars looked down at me, his finger sliding along my jawline. The moonlight reflected off his pale skin.

Taking me by the chin, Lars titled my head up and to the side, his calculating eyes positioning me just how he wanted. With a nod of satisfaction, he tightened his hand into a fist, my focus going to the ring on his middle finger. I'd never noticed it before. It was a silver band with a dark blue stripe down the middle. Gold spiders lined the stripe like a band of brothers. They turned into a blur as his fist collided with my cheekbone. Pain radiated in my eye and scalp as he yanked me up by my hair.

"Tessa!" Graham said my name so clearly. But there was nothing he could do. Ace still held the bat.

Lars dragged me back inside the house as I clawed at his thin shirt, and my feet thrashed against the ground. He slammed the door with the back of his foot. Keeping me by the hair, he guided me toward the couch, and then threw me down next to Barbie and the dog. Barbie sobbed Graham's name as he knelt on the floor, face bloody.

"Graham!" I pushed up from the couch, but just like he'd done to Barbie, Lars pressed his slimy hand against my forehead and shoved me back down.

"Stay, little girl." Lars clasped his hands in front of him and smiled a toothless grin.

We needed help.

Amá, I thought as I stroked the side of my ring, *help us.*

Reed bent at the middle and held his hand out to Ace. "Brother?"

Ace returned the bow, and then handed him the bat. Reed cracked his neck, got a sturdy grip on the bat, and swung it down on the couch next to me, making me jump and lose my concentration.

"Leave her alone," Graham said, his voice quiet and shaky from the pain.

Reed intertwined his fingers in my hair and fisted it, dragging me over to where Graham lay on the floor. He kicked the back of my legs, slamming me to my knees. The smooth, wooden bat slid against my jaw as Reed held it close. His creamy tone was low. "Tell me where your brother's stuff is, or I hit your girlfriend."

"I told you, I don't know," Graham whispered. "Please don't hurt her."

Reed frowned, his bottom lip sticking way out. "Wrong answer." He swung the bat and smashed it into my stomach, immediately taking my breath away. Unable to hold myself up, I fell down next to Graham and grappled for a huge gulp of air, the intake pressing against my lungs like a heavy weight and burning in excruciating pain.

Amá, please, I begged. *Do something.*

"I know how close the two of you were," Reed said, rolling up the sleeves of his flannel jacket. "And I know what you were up to before Greg left." He pointed the bat at Graham. "I want what's mine."

"I'm so sorry, Tessa," Graham whispered. "I'm so sorry." He stared at me, his eyes sad and unblinking. Blood dripped from a gash above his swollen eye, leaving a thin trail on his face.

Reed lifted the bat, ready to strike me again, but Graham suddenly roared and threw himself at Reed, sending them both into the old coffee table, breaking it under their weight.

Barbie cried out, but Lars backhanded her across the cheek and snarled at her to be quiet. Reed and Graham wrestled around among the debris, both fighting for control. I needed a weapon. On the carpet, next to the TV, the bat rolled to a stop. I crawled toward it, but before my hand reached it, Ace grabbed me by the arm and pulled me up.

"Not so fast there, doll." Ace pushed his torso against my back, holding me close.

Amá. Please. Help.

Cold seeped into my bones and latched on. The yellow lights in the lamps flickered, and the TV suddenly turned on, black and white static filling the screen. The volume bar went higher and higher, drowning out all other sounds in the room.

Ace dropped me onto the carpet so he could turn off the TV. The second the screen shut off, heavy metal rang from Reed's pocket. Louder and louder it went. I threw my hands over my ears to dull the noise. Letting go of Graham, Reed struggled to his feet and reached for his phone. His fingers fumbled with the side of the phone, trying to turn down the volume. Yellow and orange sparks flew from the screen on his phone.

"Oh my." Reed dropped the phone, shaking his reddened hand.

The noise cut off. A frosty wind picked up in the room, circling around Lars, Ace, and Reed, making them back into a triangle. Barbie watched, wide-eyed in horror, as she clutched Fluffsies close to her chest. Broken pieces of wood from the shattered coffee table lifted into the air, and the wind sucked them in. They slashed against the guys' skin, leaving small cuts in their wake. The sound of the wind drowned out the men's screams.

My pink scarf drifted up from the entryway and floated over to the men, slipping through the wind with ease. It encircled all their necks, squeezing tight so the fabric could make it all the way around.

The guys' matching tan work boots lifted off the ground until the Harrison brothers were being held up by the wind, the scarf strangling them.

Graham lay broken and bruised on the floor. With every ounce of strength I had left, I army-crawled to him. We had to get out while we could.

Suddenly the front door opened, and Sheriff Hayes ran in. The wind around the men disappeared, and they fell to the floor, along with my scarf. Sheriff Hayes yanked Reed off the ground, somehow slapping handcuffs on Reed in the process. Blake ran to my side, sliding onto his knees. Another deputy threw Ace against the wall and handcuffed him. Lars scrambled toward the front door, but the sheriff easily seized him by the arms.

"Are you okay?" Blake asked, his worried brown eyes looking me over.

Isn't he a gorgeous sight for Harrison-saturated eyes? DIM cooed.

I couldn't argue with her on that one – I'd never been so ecstatic to see him. "I'm so glad you came."

Blake held me tight, squishing my ribs, but I didn't care. He kissed the top of my head. "The 911 operator heard commotion through the call and sent my dad a message. Smart thinking dialing 911 and leaving the line open."

Remembering the call was still going, I reached into my pocket, sucking in a sharp breath from the movement, and ended the call. I wanted to stay in Blake's arms, but I needed to check on Graham. I pushed away from Blake and shuffled to Graham, who lay on the ground, curled up in pain.

I knelt next to him and put my face near his. "Oh, Graham." Blood covered his whole face. Tears fell down his cheeks, mixing with the blood. Both his earbuds were tangled with the strings of his hoodie, specks of blood covering them.

"I'm sorry, Tessa," Graham whispered before he closed his eyes. "I'm sorry."

CHAPTER 23

Blake drove us to the local hospital. Barbie sat in the passenger seat, her shrieking sobs providing the only sound. She kept looking over her shoulder to check on Graham. He'd laid down in the back with his head on my lap. His left arm hung over the seat in an unnatural way – it had to be broken. Blake's prying eyes watched us through the rearview mirror. I tried to block him out and only focus on Graham.

Sheriff Hayes and his deputy had taken Reed, Ace, and Lars into custody. The sheriff told me he'd come by later for a statement, something I wasn't looking forward to. I didn't want to relive the event.

Tears soaked my jeans as Graham clung to my knee. His whole body vibrated with agony, his fingers tapping along my calf. He put his earbuds back in, and suddenly the banging of drums mixed in with his mother's cries, the two surprisingly creating a well-mashed melody.

The Willow Marsh hospital was a small, white building with only one floor. Blake pulled in front of the doors with the red emergency sign glowing above it. Hospital staff were already waiting for us outside. Sheriff Hayes must have radioed it in. A lady in blue scrubs opened the passenger door and helped Barbie out, mumbling soft words to comfort her.

A middle-aged man in navy blue scrubs pushed the passenger seat forward and reached back for Graham. I gently helped Graham sit up, keeping my hands on his back as the man in scrubs wrangled him out from the back seat. As soon as I got out, I slid my arm around Graham's waist, and we shuffled into the ER.

We only made it a few steps inside when an older man with graying hair ran out, his white lab coat fluttering behind him, and took Graham from me. He guided Graham through some automated doors, away from my view. I moved to follow, but the nurse who had helped Barbie held up a small hand.

"They'll take good care of him," she said in a motherly tone. The white name tag pinned to her uniform read SUZIE. She was short, skinny, and had dark skin. Her jet black hair hung to her shoulders, curling in. She looked at me with her soft, brown eyes. "Let's get you checked out." She escorted me to a room down a short hallway covered in white. Blake's assertive voice echoed out in the hall, but Suzie put her hand on her hip. "Stay back." She waved her other hand out like she was shooing away a stray dog.

Suzie helped me change into a soft blue and white hospital gown and onto the bed, my ribs shouting their discomfort the entire time. Her hands went to the scarf wrapped around my hand, but I yanked it away.

"I want to leave that on," I said, trying to keep an even tone.

Her head jerked back. "Okay." She eyed the family ring on my finger but said nothing about it.

She poked my skin with a silver needle, giving me something for the pain, which helped me through the next hour.

Even though I said it wasn't necessary, they took a CT scan and found three broken ribs.

Dad showed up while they were doing the scan. They let him back with me since he was family. His red, puffy eyes took me in. He'd thrown a zippered hoodie over his tee and still wore his pajama pants. His tennis shoes weren't tied; he'd just stuffed his feet into them and left. He'd already lost his wife and son, so I'm sure hearing his daughter was in the hospital was too much for him.

He stood by the door the whole time and watched, looking afraid to come near me. Like if he did, I might break apart or disappear. He kept raking his fingers through his hair. Gray had started to invade his hair, which I'd never noticed before. With the wrinkles in the corner of his eyes, he looked so much older from when we'd left Skokie, and it had only been a little less than a week. I wanted to say something to him, but my mouth was thick and heavy. The pain medication was having a strong effect on me, just like most drugs.

Suzie set an ice pack on my torso. "You're going to want to keep ice on this as much as you can. Don't do any strenuous movements or activities for the next couple weeks. Your ribs need the proper time to heal." Using the remote attached to the bed, she moved the back up until it was in a sitting position. "I know this won't be fun, but you'll need to be elevated for the next couple nights while you sleep." She glanced over her shoulder at Dad. "I'll give her some deep breathing exercises, so make sure she does them. We don't want her lungs filling with mucus or for her to get pneumonia."

I scrunched my nose at everything she was recommending. I had a feeling I was in for a world of annoying pain for a couple weeks.

"Can I go home soon?" I asked. Broken ribs didn't require

a check-in to a hospital. Although, the bed at the inn wasn't that appealing to go home to.

Suzie checked my chart. "We're going to keep you overnight, just for observation." She leaned in close. "Much easier to keep you elevated on these beds, if you ask me." With a soft tap on my hand, she left the room, leaving Dad and me alone. I lay my head against the bed, unable to hold it up on my own anymore.

For a few minutes, silence hung in the air. The only sound came from outside the room as the hospital staff went about their work.

"What on earth were you thinking?" Dad asked from the doorway, his voice strained. He stepped inside and leaned against the wall, still not coming close to me.

I smacked my lips a few times, trying to get some feeling. "I just wanted to help Graham."

"You thought you could stop Reed and his brothers?" His eyes were furious.

"I thought I could stop Graham from opening the door and talking to them."

Dad pounded his fist against the wall behind him. "Let's say for a second that you miraculously stopped Graham from opening the door. Those men would have found another way into the house!"

"I'm sorry!" I wanted to yell that louder, but it came out weak. I hated pain meds so much.

"Sorry?" Dad finally stepped forward, closing the distance between us. "Tessa, sorry isn't good enough. I can't lose you, too. I just can't." He rubbed his hand down his face. "I thought I told you to stay away from Graham. Apparently, I didn't make myself clear."

My hands gripped the sheets on the hospital bed. "I'm not going to stay away from him, and I'm not having this argument. He's my friend, Dad, so you better get used to it."

"Get used to it?" He pointed a finger at me. "Tessa, you are way out of line. I'm the parent in this relationship, not the other way around. If I tell you to stay away from someone, you'll do it. Understand?"

No, I didn't. Graham needed me. He needed a friend, and I didn't abandon people. Just because there were some men trying to hurt him didn't mean I would run away. If anything, he needed a friend more than ever.

My masquerade should have been a simple, single-layered cover. I somehow turned it into multiple layers, intertwining with each other, creating a mirage of colors and patterns.

With all the messages Amá was sending, all the feelings about people, it was messing with my head and making me lose my focus. Dad wasn't my enemy. I needed to remind myself of that.

A small knock on the door made me and Dad pull our gazes from each other. I knew he'd continue the conversation later.

Sheriff Hayes stood in the doorway, eyeing the two of us with raised eyebrows. I hoped he hadn't heard anything. He didn't wait for an invitation; he just came in and approached the bed, his thumbs tucked into the top of his pants. "How are you feeling, Tessa?"

I closed my eyes and counted to ten to calm myself. I didn't need to take my anger out on the sheriff. "Sore, but overall okay."

"Good." Sheriff Hayes clapped Dad on the shoulder. "Alec, why don't you go get a cup of coffee from the cafeteria? I need to chat with Tessa for a bit. Won't take long."

Dad gave me a look telling me we'd talk about it later, and then left the room. Sheriff Hayes dragged a chair over, the legs skidding across the linoleum. He sat down and pulled out a pad of paper from his jacket. He'd put on some cologne to cover the smell of smoke, but it only made it worse. "Why don't you tell me what happened tonight? Start from the beginning."

It took a while, but I told him everything I knew. I had to pause a few times from either pain or dizziness. I wanted nothing more than to go home and sleep. But then I remembered I didn't have a home. Just a motel room with a bed that was right next to Dad's. No privacy or space. At least in the hospital, I had my own room.

Sheriff Hayes interjected a few times with questions, mostly wanting to clarify things. When I was done, the sheriff tucked his pen and pad of paper in a pocket in the inside of his jacket. "I think it's wise for you to stay away from Graham. I told you it would lead to trouble."

"How is he?" I asked, unable to make eye contact with him. "How's Graham?"

"That doesn't matter right now," he said. "The important thing is . . ."

I forced myself to look at him. "It matters to me. How is he?"

Sheriff Hayes clenched his jaw, then relaxed it. "He'll be okay. His left arm is broken and so is his nose. The healing will be a long process, but he'll recover."

"And Barbie?" I actually didn't care much about her since she usually treated Graham like crap, but I'd seen a different side of her tonight night. A side that cared for her son.

"She's fine. A couple bruises. Mostly emotional damage." He leaned forward, resting his forearms on his legs. "Tessa, you're lucky this ended when it did. If you hadn't been able to make that call, no one would have known what was happening. The three of you could have ended up worse, or even dead."

"But I did make the call." I took a deep breath. *Control. Steady. Calm.* "What happens with Reed and his idiots now?"

"They'll be released in the morning."

"What?" No mantra or drugs could hold back the anger in my voice.

He sat back up. "Barbie and Graham didn't want to press charges. We'll keep the Harrisons in jail until morning, but then we'll let them go."

"Not press charges?" My whole body pulsed with rage, so I punched it down, adding another layer to my masquerade costume. "Well, I want to press charges."

He tilted his head and sucked in a sharp breath. "It wasn't your home."

"It was *my* body." My heart pounded against my chest as my blood boiled. My fists clenched around the sheets again, so I forced myself to relax. "Reed has attacked me twice now. Lars punched me. Ace swung a bat at my stomach and broke my ribs. I want to press charges."

Sheriff Hayes didn't seem fazed by my anger. "Barbie said you entered their house against her wishes. You were trespassing."

Trespassing? Seriously? All of my limbs shook, and my lungs twisted, squeezing out the air. I needed my mom. Felix or Leya. Someone I could trust. Someone I loved.

A warm hand landed on my shoulder, calming me. *Steady, my darling girl.* Amá. She was with me. I set my hand on my shoulder, hoping to sense something, but I only felt the cloth of the hospital gown.

"She also said you assaulted her." The sheriff stood, resting his hand on his hip. "She actually wanted to press charges against you, but I talked her down. Don't make me regret that decision. Stay away from the Dixons." He rubbed his hand along his square jaw. "If Reed or his brothers attack you in an instance when you aren't with Barbie or Graham, call me. If not, you need to drop it. Let go of Graham. You have a chance to start a new life here in Willow Marsh. Don't blow it." He went to the door and used two fingers to motion to someone. Blake entered the room, standing tall. Sheriff Hayes patted his son's arm. "Keep an eye on her. She's traumatized and not thinking clearly. Maybe you should stay with her until her dad comes back."

"Of course, Dad," Blake said. He strode to my side, passing right through Amá's presence. It evaporated, leaving me cold and abandoned. The hollow feeling inside sent my stomach churning.

Sheriff Hayes shot me a warning look, then left the room.

Blake smoothed back my hair. "Shh. It's okay. I'm here."

Why do you need your mommy when you have him? DIM asked.

Panic weaved into me, clouding my mind. I couldn't get myself under control. Blake didn't have his usual calming effect on me. Instead, I trembled in fear.

I'd never felt more alone.

Amá, I thought. *Please come back.*

Silence.

CHAPTER 24

The pain medications made my nightmare ten times worse. Since the drugs had taken over me, I couldn't escape the nightmare, so I kept reliving the crash over and over.

Mom screaming in fear, and Felix bawling in terror. Part way during the night, the dream had a minor change. Instead of Felix crying, he kept shouting, "Why did you do this to me?"

Sticky sweat layered my skin when I finally woke. I wanted to get out of the hospital bed, but my world swayed when I made too large of a movement. Even though the bed was positioned so I was practically sitting up, I took hold of the bottom sheet and pulled myself fully up, keeping my eyes closed through it all so the room wouldn't spin. If I lay in bed, I'd fall back asleep, and the nightmare would continue.

"Bad dream?" Blake asked from a chair next to the hospital bed. He lowered his leg that he had draped over the arm of the chair. Dark rings circled his eyes, taking away his usual edge.

"Yes." Using my palms, I rubbed my eyes. "Where's my

dad?" He'd been in the seat Blake was sitting in when I'd finally fallen asleep.

"He had some business this morning, so he called me, and I came back," Blake said.

Suzie peeped her head in the room before she walked in, smiling at me. "Good news. You get to go home."

Blake's hand wrapped around mine, the cold startling me. "That's great."

"It would be if I had a home." I bit my tongue before I said any more.

Suzie's eyebrows bunched in confusion. Blake answered for me. "She's staying at Willow Marsh Inn until their house is renovated."

After checking my vitals and signing some paperwork, Suzie authorized my release. Without my dad there. Another reason why Willow Marsh creeped me out.

Blake drove me back to the inn, cruising slowly down the streets and holding my hand, and then helped me walk to the door. His chapped lips pressed against my forehead. "Let me know if you need anything. I'll bring you whatever you need."

My feelings about him had an on/off switch. Some moments he gave me a warm sensation, telling me I could trust him. The next, I'd get a cold, frightening feeling, warning me to be wary of his motives. I wish I knew if the feelings were from Amá, DIM, or someone else.

"Thank you, Blake." I put on a smile I hoped was sincere, and then went inside.

With a lot of effort, I hobbled over to the couch, taking my time getting into a comfortable sitting position. Surprisingly, the owners had been able to clean off all the mud and blood I'd gotten on the couch. Or maybe they'd just bought an identical one to replace it.

Dad and Sheriff Hayes had told me to stay away from Graham, but they didn't say anything about texting him.

How are you feeling?

I assumed Graham was still in the hospital since he was in worse shape than me. I wasn't sure if he'd respond because he had seemed so upset with me yesterday. But my phone buzzed a minute later.

Awful. Whole body aches.
Stupid pain meds are making
me extra twitchy.

:(I'm sore. The pain meds
made my nightmares
unbearable last night.

What are your nightmares about?

Leya knew the whole truth. I debated how much to tell Graham, but if I wanted him to remain my friend, I needed to let him in. Plus, it was a lot easier to talk about through text.

I was in a crash before I moved here.

Was it bad?

Tessa, don't tell him, DIM sang.
I slapped my forehead. *Shut up.*
Not having anyone in Willow Marsh know the truth ate away at me. It would be a risk to tell him, but I decided to take a gamble on Graham.

The car rolled. I was driving.
2 other people were with me.

They died.

Tessa, I'm so sorry. You don't
blame yourself, do you?

Of course I do.

Did I dare tell him the rest? The whole truth behind it?
The part Dad didn't know about. Only Leya did. I typed it on
my screen and read it over a few times before I deleted it.
Some things were probably best kept to myself.

You can't blame yourself. It's not
your fault. Accidents happen.

I was behind the wheel.
I'm the one who lost control.
Why couldn't they have
lived and me die instead?

You can't ask yourself those
questions. It's over and done. You
can't change the past or try to
make sense of it. You'll go crazy.

I think I already have.

Yeah, you proved it last night
by showing up at my house. I
know you're upset you lived,
but that doesn't mean you need
to try and get yourself killed.

I couldn't just abandon you.

Why do you care what
happens to me?

> Because you're my friend.
> I don't want to lose you.

What about your boyfriend?

> He's not my boyfriend.

Blake wanted to be. I could tell by the way he looked at me. I probably could be happy with him if he weren't so shady and clingy. But I didn't want to be with him.

I want to, DIM said.

And I don't care what you think, I responded. The skin on my arms rippled, pulsating up and down, as it turned a deathly blue. I sucked in a breath at the sting, like a bunch of ice jabbed at my skin. I went to the mirror above the dresser and looked past the bruise around my eye to see tiny waves of blue weaved in with my natural dark brown irises.

My phone buzzed in my hands, startling me.

Graham:
He seems to think so.

> I don't want to talk about him.

What do you want to talk about?

> Did you know your mom wanted
> to press charges against me?

What? Who told you that?

Sheriff Hayes. He said I
trespassed last night and
assaulted your mom.

That doesn't surprise me. My
mom can be a little dramatic.
You probably shouldn't come
around here for a while.

That won't be a problem. My dad and
Sheriff Hayes want me to stay away
from you. Plus, I'm too terrified to drive
and I can't walk at the moment.
Otherwise I'd be there right now.

If they told you to stay away,
why are you talking to me?

I'm not near you. I'm just texting
you. If this is how we have to remain
friends for a while, I'll take it. It beats
shutting you out, which I told you I
wouldn't do. Remember, you can't
get rid of me that easily.

I glanced at my skin, relieved to see it had turned back to
a light brown. "Sharp Dressed Man" by ZZ Top rang out from
my phone – Dad was calling me. Flinching from the pain, I
slowly went back to the couch and answered.

Dad's soothing tone was the perfect remedy for my
misery. "How are you feeling?"

"Sore. Tired." Loopy. Out of my mind. Confused. "I don't
have to go to school today, do I?"

"No." Dad took a deep breath. "I need to apologize."

It took a moment to register what he had said. "What? Shouldn't it be me?"

"We probably both do. Listen, Tess, we've been through a lot lately. We lost your mom and brother. You were almost killed. I yelled at you, and I shouldn't have. We're a team."

"A team." I slid the ring on my finger back and forth over my knuckle. "I am sorry, Apá. I know you're just looking out for me."

"If we stay mad at each other, I'll lose the tiny amount of sanity I still have in me." His voice flooded with desperation.

"I know how you feel," I whispered.

"Good news." The smile in his tone was obvious. "The house is almost done. I'm here now finishing up some minor details."

Finally, my own room. My own bathroom and bed. "Are we moving today?"

"Yep. I wanted to get it all done, so you had something to look forward to. Take it easy today and call me if you need anything." He mumbled to someone in the background, probably a worker. When he turned his attention back to the call, his tone was soft. "Tessa, I love you."

"Love you, too," I said before I ended the call. I couldn't wait to have a home.

My phone buzzed in my hands. Graham.

Thank you.

For what?

For being my friend. I haven't
had one in a long time.

Thanks for listening to me.
If you don't mind, can you keep

what I told you between us? No
one else in Willow Marsh knows.

Not even Blake?

Nope.

Your secret's safe with me.
Try to get some rest.

You, too.

Setting my phone on the couch, I used my palms to help
me stand so I could use the restroom, but the floor creaked,
causing me to stop. I limped around, testing the floor all
around the couch, finding one spot that seemed wobbly
under my feet, like someone had removed the wood below
the carpet before. Digging my feet into the floor, I pushed on
the arm of the couch until it slid over and blocked the door
to the room.

I used the window sill as a support as I knelt down,
sucking in a sharp breath from the pain. The carpet was soft
near the baseboard from lack of traffic. Gritting my teeth, I
yanked on the edge of the carpet until the nails pried away
from the wood floor beneath. I tugged the carpet back until I
reached the squeaky part of the wood.

I ran my fingers around the wood floor, but I couldn't find
a spot to lift anything. Using the window sill again, I stood
and bounced around until one of the pieces of wood popped
up. Pain tore through my middle as I knelt back down, and I
realized I was sweating. My broken ribs didn't appreciate all
the moving.

Two wooden planks lifted with some force. There,
beneath the room, sat an old, wooden box about the size of a

shoe box. Dust covered the top of it, so I brushed it away before I lifted the box out of the hole and set it on the floor. I ran my fingers across a raised piece of wood with an arrow carved into it, the wood wobbling a little underneath my touch. When I pressed down on the arrow, there was a click.

Placing my hands on both ends of the lid, I lifted it back and immediately saw a picture taped to the inside of the lid. It was of a young guy, probably around nineteen or twenty, with his arm around a girl about the same age. I ran my fingers across his face, recognizing the green eyes and long lashes. It had to be Greg. I could see the resemblance between him and Graham.

Inside the box, I found a few different things. An envelope held about five hundred dollars in cash. There was an old silver coin dating back to the Civil War tucked all the way on the bottom. Below it was another picture with two young guys, smiling wide. The oldest looked to be ten, the younger one maybe seven. Greg and Graham as kids. There was also a nice gold watch with the initials G.D. carved into the inside.

My fingers brushed along a folded piece of parchment. I carefully opened it, revealing a map of Willow Marsh from 1863. It felt weird to be holding a piece of history like that. The town was much smaller back then, with only a few stores and houses. There was a circle drawn in red ink – definitely done recently – over a section of the woods. With how much Willow Marsh had changed, I wasn't sure where it was currently located. Maybe I could compare it to a newer map. I snapped a picture of it with my phone and carefully refolded the parchment.

A camcorder took up the rest of the room in the box. I turned out the screen so I could see it and pressed power, hoping the battery wasn't dead. A green light switched on, and the screen came to life. Leaning back against the corner of the couch, I pressed play.

Greg came on the screen, wearing a light jacket and a black beanie. His smile matched Graham's.

"Hey. Your favorite adventurer, Greg Dixon, here. You're about to see the most stunning view of Willow Marsh." He turned the camera around and showed the city down below.

"Willow Marsh may not be the greatest city to live in, but you can't beat the view and the hikes in the area. The scenery is breathtaking." The camera shook as it faced Greg again. "Now I'm going to take you to my favorite spot. My brother, Graham, and I go there all the time to hang out and get away from our mom. So, hold on tight." The picture bounced with each step he took as he went farther into the woods. After a minute, the willow and birch trees opened up into a small clearing. A stream trickled nearby. Greg hopped up onto a large boulder and scanned the area. Large maple and pine trees lined the spot, different than the trees the woods held. Lush, vibrant green grass covered the ground like a pillow. I wanted to sink into it.

Greg's voice came on as he panned the area. "Told you it was breathtaking. Best place in the area, trust me. I've spent my whole life exploring everywhere around Willow Marsh, and nothing beats this."

A loud bang echoed through the trees, and the camera lowered, showing a gray boulder. "What was that?" Greg's voice bounced as he jumped off the boulder and ran back into the trees, the screen a shaky blur. He finally came to a stop and lifted the camera. His voice was barely a whisper. "I think it came from around here." He continued to slowly walk forward, moving the camera around, searching for the source of the noise.

Deep voices sounded in the distance. Greg kept going until he got closer, then stopped. The camera lowered until you could see between some trees. Three men were standing not far off, looking down at something. When one of the men moved, I saw it was someone, not something.

The girl on the ground held onto her bloody leg, crying out in pain. "I told you I don't know where it is!" She shouted through gritted teeth. From what I could tell, she looked no older than sixteen. Her long, blonde hair framed her face.

"I do hate when people lie to me." I didn't have to see his face to know it was Reed. My fingers tightened around the camcorder. I immediately recognized the other two guys as Lars and Ace. Reed had his fingers wrapped around a black handgun as he massaged the back of his neck.

"I'm not lying!" the girl yelled, her voice cracking.

Turn it off, DIM growled.

Reed sighed and knelt next to her, pressing the barrel of the gun against the girl's forehead. He wiped at his mouth with his sleeve. "It's simple, really. Just tell me the truth, and you can go."

Press stop! DIM yelled inside my head. *I don't want to watch this.* Ice flooded my veins, making it hard to grip the camcorder.

The girl just lay there, whimpering in pain. Reed nodded at Ace, who pressed his boot down on the girl's leg. A horrible, distorted scream left her mouth.

"Who are you?" Reed asked, steady and calm. He brushed some hair out of her eyes. "I will not ask again."

Please, turn it off now! DIM screamed. My hands went stiff, and the camcorder dropped from my grip.

"Delilah!" the girl yelled. "You know me. I'm not who he says I am. I'm not a Walker."

My limbs were practically frozen. Small puffs of air left my mouth, creating an icy mist in front of me. I forced through the pain and picked up the camcorder.

"I was worried you'd say that." Reed pulled the trigger, the shot cracking through the air, and the girl went limp.

A cry escaped my mouth at the same moment Greg's did on camera. All three heads turned toward Greg. He took off running, the camera bouncing out of control.

"Get him!" Reed snarled in the background. Greg ran a while longer before the feed went black.

With some force, I shut the screen on the camcorder and set it down. Reed had killed that girl, Delilah, and Greg had seen it. He'd filmed it. Was Greg's death really an accident like Graham had said? Or had he been murdered by the Harrisons?

The cold retreated from me, warmth returning in its stead. DIM crawled away at the same time. I could still feel her, in my mind, but she was hiding. Almost cowering.

Ignoring the pain from my ribs, I shifted until I could reach my phone, which had slid away. I texted Graham.

> We need to talk.
> I think I found what Reed wants.

CHAPTER 25

After he was out of school, Blake picked me up from the inn for my therapist appointment, but I wasn't in the mood to talk to Rita or see Blake. I'd created a copy of the footage on my laptop, hid the camcorder in my suitcase, and hoped no one would find it in the meantime.

All I wanted to do was talk to Graham, but it would have to wait. I wasn't even sure when I'd be able to see him. I couldn't get behind a wheel, and Graham's injuries would make it difficult for him to drive.

Blake smiled at me when I opened the door, some of my worry drifting away. His cute dimple flirted with me. His deep eyes put me in a trance that I couldn't control. I hated it.

"Hey, beautiful."

Hello yourself, DIM said.

You're back? I asked.

DIM scoffed. *Excuse me for not wanting to witness a murder. We both knew that was going to happen. It's Reed.*

Blake leaned in and kissed me on the forehead. At least

he'd applied some lip balm, so his lips weren't dry anymore. "Ready to go?"

DIM shuddered within me at his touch. Her feelings for him sent a small wave of adrenaline through my blood. I was surprised I couldn't see my skin move on the outside.

"Yep." I shut the door behind me and let Blake escort me to the car. I wanted to stay strong and not let the warmth of his hand on the small of my back get to me, but it felt good.

"How was your day?" Blake asked as we rode in his car. His hair was gelled perfectly in place.

"Boring. Just sat around in the hotel room."

He reached over and placed his hand on my leg, just above my knee. "Still sounds better than being at school. By the way, I have some homework for you from your teachers. I talked with the principal, and she said you can take as much time as you need to recover."

I liked the fact he made sure to get my homework, but he talked to the principal without asking me what I wanted. He took it upon himself like it was his responsibility or something. I forced a smile. "Thanks. That's good to hear. I'm still so sore."

His thumb rubbed my leg in a circular motion, easing my tense muscles. "I could take tomorrow off school to take care of you."

See how wonderful he is? DIM purred. *He could be ours.*

"You don't need to do that. I can manage on my own."

Blake parked along the curb outside the city building. "I know you can. Can't a guy want to spend time with the girl he likes?"

I turned to him, leaning my head against the headrest. "Why do you like me? You hardly know me."

"I know enough. I like spending time with you." He ran his long fingers through my hair. "You're easy on the eyes, which definitely helps." At the mention of eyes, something inside me shifted. Blake leaned toward me. "Your eyes. They're swirling with blue again."

An electrifying heat coursed through my veins. His touch did that to me. It did that to DIM.

When I didn't respond, Blake kissed me. Part of me wanted to push away so I could sort out my thoughts, but the other part enjoyed kissing him. His lips were so soft and perfect. My whole mind clouded as his fingers tangled into my hair, needing no encouragement from me. I'd been so distracted I forgot to pull it back in a ponytail to keep it under control.

A weird sensation flitted through my head. I wanted to stop kissing him, but something had overtaken me, making my lips move against his.

Mine, mine, mine, DIM sang.

Blake's kiss turned fierce, like he'd been longing for it. A small moan rumbled in his throat. He wrapped his hand around my back and tried to pull me closer, but my ribs pushed against the center console.

"Ow!" At the pain, my connection with DIM snapped. I sank back into the seat, placing my hand on my ribs. I should have brought an ice pack with me.

"Sorry." Blake swore under his breath. "I'm such an idiot. Are you okay?"

Closing my eyes, I leaned my head against the seat, clenching my teeth from the pain.

"Tessa." He pounded his hand against the steering wheel. "I didn't mean to hurt you. You just turn me on. I can barely control myself."

I craved fresh air. "It's fine. I'm going to be late for my appointment." Opening the door, I placed my hand on the side of the leather seat and pushed myself up and out of the car.

Blake hurried out and swatted at a vampire finch that had

landed on the hood of his car. It whistled and snapped its pointy beak at Blake. I used the distraction to limp into the building.

Why do you keep doing that? I asked.

DIM laughed, sending jagged pinpricks to my skin. *Because it's fun. You're so easy to control.*

I hated her so much. I wished I knew how to block her out. Or better yet, get rid of her completely.

The elevator doors opened just as I got to them. Reed sauntered out, putting his hands on his hips and grinning when he saw me. I swear he didn't own anything else but that ugly flannel jacket. At least the shirt underneath was clean and had no holes. That I could see.

"I'm so glad to see you again, *Tessa*," Reed said in a sugary tone. I stepped into the elevator and smacked the button for the second floor with my palm. The door started to close, but Reed put his hand out to stop it. "We need to talk."

Before I could react, he slipped into the elevator and pushed the button to close the doors. I saw a worried Blake for a second before the doors closed. I only had one floor to go until the doors would open, and I knew Blake would run up the stairs to be there when they did.

Reed pushed the emergency stop button, making the elevator halt between floors. I backed against the wall and tried to keep my breathing deep and slow to not hurt my ribs. Anxiety wrapped its warped hands around my lungs and squeezed.

I was trapped in an elevator with Reed Harrison.

He closed the gap between us and ran his finger along my cheek, his cloudy blue eyes taking me in. I tried to push his hand away, but he just grabbed my wrist and pinned it against the wall. When I tried to use my other hand, he pinned that wrist, too.

"Now that I have you alone, we can finally talk one-on-one." His breath was coated with alcohol.

"I don't want to talk to you." I tried to keep my tone steady, not wanting him to know how much he was hurting me, but my voice quivered. I stroked my bronze ring with my thumb. *Amá, help me. Protect me.*

"Well, that isn't very nice." Reed's hands tightened around my wrists, and I held in a scream. "Tessa, I run this city. I own Willow Marsh. I walked into the Dixons' house, ruined everything, and hurt you, Graham, and his mom." He quirked his head to the side, his honey tone going down an octave. "And I can do it again."

My upper lip curled into a snarl. "I'll never cower under you."

After a sigh and shake of the head, he let go of one of my wrists to backhand me across the face. Tears pooled in my eyes from the sting. "Darling, it's not nice to interrupt, okay? The only reason I'm keeping you alive is because I know you can talk some sense into your boyfriend." He poked my nose and chortled. "Just like all good girlfriends do."

Amá. Please. I need you, I thought.

His hand hovered next to my cheek, his languid eyes debating whether he wanted to touch it or not. "You tell him that we're not done. I want my stuff." He ran his tongue across his top lip. "Graham knows what Greg was up to, and he wouldn't get rid of Greg's things like that. I'm in a good mood today, so I'll give you two days." He grinned, showing his white teeth. "That's more than generous."

His hand trailed along a strand of my hair. He held it below his nose and breathed it in, his eyes going cross, seconds before he dropped it. He squeezed his hand around my chin, his fingernails digging into my skin, and pushed my head against the elevator wall. "If I don't get what I want, your dad will receive your body in pieces, and Barbie will get Graham's." He pressed his slimy lips against my ear. "Are we clear?"

All of a sudden, the lights above us flickered with a crackling sound before they dimmed. Music drifted from the speaker overhead. A piano melody – dark, tragic, and piercing.

Reed eased his hold on me and looked up, but he didn't let go completely.

The elevator jolted, powered back on, and travelled up a couple floors. Pain tore through my middle at the sudden motion.

Let her go. Ellington's faint outline watched us from the mirror on the left, his voice full of static. I wouldn't have known it was him if I hadn't seen him in the mirror. The uniform he wore was hard to see, just like the rest of him, but his eyes burned into Reed with an anger I'd never seen before. The mirror cracked in the center, the lines racing in every direction, creating an intricate design.

"Who said that?" Reed asked as his focus darted all over the elevator. His hand shook against my face.

Ellington appeared in the right mirror, his gaunt face fleshing out. His head tilted slightly to the side as blood dripped from his eyes. Horror seized my stomach when I turned to look at Reed and noticed blood trickling down his cheeks.

Reed dropped me, his hands going to his eyes. His fingers dabbed at his cheeks, and he rubbed the blood between his fingers, curiosity landing on his face. "Now, what kind of witchcraft is this?"

I started to back into the corner, trying to create a distance between us, but the left mirror cracked, sending a few broken pieces to the ground and freezing me in place.

The heart-wrenching music intensified, growing and shrinking with each beat. Goosebumps erupted on my flesh.

Suddenly, the elevator plummeted. I screamed, my arms flailing to hold on to something, but only air surrounded me. The brakes squealed against the rails as we fell, floor by floor, passing the ground floor and heading well below the earth. My stomach lurched at the thought of meeting my doom.

Reed calmly clawed at his eyes, tugging at his skin, the blood continuing to spill out and drench his shirt.

The elevator jerked to a stop, throwing me into the air. My side crunched against the ground and pushed the breath out of me. I held my ribs, desperate to get air.

Leave her alone! Ellington's static voice boomed and vibrated the broken glass on the floor.

The mirror on the back wall of the elevator shattered, daggers flying out. I threw my arms out to shield at least some of my body, but my fear turned to awe as the pieces of glass slowly descended, cascading like a waterfall, nothing touching me. The music softened to a peaceful lullaby. One Amá used to sing to me as a child.

"Amá!" She'd shown up. Amá had come to protect me.

The elevator door pinged open, revealing a dark tunnel well below the office building. The image of the rusty key I'd found in Trenton's locker flashed into my mind.

Reed was on his knees, terror finally seizing him as he screamed, his bloody hands covering his eyes. A cool breeze swept from the tunnel and into the elevator, sending a few pieces of glass spinning into the air. Reed lowered his hands enough to check what was happening, but he was rooted to his spot.

Slowly, the doors screeched closed. The elevator sprung to life, rising steadily. The music switched to a typical boring elevator melody. I didn't dare move with broken glass littering the ground. To my right, the pieces shifted, spelling something. *The path to forgiveness is here.*

We were almost to the second floor, so I took the window of opportunity and used the strength of knowing I had Amá on my side. "Reed, leave me, Graham, and . . ." I hesitated, clenching my jaw and holding in an eye-roll before I continued. "And Barbie alone."

He rocked on his knees like a child, mumbling about witchcraft and sorcery.

"You've seen what happens when you mess with me," I said in a low, threatening tone, my courage building. "So stay away."

As soon as the doors opened, Blake and Rita rushed in, the broken glass cracking under their weight. A glance back at the glass showed no more words. Reed crawled out of the elevator while Blake and Rita hovered over me, making sure I was all right.

"What did he do to you?" Blake asked, holding me in his arms. I still couldn't breathe right, so I laid my head against his chest, concentrating on his heartbeat.

Rita tried to soothe me by running her hand down my hair. I heard Sheriff Hayes in the hall, tending to Reed, who was making unearthly grunts. Blake scooped his arms under me, lifted me off the ground, and carried me out of the elevator.

"An ambulance is on its way." Rita's wide eyes took in the broken pieces of glass all over the floor, then slid over to Reed's bloody face and hands. "What happened in there?"

Blake found a cushioned chair for me to sit on in the hall. His eyes kept gliding over me, searching for wounds, but none were to be found. Amá had protected me.

"He attacked me." My voice was unsteady. How could I explain the broken glass or blood pouring out of Reed's eyes?

A paramedic in a blue uniform raced up the stairs and

over to Reed, who was still freaking out, mumbling incoherently. I watched, dazed, trying to process what had happened.

"How did the mirrors break?" Blake asked.

My voice came out in a whisper. "I don't know. The elevator dropped below the building, and all the mirrors shattered."

Rita rubbed my arm. "There's nothing below the building, Tessa." Her eyes filled with concern and doubt. She would probably write all of it down in my file the second she could. Crazy patient. Delusional.

Amá, or maybe Ellington, had shown me there was some sort of basement. Maybe no one knew about it, but now I did, and the key had something to do with it.

The paramedics carried a lethargic Reed on a stretcher down the stairs.

With a heavy sigh, Sheriff Hayes wandered over to where I sat and got down on one knee, resting his arm on the other. "Tessa, can you tell me what happened in that elevator?"

I shook my head. I couldn't explain it without sounding mad. With my therapist right in front of me, I needed to keep everything to myself, so I didn't get locked up in a mental institution.

Sheriff Hayes exchanged a look with Rita, but I didn't know what it meant.

"She's on pain medication," Blake said. "Reed attacked her. Again. Give her a break, Dad." For once, I was grateful for him. He'd stood up for me.

"We can talk about it later," Sheriff Hayes said with a nod. "When she's had some more rest."

Rita patted my arm. "Why don't you come into my office, and we can talk about it?"

My eyes went to hers. I definitely didn't feel like having a session anymore. I wanted to call Leya or Graham. But I couldn't call him.

Blake helped me stand, his arm firmly around my waist. "Sorry, Rita, but not today. Tessa needs rest."

Rita started to say something, but Blake pushed past her and helped me walk down the stairs. I leaned into him, grateful for the physical and mental support.

CHAPTER 26

The excitement of finally being in my new house drifted away, out of reach with no hope of coming back. Dad, Blake, and Sheriff Hayes made me sit on the couch and do my homework as they did all the work around the house. I wouldn't have minded if they hadn't spent the whole time talking like I wasn't capable of taking care of myself. They discussed the necessary precautions they needed to take to make sure I was safe. Sheriff Hayes was even going to talk to the principal about changing my two classes I had with Graham. Now the only chance I had to talk to him was ripped away.

Dad sat next to me on the couch, holding a large present in his hand. "Apparently, Leya sneaked this into our moving stuff. Want to open it?"

"I don't have the energy." The pain medication had worn off, letting the pain slam into me. I held an ice pack against my tender ribs.

With a pocket knife, Dad removed the wrapping paper to reveal a hand-painted wooden board. It read *"Donde quiera que moramos, siempre seremos familia"* in blue, curly lettering.

"Wherever we dwell, we will always be family." Dad held the board for me to see. "Where should we put it?"

I traced the letters with my finger, smiling. Leya always knew exactly what I needed. I glanced around the living room, my eyes resting above the brick fireplace. "Up there."

He placed the board on the coffee table. "I'll hang it up as soon as I can." He adjusted the wool blanket draped over me. "Want to talk about what happened in the elevator?"

"Not yet." I didn't know how to explain it. Where had the elevator taken me?

Dad went back to unpacking, so I finished my homework, and then texted Leya. I wanted to call her, but I didn't want the guys eavesdropping. I had to be careful what I wrote her because Blake kept looking over my shoulder, trying to read my message. I'd never have any privacy again.

"Who's Leya?" Blake asked, his voice incredibly close to my ear.

I twitched away, then grunted in pain at the movement. "Just a friend from back home."

"Huh." His eyes lingered on my phone a while longer, waiting for another text to come in, but then he finally gave up and went outside to grab another box.

After a while, I couldn't take it anymore. I peeled off the blanket, set the ice pack on the coffee table, and hobbled toward the hall.

Blake appeared in front of me before I got two feet. "What do you need? I'll get it for you." He set the box on the floor next to the couch.

"I have to use the bathroom," I said, trying to remain calm.

Don't be mad at Blake, DIM said.

Shut up, I said. *Don't ever try to take control of me again. Ever.*

DIM giggled. *Not likely.*

"Well, I can at least walk you there." Blake put his arm

around my waist and escorted me to the bathroom on the main level. Dad had replaced the sink and toilet in there, making it look new and not so terrifying. The first time we checked it, we'd found a furry critter in the toilet.

I flipped on the light and went inside, starting to close the door behind me.

"I'll wait right here," Blake said, smiling at me.

Seriously? I didn't care if I had to create an awkward moment. I needed privacy. "I might be a while. I have to . . . you know."

"K. I'll be upstairs getting your room ready. Just holler when you're done, and I'll be right down." He gave me a light kiss on the lips before he left me alone.

Shutting the door, I locked it and turned on the fan. Leya's number was dialing the second I flipped the switch.

Her face immediately filled the screen, holding her phone way too close that I could only focus on her shiny pink lips. "What's going on? You're being cryptic in your texts."

"I have zero privacy," I said, keeping my voice low.

She finally pulled the phone back, furrowing her eyebrows and trying to look behind me. "What's that noise?" She had her braids wrapped in a bun on top of her head.

"The fan. I'm in the bathroom. It's the only way I can be alone." I leaned against the door and rubbed my forehead. "Leya, I'm going to go insane. Reed has now attacked me three times, the sheriff won't do anything about it, and now Blake and Dad have decided that I should never be alone. Ever."

"Ever?" Leya twisted her lips, her eyes incredulous. "Like even at night? Is Blake going to sleep over or something? Have a slumber party? Do each other's nails? Braid your hair?"

I rolled my eyes and massaged the back of my neck. "He

better not think he can stay here. He's already so touchy feely."

Her face softened. "So, what are you going to do?"

"I don't know, Leya. I want to go home."

"Then come home." She leaned to the side, disappearing from view, then came back with a bag of Cool Ranch Doritos in her hand. "Come live with me. My parents are totally cool with it. I miss you."

"I miss you, too." Tears formed in my eyes, but I used the scarf on my hand to wipe them away before they could fall. I couldn't cry. I needed to be strong. "But my dad won't let me leave."

She finished off the chip in her mouth. "Have you actually asked if you can go? I mean, doesn't he realize how dangerous it is for you? Honestly, you look like crap."

"Thanks." I didn't hide the sarcasm in my voice. "And no, I haven't actually asked to go home. If I ever get a free minute away from Blake, I will." But I needed to talk to Graham first. "Leya, I gotta go. I need to reach out to Graham before Blake sends a search party. I'll call you later."

"Stay safe." She blew me a kiss. "Bye."

I texted Graham as soon as I hung up. He usually preferred that over talking.

> We need to talk. It's an emergency.
> I can't get away now. Blake and
> Dad watching me like hawks.

Are you safe?

It made me smile that he asked that first. It wouldn't be easy for him to drive, but I had to ask.

> For now. Can you

sneak away tonight?

Yes. When and where?

I can't go far. We're in our new
house. Meet me in the trees behind
the house around midnight.

Can I come earlier?

Not sure if I can get away. Dad
and Blake won't leave me alone
until they know I'm asleep.

Midnight it is. Tessa, if anything
happens before then, call me.
Text me. I'll be there ASAP.

Thank you. I'm so glad I have
you. You're the only one I
trust in Willow Marsh.

I'm glad I have you, too.
See you later.

I erased all the messages from Graham, just in case Dad or Blake looked at my phone. I hoped they wouldn't go that far, but I wouldn't be surprised if they did. Before I left the bathroom, I made sure to set the alarm on my phone for 11:55 PM, in case I fell asleep.

When I opened the door, Dad was walking down the hall. He stopped when he saw me. "Everything okay? You were in there awhile."

"Do you really want to know all about my bodily

functions?"

Dad grimaced, scratching at the scruff on his jaw. "Not really."

I did a quick scan of the area and didn't see Sheriff Hayes or Blake, so I went close to him. "Dad, something was in that elevator with Reed and me. It attacked him and stopped him from hurting me further."

He rubbed his hand over his face. "Have you heard voices?"

His question took me by surprise. "What?"

"Have you heard voices in your head?"

"Yes," I said, hope igniting inside. He understood. "But I think it's Mom."

Dad sighed, his eyes disappointed. Or maybe tired. I couldn't tell. "Jillian had the same problems." So he didn't understand. Jillian was his little sister. I'd never met her. She ran away from home when she was fifteen. They eventually found her and locked her up in a mental health hospital for hearing voices and seeing things.

She committed suicide when she was seventeen.

"Apá, I'm not Jillian." I put my hands on his arms. "I'm telling the truth. You have to believe me. I'm not crazy." I braced myself for Dad's tirade when I told him the next part. "It's not just Amá. There's been this ghost following me."

Dad backed away, his face scrunched together like he was fighting back tears. "Tessa, don't do this. Not now."

I stepped in front of him. "It's true. His name is Ellington and..."

"Tessa, stop." He rubbed his forehead. "Please stop this nonsense."

"I want to go home." I wiped a tear from my eye. "Leya said I could go live with her."

He glanced over his shoulder to make sure we were still alone. "This is your home now."

"This place is crazy. Dead bodies showing up. I was almost murdered. I can't stay here." I swayed from anger and dizziness, so I placed my hand on the wall to steady myself.

"I know you're scared," Dad said, his eyes soft. "So am I. But we can't keep running from our problems. I'll protect you. The sheriff will protect you. Stay around the right people, and you'll be safe."

Sheriff Hayes came around the corner holding a cardboard box that had 'kitchen' written in black sharpie on it. He paused when he saw Dad and me. "Everything okay?"

Dad put his hand on my shoulder, squeezing it gently. "Yeah. Tessa's tired and needs some rest." He kissed my forehead. "Why don't you go get some sleep?" I shuffled toward the stairs. Dad leaned in and whispered in my ear. "Everything is going to be okay."

Then why didn't it feel like it would?

CHAPTER 27

Each step up the stairs sent a jolt to my ribs. By the time I sat on my bed, I was panting. My neck, face, and ribs ached. I hadn't noticed Blake in there, shutting my dresser drawer.

"I told you to holler up to me," Blake said, coming to sit by me. He wrapped his arm around me and pulled me close. I sank into him, grateful for the warmth.

I eyed all the white furniture in the room. It all matched and looked old, yet refurbished. I loved the whole set. Dresser, bedposts, nightstand, and the bookcase. "Where did all this come from?"

"It was the previous owner's. Your Dad restored everything."

"That was quick." Way fast.

"He had help from some men in town." Blake kissed my temple. "It's late. You should go to bed." He stood, went to one of the drawers, and pulled out some flannel pants and a T-shirt. "All your lounging and sleeping clothes are in this drawer." He pointed out all the drawers, telling me what was in each one.

He'd put my clothes away for me? When he pointed to the drawer that held my underwear and bras, he winked at me, making any calm leave. He'd gone too far. We definitely hadn't reached that level of a relationship.

Blake brought over my pajamas and set them next to me on the bed. "Stand up. Let's get you changed."

At first, I thought he was joking, but then I saw his serious face, which told me otherwise. "I can do it myself."

Blake put his hands on the bottom of my shirt, ready to lift it. "I don't mind."

"But I do." I pushed his hands away. "My dad could come by at any moment." Plus, I wasn't ready for him to see me undressed. Actually, I never wanted him to see me undressed. He'd gone from hot to creepy in a day. That had to be some kind of record.

But think of the fun we could have, DIM said.

"I can shut the door," Blake said with a quirk of his thick eyebrow.

"Really, I can dress myself." My cheeks were on fire but not from embarrassment.

Blake tucked my hair behind my ear. "You're cute when you blush. What, you've never had a guy see you without your clothes?"

"No." I restrained myself from pushing him out of the room. "I'm not that kind of girl, Blake. If that's what you want, then you shouldn't be dating me." I flinched. I used the word *dating.*

He put his hands on my cheeks. "You're what I want. If you want to wait, we'll wait." He kissed my forehead, letting his lips linger longer than necessary. "I'll be right outside."

I changed as fast as my body would allow, in case he decided to come back in. The old brass doorknobs didn't have locks. I had just finished putting on the pants when I remembered the camcorder. Blake had unpacked all my stuff.

I searched the drawers, frantic to find it. When they proved fruitless, I moved to the closet, raking through the stuff. It had to be here somewhere. I checked every nook and cranny in the room, including the suitcases under the bed, which were empty.

Blake opened the door and popped his head in. "What's going on in here? I heard a bunch of noise."

I licked my lips. "Did you unpack all my stuff?"

"Yeah." He glanced around the room. "Is something missing?"

I'd wrapped the camcorder in a towel and put it at the bottom of one of my suitcases. "I had a towel in my suitcase."

"Oh. That." Blake pointed his thumb toward the door. "I put it in the dirty laundry bag you had and took it downstairs. It's in the laundry room."

I sighed in relief. He must not have found the camcorder wrapped inside. It was a small one, so it was easily concealed. I'd have to get it before Dad started the wash. I drew back the covers on my bed and slowly sat down, keeping my back straight.

Blake sat next to me. "Oh, and I took the camcorder out of the towel so it wouldn't get ruined. That was an interesting way to pack it, but it added protection."

"Where did you put it?" At least I had been smart enough to take out the memory card and had it stuffed in the side of my bra. I normally took off my bra to sleep, but I was so not going braless with Blake around.

"It's in the office downstairs."

Taking a bunch of pillows, I created a wall against the headboard and sunk into them so I could sit up while I slept. It wasn't the most comfortable position, but I hoped I'd be exhausted enough to sleep anyway. Blake draped the covers over me.

Snuggling under the covers, I leaned my head on the highest pillow. "Thanks, Blake. I'll see you tomorrow?"

He knelt down next to the bed, taking my hands in his. He fingered the scarf on my hand. "Are you going to take this off?"

I quickly shook my head. "I like having it there."

His eyes held intrigue, but he didn't bring it up again. "I can stay with you if you'd like. Keep an eye on you." He ran his hand down my hair. "Keep you warm."

I yawned. "I'll be safe with my dad."

He looked like he was debating it in his head, but he leaned in and tried to kiss me on the lips. I pulled back.

"Blake." I didn't know where to begin or what to say. I wasn't sure how he'd react. "I'm not ready for a relationship."

"I said I could wait," he said with a strained smile. Suddenly, his dimple had lost its charm, and I wanted it to go back into hiding. His thumb grazed my lip. "I don't mind."

I forced myself to not recoil from his touch. "That's the thing. I'm not sure if I'll ever be ready. You shouldn't wait around for something I can't promise."

His smile left, and his hand cupped my chin with a little too much pressure. "Do you not like me? Because it sure felt like you did when we kissed today."

That was DIM, not me. I hated where the conversation was going. I hated that we even had to have it. "I did enjoy it. But I've been through so much lately. I'm not in my right state of mind. I don't want to lead you on. Just give me time to sort through everything."

"Time." His jaw tensed as he raked his fingers through his hair. "Don't you see I can help you through this? I can be here when you need a shoulder to cry on or someone to talk to. I can protect you and keep Reed away. You already saw that he listens to me. No one else can give you the same protection. My dad's the sheriff. He listens to me, too."

"I don't mind having a friend." I tried to keep my face calm, even though inside I felt like a mess. It was a sticky mixture of frustration and longing. "I just don't want a boyfriend."

Blake leaned in, resting his forehead against mine. "I know you felt what I felt when we kissed. I've seen the way you look at me. You can't tell me you're not attracted to me."

My skin rippled in a frosty current, and my throat tingled. "I am attracted to you." Those weren't *my* words. How had DIM done that? I couldn't let her. I had to stay strong. Be clear. My hands squeezed into fists, my fingernails digging into my skin, as I took back control of my body. "I just don't know if we belong together. Not right now."

DIM fought against me, but I held in place, sending her screaming in anger to the back corner of my mind.

"I know you want to be with me," he said, pulling his head away, but keeping his hand on the back of my neck, holding it firm. "We could have something great." He ran his hand down my cheek. "Believe me when I say I'm the wrong person to cross."

I tried to push away, but he was too strong. "Are you threatening me? I don't need someone else doing that to me."

Blake kissed my cheek, his cool nose grazing my skin. Then he pressed his lips to my chin, and my insides rolled. "I'm saying that I have a lot of connections in Willow Marsh. You're new here and have a chance to join the right side. Don't be an idiot and choose Graham."

"What does Graham have to do with this?" Just at the thought of him, my heartbeat quickened, flushing me with heat and desire.

"I know you want to be his friend. But he's on the *other* side. The side of this town that doesn't get their way. He's the one who brought Reed into your life. Not me. I stopped Reed from doing something terrible to you. And if you hadn't stormed out of the car today, I could have prevented that, too. Don't be foolish, Tessa. Do the right thing."

The right thing would be leaving town and never looking back. But that wasn't an option at the moment. Masquerades were supposed to be magical, but mine was just disturbing. I would play his little game until I could figure a way out. "Okay."

His smile returned. "That's my girl." He kissed me on the lips, and I forced myself to kiss him back, even though it made me want to throw up. DIM perked up, trying to crawl forward, but I put up a solid wall in my mind. Blake left a trail of kisses along my jaw before he stood. "I'll pick you up tomorrow morning for school. My dad said I can't miss school, and your dad has to work, so you'll have to go with me so I can watch over you."

Never alone.

I shut my eyes and tried to relax until Blake finally left my room, turning off the light before he closed the door.

I needed to figure out how to end his game before my mask became permanently stitched onto my face.

CHAPTER 28

Five minutes before midnight, my phone buzzed, waking me from my regular nightmare. I sat there for a moment and tried to get my panting under control. I worked on the deep breathing techniques Suzie had given me at the hospital.

No light came from the crack under the door, which meant Dad was probably in bed, and the sheriff and Blake had gone home.

Peeling back the covers, I kept my back as straight as possible and slipped out of bed. After I put on my skull hoodie and my tennis shoes, I grabbed a drawstring bag from my closet and sneaked out of the room. There were no lights on anywhere in the house, just some moonlight shining through the windows. As I descended the stairs, I kept to the edge, hoping not to cause any of the wooden steps to creak.

My hands brushed along the textured wall in the hallway as I slowly worked my way to the office. I used my phone as a flashlight and searched around until I found the camcorder in a desk drawer. Slipping it into the bag, I hefted it over my shoulders.

A creak sounded behind me. I whipped around, sucking in a scream from the pain, and held my phone out as a light, but no one was there. My heart pounded as I crept out of the office, shining the light down the hall as I tiptoed toward the back. The house kept moaning, threatening to expose my escape. I'd have to get used to all the sounds, and I hoped Dad would sleep through it all.

As I passed the bathroom, a lightly pulsing figure stared at me through the mirror. Taking a deep breath and shutting down the panic that wanted to take over, I forced myself to go inside and face the ghost of Ellington. He wore the same navy blue uniform with gold buttons. He was so thin and fragile, like he could easily break. His sunken eyes watched me.

"What do you want from me?" My voice sounded so sure, not giving away the fear that clawed at my skin, wanting to break out.

Ellington used his bony finger to write in a deep red on the mirror. *Stop RH. Find box. Protect WM.*

RH? The only people that came to mind were Reed Harrison and Rita Hastings. Reed would make more sense than Rita.

My eyes locked on his through the mirror. "Do you mean Reed?"

He nodded.

"What box? Where is it?" I asked. He had been much stronger in the elevator. Ellington didn't have the same energy as he had then.

His words faded, and he wrote once again on the mirror, the red brighter. *I'll show you.*

Mist rose from the floor, filling the bathroom and clouding up the mirror. Whatever he had used to write dripped down the mirror. I slid my finger along the words, the liquid warm against my skin. I rubbed my finger and thumb together, examining them. Blood.

My eyes shot back to the mirror, but the entire bathroom was thick with fog. I staggered out, gasping for fresh air. I didn't dare look back as I hobbled to the back door in the kitchen. I needed out of the house. Away from ghosts and blood and nightmares.

Turning the doorknob on the back door as quietly as I could, I stumbled over the threshold, using the door frame as a support to keep from falling. The cold air immediately kissed my skin. Even though it would make it difficult to walk, I turned off the light on my phone, just in case Dad looked out his window. With each snap of a twig beneath my foot, I panicked.

The willow trees behind the house were large and thick, all their branches making it appear like they were packed together. They provided cover from the moon and stars, casting darkness all around me.

To the left, branches rustled together, the sound piercing in the quiet night. Crouching, I balled my hands into fists, ready to defend myself if necessary.

"It's just me," Graham said.

My eyes searched for him in the dark until they finally rested on his outline. I threw my arms around him, not caring he didn't like being close.

At first, he tensed, his arms hanging at my side. Then he put his arms around my back and hugged me. I ignored the pain in my ribs. The heat from his body, plus his strong hold, felt so good and comforting. I clung to him, not wanting to ever let go.

Graham held me, his heart beating as wildly as mine. I pushed up on my tiptoes to be closer, one hand on his shoulder, the other resting on top of his shaggy hair, nuzzling into his chest. His hair wove softly around my fingers. I breathed in his woodsy scent. Graham pushed his face against the side of my neck, his warm lips resting against my skin, but not quite kissing it. I leaned into him, wanting more.

Being with Blake left me feeling fuzzy and not in my right mind. With Graham, everything seemed so clear, and I could process my thoughts. I liked being in his arms. I wanted to be his friend, maybe more, and I didn't know if it was possible.

After a few minutes, I reluctantly pulled back but kept my hands on his shoulders, my fingers wishing they could touch his skin instead of his hoodie. He rested a shaking hand on my waist, and his fingertips from his casted hand rested on the other side. His earbuds were draped around his neck, but no music played from them.

"Graham, I'm scared," I whispered.

"Why?" He traced small circles on my side.

I recounted Reed's attack for him but left out the part about Ellington. I didn't know how Graham would take that part. I needed to talk to Corrine. She'd understand.

I also told him that Blake and my dad didn't ever want me to be alone. At the mention of Blake's name, Graham tensed.

I looked into his eyes. "I don't want to be with him."

"You don't?" He sounded surprised, yet happy.

"No." I played with the strings on his hoodie and rested my hip against him. "I don't feel right when I'm around him. I thought I liked him at first, but the more time we spend together, the less sure I am." DIM was the one who liked him, but I couldn't explain that to Graham.

"Then don't be around him," he whispered.

I tried to back away, but Graham held me steady. Reaching up, I placed my hand on his cheek, his skin surprisingly soft. He sighed under my touch. "I'm not sure I can leave him," I said. "Dad, Sheriff Hayes, and Blake have taken it upon themselves to run my life. They've forbidden me to be friends with you. Blake's going to drive me to and from school and to my appointments with Rita."

"You're seeing Rita?"

"Yes." The wind picked up a little, sending a chill through me. "I thought it would help to talk to someone about everything."

He blinked rapidly. "I think that's a good idea. She's nice. Helped me through Greg's death."

At the mention of Greg, I remembered the camcorder. "Graham, how did Greg die?"

His blinking increased, and his fingers created a beat on my waist. "I'm not sure. Mom wouldn't tell me. Just said he had an accident."

"I found the stuff that Reed is looking for."

He dropped his hand from my waist. "Ww...where?"

I opened the camcorder and slipped the memory card back in. "At the Willow Marsh Inn. It was buried under the wood floor in the room I was staying in."

"Room five." He'd gone back to whispering. "Greg stayed there before he died."

My eyebrows pinched together. "Why was he living there?"

"Mom kicked him out. She didn't like his girlfriend."

I remembered the picture inside the box. "He had a picture of the two of them in his box. Plus a picture of the two of you as boys."

His blinking slowed. "He did? A picture of me?"

"Yes. He cared about you, Graham."

He placed his good hand on top of his head. "He was always nice to me. Never made fun of me." He dropped his hand and looked at me. "Just like you."

I lifted the camcorder. "He also left this."

"What's on it?"

How would he react to seeing it? It could be upsetting to

watch. "I should warn you that it's pretty intense. Greg taped himself, and he saw something that I think may have gotten him killed."

His eyes went wide, his volume increasing. "You think he ww...was murdered?"

I stepped closer to him, putting my hand on his arm. "Yes. Reed said you knew what he was up to. Is that true?"

Graham licked his lips, his focus settling on the skull on my hood. He seemed to be debating, probably not sure on how much to tell me, which I understood. I'd been doing the same with him.

His voice was low. "A little, but not much. I didn't think he'd been murdered, though." His eyes met mine. "I hoped he hadn't."

I held up the camcorder. "You sure you want to watch this?"

He nodded in response. I turned so he could see the screen, pressing my back against him, molding nicely with his chest. My reluctant fingers hovered over the play button for a few seconds before I finally got the courage to press it.

Graham's fingers drummed along my waist the entire time. At least he was getting more comfortable with being near me.

When it got to the gunshot, Graham swore under his breath. His good hand rested on top of his head as he watched the rest. As soon as the screen went black, I turned I turned off the camcorder, took out the card, and placed it back in my bag.

I turned to Graham. "How are you doing?"

He ran his shaking hand through his hair. "I don't know."

Putting my arms around him, I held him close. He didn't hesitate in hugging me back. The wind intensified, and a few drops of rain landed on my head.

He released me but didn't move away. "I thought Delilah committed suicide."

"You knew her?"

His eyes settled on a tree behind me. "Delilah Morgan. She was Blake's girlfriend."

I couldn't believe this was the first time I had heard about her. "How long had they been together?"

"Years. Since junior high. Everyone thought they'd get married." He brushed some raindrops off my shoulder.

"Wait, I thought he was a player." Everyone had told me that.

"He is now," Graham said. "He took Delilah's death hard and started dating every girl in town." His lips pulled down in a slight frown. "I was surprised that Delilah would take her own life. It didn't make sense."

Coldness shook me to the core – another nasty Willow Marsh storm was on its way. "Do you think Blake knows that she was murdered?"

"I don't think so," he whispered. "He was upset for months. Until you showed up."

Blake had seemed angry and rude on my first day at Willow Marsh. The second he saw me, his demeanor had done a complete turnaround. DIM had shown up around the same time.

DIM. She didn't want to watch the video. Was she Delilah?

Ding, ding, ding, DIM sang. *We have a winner! Took you long enough. Kinda funny that you named me DIM since those are my initials.*

They are? I asked.

Delilah Isabelle Morgan.

"Reed probably killed Greg," Graham whispered. "He wants the evidence now, and he will end up killing my mom and me once he gets it."

Aren't you two just little smarty pants? DIM said. Or rather, Delilah. *You both can have a prize.*

Not now, I said. *Go away. We'll talk later.*

Fine, Delilah purred. *But for the record, Blake is so much more delicious than Graham.*

A slight tremor ran through me as she retreated to her corner. "Then he can't get it. He doesn't know I have it."

Graham put his hand on my bag. "I can't let you keep it. You're already in too much danger."

I laid my hand on top of his. "You're not taking it. Reed expects you to have it. If I keep it hidden, he'll be none the wiser. With Blake and Sheriff Hayes guarding me, he won't suspect anything." I hated the next words out of my mouth. "It means we have to keep our interactions to a minimum. No more talking in public. We have to delete any texts to each other. No calling."

"So, you're going to stay with Blake?" His eyes went to the dirt.

"For now, I have to." I put my hand on his cheek. "But know I don't want to be with him. I'd so much rather have you in my life, but that's not possible right now."

Briefly closing his eyes, he leaned into my hand.

"We'll sort through this," I said. "We need to find someone we can trust and figure out what to do with all this information. Reed has to pay for what he did to your brother."

Graham pulled me closer. "I think I may know someone I can talk to. Just make sure you hide that card somewhere Blake or your dad won't find it."

"I will."

"Text me every night. Just to let me know you're okay."

"You do the same." I lowered my hands. "Be careful, Graham. Reed will probably be keeping a close eye on you."

More rain fell, splattering against me. "I should probably get inside, and you need to get home."

He looked up at the sky, even though it was hard to see through the trees. "I wish things were different, and we could be friends. I like hanging out with you. You make me feel normal."

"You *are* normal." I flung one of his earbuds. "You're the only normal person in this town."

Graham blinked wildly again. "Can I see you tomorrow night? Here? Same time?"

"Yes. I'll text you if it won't work, but I don't see why it wouldn't." I gave him a quick hug. "Sleep well. Even though I can't talk to you at school, know I'll be thinking about you." I thought about Blake. "Just so you know, they're going to change my classes so we don't have any together."

His face fell. "But I ww...was looking forward tt...to passing notes."

"Me, too. Guess we'll have to find another way."

"Gg...guess ss...so." Graham whispered, so I wasn't sure why he stuttered. His blinking went crazy as his gaze fluttered to my lips. All he had to do was close the distance. I wouldn't stop him. In fact, I wanted him to. I would have kissed him myself if I knew he'd be okay with it.

My heart raced as he inched closer. His blinking was faster than I'd ever seen it. I swear I could hear his heartbeat pounding through his chest. His breathing matched the quick tempo.

I stood on my tiptoes and closed my eyes, waiting for his lips to land on mine.

Sorry, Delilah said, *but I've stomached this way too long. No way you're kissing this guy.*

The next thing I knew, Delilah swept over me, seizing control of every limb, every muscle, every part of me.

"I'm not interested in you like that," I said. Well, they

were Delilah's words, not mine. I couldn't believe how strong she was. No matter how hard I fought back, she just shoved me away like I was nothing.

Graham's eyes went wild, blinking uncontrollably. He stumbled away from me with his jaw clenched tight and his face a mask of horror. It was probably a mix of surprise that he'd tried to kiss me and embarrassment that I shot him down.

I wanted to speak up, tell him I didn't mean it, but Delilah wouldn't relinquish control. Not until Graham had run off, leaving me alone in the freezing woods.

"I hate you," I said with a snarl the second she let go. "Why would you do that to Graham?"

Delilah huffed. *I was doing you a favor, sweetheart. You can thank me later.*

"Never going to happen, *sweetheart.*"

I took a few shaky deep breaths before I sneaked back into the house and crawled into bed, the covers over my head. I had no idea how I'd apologize to Graham. No way I could tell him the truth.

It was nice finally knowing who DIM was, but now I needed to focus on getting rid of her before she could fully break Graham's heart.

And mine.

CHAPTER 29

Every time I saw Graham at school, I had to ignore him, which wasn't too hard because he'd scurry away like a scared mouse when he saw me. Thanks to Delilah, everything I'd been slowly building toward with him had crumbled within seconds. I'd somehow have to work my way back.

Blake held my hand or kept his arm around me the whole day. He walked me to and from classes. Kissed me whenever he felt like it. If I tried to pull away or move my head, he'd hold my chin in place, and the look he'd give me sent chills down my spine. Not in a good way.

Sheriff Hayes stayed true to his word, and they switched Graham out of my classes. I had expected them to move me since I had just started there, but they made Graham move, which upset me more.

In one of my only classes without Blake, I was able to write Graham a small note. In between fifth and sixth period, I passed him in the hall. It was so crowded that he didn't have a chance to notice me and run, so I slipped the note into his hand. I gave it a squeeze before I let go and kept on walking. Blake didn't even notice.

We need to figure this out soon. Blake's driving me crazy. Graham, I'm sorry about last night. I'm not in a good place. I hope you'll still come tonight because I really want to see you.

I wasn't sure if Graham would still show, but I hoped and prayed he would.

After school, Blake drove me to see Rita. He got out of the car first and jogged around to my side, opening the door. He put his arm around my waist and helped me inside. Workers were installing new mirrors in the elevator, so we took the stairs.

Blake had the audacity to try to sit in on my appointment, but thankfully, Rita talked him out of it.

When she'd closed the door, and we sat down, she nodded toward the door. "So, you're with Blake?" We both knew he was standing on the other side.

Looking out the window at the quiet street, I slowly nodded. I had to decide how much I wanted to tell Rita.

"But you aren't sure about it." She said it as a statement, not a question.

I turned to her. "Anything I tell you in here is confidential, right?"

"Of course."

"Are you recording this?" I adjusted the purple scarf on my hand to make sure it fully covered my scar.

She looked taken aback, but she looked me straight in the eye. "I don't audio record my sessions. I do take notes to help important things stay in my mind, but I shred them after the session. You never know if they'd somehow fall into the wrong hands."

"You don't trust people?"

Rita thought about it before she answered, an amused smile on her thin lips. "Depends on the person. I know

Willow Marsh is full of decent people, but there are also some residents I can't turn a blind eye to. It would be naive of me to trust everyone here."

I searched her eyes, looking for any sign of deceit. Trust flowed through me. In that moment, I decided to have faith in Rita. If she turned out bad like the others, well, she could just get in line. "I don't want to be with Blake."

She crossed her legs and leaned her arm on the armrest. "Then why are you with him?"

"In short, he threatened me." I pushed my back against the arm of the couch, then rested my legs on the cushions, getting as comfortable as I could. I would have taken off my shoes if it didn't hurt so much to bend in the middle. "Reed's out to get me, Graham, and Barbie. He's after something of Greg's, and he keeps attacking us. Well, me, mostly."

She scribbled something on her paper with her left hand. "How are you feeling, by the way? After your attack yesterday?"

My hand went to the marks on my cheek that Reed had left behind. "I'm doing okay. Still a little shook up."

Her eyes lingered on my cheek for a bit. "Just so you know, Reed's been banned from the building, so you're safe here."

"Any chance he could be banned from Willow Marsh?"

She chuckled, a small glint in her eyes. "Unfortunately, no." She scratched the side of her nose. "So how does Blake tie into this?"

"He and my dad don't trust Graham. They want me to stay away from him. They want to protect me from Reed, so they made a pact to never let me out of their sight."

She tapped her foot on the gray carpet. "That explains Blake hovering around you."

A bitter laugh escaped my mouth. "Understatement. He

said there were two sides to Willow Marsh, and I didn't want to be on the opposite side as him."

Her mouth fell open for a second. "Those are some bold words coming from the sheriff's son."

I slid the ring on my index finger. "I don't trust the sheriff, either."

"Why not?" Rita asked, leaning forward.

"He just rubs me the wrong way." I switched to playing with a string on my shirt. Doing something with my hands helped ease the anxiety. "The other morning when I was out running, he was driving back into town. It seemed a little weird to me for him to be coming back from somewhere else in the wee hours of the morning."

"That's the duty of a sheriff."

He'd said the same thing. "Rita, do you know what happened to Delilah Morgan?"

Her pen fell to the floor. She quickly picked it up, looking flustered. "Why do you ask?"

"She and Blake were supposedly inseparable, and then she randomly kills herself? It seems odd."

"There's probably more behind their story than we know." She glanced over her shoulder at the picture of her and her husband, a soft smile on her face. "People don't always share their bad moments. They put on appearances. Maybe they weren't as in love as people thought."

"So, you really think she took her own life?" I asked. Telling Rita about the recording would be dangerous, but I could set out little bread crumbs so she would start asking questions.

She hesitated, twirling her pen between her fingers. "Let's focus on you. How's your anxiety?"

I really didn't want to talk about Amá or Felix. My family was one thing I wasn't ready to bring into my sessions with Rita. I'd rather find out more about Willow Marsh.

When I didn't respond, she spoke. "Do you still feel like someone is watching you?"

A part of me wanted to mention Ellington and Delilah haunting me, but I wasn't sure if Rita would accept it, or want to commit me.

She leaned forward, sensing my hesitation. "Tessa, you can trust me. I won't repeat a word you tell me." She looked at the door. "And these walls are pretty soundproof. I made sure of it when I moved my office here."

My fingers fumbled with the string. This was sensitive information, and Rita was practically a stranger. But there was something in her eyes.

Rita brushed a piece of lint off her slacks. "Okay, easier topic. What are you going to do about Blake?"

I wasn't sure I'd define that as easier, but I rolled with it. "I'm not sure. Stay with him for now. Until Reed backs off, I can't risk it."

She frowned. "I desperately want to tell you that you'd be better off without him, that you'd be safe, but I'd only be fooling myself. The Hayes' men are not ones you want to cross. I'm sorry you're in this situation. I'll do what I can to help." She tucked some of her curls behind her ear. "What does Reed want? You said it was something of Greg's."

I couldn't tell her that. Not if I wanted to live. "I'm not sure. Graham doesn't know, either. But Reed will do anything to get his hands on it."

"You're lying." She leaned back in her chair. "I'm good at spotting lies. But I understand if you feel the need to protect yourself and Graham. I'm assuming whatever it is, it can get you both seriously hurt?"

"Killed."

"Can you fix it? Give it back?"

"I could give it back." But it would let Reed go free of his crimes. He'd probably end up killing Graham and me anyway since we knew the truth.

Rita pursed her lips, her eyes narrowing in thought. "But it wouldn't fix it."

I shook my head in response.

"If I knew what I was working with, I might be able to help you. I might know the right people to contact."

"I want to give Graham a chance first. I don't want to drag anyone else into this if I don't have to."

She smiled softly at me. "I understand. Before you go, one last thing. What happened in the elevator?"

If I told her, would she lock me up? Admit me to a mental ward?

Trust her. I tensed, not knowing who had said that. Amá? Or Ellington? I slapped my forehead, wanting them out of my mind.

"Tessa." Rita leaded forward and took my hand away from my forehead. "What's going on?"

I needed to open up about something, and this was the most pressing. "Do you believe in contacting the dead?"

She still held my hand. "Have you tried contacting someone?"

She didn't know about Amá. I couldn't tell her about Amá's beliefs and my encounters with her. I needed to don my mask, covering up some of the truth. "I think someone's trying to contact me. They've been following me."

Her face remained passive. "Do you know the person?"

Lie. The husky voice rattled in my head. It was different than the other. "No. But they've appeared in mirrors. They showed up twice to stop Reed."

She let go of my hand and sat on the edge of the couch near me. "In the elevator, someone else was with you?"

"Yes." I found myself trembling. She rubbed my shoulder,

her eyes holding so much understanding, so I kept going. "They shattered the mirrors and made Reed's eyes bleed."

She lowered her hand and rested it on her lap. "Have you done séances before?"

"Yes."

"With your mom?"

Coldness swept over me. "How did you know?" I hadn't said anything, had I?

A soft smile formed on Rita's lips. "By your features and your Spanish when we first met, I can see the Mexican in you, Tessa. Contacting loved ones is popular in your culture. It's part of who you are." Her smile faded. "Your mom's dead, isn't she?"

I nodded.

"She's been in contact with you." A statement.

I nodded.

Her eyes scanned her office, thinking. Pondering. "But it wasn't your mom in the elevator?"

I shook my head.

"Sometimes contacting the dead can open a gateway," she said, her eyes resting on mine. "By reaching out to your mom, you let others in. For the dead, you're easily accessible. The hard part will be figuring out who you've let in and what they want."

I did know who I let in. Ellington and Delilah. But I didn't quite understand what either of them wanted.

"How do you know all of this?" I asked.

"My friend," Rita said. "Her daughter goes to your school. Corrine."

A small chuckle rose inside me. Corrine's mom sounded a lot like mine. "I know her."

She stretched out her arm and rested her hand on the back of the couch. "Tessa, I need you to be careful. You can't trust everyone who contacts you. They only want what's in their best interest, not yours."

Deep inside, I knew that. But it was hard to sort the good from the bad. "I know."

"Have you actually seen your mom? Are you positive it's her?"

"Yes." I looked her in the eye. "I can feel it. Feel her."

Rita licked her lips, her eyes satisfied. "If someone other than your mom reaches out to you, I want you to let me know when and what they say. Maybe we can figure it out together." She stood, held out her hand, and helped me stand. "In the meantime, try to rest. You've been through so much."

I shuffled over to the door and put my hand on the knob.

She kept her voice low. "Tessa, I know you're scared right now. Life has handed you some unfair things, but what we do with our challenges shapes who we are. It can either make you a better person, or destroy you. Don't lose yourself in all of this. No matter what, stay true to yourself."

Stay true to myself. I was starting to forget who I was.

CHAPTER 30

Blake was waiting for me outside Rita's office. He immediately wrapped his arms around me.

Rita waved at him. "Hi, Blake."

"Hi, Rita."

"How are you doing?" Rita asked. She adjusted the reading glasses perched in her hair. "It's been a while since we've talked. Life treating you well?" By the casual way she looked at him, there seemed to be a history between them.

Blake stiffened. "Yes. Everything's great."

"Good." Rita gently squeezed my arm. "Let's meet again Monday after school." She went back in her office and closed the door.

Blake loosened up. "How'd it go in there?"

"Great." I looked up at him. "I really like Rita."

"Yeah, she's awesome," he said, pulling away from our embrace. He took me by the hand and steered me over to the elevator, pressing the down button. They must have finished installing the new mirrors.

"Did you used to see her or something?" I asked. Maybe

he had gone to her after Delilah disappeared. I hoped he would mention it to give me an opening to talk about her.

Blake kept his focus on the elevator doors. "She helped me when my mom died."

The elevator doors pinged open, but I stayed rooted in place. "Your mom died?" Now that I thought about it, I'd never seen his mom or sibling in person. His dad mentioned having a wife and two kids when he drove me home from my run. Blake had never talked about them.

Blake reached out to hold open the door before it could close. He gently pulled me inside by the elbow and pressed the button for the first floor. I stared at him with my jaw slightly dropped. He was now sharing this with me?

"She died when I was seven."

We stayed silent until we got to his car. He drove down Main Street, keeping at a slow speed. He glanced at me sideways. "You're probably confused."

I nodded.

"I have a stepmom and stepsister. Remi, my stepmom, wants to have you and your dad over for dinner." His tone went soft. "Maybe we could do that tonight, and you can meet Livvy, my sister. I think the two of you will get along."

"Sounds good," Delilah said for me. With being in so much shock, I'd dropped my guard and made it easy for her to take over.

I stared out the windshield, everything blurred together. I couldn't focus on anything. "What about your mom? What happened to her?"

"Breast cancer." Blake reached over and took my hand, but the warmth did nothing to calm me.

A dark presence slithered through me, seizing control of my emotions and making me irrationally upset over something so minor. The anger flared like a wildfire.

"It hit both me and my dad pretty hard," Blake continued. "Rita helped us through it. Then Dad met Remi, and he fell in love again. It took me a while to adjust and accept her. Livvy is the glue that seems to be holding my family together."

I turned to him, heat rising in my chest. "How come you didn't tell me?"

He stroked my hand with his thumb, but a frown rested on his lips from my tone. "Don't know. It never came up."

Irritation boiled inside, vigorous and steaming. I'd never been so mad, and I didn't know why. The spirit in me twisted my emotions to the point my words were actually directed at me and my secrets, but Blake was in the line of fire.

He clutched his hand on the steering wheel. "It's hard to talk about."

I choked on a bitter laugh. "Hard to talk about? Seriously?" My thumb rubbed the smooth bronze of my family ring. Talking about dead loved ones opened fresh battle wounds. With the presence lurking in the background, I couldn't stop myself from lashing out at Blake.

He checked the rearview mirror, more to keep his gaze somewhere other than me. "Why are you acting like this?"

"Why did you hide that from me?"

Blake pulled into my driveway and turned off the car. "I didn't *hide* anything from you. I told you, didn't I?"

"Sure did." I got out of the car way too fast, ribs burning, and slammed the door. He did the same. I pounded up the porch steps, and I rounded on him. "A little too late, though." I put my hand on my forehead. "I have been through hell and back, okay? My life has been ripped to pieces. I don't need more secrets in my life." My masquerade threatened to end. Layers peeling away. The truth bubbled at the surface, wanting to release. Amá. Felix. The accident. Dad. Ellington. Delilah.

A vampire finch landed on the banister, its beady eyes boring into mine.

"Why are you so mad at me?" Blake asked, keeping a safe distance from me. His face went scarlet. "I didn't know I had to pour out my life secrets to you."

The finch tilted his head and whistled. I kept my eyes on the bird as I said, "You seem to expect a lot from me."

"I'm just asking you to be around me." He threw out his hands. "I'm not asking you to tell me your deepest, darkest secrets."

Tearing my eyes away from the bird, I narrowed them at Blake. "It doesn't matter. You'll keep your leash on me no matter what." I turned to go inside, but he grabbed my arm. "Ow!"

He held it tight. "Don't do this. Don't be a bi-"

My hand flew up, slapping him hard across the face. This time, it was all me. "Don't you ever call me that."

The muscles on his arms flexed, and his grip stayed firm. His voice came out low and rough. "That's not how this relationship works."

He lifted my chin so he could look in my eyes. His demeanor softened. "Your eyes are blue again." He went pale.

It took a lot of effort, but I shoved him in the chest, wanting him away. "You keep saying you want to keep me safe, but how can you possibly do that if I don't feel safe around you?" I hadn't realized how loud I was yelling until Dad opened the front door.

"Is everything okay out here?" Dad's confused eyes passed back and forth between Blake and me.

The dark spirit inside suddenly crawled to the surface and escaped, all my emotions colliding with each other in its wake. Layers fell. I couldn't do it anymore. Lie. Hide. Forget Amá and Felix. I couldn't handle the fact that I'd killed them. My stupid choice ended their lives. The vampire finch flew onto my shoulder, pecking at my neck, but I didn't care. I hated fate. It was cruel the way it left me alive, dealing with the aftermath. My wall lowered again.

Help me. Ellington sounded far away, his voice whispering in my ear, not in my head like Delilah.

Kill yourself. Delilah said with a bored tone. *It's not so bad on the other side.*

Don't trust them. Stay safe. Stay alive. Amá spoke to my soul, warming it.

There were too many voices. My legs buckled, sending me to the ground and pain searing my ribs. The bird's lilting song echoed on the porch as Dad and Blake tried to swat it away.

Help Willow Marsh. Ellington. *Undo your mistake.*

You don't deserve to live. Delilah. *I deserved to live. I'm not a murderer like you.*

Be strong, my girl. Amá.

My hands flew to my head, pounding away, wanting them gone. Wanting everything gone.

"Tessa, stop!" Leya yelled.

Now her?

Two soft hands seized my wrists, yanking my hands away from my head. My eyes raised until they landed on Leya's light brown eyes. She was kneeling in front of me.

I was going crazy. Mad.

CHAPTER 31

Leya's warm hands went to my cheeks. "It's okay, Tessa. I'm here. You're safe. No one is trying to hurt you." She pulled me into her arms, holding me close. I threw my arms around her waist and breathed in her pineapple scent. My ribs ached. Throbbed. But I didn't care.

"Is it really you?" I asked.

"Yes," Leya said. Her voice, so sweet and real. "I'm here. I flew out this morning."

Dad knelt next to us, rubbing my back. "I knew you needed her."

"You didn't tell me she was *this* bad," Leya said in a scolding tone to Dad.

"I sensed it but wasn't positive." Dad wiped some tears off my cheeks. "I sent Blake home. It's just the three of us."

It took a while to calm down. When I had, they helped me stand and took me inside. Leya sat with me on the couch while Dad got me some water.

I kept looking at her, touching her arms and face. She had on a thick beige headband with a gold flower, holding her black, curly hair back from her face. She wore a white tee that had 'Haitian and proud' written in a glittery pink.

"You really need to stop doing that," she said as I placed my hand on her smooth, flawless cheek.

"I can't believe you're here."

She smiled, showing off her dazzling white teeth with a small gap in the middle, and held out her arms. "Well, I am. I was hoping for an awesome surprise where you ran into my arms, laughing and happy to see me. Not having a … whatever you were having, falling into my arms and freaking out."

Dad joined us in the family room and handed me a glass of water and an ice pack. "Now that Leya's here, we need to talk about what's going on with you, Tessa."

"I don't know." I took a drink of water, savoring the coolness against my throat. With my other hand, I held the ice pack against my ribs.

Dad sat in my abuelo's oversized brown armchair next to the couch. It was my favorite chair, not just because it was super comfy, but because of all the memories it held. Dad didn't want to bring a lot of furniture to Willow Marsh, but I made him bring the chair. The leather was scratched in a couple places, but other than that, it had held up well over the years.

Leya sat back on the couch, put her sandaled feet up on the coffee table, and crossed her ankles. "So, what's with the creepy sixties house?" Her large eyes scanned the room. "It's pretty pathetic."

A smile landed on my lips, warming my heart. Elated didn't even begin to describe how I felt having her there next to me. "You should have seen it before Dad fixed it up."

Metal clanged against the front door, making Leya jump in her seat. "You know doorbells exist, right, Mr. Isaacson? The knocker you picked is slightly disturbing." When it rattled again, she shivered. "And by slightly, I mean extremely."

Dad stood to answer the door. "It came with the house." He disappeared into the hallway.

Leya looked at me. "Doesn't mean you have to keep it. There are trashcans and bombs and stuff to help you get rid of it."

Corrine sauntered into the room, a sulking Jade with her hood up at her side. Corrine motioned for Leya to stand. "You must be Leya." They hugged, and then Leya returned to her seat while Corrine sat across from us on the love seat. She patted the seat next to her for Jade. "Either have a seat or leave if you're going to be pissy."

Jade muttered under her breath as she sat and wouldn't make eye contact with me. Wrapping her jacket tight around her, she folded her arms and put her gaze on the ceiling.

"You called them?" I asked Leya.

Leya held up a finger. "I called Corrine. When your Dad told me about Ellington, I knew this was beyond anything I knew. I thought Corrine might be able to help."

"I told Jade to stay home," Corrine said, narrowing her eyes at her. "But she got in the car. Marcel tried to get in, too, but he actually listens when I tell him no."

Dad came into the room and set some bottles of cream soda on the table. "Help yourself, ladies."

Leya snatched one up. "Did you order dinner? I'm starving." She took a sip of her drink. "I hate flying, so I didn't have anything to eat before I left or on the flight."

"Pizza is on its way," Dad said, taking a seat in the armchair.

"So, who's Ellington?" Corrine asked. "His name sounds familiar." She clicked her pink tongue ring against her teeth, and then quickly stopped herself. "Bad habit."

Dad opened his mouth, but Jade cut him off. "Why did

you stop talking to us?" She finally had the courage to look me in the eye.

I pointed to Dad. "He told me I had to hang out with Blake."

Jade's piercing eyes went to Dad. "Why? He's a jerk."

"I'm not a fan of Graham," Dad said. His eyes danced with amusement. I think he liked Jade and her abruptness. "She's my only daughter. I want her safe."

"Then don't leave her alone with Blake." Jade clenched her fists. "Dixon's a good guy, not Blake."

Corrine slapped Jade on the arm. "Be nice." She tried to yank Jade's hoodie down off her head, but Jade growled at her, revealing her teeth, and Corrine scooted away.

Dad ran his hand down his face. "Let's not talk about Graham or Blake. They don't matter right now." He looked at me. "What matters is Tessa seeing things."

"I'm not seeing things." My focus went to Jade. The ice pack froze my hand. Dad had forgotten to bring me a towel to provide a buffer for my skin. "I'm sorry. I'd much rather hang out with you than Blake and his friends. It's complicated, so you'll just have to trust me." I took another drink of water and sat back on the couch. "I contacted Amá, which I think opened up a gateway to the other side."

Corrine nodded. "That's possible. But nothing happened in the woods when we tried."

Dad's jaw dropped. "You've done a séance together?"

"Something did happen in the woods, Corrine," I said, ignoring Dad. "I contacted Amá before that. Multiple times." Dad had a skeptical look on his face. "It's true. You know Amá taught me how to contact the dead. I wanted to apologize to her."

"For what?" Jade asked.

Dad clenched his jaw. "Maybe this was a bad idea. I think Jade and Corrine should leave."

"No, Apá."

He rested his elbow on the armrest. "I don't think you're ready to tell everyone what happened."

"Ignoring it won't change the fact that it happened." I eyed Amá's pink dahlia on my finger. The ring had been passed down from generation to generation. Amá always claimed it had special powers, but I believed she meant it held a family bond. A way to keep us all connected to one another. "I have a mom and a little brother. Had. Felix was nine. We were on our way to Felix's recital. He played the ukulele. It was stormy that night. I..." Tears formed in my eyes. They trickled down my cheeks, the salty water landing on my lips.

Leya continued for me. "Unfortunately, they were in a car accident. Tessa was driving, which is why she wanted to apologize. She contacted her mom on the other side, opened up a gateway or something, and now other dead people are messing with her head." She looked at me. "Right?"

I nodded, trying to process everything Leya had just revealed. "Uh, yeah. Another guy has contacted me. Ellington."

Corrine rubbed her forehead. "Do you know who this Ellington guy is or what he wants?"

Dad leaned forward. "Ladies, we're talking as if Tessa actually saw a ghost and spoke with her *dead* mother. That's not possible. We need to figure out how to help her."

Corrine shook a skinny finger at Dad. "You *can* contact the dead. I believe Tessa. She does need help, but with trying to figure out what this Ellington guy wants." She tapped her glossed lips. "Where have I heard that name before? It's bugging me. Like, it's right on the tip of my tongue."

"There's someone else as well," I whispered.

Leya took my hand. "Someone else has talked to you?"

"Yes." I took a drink of water, gulping it down. "Delilah Morgan."

Corrine's bottle of cream soda fell from her grasp and landed on the wood floor. A stream of foamy liquid drifted down the cracks between the wood planks. "Oh my." She made the sign of the cross.

"Uh, who's Delilah Morgan?" Leya asked.

Jade had gone pale. Her wide eyes stared at me, her terrified expression adding to my worry. "Blake's dead girlfriend."

CHAPTER 32

The clang of the knocker on the front door made Corrine and Leya scream out, and Jade jump in her seat. If Dad hadn't looked so angry, he probably would have laughed. He stood and walked toward the door. "It's just the pizza guy."

"Seriously, that was the most perfectly imperfect timing." Leya set her cream soda on the coffee table. "So, Blake has a dead girlfriend?"

"Killed herself." Jade stared at the river of cream soda beneath her. She propped her black work boots against the edge of the coffee table to keep them out of the river. "Probably couldn't stand the thought of being with Blake."

Corrine pulled her rosary beads out of her pocket and stroked the tiny beads. "Now she's haunting Blake's new girlfriend."

I stood with a little too much force. "I'm not his girlfriend."

Dad stormed into the room and threw Corrine a towel to clean up her cream soda mess. "Pizza's in the kitchen. If anyone talks about ghosts or séances or any of that crap, you'll have to leave my house." He disappeared down the hall.

All three girls glanced at me with wide eyes, but I just shrugged. After we helped Corrine with the soda, we joined Dad in the kitchen. Each of us grabbed a slice of pizza and sat down at the table, eating quietly. Dad had bought a new white wood kitchen table and chairs to match the cupboards.

After a few minutes, Corrine spoke. "So, Tessa, you're team Graham?"

"Against my wishes," Dad said, wiping his face with a napkin. "I don't trust Graham."

"He's a good guy." Jade finished off the piece of ham and pineapple pizza in her mouth. "I don't think he killed his dad, if that's what you're worried about."

Corrine tsked and held up her palm. "Don't even go there, Jade. None of your nonsense."

The pizza slice in my hand fell onto the table with a splat. "Uh, what?"

Leya's jaw dropped, and her slice of pizza sagged in her hand. She swallowed. "What are you talking about?"

Jade leaned forward, ignoring Corrine's glare. "You didn't know? His dad's death was ruled an accident, with Graham as the killer. He was just a kid at the time, so he wasn't charged with murder or anything."

Thick silence hung in the air. I couldn't believe what I was hearing. Graham had killed his dad? I took in the scarf covering my scar. If it was an accident, we had way more in common than I thought.

I sat back in my seat, processing it all. Graham wasn't a murderer. If he had been involved, it had to have been an accident. A terrible, horrible accident that he'd lived with all these years. My hands tightened around the napkin in my hand. Blake had mentioned an accident at school. Is that what he was talking about? That if I was friends with

Graham, I could accidentally end up dead as well? Well, the same could be said about hanging out with me.

Dad's fist pounded on the table, making all of us jump. His nostrils flared. "Now you're definitely not hanging out with him."

I turned to him, frowning. "How can you say that? I did the same thing. Only it was my mom and brother."

Jade snatched another piece of pineapple pizza from the box and sat back, lifting her foot onto her chair so her knee was up in the air. "I honestly don't think he did it."

Leya licked her lips. The cheese and pineapple had slid down on the slice she still had raised in the air. "Who do you think did?"

"Barbie." Jade took a bite of her pizza.

"You have proof of that?" Dad asked, his eyebrow raised. His anger had somewhat subsided.

Jade shook her head. "I just know it." She talked with her mouth full of pizza. "I think she killed her husband and blamed it on her over-blinking, drumming, twitching son." She wiped her mouth with the sleeve of her jacket, even though there were napkins right in front of her. "He's perfectly normal, by the way. She's just played up his dumbness over the years so people will buy into her story. She probably killed Greg, too."

She hadn't killed Greg. At least, I didn't think so. It made more sense for Reed to have killed him. Greg had evidence of Reed murdering Delilah.

I was surprised Delilah hadn't made an appearance. She rested in the back of my mind, quietly humming songs from *Phantom of the Opera*, but she hadn't spoken or tried to interfere with the conversation.

Delilah?

Silence.

Corrine opened her mouth to say something, but then

looked at Dad. She immediately stuffed her pizza in her mouth and slouched in her seat.

Everyone ate in silence until Dad got a phone call, and he excused himself, retreating to the hallway. He was still close, but he was mostly distracted.

Corrine and Jade got into a whispered, heated debate. 'Barbie' was the only word I could hear, probably because Jade said it with so much venom that it enunciated her name.

I took the opportunity to text Graham.

Leya's here.

That's awesome. I'd
like to meet her.

"I want to meet him, too," Leya whispered over my shoulder. "I'm dying to know what he looks like."

I was so happy Graham texted me back. Delilah hadn't completely scared him away. I needed to be stronger when I was around him to make sure she didn't take over again.

Are we still meeting tonight?
Do you care if she comes?

Yes, to both questions.

I'm so sorry about the other
night. I was nervous.
I miss you.

I miss you, too. We'll get some
time to ourselves, right?

I blushed, even though he couldn't see me. I hadn't lost

him. I wanted more time with him that I knew I couldn't have.

Of course. I'll see you tonight.

Looking forward to it.

Before I put my phone in my pocket, I deleted all the texts.

Leya frowned. "I can't believe you have to do that."

"No one can know." I sighed, wishing so badly Graham could be here with us, having dinner like we were normal. I was getting way too attached to Graham, something I couldn't do.

Blake's better, Delilah whispered.

So now you'll talk?

Only when it's something worth talking about.

"What are you thinking?" Leya asked. "You have this faraway look in your eyes."

I turned to her, making sure to whisper. "I hate that I have to do this to Graham. We shouldn't have to sneak around. He doesn't deserve it."

Leya leaned her head against mine. "I know, Tess."

Graham's not worth it, Delilah said.

You're wrong, I said. *He's amazing.*

Someone knocked at the door, giving me an excuse to leave the table and hopefully get Delilah to shut up with her Blake nonsense.

Too bad Blake stood on the other side of the door. He wore a tight green shirt that showed off his muscles. He rubbed the back of his neck and spoke in a hesitant tone. "Can we talk?"

I went out onto the porch, shutting the door behind me and keeping a considerable distance from him. "Sure."

He rubbed his elbow. "Who was that girl here earlier?"

"A friend of mine." I couldn't hide her from him anymore now that he'd seen her. "She's just here for a little visit."

With a slight nod, he took a tentative step toward me. "I need to apologize."

"So do I."

He drew a deep breath. "I shouldn't have called you that word or grabbed you." He looked down at his custom Nikes, his hands in his jacket pockets. "I should've told you about my mom. Sometimes I try to forget her because I think it'll be easier than missing her every day." When he looked at me, tears were in his eyes.

My heart ached for him. I knew exactly what he was feeling. But it didn't excuse his behavior. Although, I hadn't been making it easy for him with my dark spirit passengers.

"I know I've come on too strong," he said. "I was wondering if you'd give me another chance. I promise I'll be better. If you need space, I'll give it to you." He wiped some tears off his cheek. "Living here is hard, which you've realized. It really messes a person up. I act tough, but sometimes that's all it is – an act." He'd been holding a masquerade, just like me. "But then you come along and make me feel something I've never felt before."

Smack him, Delilah said. *He should be saying those things to ME.*

Yeah, well, you're dead, so. I pushed her back into her corner, and she didn't fight it.

Twisting his lips to the side, Blake took a small step forward, glancing over my face for a reaction. "I was jealous of Graham and how much time you spent with him. With my dad being the sheriff, people don't normally say no to me. I can get away with just about anything." He took another step, his eyes pleading. "I made a huge mistake with the way I treated you. Say you'll give me one more chance."

Looking in his deep brown eyes, that feeling I felt the first day with him rushed back and overwhelmed me. He seemed so sincere. I understood how this town could mess someone up.

I folded my arms. "I need you to trust me, Blake. I need to be treated with respect."

He swallowed, running his fingers through his hair. The gel had loosened, letting a few black curls hang on his forehead. "I know. I do trust you."

Even though I would dump him the moment everything ended with Reed, I wanted to see how serious he was. "Switch Graham's classes back."

Surprise swept over his face, but he slowly nodded. "Okay. If that's what you want."

"You have to let me hang out with him, too."

"No." He closed his eyes, taking a deep breath. When he opened them back up, pain enveloped them. "It's not because I don't trust you or want you to be around him. I don't think it's safe right now. Not with Reed. You can talk to Graham at school and in your classes, but not outside of school. Not until this gets sorted out. Once Reed drops everything, then you can hang out with Graham as much as you want."

So glad to have his permission. I bit my tongue, though, and put my hand on his arm. "Thank you, Blake. That means a lot to me."

He gave me the smallest smile. "Would you still be willing to have dinner at my house? I can't tomorrow, but what about the next night? I'll be on my best behavior, I promise."

"Sounds good. Can my friend come?"

"Sure. Any friend of yours is welcome in our home." He pursed his lips, probably thinking about Graham and wishing he could take back those words.

I changed the subject. "I can't wait to meet your stepmom

and sister." The smile that formed on my face was surprisingly not forced. "What was she like? Your mom?"

Blake stared at the wood panels beneath our feet. "She knew everyone in town by name. She genuinely liked them and wanted to know them." He put his hands in his jeans pockets. "She loved to sing. Her voice was amazing. I always looked forward to her tucking me into bed because it always involved a song."

A small smile pulled at his lips as he continued, more vulnerable than I'd ever seen him. "Oh, and theater. She *loved* it. We used to have community plays. The place would be packed." His bright eyes met mine. "Mom was putting together a performing arts program at the school before . . ." Tears welled in his eyes.

I pulled him into a hug, and we held each other for a long time out on the porch in the cold air. The impact the loss of a parent had on a child wasn't something you could explain. You had to experience it.

An experience I would never wish upon anyone.

CHAPTER 33

The new porch lights lit up the area well enough that the front of the house didn't have as creepy a vibe as it had before. Dad said he'd install a swing when he got the chance, which would definitely help. For now, he'd stained the wood a rich, dark brown, so it at least looked new.

Leya, Corrine, Jade, and I were outside so we could talk without Dad listening. We huddled on the porch steps to keep warm.

"What does Delilah want with you?" Corrine asked, sweeping her red bangs away from her eyes.

"She won't tell me." Taking hold of the scarf on my hand, I rubbed the silk material between my fingers, loving the feel. "But from what I can gather, she wants to be with Blake."

Jade scoffed. "Wow. She had no brains before she died, and that still hasn't changed. She's dead. She can't *be with Blake.*"

I adjusted myself so my ribs weren't squished. "She's using *me* to be with him."

All three of them stared at me, eyes wide. Leya moved my

chin so I was facing her. "What do you mean she's using you? Has she, you know, taken possession of your body or something?"

It made me uncomfortable to talk about, but I needed to share it with someone. "Yeah. To kiss Blake." Not to mention all the other times.

Jade gagged. "You've kissed Blake?" She rubbed her arms. "That's just wrong."

"What's wrong is Delilah taking control of Tessa." Corrine ran her hand over her spiky hair. "I can't believe she'd do that." She rolled her eyes. "I mean, I can. She's always been a control freak. But to stoop so low as to use Blake's new interest to get back with him? That's not right."

Leya scratched my back with her acrylic nails. "So, what do we do? Can we make her cross over to the other side or something?"

Corrine shook her head, swinging the silver cross pendant on her neck. "It's not that simple. Delilah has to *want* to cross over."

"Well, that's just wonderful." I flicked a tiny, black bug crawling by me. "She seems pretty content using me as a host body. There's no way I'll get rid of her."

"What about an exorcism?" Leya asked.

I straightened my back. "I'm worried that will make things worse." Especially after having another spirit enter me. What more could I let in?

"We'll think of something," Corrine said. "I'll talk to my mom about it. She might know what to do. She's done that kind of thing before."

Jade gawked at the three of us. "I can't believe you're just talking about this like it's normal. Like it's real."

I held my hand against my ribs. "Trust me, it's real. I've had to live with this nightmare. I want her and Ellington gone."

"So, who's Ellington, exactly?" Corrine asked.

"I don't know." I sighed. "He doesn't speak to me as clearly as Delilah. With her, she's in my head. In my body. Ellington is nearby, trying to communicate with me." I suddenly remembered the night I'd met with Graham out in the woods. Ellington had talked to me, and I'd completely forgot about it. "He's written something."

Leya scrunched her face. "Like on a paper or something?"

My eyes went to my fingers, remembering touching the blood. "He wrote it on a mirror. It said: *Stop RH. Find box. Protect WM*. RH are Reed's initials."

"Protect Willow Marsh from what?" Leya asked.

Corrine played with her tongue ring, thinking. She finally sighed. "I can understand about stopping the Harrisons. I think they're behind a whole bunch of murders. But what box? And how is Tessa supposed to protect Willow Marsh?"

"So, you believe Tessa?" Jade asked, looking at Corrine. "Just like that. She could be some freak."

"Yeah, right here," I said, pointing at myself.

Jade clucked her tongue. "What? This is crazy. You all sound completely insane."

A vampire finch landed on the banister behind Jade's head. It whistled, making Jade jump from her seat.

"It's been following me," I whispered. The finch whistled again, flew down, and perched itself on my leg, staring up at me.

"That's the bird from earlier." Leya leaned toward the bird. "Hey, birdie. Why are you following my BFF around like some creepy stalker?"

The finch tilted its head to the side, eyeing Leya. It sang out a beautifully tragic song and jumped around on my leg.

"That's so freaky." Jade stepped backward down the porch steps. "Corrine, can we leave?"

Corrine grabbed Jade by the arm and yanked her back

down on the steps. "For someone who acts so tough, you're the biggest wuss I know."

Jade swore a few times, folded her arms, and leaned her back against the wood banister. "Whatever."

"Can you just talk to them whenever you want?" Leya asked me.

I shook my head. "It doesn't work like that with Ellington. He only shows up when he wants. I could try to summon him."

"No." Corrine put her hand on my knee. "No more séances until I talk to my mom. If you've already invited your mom plus two other spirits into this world, another séance could bring so many more."

I couldn't handle more people in my head.

Corrine shifted her back so it was pressed up against the railing. "Maybe if we go to the spot where the magic is strong, we can find more answers."

Jade threw her head back and groaned. "Seriously, why am I your friend?"

Corrine punched Jade on the arm, not taking her focus off me. "There's some crazy, awesome, magical powers here in Willow Marsh that *some* people don't like to talk about, but it's true. My mom says we're totally connected to the other side, which makes her job easy. It would seriously explain everything you're going through."

I pulled my phone from my back pocket and scrolled through my images until I found the picture of the parchment with the map. I handed my phone over to Corrine. "Do you know where that is?"

Leya peered over her shoulder so she could see, too.

"What is this?" Corrine scrunched her eyes at the photo and used her fingers on the screen to zoom in. "This is way old and so cool!"

"I found it in the hotel room we were staying in." I hadn't

really thought about it with everything that had been going on. But maybe that spot held answers as well.

Jade shifted so she could see the photo. "Is this some sort of treasure map? Are you going to become a pirate now? A magical, ghost-seeing pirate?"

Corrine's fingers moved across the screen of my phone. "I sent it to myself." She handed me back the phone. "My dad is way into history and knows everything about Willow Marsh. I'll ask him about it."

"Even your family are complete nerds," Jade mumbled.

My eyes drooped.

"Looks like I need to get Tessa to bed." Leya held out her hand and helped me stand. "It's been a long day."

Corrine stood and brushed off the back of her pants. "I'll talk to my parents and let you know what they say."

"Thanks," I said. I gave Corrine a hug. I tried to give one to Jade as well, but she walked toward Corrine's car without saying goodbye.

"It's past her bedtime," Corrine said with an eye-roll. "Night."

"Night," I said.

I had to find out what Ellington wanted and how to send Delilah to the other side.

Ellington? I asked.

Silence.

It was worth a try.

When I yawned, Leya escorted me into the house. "Come on, hun. We need to get you upstairs before you pass out. I'm so not carrying you up there."

I put my arms around her. "I'm so glad you're here."

"Me, too," she said, hugging me. "My parents were pissed I left during the school week, but they understood that you needed me. I'll always be here for you."

I'd never been more grateful for having her as a best friend. I needed her now more than ever.

CHAPTER 34

Leya found Felix's ukulele buried in my closet. She took it out of its black case and traced Iron Man's red and gold mask on it. "I miss him playing this."

"Me, too." I sat on the bed, fluffing the pillows to get comfortable, though it did nothing to ease the pain in my torso.

Leya sat next to me, handing me the ukulele. "Play something for me."

I took it from her and strummed a few notes to reacquaint myself. My scarf made it difficult to feel the strings, so I took it off and set it next to me on the bed. Leya knew about my scar, so there was no point in hiding it from her. With a deep breath, I played one of Felix's favorite songs, "Could You Be Loved" by Bob Marley.

She took a black clip sitting on the nightstand and pulled back her braided hair, letting a few braids hang loosely around her face. "Oh, how I've missed that sound." She sunk into the pillows, clasping her hands behind her head and smiling. She hummed along.

My heart ached for Amá and Felix. Had she heard my

apology? Did she know how truly sorry I was for my choice that cost her and Felix their lives? How could someone ever get past the sorrow? The consequences?

"Stop doing that." Her eyes were closed, her feet bouncing along with the rhythm, her pink toenails wriggling around.

"Stop what?" My fingers changed chords, switching to a song I'd never heard before.

"Blaming yourself." She opened her eyes and looked at me. "You didn't know what would happen. It was an accident. At some point, you need to let go and move on. Forgive yourself."

My fingers worked flawlessly, creating a heartbreaking melody. "I can never forgive myself, Leya. You know that. Moving on is one thing. Forgiving myself for their deaths is entirely different. I stole two lives."

She turned toward me, propping herself up with her elbow. "What song is that? It's depressing."

"I don't know." My fingers had moved on their own like someone whispered to them.

She put her hand over mine to stop the strumming. "Tessa, knock it off." She sat up completely, her eyes more serious than I'd ever seen them. "Do you want to go to jail? To punish yourself?"

"I deserve it." I laid the ukulele next to me. "I deserve to be dead."

Leya put her palms on my cheeks, forcing me to stare into her brown eyes. "Tessa Isaacson, you need to stop that kind of talk. You can't change the past. But you can make your life better and make something of yourself. You're obviously still alive for a reason."

She lowered her hands. When my gaze dropped, she put her hand under my chin and lifted my head. "I know you regret what you did. But I'm not going to sit here and watch you throw your life away." Her hand went to my heart. "Felix and your mom, they're still in here, Tessa. They're watching over and protecting you. They still love you, and they've forgiven you." A few tears fell down her cheeks. "I'm not asking you to forgive yourself. I just want you to turn your problem into a solution."

Letting my tears fall, I lay my head in her lap and cried until I had nothing left inside me. Leya stroked my hair, her long nails massaging my scalp, and every now and then, her own tears fell onto my head.

I wasn't sure how long I lay there crying. At one point, Leya lay down next to me, and we fell asleep.

Amá came to me in my dream.

Tessa, be strong. Her dark curls framed her face. She looked so real and vibrant. *I love you. I'd say I forgive you, but there's nothing to forgive. It was an accident.*

Felix ran up, throwing his arms around me. *Tessa!* He squeezed me tight.

Amá smiled at me and joined the hug. She ran her hand down my hair. *You have your father's hair, not mine.* When I laughed, she put her hand on my cheek. *Oh, but you have my laugh.*

I miss you so much, Tessa. Felix said.

I miss you too, Felix.

Felix's brown eyes stared up at me. *Will you come visit us more often?*

I started to say something, but Amá cut me off. *No, dear. Tessa needs to stay in the land of the living. She needs to watch over your father.* She looked me straight in the eye, her face serious. *Be wary of Ellington, but find the box.*

What's in the box? I asked.

Amá smiled. *A chance at a new life. You belong in Willow Marsh, mi amor.* She kissed me on the forehead. *Remember to stay strong. Don't give up. Live your life.*

Felix hugged me again. *Bye, Tessa. I love you more than anything.*

I love you, too, Felix. I squeezed him back.

Amá and Felix stepped back into a white mist, fading away.

I woke with tears streaming down my face. Making sure to be quiet, I went through my closet until I found Felix's dinosaur. I sat down on the floor, keeping my back straight, and hugged it tight.

In my heart, I knew Amá and Leya were right. I needed to move on and let go of the things I couldn't fix. I'd love to join Amá and Felix on the other side, but I couldn't leave Dad alone. I wasn't ready to leave Leya. Or Graham.

Outside, a bird whistled near the window. I set the dinosaur on the wood floor next to me and stood, walking toward the window.

"What are you doing?" Leya sat up on the bed, rubbing her eyes. She looked at her phone. "Oh. It's almost time to meet Graham. We should head outside."

I stared out the window, searching for the bird.

"Tessa?" Leya appeared next to me and waved her hand in front of my face. "You're not like chitchatting with Delilah, are you?"

"Huh?" I turned to her, seeing worry in her eyes, and forced a smile. "No, sorry. Let's go see Graham."

I put on my maroon hoodie, gritting my teeth from the pain tugging at my torso, and we went outside. As I passed the downstairs bathroom, my eyes went to the mirror, but thank goodness Ellington wasn't there to greet me.

Leya stayed close to me, her arm linking through mine after we'd only gone a few steps outside. "This place gives me the creeps."

We walked into the trees, the thick branches blocking out the moonlight. Leya trembled at my side, her grip around my arm getting tighter the farther we went into the woods.

"I so thought this would be romantic," she whispered. "You, meeting a guy you love in the trees outside your house." Her eyes darted all around us. "But it's the complete opposite."

"I don't love him." I hadn't sorted out my feelings for him. I enjoyed being with him and preferred him over Blake. But love? Just like all the other four-letter words, I didn't use it lightly. They came heavy on my heart, full of passion and emotion.

Leaves rustled in front of us. Leya covered her mouth to dull her scream. I held in a laugh as Graham came out from behind a tree.

"I ss...seem tt...to always ss...scare people," Graham said. His blinking eyes landed on Leya. He had his good hand shoved in his hoodie pocket, the casted one hanging down against his side. The skin under his eyes was bruised and swollen from his broken nose.

Leya let out a strained laugh. "You didn't scare me." She put her hand on her heart. "Yeah, okay, you did. This place is beyond spooky, okay?" She took a few deep breaths before she smiled. "You must be Graham. I'm Leya."

"Hi." Graham's eyes didn't slow when they settled on me. "How are you feeling?"

I put my hand on my ribs. "Still sore. I can't handle the pain medications anymore, though, so I'm just suffering through it."

Graham nodded as he whispered. "Me, too."

"Is this where you found the body?" Leya asked, looking around on the damp ground. The soggy leaves were smashed into the mud.

"It's east of here," I said. "Near the inn."

Leya shook out her hands. "I so wouldn't have survived. I

would have had a heart attack right then and there." She scooted closer to me. "Did they ever find out what happened to the family?"

Graham's focus went to the ground.

"All I heard is that they were murdered," I said, my voice quiet. The woods made me keep my voice low. It always felt like I was surrounded by so many creatures and unknowns. "I'm placing my bet on Reed, though. I just don't know why."

"Maybe they saw him do something," Leya said with a shrug. "Like Greg."

Graham stepped back, turning to the side, his hand grasping at his earbuds hanging against his chest.

Leya swore under her breath in Creole. "Sorry. Apparently, Tessa didn't warn you that I say what's on my mind."

"Greg sided against him." Graham's voice was barely audible.

Both Leya and I shuffled closer so we could hear.

"This town has always been divided," he whispered. "Those who agree with the Harrisons and those who don't. Trenton's family sided against them. Mr. Barnett was very vocal about it."

I let go of Leya and stood in front of Graham. "Maybe. But everyone in town said the Barnetts moved. Why would they think that?"

He clenched his jaw, the muscles pulling tight. "Because the sheriff told them. Sheriff Hayes is under Reed's command and covers up all his crimes. Including the murders."

"And we're going to the Hayes' house for dinner?" Leya clapped her hands in fake excitement. "Oh joy!"

Graham's eyes flashed to Leya before they snapped back to me. "You're going over there?"

Leya took a step away from us. "I think that's my cue. Nice meeting you, Graham. This place is officially creeptastic. I'm freezing. I'm going inside where it's warm." She blew me a kiss. "Don't be long, sugar." With that, she turned and ran back toward the house.

I reached my hand out to Graham, but he stepped back.

"It's complicated," I said.

"You say that a lot." His voice was low, but I could hear the anger. His fingers on his casted hand drummed along his leg, getting more agitated with each beat. He turned. "I don't know why I even came."

I ran in front of him, ignoring the pain at the quick movement, and gently placed my hand on his chest. "Graham, don't go. I need you."

"You have Leya." He ran his shaking fingers through his hair. "And Blake. You don't need me. Besides, you don't like me like that, remember?" He pushed my hand down and walked away.

I needed to stop him from leaving before I lost him for good. It meant making myself vulnerable, but I had to do it.

"Delilah Morgan is haunting me."

Graham stopped, stumbling a little. "Ww...what?"

"She's in my head." I sighed and rubbed my arm. "She takes control of me sometimes."

His narrowed eyes searched mine. "Are you serious?"

"You want to know everything?" I threw my arms out. "I'll tell you everything."

I searched for a place to sit, but there were only damp leaves and dirt all around. Graham took my hand and led me farther into the woods. We found a fallen log and sat on it. Under the clouded sky, I told Graham everything.

About Amá and Felix. Ellington. Delilah. My contacts with them. My dreams. The key. The box. The elevator.

Everything except for the part of the crash only Leya knew about.

Graham sat in silence, his blinking eyes not slowing down once.

When I finally stopped, at least a half hour had passed. We sat in silence for the longest time. Graham kept looking at the ground, the sky, at me, and repeating the process.

"And now you think I'm crazy." I shouldn't have told him. It was too much to take in. Most people didn't believe in contact with the other side.

"No." Graham's hand wrapped over mine, sending tingles through me. "I'm surprised you trusted me enough with all that." His steady fingers brushed along mine. "No wonder you freaked out at the bowling alley. I wish I would've known." He shook his head, causing his shaggy hair to bounce. "Not that I could have done anything. But at least I would have known what you were going through."

My stomach fluttered. "Wait, you believe me?"

He jerked his head back. "Of course I do. Why would you lie about that?" He let go of my hand and slipped his into his hoodie pocket. "They're always talking about a Roy Ellington at school. He founded Willow Marsh. Think it's the same guy?"

It would make sense as to why he was so attached to the town. "He wears some sort of old, blue uniform, like he was a soldier of some kind."

"Roy Ellington was a general in the Civil War. For the Union. They wore blue."

Ellington? I tried to get his attention. *Would your first name happen to be Roy?*

Silence. It wasn't like talking to Delilah. She was always with me. Ellington just came in the vicinity when he wanted something.

"Maybe I could do some research," I said. "The library or internet would have pictures of Roy Ellington, right?" Maybe if I knew more about him, I'd be able to help him.

Graham nodded, and then stared off into the trees. "I

talked to some locals and told them what we found. They've been gathering evidence against the Harrisons, so we can add this to it. I think we're finally getting close to stopping them."

"I really hope you can," I said. "This town has been through too much."

He cleared his throat. "So, last night when you said you weren't interested in me like that . . ."

I quickly cut in. "Delilah, not me."

Ugh, Delilah whined. *So not kissing him. Don't even try it.*

She'd overtaken me so many times. If I couldn't fight her off just to kiss someone, I had no hope of fending her off for good. She pushed at me, tingles erupting everywhere as she fought for control.

Graham's blinking eyes were on my lips. He kept licking his as his fingers pounded his knee. Anger rose at the thought of Delilah ruining my moment with him. I latched onto that feeling and used it to fuel me.

With all my might, I shoved her into the back corner of my mind and built a cage around her. She screamed in protest. I had no more strength to shut her up, so I just had to deal with it. Luckily, the thudding of my heart dulled it somewhat.

Graham still hadn't moved toward me. He was probably terrified from last time we were out here. I had to take matters into my own hands.

I leaned in, intertwined my fingers in his hair, and pulled him close, our lips just a breath apart. I brushed my nose against his, seeing if he'd retreat, but he stayed firm. Closing my eyes, I kissed him softly on the lips. His whole body stiffened, including his lips, before he pushed away.

I wondered if he'd kissed anyone before. If it hadn't been for Delilah, Graham would have been my first kiss.

His breaths were deep, his eyes on my lips, telling me that

he wanted more but couldn't get himself to move. A smile pulled my lips apart. He was beyond adorable.

I slowly leaned in, placing my hand on his cheek and caressing it. His whole body shook under my touch. I pressed my lips to his, and a fire ignited in me. For the first time, Graham didn't stiffen or hesitate. He kissed me back, his lips moving softly on mine, gently holding me, being careful not to hurt me.

His hands seized the sides of my waist — his cast doing nothing to slow him down — and he lifted me off the log, setting me firmly in his lap. He ran a trail of kisses along my neck and jaw until his lips came back to mine. I wanted to taste him forever.

I lost track of time as we sat in the woods, holding each other, kissing, whispering, smiling, and laughing.

For once, I didn't need a mask or to pretend like I was someone else. I felt sane. Safe. In Control. Steady. Calm.

CHAPTER 35

I fell asleep quickly when I finally went back inside the house. My dream was perfectly clear, like I was reliving the event.

A few months ago, I'd had a really bad day at school. I wanted the pain to go away and wanted to stop feeling. So, I took a handful of my anxiety pills. Felix had a recital that night, Dad was stuck at work, and Amá had a terrible headache, so she asked me to drive. I knew in the back of my mind that I wasn't in the right state, but I drove anyway.

I sat in the front seat, hands firmly around the smooth wheel, driving down a wet road. Felix leaned forward and begged Amá to turn up the volume. "Could You Be Loved" by Bob Marley blasted through the speakers, vibrating the plastic covers. Amá cranked up the heat in the car. The smell of lilacs filled my nose.

The medication had taken over me. My arms and legs trembled as my vision went in and out of focus.

Rain pounded against the windshield, threatening to shatter the glass. I turned the wipers as fast as they would go. Fog crept up, so Amá turned on the defrost – I didn't want to take my hands off the wheel. Wind pushed at the car, making my hands tighten to the point they hurt. Felix sang from the back seat, his tone rich as honey. Amá danced along with the music and mouthed the words.

Wind rocked the car. I leaned forward in my seat, even though it wouldn't help me see clearer. I just hoped it would. Lifting my foot off the gas, I let the car slow. If we were late to Felix's recital, so be it. I didn't want to risk their lives.

My vision blurred for a moment, so I shook my head, blinking like crazy. Everything came back in focus, and a shape stood in the middle of the road. I leaned closer, straining my eyes. A distorted gray and brown deer – its edges sharp and not quite natural – with beady eyes like a vampire finch's, stood there, staring at me.

I slammed on the brakes and turned the wheel to the left. The car hydroplaned over the lanes, tilting in the air. The passenger side collided with the ground, screeching across the wet surface for a moment before the car flipped, flinging my head all around. The car rolled, each impact a new jolt of anguish through me, pushing all my air out. Even though it lasted seconds, it dragged on like it would never end.

Felix cried in the back seat. Amá screamed, the sound piercing my soul. When the car finally stopped, we were upside down on the side of the road. Rain beat against the car like bullets. Bob Marley continued to sing. Felix's cries turned into whimpers.

Amá was silent.

I tried to turn my head, but I blacked out before I could see her.

When I woke the next morning, sweat soaked my clothes and bedding. I clutched the sheets in my fists as I panted. A deer had been in the road. A weird, creepy one, and not just in my dream. It had stared at me like it had been waiting for me.

I sank into the fluffy pillow against the headboard and traced the scar on my hand made by a jagged piece of glass. The deer was why I had crashed. Not me. I must have blocked the memory, wanting to blame myself for their deaths. But there had been something wrong with the deer. It didn't seem entirely . . . earthly.

Instead of going back to sleep, I decided to do some research to get my mind off the dream and questions I couldn't answer. A simple internet search proved Graham correct. It was Roy Ellington, the founder of Willow Marsh, haunting me, but I still didn't know *why*. Knowing who he was, though, was a step in the right direction. Maybe he'd open up to me more when he came to visit.

My phone vibrated in my hand. It was a message from Corrine. She'd talked to her parents and had news.

I glanced over at Leya on the bed. She was on her back, sound asleep. I hated that she had been dragged into everything, but with her here, my sanity had a better chance of surviving. I smiled at the prospect of finally getting some answers.

Leya and I spent the day watching movies and relaxing. When we sneaked out of the house late that night, I was pretty refreshed. Dad's car wasn't in the driveway, surprising me. Hopefully, he wouldn't check my room if he got back before me.

Corrine picked us up but thankfully didn't tell Jade what we were doing. I wasn't in the mood for her negative attitude.

I slid into Corrine's old, two-door Honda. Though the outside was rusted, and the beige seats were falling apart, the inside of the car was immaculate.

"A cluttered life is a cluttered mind," Corrine said, watching me look around her car.

"If you say so." Leya leaned forward from the back seat. "Don't ever tell my mom that. I don't need her getting ideas on how I need to keep my room."

I tried to shift myself in the passenger seat so I was somewhat comfortable, but no matter where I turned, my ribs hurt. I finally straightened out, my butt on the edge of the seat. "Where are we going, Corrine?"

She had the radio turned off, the only sound coming from her rumbling engine. "So, that map? It's the exact location where the magic is strongest here. It's in the woods, not too far from the Hayes' house, actually."

Leya rubbed her hands together. "There's really magic in this eerie town? That's creeptastic."

Corrine glanced over at me. "My dad was freaking out when he saw the picture. He wants to know if you still have the parchment."

"I know where it is," I said. "I'm sure it hasn't been moved."

Corrine turned onto a dirt road. The car bounced through the rocks and potholes as it climbed up hills, and pain exploded in my torso. I clenched my teeth and gripped the handle above the door, doing everything I could to not let the swear words fly.

When we arrived at the end of the road, it took me a second to shuffle out of the car and onto my feet. Corrine grabbed a black bag from the trunk. She flipped on a hand-held flashlight, illuminating the area in front of us. She tossed another flashlight to Leya.

"Follow me." Corrine took off between the willow trees, and we followed, walking in silence.

For once, there wasn't a cloud in the sky. The almost full moon, plus all the white stars, lit up our path. Soon we arrived in a clearing in the trees, and I let out a gasp.

Corrine whipped around, shining the flashlight at me. "What?"

I shielded my eyes with my hand. "Will you not shine that in my face?"

She turned the light, showing the clearing. Lush, green grass carpeted the ground. Maple and pine trees circled the area, the trunks, branches, and leaves flawless, almost like they were painted. The white lights from the sky added a magical glow.

And I'd seen it all before. "Greg came here." Forcing through the pain, I got down on my knees and ran my fingers along the soft grass. "It was his and Graham's favorite spot."

Leya spun around, taking in the scene, awe on her face. "It's so beautiful. How is everything so ... perfect?"

Corrine set her bag on the grass in the center of the clearing. "No one knows for sure, but most townsfolk think it's because the magic is centered below this spot."

Leya froze, her arms and fingers splayed out. "Are we going to get special powers or something?"

I chuckled. "Probably not."

She dropped her arms and frowned. "Well, that's lame."

Corrine took a seat in the middle of the clearing and motioned for us to join her. Instead of standing back up, I crawled through the grass and got situated into a not incredibly painful position next to her.

"So, I did some research." Corrine's red hair was more

spiky than usual. "And I know why the name Ellington sounds familiar."

"He's the founder of Willow Marsh." I might not have had superpowers, but my spidey senses were on high alert. I scanned the trees around us, feeling like we were being watched, but couldn't see anything.

"Right," Corrine said. "Legend has it, there are Civil War relics buried under Willow Marsh. No one has ever been able to find them." She scratched her nose. "Plus, about fifty years ago, the other founding families, the Harrisons and the Walkers, created a law that prohibited anyone from searching for the treasure."

"Why?" Leya asked. She wrapped her jacket tighter around her. It had gotten colder since we'd sat down.

"Preserving the sanctity or something along those lines." Corrine played with her tongue ring, running it across her glossed lips. "Which I think is a load of crap. I think the founding families hated each other too much, and the rivalry was getting way heated to the point some people were killed."

"So, kind of like a peace treaty?" I tightened the scarf holding my hair back.

"Yep," Corrine said. "Anyway, this box Ellington wants is probably a relic."

I held in a groan and threw up my hands. "That's just great. He wants me to get something that no one has been able to find and is illegal to search for." I stared up at the starry sky. "Thanks a lot, Ellington."

The vampire finch landed on a branch of a maple tree near me, its tiny head cocked to the side.

Corrine retrieved some candles from her backpack and filled the area between us. There were at least twenty red candles. "That's why we're going to reach out to him."

Leya opened her mouth, probably to protest, but Corrine held up a hand and spoke. "I'm not letting Tessa do it. I will."

She narrowed her eyes at me. "We don't need you bringing any more ghosts into our realm."

I folded my arms. "You don't think you will?"

"I don't have the freaky powers you have," Corrine said. "After talking to my mom, she's convinced you're connected to the other side in some crazy way."

Leya sat tall, stretching her back. "What's the plan? You're just going to summon Ellington? Do you think he'll even talk to you?"

"There's only one way to find out." Corrine shook out her hands and body. "I also want to see if we can find out what happened to Greg and the Barnett family."

I pursed my lips. "Why would Ellington know that?"

Corrine reached forward and lit the candles with a lighter. "I was thinking more of reaching out to Greg and the Barnetts themselves. Hopefully, at least one of them hasn't completely crossed over to the other side."

Leya took deep, exaggerated breaths, shaking her chest.

"What are you doing?" I asked, trying to hold back the laughter.

"Shaking all the bad vibes out of me," Leya said with her eyes closed.

My phone vibrated in my back pocket. Dad had texted, which meant he had come home and saw my empty room.

Dad:
Where are you?

Tessa:
With some friends.
I'll be home soon.

Now, Tessa. We need to talk.

I silenced my phone and tucked it back in my pocket. He'd just have to wait.

We all clasped hands and took a collective breath.

"Roy Ellington?" Corrine's calm voice hugged the night, inviting it in. "Ellington, we'd like to talk to you. We need some help here in Willow Marsh."

A slight wind picked up, rustling the leaves, but nothing else stirred.

Corrine inhaled deeply. "Mr. Ellington, if you can hear me, show us a sign."

The vampire finch whistled and flew down, landing on my shoulder.

"Creepy," Leya muttered under her breath. Her eyes went wide. "Do you think that bird *is* Ellington?"

The bird shook its head back and forth like it understood her.

Corrine leaned toward the bird. "Maybe it's like his spirit animal or something. He's linked to Ellington. I've heard of things like that happening."

The finch moved its tiny head up and down in a nod.

"Well," Leya said, scooting back. "That's officially the most disturbing thing I've seen to date. So, yay me." Her grip on my hand tightened.

The bird bounced a little on my shoulder, and then craned its neck toward Corrine, whistling once.

"Mr. Ellington," Corrine said, closing her eyes. "Why do you need Tessa? Or are you just using her as a channel to get to someone else?"

I hadn't thought about that. Ellington never mentioned wanting me to contact someone else. He just said he needed my help.

A snap of a twig behind me made all our heads whip that way.

"Is someone there?" Corrine had no fear or waver in her voice, just a calm confidence.

Only silence answered. I looked through the trees but saw nothing out of the ordinary.

Heat tickled my neck. I turned back around to see the flames rising, all connecting, calmly weaving beautiful patterns. First, the key. Then a vampire finch. Followed by a willow tree. Wind swirled around us, sending my ponytail and scarf whipping fiercely. The tornado created a wall around us, blocking the outside world.

Tessa. Ellington's voice echoed all around us. *Find the box.* Static crinkled, interrupting the connection. *I can take you there.*

"We need answers," Corrine yelled. "Tessa won't help you until you help us."

What do you – crackle – *want?* Ellington sounded eager, like he wanted to help.

"What happened to Greg Dixon and the Barnett family?" Corrine asked.

The wind picked up, swirling faster, making it hard to keep hold of each other's hands. It yanked and pushed at us all at the same time, the whistling of the wind almost deafening.

Harrison. It was all Ellington said, but it confirmed what we'd thought all along.

"Can you find out where Greg is, Ellington?" I wasn't supposed to talk, but I couldn't stop myself. If we could find his body, we might find answers, or at least something to connect Reed to him. Evidence.

The tornado wall dropped, blasting out on the ground through the trees. The bird took flight and headed into the woods behind Leya. We scrambled to our feet to follow.

It weaved through the trees with no hesitation. I ducked

under hanging branches, pushing them out of the way. The finch landed on some disturbed earth near a willow tree.

The three of us stopped, staring down at the dirt. Was Greg really here? How had Ellington found out so quickly? Unless he'd already known. Everything could have been connected in a way I didn't quite understand.

Ignoring the pain, I knelt and clawed at the earth. I tossed dirt to the side and out of the way. Corrine and Leya joined me, and we dug as fast as we could.

"We need a shovel," I said.

Suddenly, the finch went wild. It whistled uncontrollably, and so loudly that I had to cover my ears with my hands. The finch's beady eyes stared behind me. I slowly turned around, afraid of what I'd find.

A tall figured loomed in the shadows, casually leaning against a tree, holding a gun.

Reed.

CHAPTER 36

My gaze darted around for his brothers, but Reed was alone. Unless they were hiding somewhere. But they always liked to be part of the action.

It took Leya a second to notice I had stopped digging. Corrine was practically rooted to the ground, staring at Reed, her arms spread out like she was using them for balance, so she didn't fall over from shock.

"Are you in pain?" Leya asked me.

Swallowing, I shook my head and pointed a wobbly finger at Reed. Leya whipped around, her eyes going wide in fear.

Reed used a shirt sleeve to wipe at his nose before he turned the gun back at us. "Seems like some naughty little girls have been digging around where they don't belong." He pushed away from the tree, his body leaning a little to the side. "I do hate wasting time, so I'm going to make this clean and simple. I need Tessa alive, but you two," Reed said, whistling and waving the gun at Leya and Corrine, "are unfortunately not needed." He pointed his gun at Leya, his finger on the trigger.

I jumped in front of Leya and pushed her behind me. "You're not killing anyone, Reed."

He chuckled like I'd just told the most adorable joke. "Is that so?"

I needed to figure out a plan – a reason why he'd want to keep them alive.

"I don't want to die," Leya said quietly. Then she let out a blood-curdling scream that sent all my hairs on edge. I almost asked what she was doing, but then I realized she was probably hoping someone would hear us. The girl had a very powerful set of lungs.

With a disappointed shake of the head, Reed shot the gun into the air, and Leya immediately stopped. She linked her arm through mine, trembling.

We weren't far from the Hayes' home. Maybe they heard and would come to check it out. But would the sheriff stop Reed? If he was on the Harrisons' payroll, the sheriff might possibly *help* him.

In the meantime, I could get some answers, even if I'd never be able to use them. I knew why he killed Greg. I had the evidence of that. "Why did you kill the Barnett family?"

He rubbed his eye with his palm. One whiff of the alcohol radiating off him told me he was plastered. "Not your business, dearest Tessa."

"It's mine," Corrine said, standing tall, her chin up. She lowered her arms to her sides. "Trenton was my friend. Their family never harmed a soul."

"It's not always actions," Reed said, his tone thick as honey, "that get in our way. Words are powerful, too." He hiccupped.

"How can I be scared and grossed out at the same time?" Leya whispered behind me.

Reed shook out his head like a dog trying to clear things

off. "I can't have you blabbing this around town. Not after I've gotten this far. I'm so close."

So close to what?

His drunken gaze shifted to Corrine, so I took off towards her. Tilting his head, he pointed the gun at her and pulled the trigger seconds after I rammed into her, sending us both to the ground. I was hoping with him being drunk, his aim would be bad.

We fell on the dirt, and pain raged through me. I held my arm across my middle and squeezed my eyes, trying to regain my breath.

Leya cried, the sound piercing through the woods. If the sheriff and Blake didn't hear the gunshot, they would definitely hear her wail. I got up slowly, looking around. Leya was unharmed. Corrine panted next to me but had no obvious injuries. Relief washed through me.

"Tessa," Reed said, taking the hand that held his gun and pounding the back of it against his forehead. "I need you to stop interfering with my plans. I had everything lined up perfectly, and then you . . ." His wet upper lip curled into a distorted smile. "You come along and set me back. I can't in good conscience sit back and let that happen. This town needs me as a leader."

His drunken ramble made no sense. He wanted me to let him roam around, beating up and killing whoever he wanted? How could that possibly help the town?

"Hello?" Sheriff Hayes' firm voice sounded in the distance, distracting all of us for a split second.

Corrine scrambled to get up and ran at Reed, tackling him to the ground. The gun went off, the loud pop cracking in the air, and I slammed my palms over my ears. Corrine lay on top of Reed, covering him from view.

I took an unsteady step toward them, hands still hovering near my ears. With a grunt, Reed pushed Corrine off him and stumbled to his feet, staggering around. Blood pooled on Corrine's stomach as she stared at the sky, convulsing.

"No!" I ran to her, not caring that Reed was right there, and dropped to my knees. The dark red blood gushed from a quarter-sized hole, so I pressed my hands against the wound. Her eyes fluttered. "Stay with me, Corrine." Her warm blood soaked through the scarf on my hand. I yanked the other scarf out of my hair and pushed it against the wound as well.

Fallen leaves crunched under pounding footfalls. Sheriff Hayes was almost to us.

"This isn't over, Tessa." Reed's silky, sweet tone sounded surprisingly sober. He took off running, disappearing into the woods.

Sherriff Hayes and Blake broke through the trees seconds later. Leya pointed in the direction Reed had run. "He went that way. Reed Harrison."

Sheriff Hayes motioned for Blake to stay with us, then used the radio on his shoulder to call for an ambulance and took off running after Reed.

In one of Corrine's hands, she held her rosary, her bloody thumb slowly moving over the beads. Tears streamed down my cheeks as I kept my shaking hands on her wound. "Please, Corrine."

Blake tried to drag me away, but I pushed at him until he sighed and stood.

I watched as Corrine's thumb went still, falling limp on the ground next to the cross. I ran my hand down her hair as her lifeless eyes stared into the starry sky.

"No!" I clung to her and sobbed.

She was gone. She wasn't supposed to die. No one was supposed to die.

"What's here?" Blake asked from somewhere behind me. Why was he talking about something other than Corrine?

Leya's voice was so soft, I could barely hear it. "We think it's Greg."

At the mention of Greg's name, I snapped back to reality. I wouldn't let Corrine's death be in vain.

I gently laid her back on the ground, smoothing out the hair around her face. I crawled to the hole and dug, using my hands to shovel the dirt.

Blake reached down to stop me, so I shoved his chest. He hesitated before he dropped next to me and helped me dig. A minute later, Leya joined us, tears streaming down her face as she choked on her sobs.

I hated that dead bodies were becoming a common element in Willow Marsh, and that Leya was so wrapped up in it. She didn't belong here. She should have been safely at home in Illinois, away from the craziness.

Blake gasped. I turned to see decaying toes protruding from the earth.

We kept digging.

It wasn't long until Sheriff Hayes came back, saying he'd lost Reed. He screamed something about contaminating a crime scene, but soon realized it was too late, and we wouldn't stop, so he got down on his knees with us.

The putrid smell became worse as we dug, but we slowly uncovered more of the corpse. Between the stench and the pain, I had to twist behind me to vomit, emptying everything from my system. Wiping my mouth, I noticed a complete silence had washed over the digging site. I slowly took a deep breath and gathered the courage to look at the face.

His round jaw line and brown hair reminded me of Graham.

I backed away, pulling my phone out of my hoodie pocket and calling Graham, the blood and mud on my fingers smearing across the screen.

He picked up right away. "Tessa?"

I tried to talk, but I couldn't find the words. Leya took the phone from me. "Hey, Graham, it's Leya." She sniffed, and her voice was shaky. "I'm so sorry to have to tell you this, but we found your brother's body."

Blake's arms wrapped around me, pulling me close to his chest. Out of the corner of my eye, I saw Corrine's beads laying in her limp hand. I sobbed for her loss. I'd barely met her, and she was gone – taken too soon. I cried for Greg and his family, and for Delilah, who should have been in Blake's arms instead of me.

When would it end?

CHAPTER 37

Blake escorted me back to his house and up to his room. He tugged my wet hoodie over my head and tossed it in a pile of clothes on the floor. I was in a stunned stupor, trying to process everything that had happened.

A wool blanket wrapped around me, and I held on tight. I pressed the blanket against my nose and inhaled the tropical scent Blake had left behind.

He sat down next to me on his bed, draping his arm around me.

I swallowed, trying to work moisture back into my mouth. "Where's Leya?"

Blake's nose pressed into the side of my head, right above my ear. "Talking with my dad. I wanted to get you out of the cold and make sure you're okay."

"I'm not," I whispered over my dry lips. "I can't believe Corrine is gone." My chest shuddered as I pictured her lifeless eyes staring at the sky.

His sure arms pulled me into him. "I'm so sorry, Tessa." He said my name so soft and gentle, a reverence I'd never heard from him before. He leaned back, placed his warm hand on my cheek, and turned my face toward his. "You'll be okay. I promise." His focus fluttered to my lips.

Kiss him, Delilah said.

I pushed away from Blake, stumbling to stand. The blanket fell to the floor in a heap. *Seriously, Delilah? Corrine just died, and you want to kiss Blake? What's wrong with you?*

Blake stood and brushed his finger along my lower lip. "What's going on?"

Tessa, Amá whispered. *Leave, sweet girl.*

I wanted to, but my feet were tethered to the ground, an invisible force keeping them there. I pushed my palm against my forehead. What was wrong with me?

Blake yanked my hand away from my head, and for a moment, he faltered. The confusion left his face, replaced by longing. He pressed his body against mine and stared into my eyes, daring me, pushing me.

Kiss him, Delilah said.

Taking hold of the back of my neck, he smashed his lips against mine, kissing me fiercely. His hand slid up my back and stopped at my neck. He pulled the scarf from my hair, letting the silk material fall to the floor.

Everything clouded, reality and fiction merging together. The true me wanted to run and get as far away from Blake as possible. But Delilah shoved him onto the bed and jumped on top.

"Hey, baby." The words came from my mouth, but it wasn't me, nor did it sound like me. It was throaty and sultry.

"Delilah?" Blake asked. He sat up, his firm hands landing on my thighs and straddling me in his lap.

Delilah tried to force more words out of my mouth, but I fought to keep them in. My blood flowed like waves through my veins, slowly turning to ice.

Blake looked deep into my eyes. "Is it really you?"

I lost control as she slowly seized my limbs. "Yes, it's me."

"I could see it in Tessa's eyes." His hand caressed my cheek. "Your beautiful blue would mix with her brown. But it just didn't make sense." He kissed my lips. "I've missed you so much."

Delilah took complete control, turning my muscles into ice. She ripped off Blake's shirt. Then mine. I tried to fight back and stop it. I pushed back with every bit of strength I could muster.

Please, Delilah, I begged. *I don't want this. I don't want Blake. I love Graham.* How could Blake even want to? Especially after what we'd seen in the woods. What we'd uncovered.

Too bad for you. Delilah giggled. *We're going to have some fun, fun, fun.*

In my head, a war started. A battle I couldn't control. All I knew was at that moment, Delilah was about to win.

Blake kissed me, and as much as I fought, nothing worked. Delilah kissed him back, my fingers tangling in his hair. She paused for a second, pulling back from Blake and panting. A smirk fought onto my lips as she reached over and grabbed his phone.

"We should get a picture of our reunion," Delilah purred.

As Blake switched his camera to selfie mode, Delilah kissed him just below his ear, which was the exact moment Blake took a picture. He dropped his phone and found my neck, his warm lips trying to kiss every inch.

Delilah pushed forward, moving my arm toward the phone. I struggled against her, but it was like I was watching everything from afar with absolutely no control. While Blake continued to kiss my neck, Delilah sent the picture of Blake and me – both of us with no shirts on and me kissing him – to Graham with the caption: *I can't believe you actually fell for the possession story.* She'd moved so fast that I didn't have time to try to fight it.

How could you? I snarled.

It only made her laugh. *Now Graham will think that you made up everything about me and that you chose Blake over him. And since it came from Blake's phone, well, he'll believe it.*

She was right. If it had come from mine, Graham might have suspected Delilah was behind it. But with "Blake" sending a picture of "me" kissing him, seemingly unaware that a photo was being captured, Graham could think it was real.

Blake unzipped my jeans, brutally bringing me back to my situation. Tears escaped down my cheeks, but Blake was too busy taking off our clothes to notice.

Delilah, I cried. *Please.*

He yanked off my jeans and pinned me to the bed, kissing my neck and chest. I couldn't let Delilah win or let Blake do this to me. As much as he'd try to deny it, it was rape. I wasn't myself. His lips came back to mine, and Delilah didn't hold anything back. I was boxed in, chained up against my will.

His fingers brushed down my back, heading for my bra strap. Anger seared through me, melting the ice in my veins.

What are you doing? There was a slight panic in Delilah's voice.

Not letting you win, I said. It was my body, not hers. I shoved at her and fought for control of my limbs.

In an easy, swift motion, Blake had my bra unfastened. But I was still covered, and I would not let him go farther. With a mighty roar inside, I slammed into Delilah, sending her tumbling to the back of my mind.

The door opened. "Oh!"

Blake jumped off me, and I seized the opportunity to sit up and refasten my bra.

A lady stood in the doorway, her face flushed. It must have been his stepmom. "I'm so sorry. I didn't . . ." She looked at Blake and me, both half dressed. The embarrassment on her face turned to anger, and she pushed the door open farther. "This door should remain open at all times."

She and Blake argued about rules and staying dressed, but I ignored them, rushing to put my clothes back on.

I paused at the door and looked at his stepmom. "I'm sorry. This won't happen again." My eyes went to Blake's – the rage in them flaring – and I could feel Delilah laughing, slightly strained from anger, in my head. "Ever."

Without waiting for a response, I ran out of the room, down the stairs, and out of the house.

CHAPTER 38

Instead of going back to the crime scene where my dad and Leya probably were, I headed toward home. The pain in my ribs kept my pace slow. I roamed the darkened streets, trying to stop the tears from coming. I couldn't believe Delilah had taken full control of me like that. I had absolutely no power. If Blake's stepmom hadn't shown up, what would have happened? Would I have been able to stop Blake? Even with control of my body, he was a lot stronger than me.

You were embracing your true self, Delilah said. *Just admit it. You're exactly like me. It's why Blake likes you.*

He likes YOU, I said. *He could see your eyes in mine. That's why he wanted to be near me. He missed his dead girlfriend.*

You're saying all of this like it's a bad thing. We could be happy with Blake. He'll love you and take care of you. You have to admit, he's an amazing kisser.

Graham's better.

Delilah huffed. *I was there for that kiss as well, dear. Blake's better.*

Guess we'll have to agree to disagree. I needed her out of my head. *What was the point of sending Graham that picture? Why would you hurt him like that?*

With the truth? It needed to be told.

It wasn't the truth! I shrieked. How could I possibly explain it to Graham?

Graham. His brother's death had just been confirmed, and then Delilah went and did that. I wanted to be with him, but I was probably the last person he wanted to see. And after everything that had just happened with Blake, I felt so . . . gross and ashamed.

My mind wandered to Ellington. Did he know more than he was letting on? Had he been involved in Greg's or the Barnetts' deaths? I rubbed my eyes, wishing I had a way to talk to Ellington directly.

The sun was almost up by the time I made it home. I'd made some wrong turns with the cloud of confusion in my mind.

Leya stood on the porch, waiting for me. Her fists were clenched tight, and her eyes were narrowed, the irritation radiating off her almost blinding. It was like she knew what had happened between Blake and me. She helped me up the porch steps and into the house.

Dad was in the family room waiting for us. He stood, arms folded in front of him and shoulders squared.

"Where were you?" Dad asked.

"With Blake." I sat down in my abuelo's chair, trying to keep my back straight and scrubbing at my arms like I could wipe away what happened.

"Is your phone broken?" Dad asked.

I pulled it out from my pocket and held it up for him to see. It was drowning in notifications from the two of them. "Nope. I can see all the missed calls and texts." My body went numb, just like my brain. It was like everything shut down.

He ran his hand across the scruff on his cheeks. "This is

not a joke, Tessa. Where were you?" Anger boiled behind his eyes, but I was past caring.

I kicked off my dirty tennis shoes in a haze. "I was with your precious Blake. The guy you want me to be around, remember?"

"Don't twist this." Dad sat down on the couch, wringing his hands together. "Things have changed. This is why I told you to come home earlier. I know so much more now. You need to stay away from him!" His shoulders slumped. "You're all I have left. I can't lose you."

I furrowed my eyebrows, some clarity coming back. "What are you talking about?"

He stared at his sneakers. "I found out that Sheriff Hayes is on the Harrisons' payroll."

"How?" I asked. I'd had a feeling he was, but it still made me sick to my stomach to have it confirmed. He'd probably let Reed get away in the woods.

"I've been talking with some people in town," Dad said. "Trying to figure out everything that's been going on. Hal Hastings has told me a lot of eye-opening things."

Rita's husband. If Dad believed Hal, then that was a good thing. I trusted Rita. Maybe Dad would finally let me hang out with Graham. My heart ached at the very thought of him and what he was going through.

Leya stood near me, her arms folded and tapping her foot. She looked like she hadn't registered anything my dad had said. Something else was bothering her. "Why did you take off with Blake and leave me all alone? Tell me now, or so help me..."

"I need to start from the beginning." It wouldn't be easy, but I had to open up, especially to my dad. He wouldn't understand, or accept, the possession, but I could work another angle to get him to loosen up to the idea. I looked at him. "Your sister, Jillian, went crazy, right?"

He slowly nodded as surprise flashed in his eyes. "She had a mental breakdown."

I ran my fingers through my hair. "So, she was crazy."

Leya threw up her hands. "What does that have to do with anything?"

"It has everything to do with this." I leaned my head against the back of the chair. "Voices in her head. Drug addiction. Suicide."

Leya knelt next to me. "I thought you said you stopped taking the pills."

Dad's eyes swept between Leya and me. "What pills?" He stood, coming over to me. "Tessa, are you really contemplating suicide?"

It took so much energy, but I confessed my overuse of the anxiety meds, the truth behind the night of the crash — including the part about the psycho deer — and how tempting ending my life had seemed.

I hesitated about explaining the possession and ghosts. Dad would have the hardest time with that. But I couldn't hide the truth anymore, whether or not Dad wanted to hear it. I told them about the nightmares, Ellington, and Delilah — even about the dark spirit that had snuck in a couple times.

When I got to the part about Delilah taking control, I had to stop. They both waited patiently. I didn't want to admit it or talk about it. But keeping it to myself wouldn't help anything. They had to know. So I told them.

Tears ran down Dad's face. I leaned forward and wiped them away. "I don't want to end my life anymore. I can be happy here in Willow Marsh." In a weird, twisted way, I knew it was true. Once everything was sorted out, I believed Dad, and I could have a happy life here.

"And the pills?" Dad asked.

"I haven't touched them since the night of the crash." I

rubbed my forehead. "But I'm not sure I made the right choice."

His eyes softened. "Jillian never sought help. But you have. You've seen Rita. You're trying to control your medication intake. You're on the right track, Tessa." He took my hand. "Whatever you need, I'll do it. If you need to see Rita daily, then I will take you myself. I can administer your anxiety medication, so you don't feel the need to overuse. If someone tries to take control of you again, please come tell me. I'll listen. I'll help. I won't judge or think you're crazy."

I knew how hard all of that was for Dad. I threw my arms around his neck. "Thank you, Apá."

Dad held me, whispering how much he loved me and what I meant to him. He apologized for not understanding and not listening.

Leya joined in on our hug. I loved my family more than anything. The two of them were all I had left. I'd been pushing them away instead of pulling them closer.

You'll always have me, Delilah said.

Not if I can help it.

She laughed. *Well, seeing how much control you lacked an hour ago, I think it's safe to say I'll always win.*

I needed to contact Ellington and find out where the box was. Then I needed to make him and Delilah cross over to the other side and end the madness. Everything was a chaotic mess of unanswered questions, but I did know one thing for sure: my masquerade was about to be sent to its grave.

CHAPTER 39

I fell asleep in my bed with Leya sprawled out next to Dad and me in a sleeping bag on the floor. He didn't want to leave my side. Multiple times I told him I wasn't going to kill myself, but he insisted on watching over me. Before, I had underestimated my love for Dad. He meant the world to me, and I was lucky to have him.

My nightmare never came. Now that I finally knew the truth about that night, I had nothing to haunt me anymore. I slept like the dead until something pecked on my window. Sliding out of bed, I tiptoed over to the window, pulling back the thick curtain to look out. A vampire finch sat on a branch of a nearby willow tree, looking directly at me.

I turned to see if Dad or Leya stirred, but they both were sound asleep. It was the perfect time to contact Ellington without their interference. I wanted nothing more than to shut him and Delilah out forever.

I threw on some jeans, a pink hoodie, and my Chuck Taylors, grabbed my phone, and headed down the hall.

In here, Ellington said from the upstairs bathroom in a clear, authoritative voice.

In the center of the bathroom, a levitating candle flickered, drawing me closer. I slipped in and shut the door quietly behind me. The finch perched itself on a tree outside the bathroom window, watching me.

It's time. Ellington stared at me through the mirror. Somehow, he looked more real. More distinct. His navy blue Civil War uniform was perfectly pressed, the gold buttons shining.

The candle floated down and landed on the lid of the toilet. I checked around me, but I could only see Ellington through the mirror.

I tightened the scarf wrapped around my hand. "Time for what?"

To find the box. Find what's ours.

"What's in the box?"

A chance at forgiveness.

I hated how vague he always was. I tried to mask the annoyance in my tone, not wanting to upset him. I didn't want him to change his mind about showing me the box. "Where is it?"

His smile lit up his eyes. *I can take you there. Tonight.* He moved his hand, placing it on my shoulder. Tingles erupted in the spot. He was much stronger than he'd ever been.

"Why do you care so much?" I tried to hold still, even though the touch sent shock waves through me. "You're dead. You can't use whatever's in the box."

Ellington's excited grin stretched from ear to ear. *Oh, but I can. There is something there of great importance, Tessa. It can help you as well.* He finally removed his hand from my shoulder.

I took out a pink silk scarf from my hoodie pocket and tied back my hair. "How?"

It could bring your mom and brother back from the dead.

I'd been lowering my hands, but they froze in midair. "What? How?" It was impossible. No one could be brought back from the dead.

There's a power inside the box that will fix your life. He watched me through the mirror. *Let's undo your mistake, Tessa.*

I rested my hands on the porcelain sink to support my weight. He was talking nonsense, but I needed him to continue. "How did you know where Greg was?"

He lifted his chin ever so slightly. *I know everything that happens in Willow Marsh. I would have shown you earlier, but sometimes it's hard to communicate.* He beamed. *But you make me stronger. You helped find him.* He rubbed his old, wrinkly hands together. *Now, are you ready?*

A part of me was still wary of him, but he needed to be sent to the other side. I had to don my mask and play along. "Yes. How do I get there?"

The unearthly glint in his eyes made my stomach roll. *Go to the elevator. I will do the rest.*

I turned toward the door, knowing I couldn't go it alone. "I need to just wake my Dad and..."

No. Only you can come. You can't trust anyone else. He grew in size until he towered over me. *They lack the power, Tessa. They don't believe like you do.*

I cowered back, surprised with his sudden change. The back of my feet banged into the bathtub. "They'll listen to me. I just need to explain it to them."

Someone laughed, sharp and grating, making my skin crawl. *They won't.*

"Who said that?" I asked, my voice trembling. Ellington had faded away.

They only said those things to stop you from hurting yourself, Delilah said, agreeing with the new voice. *They think you're crazy. You'll be locked up.*

"No. They believed me." My eyes searched the room for the other voice. "They care about me."

No, they don't, Delilah said. *Go with Ellington. Prove to them that you have the power to get the treasure and stop the Harrisons.*

Think of the glory you'll have. Ellington reappeared, though not as clear as before.

"Where did you go?" I asked through the mirror.

His eyes darted all over the room. *Someone pushed me out. Tessa, your dad and friend can't stop the Harrisons, but you can. You could be in charge of Willow Marsh and have complete power.*

I shook my head, slapping my palms against my forehead. None of it made sense. "I don't want power. I want justice and to stop the killings."

The temperature in the bathroom dropped dramatically as ice crackled across the mirror. Frosty breaths puffed from my mouth. Trembling, I tried to open the door, but the handle wouldn't turn. "Open the door, Ellington."

It's not me, he said in a strained voice. *Someone else is here.*

A shrill cackle echoed on the tiled floor, bouncing on the walls around me. *I'm bored. Let's play.*

Suddenly, the mirror shattered, spraying glass all over the bathroom. A piece sliced my arm, sending blood trickling down.

Who's there? Ellington asked, his tone firm. *Show yourself.*

Black smoke drifted up from the tile, weaving through the air in thick tendrils. It caressed my cheek, searing the skin, and I flinched away.

Ellington disappeared again.

Freezing water sloshed over my feet. My gaze went to the floor. There was at least an inch of water on the tile, and it continued to rise. The cold took away most of my strength, but I yanked at the doorknob, trying to free myself.

The water stopped when it reached my ankles. In the corner, the water froze, cracking its way toward me. Before I could react, my feet were in solid ice. I had moved just out of reach of the door, even with my fingers out as far as they would go.

"HELP!" I yelled. I went to shout again, but a force

wrapped a solid wall around my throat, blocking the sound. I tried to grab my phone from my back pocket, but wind came from nowhere and whirled around, keeping both arms from moving.

Tessa, someone else... Ellington's shaky voice cut off.

The black smoke swirled around me, mixing with the wind, radiating heat. It whispered. *Tessa, pretty Tessa.* A flow of air ran down my hair like it was being stroked. *Pretty head. Pretty girl.*

I moved my neck from side to side, but I couldn't shake off the smoke. It slithered into my ears and nose. A hot fire coursed through my veins. Something crawled under my skin, expanding in small waves.

I wanted to scream, but the force still blocked my vocal chords.

Tessa, Ellington whispered. *Push them out before they completely take over your body.*

How? I asked.

Light, Ellington said. *They hate the light.*

Tiny balls of white light appeared, floating in the air. They surrounded me, their warm layer sucking at my skin. Inside, the dark presence squirmed and fought against the light. The balls divided to create more, covering every inch of my exposed skin. Black smoke puffed out of my pores, disintegrating in the light until only a trace remained in me, and the balls of light evaporated. There was a small tremor in my arm, the dark still lingering, but the light had at least stopped it from taking over my body.

Thank you, I said to Ellington.

Outside, the bird sang, and the force blocking my voice freed.

We must hurry, Ellington said, his tone eager. From my angle, I could only see part of him in the mirror. *Before another dark spirit has a chance to enter.*

Someone knocked at the bathroom door. I strained to reach the doorknob, the ice around my feet keeping me rooted in place.

"Tessa?" Dad said in a groggy tone.

"Help me!"

Dad wiggled the doorknob, but it didn't budge. The door shook as if Dad had thrown his whole body against the door. I heard him yell something to someone else, but I couldn't make out the words.

Come with me, Tessa, Ellington said. His form floated between me and the door.

I couldn't handle another day with Ellington and Delilah in my life. "Okay. I'll go with you."

Ellington's mouth turned into a smile. The ice around my feet melted, the water dissolving into the floor. Warmth took over the bathroom, and he evaporated.

CHAPTER 40

Dad surprised me by driving us to the office building on Main Street. So much uncertainty sat behind his eyes, but he didn't question me. Leya sat next to me in the back seat, holding my arm and shaking. Every couple of minutes, a small patch of heat would flare in my lower right arm, but then it would subside seconds later.

Rita stood in her flannel pajamas, waiting for us outside the main doors. Dad had called her and asked her to meet us there since she had a key to the building. Rita's alert eyes glanced at Dad before she put a steady arm around my shoulder. "Tessa, why don't you and I go up to my office and have a little chat?"

"What? No." I hurried inside and repeatedly pushed the button for the elevator. "I have to go downstairs."

Rita put her hand on my arm. "Tessa, sweetie, I checked the elevator while I was waiting. There's no option for a floor below ground level. I also checked for a staircase leading downstairs. Nothing."

Leya, Dad, and Rita all stared at me, their concern reeking so strongly that for a split second, I doubted myself.

But then I remembered Graham. I turned to the elevator and pressed the button again, my sweaty palm sliding over it. "Ellington said he could help me." In the door's silver reflection, I saw Rita and Dad share a worried look.

I told you they'd think you were crazy, Delilah sang.

You can't trust them, Ellington whispered from somewhere nearby.

Remember what your mom said, Delilah said. *Trust no one.*

The doors pinged open. I stepped inside the elevator, looking over the buttons. Nothing for underground. "Ellington, take me down there."

Dad stepped on the elevator with me, scratching at his short beard.

Not with him here, Ellington said.

My gaze slid to Dad as I scratched at my arm. "You need to step off the elevator for a minute."

"No way," he said, sweeping out his hand. "I'm not leaving you alone. You need help, Tessa."

"Ellington won't help me if you stay," I said. Dad opened his mouth, but I cut him off. "I can't take another day of this possession. I need to send them back to the other side."

Leya took a hesitant step forward. "Tessa, maybe we should talk through this. You're not making much sense."

The patch of heat in my forearm blazed, expanding past my elbow and heading toward my shoulder. I tightened my hand into a fist. Why wouldn't they just listen to me? "I know what I'm doing."

"I know we need to exorcise Delilah and Ellington," Leya said, her eyes confused. "But how would going into some crypt . . ."

"Back off!" The snarled words left my throat with a rage I couldn't explain.

Leya stumbled back as if my words had slapped her. In a way, they had.

My arm shook with a fire that wanted to escape. The darkness slithered through me like it owned my body.

Dad ran his hand down his face. He rolled his eyes, and then cleared his throat, his face saying he couldn't believe what he was about to do. "Sorry, Ellington, but I'm not leaving my daughter alone with you. You have to take both of us."

Ellington's voice boomed across the lobby. *Sorry, Daddy, but just like your ancestors before you, your journey ends here.*

Dad's, Rita's, and Leya's eyes practically sprang out of their sockets as they stared past me at Ellington's outline. He'd finally made himself known to them.

A strong gush of wind swept into the elevator and shoved Dad in the chest. He flew backward, landing hard on his back on the carpet outside the elevator doors. Before anyone could stop them, the doors closed, leaving me alone in the elevator.

A soft jazz tune played from the speaker overhead as the elevator descended. Ellington's form leaned against the mirror, his arms folded, fingers tapping along with the beat.

The bitter anger inside me retreated to a corner but didn't fully go away.

"What did you mean about my dad's ancestors?" Another question instead of an answer.

They're your ancestors, too. Your roots are deep in Willow Marsh. When the elevator stopped, Ellington smiled at me. *I'll take you to the crypt where your ancestor is buried. Inside, there are treasures beyond your imagination. I only want one thing.*

I watched my arm, expecting it to turn red from the flames, but nothing happened. "Let me guess. A box?"

Yes. All I need you to do is open the box. Then you can have everything else.

"What's so special about this box? What's in it exactly? And none of the vague crap." I suddenly remembered him mentioning bringing Amá and Felix back to life.

Ellington smiled like he knew what I was thinking. *It's a portal, Tessa. One that can connect our worlds.*

"That sounds dangerous." Especially after what had happened in the bathroom and what was currently snaking through me. It felt rotten and evil.

No, Ellington said. *It's not. I promise. I can return to the living and help you with Willow Marsh. I can help you end the Harrison reign.* His smile twisted. *We can bring back your mom and brother. Your family can be whole again.*

This is everything you've wanted, Delilah said. *Having your family back together. Wait, can it bring me back, too?*

A part of me loved the idea of having Amá and Felix back, but the other part feared the unknown. If the portal could let in Ellington, Amá, and Felix, who else could it let in? It could be so much worse than the black smoke from the bathroom. Or Delilah.

Think of it, Ellington said. *You'll have both of them back. Physically. Doesn't that sound wonderful?*

My heart thrummed in my chest and ears. "Yes. But it sounds impossible. Too good to be true."

Let me show you, Tessa, he said in a silky-smooth tone. *I can prove how perfect it can be.*

The elevator doors pinged open.

CHAPTER 41

Darkness filled the area outside the elevator doors, masking the truth of what lay ahead.

You're almost there. Ellington's voice calmed me. *Keep straight. Don't look back.*

I stepped off the elevator, the cold filling my lungs. The heated darkness inside me push against the walls of my skin like it was trying to retreat. My breath drifted out in icy clouds as the doors closed behind me, cloaking me in a sea of black. When I took a candle out of my pocket, the matches fell to the floor. I bent down, trying to find them, but the wick lit on its own, giving me a dim view of the man-made tunnel that had been dug years before.

The frosty air soaked through my hoodie, pricking at my skin. Each unsteady step took me farther into the passageway, so far I was surprised I hadn't run into a dead end or turn.

A ding from the elevator echoed down the tunnel, so quiet I could tell I'd gone a far way. The only person who had been capable of breeching this floor was Ellington. But he didn't need to use the elevator. Had Dad found a way down?

"Dad?" My voice echoed against the rocky walls. Only silence answered.

The candle shook in my hand, sending wax trickling down the side and onto my hand. I welcomed the warmth. My feet and head fought on which way to go. Farther into the tunnel to find the crypt, or back to the elevator to see who had followed me?

Keep going, Ellington said.

Don't look back, Delilah said.

The crypt won the battle. I kept moving, each step across the uneven ground quicker than the last. I rounded another corner when I heard footsteps pattering behind me. Turning, I held up the candle, my eyes searching the darkness.

"Hello?" My voice was surprisingly steady. I waited a minute before I gave up and continued through the tunnel.

The stale air thinned out the farther in I went, and I worried about how long I could be down there. After at least five minutes – and me checking over my shoulder numerous times – the tunnel opened into a cavern. The airflow seemed much stronger in the open area.

Using my candle, I lit a torch on the wall. I walked around the circle, lighting each torch until the entire cavern lit up.

I gasped in surprise. The whole crypt was full of relics. Swords, knives, handguns, and rifles. A rusted Gatling gun sat in the corner, and wooden chests lined the walls. Three caskets lay in the crypt. I walked over to one, running my fingers along the dusty top layer. Cool metal brushed against my skin. Removing some dirt, I read a plaque on the casket. *Joseph Walker.* I checked the entryway to make sure no one had come in before I set my candle on top of his casket.

Your ancestor. Ellington floated next to me, his figure getting brighter. *You're a Walker, Tessa.*

They'd thought Delilah was a Walker, too. I so didn't want to end up with her fate.

The other two caskets revealed the names *Albert Harrison* and *Roy Ellington.*

That's me, Ellington said, his thin hand patting the top. *My body lies in that casket.*

"That's so weird." My gaze flitted to the empty archway. I was still alone.

I went over to one of the chests and tried to open it. Locked.

The key, Delilah said.

Before we left the house, I'd grabbed the key I'd found in Trenton's locker – I'd had a feeling I'd need it. Pulling the key from my back pocket, I slipped it into the lock, but it wouldn't turn. I scanned the crypt, looking for something I could use to pry the chest open.

My gaze stopped in the center of the room, where a wood carved pedestal stood with a copper box resting on the top. Something echoed out in the tunnel, like a small rock being kicked against the wall. I had to hurry.

My hand inched out toward the box, fingers grazing it, when a figure jumped from the tunnel, crashing into me and sending us to the ground. Two sturdy hands wrapped around my neck. Reed Harrison. He squeezed tight, closing off my airway. My legs thrashed around in a pathetic attempt to wriggle free.

"So very kind of you to lead me to the crypt, Tessa." Reed's tone was tranquil as his hands tightened around my throat. Scratches surrounded his eyes from his encounter with Ellington in the elevator.

Knowing his eyes would be sore, I shoved my thumbs into them as hard as I could until he loosened his hold on me. I kicked his stomach with all I had, and Reed rolled off me. I stumbled away, creating a safe distance between us.

"How did you get down here?" I asked, holding an arm

across my ribs. Inside me, the darkness came back to life and hummed through me.

Reed's watering eyes found mine. "Just like you did."

A silver candlestick lay on the floor near my feet. Picking it up, I chucked it at Reed's head, connecting with his cheek. "That's not possible."

He stretched out his neck before he ran at me with a low, guttural sound. I barely avoided him, going around Ellington's coffin to create a barrier between Reed and me.

"We have a mutual friend." Reed took a tentative step toward me, his hands held out in front of him, reading for an attack.

He lies! Ellington hissed.

"Oh, Ellington, you know I'm not the one lying." Reed's eyes were locked behind me.

Slowly turning, I saw Ellington's opaque form hovering above Joseph Walker's casket. Ellington ran his hand over the flame from the candle. *I can almost feel the heat.*

"You can see him? Hear him?" I asked Reed.

Reed scoffed, amusement in his light blue eyes as he ran his hand along his beard. "Of course I can. He's quite helpful when he wants to be."

My eyes went back to Ellington as denial welled inside me. "You've been helping him, too?"

Ellington's one-sided smile filled me with dread. *I need both of you.* He swept out his hands. *Here we are. An Ellington, a Walker, and a Harrison.*

"Why did you help us separately?" I asked, looking between the two of them. "Why not just do it together?" The darkness scratched at my muscles, itching to take over.

Ellington pointed his fingers at us. *I could never get you two together without one trying to kill the other.* He looked at the ground, a slight frown resting on his opaque lips. *I'm not as strong when I work with you individually. Especially with Reed. I couldn't relay the messages I wanted.* He clapped his hands and intertwined his fingers, his smile returning. *Doesn't matter now. We're here.*

"Why do you need me?" I wanted to hear it from his mouth and finally get some answers.

He held his clasped hands up, both his index fingers pointing at me like a gun. *You're a descendent of Joseph Walker. You hold the power Delilah lacked.*

"What do you mean?" I asked as I fought to keep the darkness at bay.

His form shrugged. *Thought Delilah was a descendent of a Walker. Turns out she wasn't. Oops.*

Oops? Delilah shrieked. *I died because of his mistake!*

"Well, FYI," I said, folding my arms. "She's pretty pissed at you. As she should be." The darkness caressed my skin, so I squeezed my arms tighter, hoping to block the passageways. "Are you positive I'm a Walker? I mean, you thought Delilah was, and look how that turned out."

Reed grinned, massaging the back of his neck. "The world doesn't miss her." He leaned his back against Albert Harrison's casket, his tone caramel sweet. "When I first heard your name, I thought it sounded familiar." He scratched his beard along his jaw line. "Turns out, Joseph's wife?"

Ellington cut in. *Her maiden name is Tessa Isaacson.*

CHAPTER 42

Goosebumps crawled up my arms, contrasting with the heat flaring inside. I knew I'd been named after Dad's grandma, but I really hadn't done much research on the matter. I realized I knew so much about Amá's side of the family, but not my dad's.

I pulled out my phone, wanting to do a search of Tessa Isaacson Walker, but I had no service down in the crypt.

It's true, Tessa, Ellington said. *Joseph and Tessa Walker are your great-grandparents.*

"So, you need my blood?" No way was I letting that happen.

Ellington motioned to the box. *With blood from me, Joseph, and Albert, I was able to forge the box using the magical powers here in Willow Marsh.* He smiled softly at me, almost like a proud grandparent. *I've been waiting years for the right person to come along and help me. I needed someone with your strength, Tessa.* He started to fade, and panic flooded his eyes. *We're running out of time. I've led you both to your treasure. Now help me.*

Reed leaned to the side as his twisted smile lit up his baby blue eyes. "I'm not helping you. I have what I want. I'll kill

Tessa, you'll disappear, and I'll be rich. I'll finally do what no one else in my family could."

Killing her won't end me. His wavering eyes didn't convince me.

"She's your link." Reed smoothed out his wrinkled flannel jacket. "With her dead, your power is gone."

Kill Reed, Delilah said. *Before he kills you.*

Reed sauntered toward me, hunger burning in his eyes that matched the darkness lurking inside me. I backed away, going around the coffin to keep the barrier. "How did you know where we were the other night?"

He stopped walking, folding his arms on the casket and leaning toward me. "I had help." His eyes flickered toward Ellington for half a second. "I'd been communicating with my grandpa." He stuck out his bottom lip in a pout. "He told me how naughty you were being and that you'd expose the fact that I killed Greg."

I spotted a sword in the corner, but I probably couldn't get to it before Reed stopped me. And I had no idea how to even use it. "And me? Why did you try to kill me?"

"He told me you and your family would threaten me, so I knew I had to take action." His creamy tone was almost hypnotizing. "But then Ellington told me that we needed you and your Walker blood, so I changed my mind. I knew Ellington wouldn't bring me here without you." He looked past me. "You're stronger than me when it comes to the other side." He pulled a small handgun from his pocket and gently set it on the casket. "Enough small talk."

On a wooden crate to my left, I saw a silver knife with a wooden handle. "Yeah, I've seen your aim," I said, taking small steps toward the knife. "It sucks." The darkness pushed against my muscles, helping me move.

Reed grinned as he rapped his knuckles on the casket. "Like all those times I've been *drunk*." There was a weird edge to his syrupy voice. "You know how easy it is to pretend you're wasted when you're not? I wanted people in the town to fear me. Let them know I can be dangerous when I've had one too many. It's an easy ruse."

"I've smelled the alcohol on you," I said. Every time his gaze left me, I took another step, which caused the dark spirit to pulse with life.

"Easy to pour a little beer or whiskey on my clothes." He stared down at his tattered, stained flannel jacket and sighed. "I will say it'll be nice when I don't have to wear this again. I can go back to my normal sober self. Everyone will think I've cleaned up my act and trust me."

I was almost within reach of the knife. "You still squandered all your money. You're careless."

He smirked and rubbed his hand over his thick beard. "Did I now? Huh. Again, appearances can be deceiving." He picked up his gun, his finger sliding to the trigger. "As much as I love an occasional repartee, I'm getting quite bored with this idle chitchat."

I moved toward the knife seconds before his gun went off, firing a shot at me. Ellington had hurled a blast of air at Reed's hand, moving the gun enough to throw off his aim. The bullet sped by me, lodging into the crypt wall.

My hands flew to my ears, even though it was too late to dull the loud crack from the gunfire that echoed off the rock walls. Snatching up the knife, I ducked down and hid behind the coffin. I turned the small knife over in my hand. I'd have to get close to Reed to use it, and I wanted to avoid that if possible.

The guns, Delilah squealed.

No, I said back. *They're old. They won't work.* Inside, my dark passenger gripped the knife, its longing to use it almost overpowering.

Try one, Delilah said.

They probably don't have bullets, I said.

Reed sprang around the corner, firing another round. Ellington heaved another gust of air to throw off the aim, but he was a little too slow, and the bullet grazed my cheek. Tears pooled in my eyes from the sting, so much that for a moment, everything looked like we were underwater.

Blood trickled down my skin, but I didn't have time to wipe it away. I dove toward a revolver, my hand wrapping around the old, brown handle.

Ellington's form stood between Reed and me. *Enough! You can both live. Share the treasure.*

"She knows too much." Reed pulled the trigger. The bullet went right through Ellington's ghost and over my head. "Do you know how hard I've worked to get here? What I've had to do to claim what's rightfully mine? I will not let some stupid teenage girl ruin everything for me."

I ran to Walker's casket and hid behind it, my back pressed up against the cool stone. Any hope I had vanished when I got a good look at the gun. Rusted. With some force – and I'm quite certain the aid of the dark spirit – I pushed open the cylinder to check for ammo. Two rounds.

Kill Reed, Delilah said.

"This won't work," I said through clenched teeth. "It's completely rusted."

It will work, she sang.

"It could blow up in my hand!" My passenger used my thumb to stroke the handle of the gun like it was petting it.

Trust me, Delilah said.

Amá whispered in my ear. *Don't trust her or Ellington, mi amor.*

"Are you sure?" I asked, fighting to keep control of my limbs.

Suddenly, Ellington was sitting next to me. His figure pulsated. *Who are you talking to?*

My hand tightened around the revolver. "None of your business."

"Let's end this." Reed's sugary voice came from the other side of the casket. "You can't win this battle, Tessa. I'll give you a little history lesson: The Walkers always lose."

That is true. Ellington shrugged and straightened out one of his gold buttons. *But that could change today. We don't need him. Just his blood. Kill him. Then the treasure will be entirely yours.*

I glared at Ellington. "Why should I trust you? You've been talking to both of us!" The darkness slithered through my veins, desperately wanting to destroy me from the inside out. It worked its way up my neck, heading for my eyes.

I thought we could all work together. Reed is turning out to be more problematic than I thought. Ellington sighed. *All the Harrisons are like that.* His hand flew out just as Reed came behind the casket and fired his gun. The bullet lodged into the coffin, right next to my head.

Biting through the pain in my ribs, I crawled away just as another round went off. Ellington stayed close to me.

"Stop this chase." Reed's tone twinged on madness. He fired a shot at Ellington's casket, the sound thunderous. I worried I'd be deaf at the end of it all.

Kill him! Ellington roared.

Do it, Delilah chanted.

"What if the revolver explodes?" I stared at it. The rusted metal contrasted with the silk scarf wrapped around my hand.

It won't. I promise, Delilah said. *It will work. Just point and shoot.*

The revolver shook in my hand. The thought of killing another human being made my stomach queasy, even if he was trying to kill me.

My dark passenger hissed past my ear. *Let me help.*

I shivered despite the raging fire inside.

You've done it before, Delilah said with a huff.

"No." I licked my lips, eyeing the scarf covering the scar on my hand. "That was an accident. If the deer hadn't been in the road..."

You still would have crashed. Delilah drew out the next words. *You were high on drugs.*

"Maybe. Maybe not." I realized I hadn't heard Amá in a while. "Amá? Are you still here?"

She can't help you. Ellington pointed a lanky finger into his chest. *Only I can.*

Flames from the darkness licked my throat from the inside. The spirit expanded to my toes and fingers, making them throb with my heartbeat.

I pressed a fist against the side of my head. "She can help me!"

Yet I am here. She is not. Ellington hummed a song I didn't recognize.

She's left you all alone, Delilah said. *Proof she hasn't forgiven you.*

"Amá!" My whole body shook, fighting off the dark spirit. "I need you, Amá."

Tessa... Her voice was faint, echoing in the room.

Ellington quirked an eyebrow. He'd heard her. *Not now, mommy dearest. We're busy.*

Kill Reed, Delilah said. *He killed me, remember? Justice. Kill. Kill. Kill.* She said the last words quickly together, like a song.

Ellington faded until I couldn't see him anymore.

"Ellington?" I wheezed.

Reed rounded the corner, head cocked to the side, his gun raised, pointed straight at me. "He can't help you forever."

Use the revolver, Delilah screeched. *Do it! Pull the trigger!*

"No. I can't." I wouldn't. No matter how much I hated Reed, I wasn't a murderer. There had to be another way.

"Oh, looks like we might be back to an interesting topic."

A smile tugged at Reed's lips. "Are you still talking to Ellington, darling Tessa?"

Let go, the dark passenger taunted in a fizzy tone. *Stop fighting me, and I can help.*

"Shut up!" I slapped my free hand against my forehead. "Just shut up!"

Kill. Kill. Kill, Delilah sang.

"Looks like someone is going crazy." Reed's body leaned to the right. "What are the voices in your head telling you?"

Lowering my hand, I looked him in the eye. "To kill you."

Reed chuckled. "With what? That old gun in your hand? You know it won't work."

It will. It will. It will, Delilah said in a singsong voice.

Do it, the dark spirit hissed.

"Delusion runs in the Walker family." Reed kept the gun pointed at my chest. "Like your Aunt Jillian. It's why my dad failed with her. It's why the Walkers were never fit to run Willow Marsh."

My insides churned. "What do you mean, your dad failed with Aunt Jillian?" How did he know about her?

Jillian. Had she not been crazy? Was the voice in her head Ellington?

"We've been trying to find a Walker for years so Ellington would take us down here," Reed said. "Dad thought he was getting somewhere with Jillian. With the help of Ellington, he convinced her to move here." He rolled up his sleeve and pointed to the scar on his arm. "This is thanks to her. She tried to escape. If I hadn't been so young, I probably wouldn't have walked away with a scar." He rolled his sleeve back down. "Like all the others, she failed." He waved his gun at me. "You are much stronger, thanks to your mom."

We can do it, Delilah said.

Yessss, the darkness said. It tapped along the bones in my hand holding the gun.

"Harrisons were always meant to be in charge." Reed took a step closer to me, his voice steady. "It's why we've thrived while the Walkers . . ." He ran his fingers through his beard. "Are dead."

Delilah snickered. *Goodbye, Reed.*

Ice flooded my veins, taking over the fire from the darkness. I watched in horror as my hand tightened around the revolver. My arm lifted, pointing the gun at Reed. Delilah had overtaken me, her spirit even stronger than my dark passenger. With my other hand, I placed it against my arm and tried to lower it, but Delilah was too powerful.

"Go ahead," Reed said, opening his arms wide, his gun now pointed at his ancestor's casket, and his finger hanging loosely on the trigger. "Pull the trigger. Either nothing will happen, or you'll blow your hand off."

Pull. Pull. Pull, Delilah sang.

My hand shook, trying to fight off Delilah. "I can't."

Then he will kill you. Delilah clucked her tongue. *You or him. You or him. You or him.*

"Pull it." Reed's light blue eyes danced. The arrogance in his stance astounded me. He thought he was invincible.

Pull. Delilah and the darkness whispered in unison.

The sound of the gunfire echoed through the crypt as smoke wafted from the barrel in a slithering gray cloud. The gun slipped from my shaking hands and clanged on the hard ground.

Reed stared at me with his jaw dropped. He slowly fell, landing on his knees. His wide, milky eyes never wavered from mine as his gun fell from his grip, and his body slumped down to the ground.

Told you it would work, Delilah sang.

The bullet had hit him near the heart. I didn't think the gun would fire. It was too old and rusted. The possibility was slim to none.

You had me to help, Delilah cooed. Her ice stayed in place, holding the darkness at bay.

My steps were shaky as I moved toward Reed, who twisted on the ground and choked on his blood. I stood over him in shock, watching the life drain from his eyes.

I'd killed Reed Harrison.

CHAPTER 43

I'd never intentionally killed someone before. The first two were accidental. My head didn't know how to comprehend the situation. None of it seemed real.

You did it. Ellington came into focus, resting on top of his casket. *Good girl.*

"Where did you go?" I forced the words from my dry mouth as I stared at my hand that had held the gun.

He pointed his finger at me. *You pushed me away.*

I shook my head. "No, I didn't."

You need to make me whole. He hopped off the coffin. *I saved you. Now you save me.*

My gaze turned to Reed's dead body. Nausea rose in my stomach, and I placed a shaking hand to my lips. A layer of fog lifted from the ground until it completely covered his body.

My focus went to Ellington. "How can I save you?"

He nodded his head toward something behind me. I slowly turned, seeing the wooden pedestal. On top of it sat a copper box, roughly the size of Felix's ukulele, in the shape of a family crest. Images and words had been carved into the top and sides. The Ellington family crest. I reached my hand out, hoping to touch it, but an electrical current flew from the box the closer my hand got.

The darkness zapped away from it, sizzling in pain. My own power deep inside me ignited, a brilliant orb full of goodness and light. It began to grow, snuffing out the darkness until it was a tiny speck near my heart.

Open it. Ellington's low whisper had a slightly strained edge. *Connect our worlds.*

What about me? Delilah asked with hope. *Can this bring me back, too?*

"Will this work for Delilah, too?" I asked Ellington.

His head jerked back. *What does she have to do with this?*

I looked at my hands, which were glowing a faint blue. "She's in my head. In my body."

Ellington flinched but covered it up just as quickly. *Then, of course. Delilah will come back since she is with you. You can have Amá and Felix back. You can undo your mistake.*

No, Tessa, Amá said in a gentle tone. *Destroy the box.*

"Amá?" She was back.

Don't listen to her! Ellington bellowed.

My hands went to my head, wanting to stop the voices, but I couldn't. Wind circled the room, trapping me and the box in a barrier.

White light filtered out through the cracks of the lid, glowing brighter with each passing second. The speck trembled behind my heart, afraid. Inside, my lungs constricted, closing off my airway.

Do it. Ellington's ghost appeared behind the box. *Lift the latch.* His eyes were hungry and wild.

Help me, Tessa. Felix. Set me free.

I took a trembling step forward, closing the distance between me and the box. It quivered on the pedestal.

Tessa, listen to me, Amá's sweet voice said. She continued to talk, but I tuned her out.

My hand itched to flip the latch up and release the power inside. To see Amá again. To hug Felix and hold him in my arms. Hear him play his ukulele and see Amá's smile.

The hole in my heart yearned for it.

Shouts sounded inside the wall of wind. I thought I heard my name, but the wind blew it away. The wall rose higher, reaching floor to ceiling, the current growing stronger.

Ellington watched me, his eyes beckoning me to move closer. Daring me to.

Tessa, I need you. Felix laughed, the sound horribly distorted.

Amá appeared beside me in her angelic form, her warm hand landing on my arm. The second it did, the speck of darkness popped, leaving no trace of the dark passenger inside me.

Tessa, mi amor, Felix isn't here. He's moved on. You need to as well.

I'm here! Felix's voice pleaded.

Amá's hand brushed along my hair, sending a flow of strength through my bones. *Your head deceives you. Be strong.*

My watering eyes sought out Ellington. "Will this really bring them back?"

Yes, he said. *It will make our souls more defined. We can walk with you on solid ground.*

Amá moved so that she stood between Ellington and me. *Listen to me. The power in that box will destroy you. It will give Ellington power no soul should have. It will only help him, no one else. It was designed only for Ellington family blood.*

She lies! Ellington yelled.

Amá smiled, the gesture reaching her loving and kind eyes. *My sweet Tessa, I love you more than words can say. I don't blame you. It was an accident. You're strong and smart. You have to let go of the past and move on. Felix and I will be waiting for you when the time comes, but, my darling girl, that time isn't now. Donde quiera que moramos, siempre seremos familia.*

Wherever we dwell, we will always be family.

Ellington tried to move toward us, but Amá's soul was too strong. It was pure. Full of love and hope.

Destroy the box, Amá said, her hands clasped calmly in front of her. *Overcome your demons.*

Tears slid down my cheeks. "I don't want to let go."

I know, Amá said. *But you must. Now.*

The box glowed bright, shaking and bursting at the seams. "How would I even destroy it?"

NO! Ellington yelled.

Amá swept her arm toward him, sending Ellington's soul flying through his casket. Her kind eyes turned to me. *Your blood, it's strong, Tessa.* Her focus went to the family ring on my finger. *So is the power inside of you. Four drops of your blood on top of the box.* She motioned to my candle on Walker's casket. *Four drops of wax to seal the blood.*

Ellington wept. *Please, Tessa. Save me. Help me. Don't condemn my family.*

Do it before your power opens the box forever, Amá said.

I searched the relics until I found a knife. Even though I shook, I forced myself to walk to the box and stand in front of it. The light pouring from the cracks was almost blinding.

Think of Felix, Ellington said in a desperate plea.

Taking the blade, I slashed my left palm, grinding my teeth in pain. I let the knife fall to the floor.

What are you doing? Delilah sounded grossed out. *That knife is so not sanitary.*

"I have to." My voice quavered. I held my palm over the box, a drop of blood falling into each section of the crest. A willow tree. White. A vampire finch. Black.

The images from my vision the night I summoned Amá for the first time.

Inside my body, the electrical current pulsed through my veins. Being so close to the box gave me a power I couldn't explain.

See how good that feels? Delilah purred. *Don't destroy the box. Use the power yourself.*

Fight it, Amá said.

The key grew warm in my jeans pocket. I took it out, running my thumb over it, and it glowed. The box pulled at the key, the force strong.

Use the key, Ellington said with reverence. *Unlock the box. See Felix. Erase your mistake.*

Open, open, open, Delilah sang.

"No." I put the key back in my pocket, grabbed the candle from Walker's casket, and forced my aching body back to the rattling box.

Seal the blood, Amá said.

With a shaking hand, I poured a drop of wax on the blood on the willow tree, and then the white. Delilah fought me. With my other hand, I shoved with all my might until the candle was over the box again. Another drop of wax fell onto the blood on the vampire finch. It sizzled on impact.

Ellington fell to his knees, his hand on his chest. The wall of wind sped up, swirling my hair and scarf.

In my pocket, the key heated even warmer. It burned through my jeans pocket, scalding my skin. I yanked it out as fast as I could and threw it. The key caught in the wind, circling around me.

Get the key! Ellington yelled.

Key. Key. Key! Delilah shouted.

You'll die if you don't! Ellington said. *The power will consume you.*

Do you want to die tonight? Delilah asked.

I pounded my free hand against my forehead. "LEAVE ME ALONE!" Taking the candle, I hovered it over the last section of the box. Before the wax could fall, the fire from the wick suddenly sprang up and twisted, turning until it connected with the scarf on my hand and ignited it.

Dropping the candle, I unwrapped the scarf and threw it into the wind, the fire blowing out. My scar throbbed with pain, the area around it bright red. The reminder of what I'd done to my mom and brother taunted me. I fisted my hand. I couldn't bring them back, but I had a chance to make things right.

The candle rolled along the floor, somehow still lit. Forcing through the pain in my ribs and Delilah's fight for control, I retrieved the candle from the ground and held it over the box. Wax slowly plopped onto the last drop of my blood. Together, the blood and wax spread, covering the whole box, slipping into every seam.

What did you do? Ellington's eyes were wide with terror. He started to fade.

Destroy it, Amá said.

"With what?" I asked.

Your power, mi amor. Amá's voice soothed my soul and calmed the wind around me.

With both hands, I reached for the box. Strings of electricity flew from it toward my hands. Toward my ring. The moment I touched it, the box warmed, burning hotter and hotter. Inside my body, my blood boiled. Every muscle tingled. I wanted to let go, but I held on tight. Ellington and Delilah continued to yell at me, but I pushed them out, focusing all my thoughts and energy on the box. I didn't care if it killed me. I would never let Ellington or any other soul have that kind of power.

Te amo, Amá said, so clearly.

The box burst, the copper remnants flying all around me

as Ellington and Delilah howled. The wind came to a halt, disappearing like it had never been there. I stared at myself, expecting to explode with the power glowing through my skin, but it slowly dissolved until I returned to a normal state.

I stood alone in the freezing crypt. The box shattered. Amá silent. Reed dead.

Ellington gone.

Felix gone. Only, he'd never been there. That had been Ellington toying with my emotions. It all became so clear. He had used Reed and me.

I ran a finger along my scar. At least I knew Amá and Felix were in a safe place. A better place. I'd see them again, but my time on earth wasn't done. Not yet.

The key sat on the floor near Ellington's casket. I picked it up, surprised to find it cool to the touch. I'd just grabbed my candle, ready to leave, when something made me stop and pick up the sword – like I needed proof of where I'd been.

Shaking, I made the long walk back to the elevator, in way too much shock to process everything that had happened. There were no buttons lining the wall. Ellington couldn't help me. I could feel in my soul and bones that he'd moved on to the other side at last.

I twirled the key in one hand and used the other to move the candle along the wall. To the right of the elevator, I saw a key hole. I inserted the key, twisted it, and the elevator doors pinged open.

Classical music played as I rose to the main floor. I held the sword at my side as I leaned against the elevator wall, tears wanting to come, but emptiness holding them back.

I searched my head for Delilah, but she was silent.

Gone forever.

CHAPTER 44

The second the elevator doors opened on the main floor, I took a step back in surprise. I wasn't sure what I had been expecting, but it hadn't crossed my mind that the place would be flooded with people. They probably hadn't been expecting the elevator doors to suddenly open, and there I was, disheveled, tired, and holding a sword.

Rita and her husband, Hal, stood in the corner of the lobby. Police were taping off areas and setting those little yellow crime scene numbers on the ground. City workers were with the sheriff, hovering over a plastic table covered in maps. To my surprise, Sheriff Hayes let out a huge sigh of relief at the sight of me.

Jade and Marcel were near the front doors having a heated debate until they saw me, and Jade broke out in grateful tears.

I only caught a blur of Leya before she threw her arms around me, her swift motion causing the elevator to bounce a little. I dropped the sword and hugged her back. The doors started to close, but Graham held out an arm to stop it.

Graham. When we locked eyes, I was expecting anger,

disappointment, something along those lines, but all I saw was concern and elation swirling together.

A police officer stepped onto the elevator and locked it in place. I heard the sword being lifted from the ground, but my focus was on Leya in my arms.

She sobbed into my neck as I held her close. Inhaling her pineapple scent, feeling her real, live, human form, confirmed that I'd made the right choice by destroying the box. Amá and Felix would never come back to me, but I still had people here worth staying for.

And I knew in my heart I'd see my mom and brother again. Just not in this lifetime.

Sheriff Hayes approached the elevator, his somber eyes on my bloody cheek. "You're hurt."

Shaking my head, I dropped my arms from around Leya, but she stayed right by my side and held my hand. "I'm fine. Only grazed." I scanned the room again, but my dad was nowhere in sight. I swallowed, trying to find the energy to talk. "Where's my dad?"

Graham's eyes went to the floor, and Leya's hand tightened around mine. Jade and Marcel walked closer, Jade's teary eyes on me. They stopped next to Graham.

The sheriff held up a palm. "Let me start with, he's safe."

My eyebrows furrowed. "Safe from what?"

"When Reed showed up earlier, he shot your dad," Sheriff Hayes said. When I gasped, he leaned toward me. "He's fine, Tessa. The bullet went through his leg, but no major arteries were hit, and we got him to the hospital quickly. He'll be okay."

Reed had shot him? That made me feel slightly better about shooting Reed. At least Dad hadn't been killed. "He'll be okay," I said, more to myself than anyone else.

A deputy handed the sheriff the sword I had brought up.

Sheriff Hayes looked it over, his thick eyebrows shooting up. He looked at me. "Where did you get this?"

"Where were you?" Leya finally spoke. Tears stained her cheeks and soaked the top of her sweatshirt.

"What happened?" Marcel asked, eyes eager.

Jade hiccupped. "Don't ever do something like that again!"

"You don't even know what happened," I slowly said.

Jade wiped at her nose with the sleeve of her jacket. "You disappeared! Reed went after you with a gun! Right after Corrine was . . ." She leaned her head on Marcel's shoulder. He put his arm around her and held her close.

"I want to see my dad," I said, looking at the sheriff.

He held out the sword. "After you tell me where you got this. And where Reed is." He sighed. "And where you've been."

I could feel Graham staring at me, but when I looked at him, his focus went back to the ground. He was slumped against the wall like he was in pain or upset. It was hard to get a good feel on the right mood.

Everyone – aside from Graham – watched me, waiting for the story. I was too tired to tell it all, and I really wanted to see my dad, so I decided to give a brief recount. "Your town . . ." I paused. It was my town now, too. "Our town has a crypt below this building."

I ran my finger over the key in my pocket. There was a good chance that when I handed the key over to the sheriff, he'd walk away with all the treasure. I glanced around the room, taking in all the witnesses. Maybe if everyone knew about it – plus having Reed dead so Sheriff Hayes could no longer be on his payroll – would help the sheriff soften.

Taking a gamble, I held out the key to the sheriff, who took it hesitantly into his hand. "That will get you down there," I said. "There's a bunch of relics from the Civil War." I motioned to the sword. "Just like that." My fist opened and closed, remembering the weight of the gun. "You'll find Reed down there. He attacked me, and I . . ."

I killed the man.

"He's dead?" Leya whispered.

I slowly nodded.

Sheriff Hayes threw his head back, rubbing his thumb and forefinger on his eyes. His whole body relaxed, almost like he was relieved. Maybe the sheriff hated the Harrisons as much as everyone else. There was a chance he never wanted to be on their payroll. But it wasn't like I could ask. It did make me feel better about my choice of giving him the key.

"How did you find the crypt?" Sheriff Hayes finally asked. He turned the key over in his hand. "And where did you get this?"

I rubbed my forehead. "It's a long story, and I promise I'll tell you later. Right now, I want to see my dad."

The sheriff stared at the key for a long moment before he responded. "Fine. We've got a lot to do here anyway." His gentle eyes found mine. "But I want the full story tomorrow morning." It was weird to see such a different side of him – but I liked this version. It gave me hope that I made the right choice.

With a nod, I stepped off the elevator with Leya at my side.

"Hey, Tessa," the sheriff said.

I looked over my shoulder at him.

He smiled softly. "I'm glad you're okay."

When I turned back around, Jade hugged me, squeezing way too tight for my ribs – and in general.

She let me go after a while, and then punched my arm. "I'm glad you didn't die."

I rubbed my arm where she'd struck me. "Yeah, me too."

Marcel patted my shoulder. "Do you need a ride to the hospital?"

"No." I turned to Graham, wanting to ask him for a ride, but he was headed outside. I jogged after him, leaving the others behind.

He'd barely stepped out onto the street when I caught him. Flashing lights from cop cars lit up his sad face.

"Will you give me a ride to the hospital?" I asked.

His jaw tightened. "You should ask your boyfriend." He shifted his eyes past me, so I glanced over my shoulder.

Blake stood near some of his friends, and with a lot of the town. They were all gathered in the street, mumbling to one another. Blake smiled when he saw me, giving me a little wave, but when I snarled at him, he lowered his hand and took a step back, his smile shattering on the asphalt. Now that Delilah was gone, it was going to be so much easier to shut Blake out of my life.

I turned back to Graham, wanting to talk, but he was already a block away, heading toward his truck, which was parked along the curb. Even though I ached everywhere, I ran, getting to his truck at the same time as him and putting my hand on his arm.

"You got the text," I said.

He pounded a fist against the side of the truck. "Ss...sure did."

I pointed to the building. "But you looked happy to see me when the elevator opened."

He stared at me incredulously. "Of course I ww...was. I don't ww...want you to die." He wrapped a fist around the handle and opened the driver side door. "But I don't do love triangles."

I couldn't help the laugh that rumbled up my throat and out of my mouth.

Graham pulled back in surprise. "You're laughing? How could you laugh at this?" He stepped close to me, his voice low. "I care about you, Tessa. A lot." Shaking his head, he ran his fingers through his shaggy hair. "But I can't just sit around while Delilah uses you."

I swallowed. "You knew it was her? Not me?"

"Of course. You're not cruel like that, Tessa." He took a deep, shaky breath. "Do you know how hard it was to see that picture? To see you kissing Blake? In your . . ." His cheeks flared as his gaze dropped to my chest. Graham was probably thinking about my bra. "Until she's gone, I just can't. I'm sorry."

I leaned against his truck and stared at my hands. "Do you know what it's like to be chained up in your own body? I had absolutely no control. I had to watch as Delilah sent that text."

His eyes softened, the hurt chipping away.

I let out a shaky breath. "If Blake's stepmom hadn't come in the room . . . Blake . . . Delilah . . . they would have . . ." I thought back to our bodies tangled on Blake's bed, and I shuddered.

Graham's strong arms wrapped around me and pulled me against his chest. The side of his lips pressed against my hair. "I'm so sorry she did that to you."

I clung to his hoodie, the material scrunched in my fists so tightly, I would probably leave permanent marks. "I hate her. I hate him. So much."

His steady hand stroked my hair. "You have to get rid of her. Things can't go on like this."

"She's gone. She's crossed over to the other side."

He jerked his head back and looked at me. "What? When?"

"Down in the crypt. I felt her leave."

His whole body sighed in relief.

I placed my hands on his cheeks. "You're the one I want. You always have been."

He leaned his forehead against mine and whispered, "You've had my heart since the day we met."

My smile interfered with his kiss at first, because it wouldn't lessen or go away. He kept pressing his lips to mine, giving me small kisses.

"How do I get you to loosen up?" he mumbled against my lips.

I let go of the back of his hoodie so I could slap his chest.

"That's not what I meant," he said. "I just want you to relax."

He placed his warm hands firmly on my cheeks, looking deep into my eyes like he was staring straight into my slightly off-colored soul. His nose brushed against mine, knocking the smile off my face. Tingles erupted on my skin, my heart on the verge of shattering my ribcage, heat flaring in my neck and cheeks as blood rushed everywhere.

His perfect lips kissed mine as his hand slid behind my neck and into my hair. Lifting onto my tiptoes, I pushed our bodies closer, feeling his heat soak into me as our lips moved against each other. His other hand landed on the small of my back, holding me steady.

He kissed me like I was the only thing that mattered in the world.

"You two were made for each other." Leya's voice rang out in the still of the night.

Graham grunted, but pulled away, taking my hand in his.

Leya stood in front of the truck and folded her arms. "Seriously. Tessa went below the building to do who knows what, her dad got SHOT by freaking Reed Harrison, and instead of heading straight to the hospital, you two decide to cozy up on the street and make out." She waltzed to the passenger side of the truck.

"So weird," she continued. "You're like twisted soul mates. It's disturbing and downright romantic at the same time." She opened the passenger side door of Graham's truck and stared at us, a small smile pulling at her lips. "Why am I happy? This shouldn't make me happy, but it does." She hopped inside the truck.

Graham helped me in through the driver's side, and I slid to the middle. I squeezed his hand. "Why did you even come here?"

He drummed his fingers along my leg. "Leya called like a thousand times. Even though I was mad about the picture, I still didn't want anything to happen to you."

"Let's not get all dramatic," Leya said. "It was more like a hundred." She pointed to Graham. "Thank goodness he showed up when he did. He saw Reed holding the gun and totally sprang at him, throwing off the aim. If he hadn't done that . . ."

I turned to Graham. "You saved my dad."

He started up the truck. "I couldn't let Reed take someone else that matters to you. To anyone. But he scrambled into the elevator before any of us could stop him." He stared at the steering wheel. "Just do me a favor and maybe take a break from séances?"

I pressed my lips to his cheek. "Deal."

CHAPTER 45

I barged into Dad's hospital room, not caring that a nurse was checking his vitals, or that another nurse was running after me in the hall because I'd gone back without permission.

I immediately went to him and threw my arms around his neck. We hugged and cried until the nurses made us separate. Suzie, the nurse from my previous stay, tended the wound on my cheek from the bullet and my arm from when the glass had shattered in my bathroom.

After she and the other nurse left, I told Dad, Graham, and Leya everything that happened in the crypt. It took a while, especially when I got to the part about shooting Reed.

Dad ran his hand down his face. "Another Harrison we don't have to worry about." He must have seen the heartache in my eyes. "Don't beat yourself up." He flinched, hesitating on the next part. "Delilah took control of you. You did what you had to do to survive. He would have killed you if you hadn't." For him to believe that was a huge step.

Leya's eyes were wide. "I can't believe you killed someone.

I mean, I know it was self-defense and like possession and all of that, but oh my! That's just crazy. Was it weird?"

"Yes," I said, trying to hold in a smile. She cheered me up without trying. "I wouldn't recommend it to anyone."

"Especially ww...with a rusted gun." Graham rubbed the back of his neck. "You're lucky you didn't gg...get hurt."

Dad adjusted his hospital robe. "I can't believe it worked after all these years."

"Fate, people," Leya sang. "It was on her side. Good always triumphs over evil." She batted her eyelashes at Graham and me. "Graham triumphed over Blake."

Dad's jaw clenched, his eyes darting between Graham and me. "Are you two . . . together?"

Graham took a step away from Dad, his blinking eyes showing no signs of slowing down. "Uh." Raking his fingers through his hair, he wet his lips and tapped his other fingers against his leg.

I took Graham's hand to pull him toward me, but he tried to step farther away. I ended up yanking him so hard, he stumbled toward me. He quickly righted himself, his face bright red.

Leya snapped a picture with her phone. "So uploading this and all its awkward glory."

"Dad, Graham and I are together."

Dad's hand tightened around his hospital robe. "Are you now?"

I squeezed Graham's hand. "Yes. Don't kill him, okay? He's a good guy."

"What happened to your father?" Dad asked Graham.

I flinched at the sudden change in topics. The red drained from Graham's face.

"I'm just going to go do something that's not in here." Leya pranced out of the room without looking back.

With my foot, I pulled a chair toward me and pushed Graham down in it.

Dad sat up tall in the hospital bed. "Graham, Tessa's my little girl. The only family I have left. I can't trust her with just anyone. I need someone who will respect her. Someone who would never hurt her."

"I would never, ever hurt Tessa," Graham whispered. "She's the only person in this world I care about." He beat his fingers on the chair's arm. "I'm sure you've heard the rumor that I killed my dad."

"I have," Dad said. "Is it true?"

Graham's blinking eyes stared at the floor. "I can't." He sighed. "I can't talk about it. I promised I wouldn't."

I hopped off the bed and knelt in front of Graham. "You can trust us with anything, Graham. You know we're no saints. We've all made mistakes. It's okay."

"She'll kk...kill me," Graham said.

"Who?" Dad asked.

"Your mom?" I asked.

Graham nodded. "I promised to never talk about that night."

Dad tried to move closer to us, but all the cords kept him in place. "Graham, whatever it is, you can tell us." I moved Graham's chair even closer to Dad. He placed his hand on Graham's arm.

Graham relaxed under his touch, his body letting out an obvious sigh. "They were having another argument, which led to physical fighting. I sat there on the floor watching my dad beat my mom." He covered his face with his hands for a second. "I know everyone thinks she's awful and rude, but she does it to keep people from asking questions. Everything my dad did to her, it made her put up a tough wall that's hard to break through." He flicked the earbuds hanging against his chest. "I didn't want to watch her die."

"So, you did kill him?" I asked.

He leaned forward, shaking his fists. "I just wanted him to stop hitting her. So I grabbed the bat he kept by the front door and whacked him over the head. I was so small that the hit alone wouldn't have killed him. But he stumbled back and fell, the corner of his head hitting the edge of the end table on the way down." He rubbed his forehead like he was trying to picture the memory.

"He had a gash at the back of his head. Mom panicked. She grabbed a pillow from the couch and smothered his face until he stopped breathing." He rubbed his hands up and down his arms. "I was so young, I didn't quite grasp what had happened. Mom was just trying to protect me. She knew if he lived, he'd kill me once he healed."

Silence hung in the air as we digested it all. I couldn't believe he had to go through something so terrible and at such a young age.

"Graham, I'm sorry," Dad finally said. "No boy should ever have to face those kinds of decisions. You're a good man."

Tears pooled in Graham's eyes, but he wiped them away. He'd kept his whisper, making it easier for him to speak. "Thank you. It feels so good to get that off my chest."

Dad gripped Graham's shoulder. "You also saved my life. Thank you for that."

A small smile landed on Graham's lips. His blinking and drumming slowed until his fingers remained still on his knee.

Dad suddenly grunted and sucked in his breath. "The pain is coming back. Suzie! I need some morphine!"

EPILOGUE

I sat on a boulder, looking out over my town. Willow Marsh. A place I'd been nervous to enter. My gaze flitted over to a memorial for Corrine. A bunch of students from the school constructed a memorial site for her up on the hill. There are candles, pictures, flowers, rosary beads, and stuffed pandas everywhere. Apparently, she had a thing for pandas. One of the things I never found out when she was alive, because she was taken too soon.

Corrine was the first person to be genuinely excited that I moved to Willow Marsh. She'd made me feel included and wanted.

Sighing, I pulled my legs into my chest and rested my chin on my knee.

Change, new friends, and letting go were hard, but it had to be done.

Although, I'd never truly let go of Amá and Felix. They would always be in my heart. A few times, I thought about trying to contact Amá again, but I didn't want to let in another soul like Ellington or Delilah. Plus, I'd promised Graham I'd lay off the séances.

I'd found a place where I belonged. There were lots of dark, twisted souls in Willow Marsh. I could relate. We all have a certain amount of crazy in us – balancing it was the trick.

Leya had to go home, which broke my heart, but she couldn't stay with us forever. Dad said she could come back for the summer. Leya called me the second she got home and told me she was already looking up flights.

Rita became my release. I could talk to her about anything and everything. She never judged and kept an open mind – believed me and trusted me. Never once did she look at me like I was crazy.

Jade took Corrine's death hard, but she turned to me, and we became good friends. I understood what she was going through.

Graham. My perfectly imperfect companion.

Dad and I had grown close. He let me talk to him about my problems and my feelings. He took me to see Rita with no complaints or snide remarks. He started seeing her as well, which brought us even closer.

Amá and Felix. My lifeline. My blood. My heart.

Every part of me wanted to come up with a rational reason for why I lived and they didn't. It took me a while to figure out I couldn't rationalize fate.

I was just along for the ride.

Standing, I brushed off the back of my jeans and headed down the hill toward my car. Dad got me an old Corolla once I was brave enough to get behind a wheel again. So far, driving had gone well. Although, I never let anyone ride with me. I wasn't ready for that yet.

I was almost to the car door when a small pocket of heat came to life in a little crevice behind my heart. It flared, pulsating along with my heartbeat, and igniting a fire in my veins.

THE END

If you enjoyed Willow Marsh, would you do us a solid and leave Jo an honest review? You can leave one on any book retailer or review site online. The more reviews Jo gets, the more visibility she has. Then, she can connect with even more fantastic readers like you!

ACKNOWLEDGMENTS

Cammie Larsen, I love your brain. It's amazing. Thank you for helping make this story much more awesome than I could have ever imagined. You talked me through the dark moments when I felt like giving up, and you brought out so many things in me as a writer that I never knew I was capable of. And the cover? Brilliant as always. You're like the triple threat in the writing world: writer, editor, and graphic designer.

Thank you to Mary Gray, Cammie Larsen, and Monster Ivy Publishing for giving my story a chance. You understood Tessa's journey from the beginning and helped make her shine. I love being part of the MIP family, and I'm going to do my best to always make you proud.

Douglas, thank you for all your sacrifices so I can continue to write and do what I love. It looks like our leap of faith just might pay off. You're my hunky knight in shiny, bullet-proof armor and I love you more than Dr Pepper.

Speaking of Dr Pepper, thank you, DP, for fueling my writing. You're a hero swimming in 23 delicious flavors. I'll always be a proud member of the #PepperPack.

To my mom, dad, siblings, family, and friends, thanks for your unwavering support. I've been blown away by all the love and encouragement. Not all writers get that, so I know how lucky I am and I hope I never take it for granted.

Princess Buttercup, you helped a lot with the editing of this book. And by help, I mean you sat on all my papers and rolled around demanding attention. But thank you for being such a loving kitty and being my writing companion for better or for worse.

Thank YOU, reader, for giving me a reason to keep on writing. I love sharing my stories with you, and I hope to continue to do so for many, many years.

A very special thanks to Heavenly Father for helping guide my journey and lighting up the paths I needed to take. I would be lost without you.

And to my angel niece, Kaleya, thank you for being the brightest star of them all. You showed our family the true meaning of love, happiness, loyalty, and bravery, with a dash of sass. I'll make sure to give everyone in the family a kick in the fanny for you. I love you, Kaleya, and I can't wait to see you again!

ABOUT THE AUTHOR

Jo Cassidy grew up in sunny Southern California but now lives in snowy Northern Utah with her husband and their crazy cat. She loves all things creepy – Bates Motel, Stranger Things, and Criminal Minds are a few of her favorite shows. She believes Stalker was canceled way too early and would love to see it come back. You can subscribe to her newsletter at www.authorjocassidy.com.

DISCUSSION QUESTIONS

1. While we don't recommend doing séances to contact the dead, how can being in touch with your family history help you through personal challenges?

2. Despite being nervous about moving to a new town, Tessa makes friends fairly quickly. What about her personality helps her do this?

3. What are some of the ways Tessa deals with losing Felix and her mom? Would you consider these healthy outlets? Why, or why not?

4. In what ways did Cassidy create a creepy atmosphere in the town? Would you want to live in Willow Marsh? Why, or why not?

5. If you were to describe Graham to your best friend, how would you do it? Can you see how when we get to know a person, we often want to focus on their strengths as opposed to their weaknesses?

6. Leya's playfulness helps break down some of Tessa's nerves, while Reed amplifies her anxiety every chance he gets. What can this tell you about the types of people you want in your life?

7. Tessa's family motto is, "Wherever we dwell, we will always be family." Does your family have a motto? If not, can you create one?

*Enjoy delving deeper? Join the Monster Ivy Book Club Facebook Group, where we read and discuss our latest releases with live Q&A sessions, host giveaways, and offer insights on how to host your own perfect book parties.

Good Girls Stay Quiet - Fifteen-year-old Cora has a secret only her "daddy" and journal know about... until a blackmailer finds out the truth and demands test answers and money.

GOOD GIRLS STAY QUIET

CHAPTER 1

I ran my fingers along the white eyelet canopy surrounding my bed. Daddy said it would protect me at night while I slept but still allow me to breathe. Sometimes I liked to sit on the bed with the canopy closed, soaking in the comfort and safety it provided.

I'd already finished my homework for the day. It was always the first thing I did when I came home from school so I'd have the evening free to spend with Daddy.

My leg bounced, my fingers drumming along with the motion. I glanced at the twin bell alarm clock on my nightstand. Only twenty more minutes until Daddy came home and unlocked my bedroom door. I could hold my bladder that long. I'd done it before. I needed to distract myself so I wouldn't think about it.

I leaned over the side of my bed, the canopy draping over my hair, and retrieved the journal tucked under my mattress.

Noah, my stuffed elephant, cleared his throat, which did nothing for the rasp in his tone. "Oh, Cora dear. You know not to write in that during the day. *He* may come home and see it."

I glared at the elephant sitting on my bed, his bright, blue eyes staring back at me. "I know that, *Noah dear*. I was just seeing how much room I had left." I thumbed through the empty pages in the back. "I'll have to steal another journal soon."

Noah guffawed. "So you can write more thrilling stories about me?"

Whoever manufactured the stuffed animal didn't bother with getting the facts straight. I'd never seen an elephant with blue eyes that sparkled. It certainly didn't match with Noah's sometimes rough and sarcastic demeanor.

Daddy had bought him for me when I was eight. He'd said the elephant's eyes matched mine. Little did he know, he'd brought me home an elephant with a soul that came alive when we were alone.

"Or is this about brushing up on your shoplifting skills?" Noah asked.

I put my hand on my hip. "Please don't judge me. There are extenuating circumstances."

"Keep telling yourself that." He laughed louder, though his stuffed body remained completely still on the bed.

I was about to flick his trunk when I heard footfalls in the hallway. Daddy was home early. Shoving the journal back under my bed, I surveyed the room to make sure nothing had been left out that I didn't want Daddy to see. I fumbled to refasten the top button on my shirt so only half of my neck was exposed. Then I rolled down my sleeves and buttoned the cuffs. Daddy liked his little girl to look a certain way.

"Are you going to start hiding me?" Noah asked.

Daddy didn't know about my relationship with Noah, and I wanted it to remain that way. Luckily, I was the only one who could hear Noah. It was the main reason our relationship was special and why I confided in him so much.

Right as the lock unlatched on the outside of my door, I

settled into place on my bed holding a regency book I'd brought home from the school library. At the last second, I moved my braid so it rested on my right shoulder. The door opened, and Daddy stepped inside the room. He still wore his blue work coveralls, and I immediately took in the scent of grease and sweat. I noticed his pomade had held his perfectly brushed hair in place all day.

Even though his presence caused unease to swirl inside, I plastered on the smile he loved so I wouldn't have to deal with his explosive anger. It was why I referred to him as Daddy in my head. I never wanted to accidentally call him something else to his face.

"Hi Daddy!" I set the book on my nightstand and went to him. I put my arms out to hug him, but he took a step back.

"I need a shower." He rubbed at his tired eyes. "My last appointment was a bit of a mess."

"Why don't I cook dinner while you wash up and then you can tell me all about your day over our meal?"

Daddy leaned forward and kissed my forehead, his dry lips causing my stomach to roll. "What would I do without you, Cora?"

"Not be such a creepy old man?" Noah offered in a haughty tone.

It took everything in me to not turn around and scold Noah. He shouldn't talk about Daddy like that. Thank goodness Daddy couldn't hear him, or we'd both be locked in the basement for the night.

"I could really use a decent BLT," Daddy said.

"Consider it done." My tone was as sweet as honey, but my insides were heavy like molasses.

He turned to leave, but then faced me and raised his eyebrows. "Make sure the bacon is crispy, but not over-cooked." He placed his hand on my arm and squeezed as a small storm brewed in his eyes. "Last time it was practically burnt."

I clasped my hands tightly in front of me so I wouldn't flinch from the pain. "Of course, Daddy."

The storm in his eyes retreated, and Daddy left the room. I wanted to yell at Noah, but I really needed to use the bathroom. It had been hours. As soon as I finished, though, I headed back into my room.

"Don't say things like that about him," I hissed. When it came to Daddy, Noah and I didn't see eye to eye. He didn't like the way Daddy treated me.

"The truth?" Noah whistled. "Fine. I'll feed myself lies like you do."

Going to the bed, I put my face in front of his. "Being nice to him makes him happy. He's done so much for us, Noah." I poked his trunk. "Remember that."

"That's right. All the things he does out of *love*. Well, if you want him happy, then you should start dinner and stop lecturing me."

I gave him one last glaring look before I went into the kitchen to prepare dinner. I put on an apron so the grease wouldn't splatter my shirt. That would make Daddy real mad. I kept a close eye on the bacon, making sure every inch turned brown but had no hint of black. Once it was perfectly cooked, I took the plate of bacon and gently placed it on the table. I used a towel to wipe away a drop of grease on the edge of the plate.

After smoothing out a wrinkle in the tablecloth, I used my hand to measure the length of the material hanging over the edge, double checking it was even all the way around, just how Daddy liked it. We had a round table so the chairs could be spaced perfectly apart; far enough so Daddy could look at me, but not too far so he could reach out and touch me if he needed to. It had been almost a year since I'd stepped out of line at the dinner table and he'd sent me to timeout. I planned on keeping it that way.

The white ceramic plates and bowls were on their place-mats, with a fork on the left, fork above for the salad – even though we weren't having salad, it always had to be there – and a spoon and knife to the right. The glasses were up and to the right, with the cloth napkins flawlessly folded in a standing triangle on the center of our plates. It was perfect.

"Smells delicious, angel," Daddy said, joining me in the kitchen. He'd switched to his usual button-down shirt tucked tightly into his casual slacks. His shirt was buttoned all the way to the top like mine. My chest tightened at the sight of his leather belt.

He wrapped his arm around my shoulder and kissed the side of my head, my hair creating a barrier between his lips and my skin. His sweat and grease stench had been replaced by soap and Selsun Blue shampoo and his brown hair hung down, still wet from the shower. I preferred that look to his perfectly sculpted hair. It made him appear carefree.

"So, tell me about this last client of yours," I said, hanging up my apron in the pantry and softly closing the door.

Daddy grabbed a bottled beer from the fridge. "Not much to tell. A guy inherited everything in his dad's garage, which included some tools that hadn't been used in a very long time."

Keeping my hands steady, I pulled out his chair for him. He sat down, his thin lips turning into a smile as he did. I returned the smile, though my stomach fluttered. I hoped I cooked the bacon just right.

"Did you get them working again?" I sat down and tucked my napkin into the top of my shirt, just like Daddy had done. Then I made sure my braid hung over my right shoulder.

He winked. "Always do."

I grabbed two pieces of bread and spread mayo on them. *"Never leave a client unsatisfied."*

He laughed. "So you *do* listen to me."

I tilted my head to the side and winked at him. "Always do."

The laughter reached all the way to his eyes and some of the tension released inside me. His eyes were much kinder when they weren't housing a storm.

I loaded up his sandwich with bacon, lettuce, and fresh tomatoes I had picked from the backyard the day before. I tried to keep my hands stable as I placed the BLT in the center of his plate.

Clasping my hands in my lap, I waited patiently for Daddy to take a bite of his sandwich.

"It's perfect, angel." He wiped his mouth with the napkin and nodded at the bread. "Go ahead and make yourself a sandwich now."

My heart calmed. "Thanks, Daddy."

"You deserve it," he said. "Having you gives me a reason to wake up every morning."

Tears welled up behind my eyelids. I was lucky to have a father who loved me so much.

After dinner and cleaning up under Daddy's watchful eye, I grabbed the playing cards from the closet in the hall. It was tradition to play every night. I let him win all the time because he hated to lose. The last time I won, he didn't let me out of the basement for two whole days.

Continue reading...

www.ingramcontent.com/pod-product-compliance
Lightning Source LLC
Chambersburg PA
CBHW070827190726
48292CB00006B/2128